SECRETS
OF A
WHITBY GIRL

SECRETS
OF A
WHITBY GIRL

Jessica Blair

piatkus

PIATKUS

First published in Great Britain in 2011 by Piatkus

A CIP catalogue record for this book
is available from the British Library.

ISBN 978-0-7499-4289-2

Typeset in Times by M Rules
Printed and bound in Great Britain by
MPG Books, Bodmin, Cornwall

Papers used by Piatkus are natural, renewable and
recyclable products sourced from well-managed forests and certified
in accordance with the rules of the Forest Stewardship Council.

Mixed Sources
Product group from well-managed
forests and other controlled sources
www.fsc.org Cert no. SGS-COC-004081
© 1996 Forest Stewardship Council

FSC

Piatkus
An imprint of
Little, Brown Book Group
100 Victoria Embankment
London EC4Y 0DY

An Hachette UK Company
www.hachette.co.uk

www.piatkus.co.uk

For Jill
whose friendship is so important to me

PROLOGUE

13 August 1901. I am going to write 'Finis' after this entry and close my diary for good. I started writing it when I was sixteen. Now I am eighty-five I think there is no more for me to record. What has been the point of it? What has it achieved? Only a measure of self-satisfaction. I soon realised I could not show it to anyone – it contains secrets which could bring distress to others. I should perhaps have stopped when I realised that, but it had become a habit for me to record the major events within my family. It is not a daily account, which is why there are only three volumes.

What should I do with it now? Give it to Esther, my great-niece, who always wants to know about her ancestors? I've told her some things, but should she know everything that is written in these pages? Maybe I'll get Jenny, my maid, to burn the three volumes in the grate in my room, then I'll know they can do no harm. But even as I watch them burn, will I start to regret that I have not left behind a true record of the family story?

Sarah Brook laid down her pen, closed the notebook and let her gaze rest on it for a moment before drawing herself stiffly to her feet. Once she was upright she carefully smoothed her pink silk dress, cut to draw attention to her small waist. Throughout her long life she had always taken pride in her appearance and was not going to let standards slip now, not even at this age. And she wanted to look her best for her favourite great-niece, Esther, whom she knew would be calling later in the day.

Sarah was delighted that Esther's dress sense turned out to have matched hers. They enjoyed discussing the latest fashions and Esther had promised that today she would wear the outfit her great-aunt favoured most: a waist-length jacket of dark blue, with high collar and gigot sleeves, contrasting with the pale blue of the skirt fitting snugly at her hips and gently flaring to the top of her black button shoes.

Sarah picked up the diary. With the aid of her walking-stick, she moved slowly to the armchair placed at one side of the window. From her house on Whitby's West Cliff she could gaze across the River Esk to the town's East Side. Still holding the diary, she sat down and allowed her gaze to roam freely across the river and slide upwards from red roof to red roof until it rested on the ruined Norman abbey set on the clifftop, its command-ing position making it a reference point for Whitby's sailors returning home over the sea. From the abbey her gaze drifted down to the river mouth and settled on the bustling quays with their ships and stevedores and sailors. She sighed, a regretful sound; the port in 1901 was not as she had once known it. Whaling, fishing, alum, ironstone and all manner of everyday commodities had brought wealth to this port. Its ship-building indus-try was renowned – hadn't Captain Cook used Whitby-built ships to sail the world? Its ships had once plied a lucrative coastal trade around Britain as well as sailing to far horizons. But fashions in trade shifted, and whaling had moved away from the Yorkshire ports. New processes introduced into the manufacturing world made shipping alum from the town no longer a profitable proposition, and ironstone was mined closer to the furnaces of Teesside. Whitby's fortunes had altered along with these changes but Sarah's family had always managed to survive the hard times and prosper in the good, thanks to the acumen of her father.

The great days of the town seemed very close again as she gazed out of the window, eyes unseeing now. A tear trickled down her cheek as she remembered the anniversary of Jim Barbour's death. With it came a vision of two whirling figures, she in his arms, laughter and love on both faces. Unaware of the rest of the world, they danced for the joy of the love they had just declared for one another.

She glanced down at the book. Her arthritic fingers stroked it lovingly. The passing years were clear enough in their gnarled and twisted appearance. Yes, those fingers had written enough – the important things; not the frivolous ones. It had been a labour of love, conducted largely for her own satisfaction, a faithful record. No one else knew about it. What should she do with it now?

She started, hearing a noise downstairs. Voices . . . Esther! Sarah glanced at her fob watch. Goodness, she was early! The diary! Must put it out of sight . . .

Sarah struggled to get to her feet. Her walking-stick slipped and rattled to the floor. She reached out for it. The book slithered from her grasp and fell with a thud that, in her panic, she was sure would be heard throughout the house. She pushed hard on the arms of her chair but her right hand slipped and she fell sideways, jarring her spine. She gasped for breath, face screwed up against the pain.

The door burst open.

'Aunt!' Alarm heightened Esther's greeting as she hurried across the room. She dropped to her knees beside Sarah.

'I'm all right, don't fuss,' insisted Sarah, trying her best to sound unconcerned.

'Just sit quietly,' said Esther, knowing that her great-aunt abhorred being a nuisance to anyone. Seeing that her aunt was settling, she called over her shoulder to the maid who had followed her into the room and waited to be of help. 'A good cup of strong sweet tea, please, Jenny.'

'Yes, ma'am.'

'Now, Aunt, what were you trying to do?' queried Esther as she retrieved the walking-stick and placed it next to her aunt's hand.

'I was trying to get up and the stick slipped.'

'Seems something else fell,' said Esther, picking up the book. Automatically she glanced at the page that had opened when it fell. She stared at the hand-written entry where she had expected to see a printed page.

Looking back, I realise now what sacrifices Arabella made. If I had only known at the time maybe I could have helped her more . . .

'Give that to me!' Sarah's voice was firm and commanding. Esther looked up at her aunt in surprise.

'I'll take that.' Sarah's voice had grown quieter but it was still authoritative, her tone the one Esther had known throughout her forty-three years and had rarely disobeyed. But now, favourite niece or not, she felt an urge to be disobedient.

She flicked to another page and briefly scanned the familiar writing. It was long enough for her to realise what it was she was holding. 'This is a diary. You've been keeping a record of . . .'

'It is not for other people's eyes!'

Esther ignored this and went on, '. . . the family. This entry mentions your sister Harriet; the other one my grandmother Arabella.' Excitement came to Esther's voice. 'Will this tell me all about the family?'

'I've told you all you need to know.' Sarah's tone was forbidding. She wanted to discourage Esther's questions.

'But I think there is a lot more. Aunt, I want to know it all.'

'I've told you, it's not for other people's eyes.'

'Then why have you kept it?' Sarah read something of herself in Esther's defiant tone then. She knew she would have posed exactly the same question if she had been in Esther's shoes. And she knew how she would have followed up that question, so it came as no surprise when her niece did exactly the same thing. 'You've got to let me read it, Aunt. You know how much I want to learn about my ancestors. Mother is not interested in the slightest, and from the little she has told me knows nothing of any consequence. So you are the only one who can tell me. I think you have not been truly forthcoming. This diary proves that there must be more to be learned, or why keep a record?' She flicked through the pages again so that she could read the date of the first entry. She looked up at her great-aunt with such an intent gaze then that Sarah could not evade it. 'Judging by this date, I believe there must be other diaries. Aunt, please, you've got to let me read them.'

Sarah set her mouth in a grim line.

5

'Please, Aunt. Why keep the diaries if no one else is allowed to read them? What were you going to do with them?'

'Burn them.'

'What? Aunt, you can't!' Esther protested. 'Please don't destroy them when there's so much inside them I need to know.'

'Esther, don't pursue this,' Sarah told her in a warning tone.

'Why not? If you burn them without letting me read them, I'll only be left wondering what was so important or terrible it couldn't be told.'

Sarah looked perplexed. 'If you hadn't arrived early today, you would never have known about my diaries and would have accepted my explanation that there was nothing to be told.'

'Then fate played its part,' replied Esther. 'I am *meant* to know what you have written. Don't you see, it's the only way for me to find out the full story of our family? Mother certainly won't tell me it.'

'She knows nothing,' Sarah said sharply.

'Then there's something in the past . . . A scandal? Wrongdoing? What is it, Aunt?' The earnest desire in Esther's voice was not lost on Sarah.

She eyed her niece thoughtfully. If she allowed Esther to see the diaries she could lay down conditions, but would her favourite relative abide by them when she knew what the diaries contained? Could Sarah trust her? She was shocked by the doubt in her own mind. It seemed to her it would be better that Esther should never be put to the test. Better to burn the diaries than that . . .

She gave a little shake of her head, an automatic

reaction as she tried to reach her decision but one that Esther misinterpreted as her final answer.

'Very well, Aunt, if that is your decision then I am bound to say I will not visit you again.' Her expression was so resolute that Sarah knew Esther meant it.

She reeled from the shock of it: her favourite niece taking this stand against her; questioning her judgement. Esther, who had been her faithful visitor throughout the years. The girl she had watched grow up with pride, understanding and love; the person whose welfare was of the utmost concern to her, though she never interfered in her family's affairs, and was therefore loved all the more by Esther's mother and father. Would all these treasured memories be marred or even lost to her forever if she refused Esther's request now?

She looked hard at her niece but there was no condemnation in Esther's eyes, only pleading. 'That wasn't a sign of my refusal. I'm still deliberating. You were over-hasty,' Sarah told her.

Guilt-stricken, Esther dropped to her knees beside her aunt's chair and gently took hold of her frail, arthritic hands. Her own eyes were damp as she said softly, 'I'm sorry, Aunt. So sorry.'

Sarah met her tear-filled gaze. She reached out and stroked Esther's cheek lovingly. 'We all say things we don't mean in the heat of the moment.' Her gentle tone matched the forgiveness in her eyes. She paused for a moment then asked, 'Does it really mean so much to you to know about your family's past?'

'It does, Aunt, it really does. I feel the lack of something . . . have always felt it. Perhaps reading the diaries will finally settle my restless urge to know myself.'

Sarah gave a nod, but silently wondered if it would.

7

'Let me have a little time to think. Come back tomorrow. I will give you my decision then.'

Esther stood up and kissed her. 'Thank you, Aunt. I do love you.'

As the door closed behind her, Sarah opened the diary and gazed at the first words she had written so long ago.

1

3 April 1832. We buried Mama today. This is a strange way for a sixteen-year-old to start a diary but I feel compelled to do so; not to record the everyday events but the truly memorable things that happen to our family. Each one of us, Arabella, Harriet, myself and Charley, will miss her terribly. She was kind and gentle but would stand up to Father if she thought he was being too strict. Life will change for us now, as it does for anyone who loses a person they love.

P.S. I didn't approve of the way Harriet flounced around, trying to be noticed even in her mourning dress.

P.P.S. I was pleased to see Jim among those who had come to pay their respects.

The final sympathisers having left the family home in New Buildings on the West Cliff, Benjamin Brook had ensconced himself in his study with the Reverend Arthur Bosworth, Vicar of the ancient Parish Church of Whitby which was situated close to the ruined abbey. Sarah had gone to her room. When Harriet saw Arabella and John Sharp step out into the garden, she felt obliged to stay with Charley.

'Thank you for staying behind, John,' said Arabella,

9

casting a sideways glance at him as they strolled down the path together.

'I did it for you, Arabella,' he replied, squeezing her hand in his.

'You gave me such encouragement and strength.'

'I wish I could have done more. After all, your family is like my own since I have no siblings, and your house became a second home to me after Mother and Father were killed. It doesn't seem like four years ago . . .'

'I feared you might leave us then.'

'Where would I have gone? The house two doors away became mine, a place to return to from the sea, though it was always your house I pictured in my mind while I was shipboard. I could never have ceased coming here. But I fear I must sail tomorrow. I wish I could stay longer . . .'

'Will you be able to make up time?'

'I hope so. It will depend on the weather, where the whales are and the conditions of the ice.'

She stopped walking and turned to face him. 'Mother was proud to see you become a captain at twenty-four. She had such faith in your ability.'

'I hope I can always live up to that.'

'I'm sure you will. Take care. You sail dangerous waters.'

'I will. I've a lot to come back to.'

He pulled her to him then and kissed her, feeling pleased that she responded in a way he would remember when he was far away. He held the kiss, sending Arabella's pulse racing and making her yearn for him to stay beside her instead of courting danger in the waters of the cold, lonely North.

'I must go,' he said regretfully. 'I've some business to see to before we sail tomorrow.'

'I hope, in spite of the rules of mourning, we can still persuade Father to allow us to watch you set sail. If so, I'll be on the cliffs as usual.'

'With Harriet, no doubt?'

'No doubt. And I couldn't stop Sarah and Charley from coming either. He hero-worships you. Talks to me of nothing else but joining the whale-ships like you.'

John smiled and looked earnestly down at her. 'When I leave, you are always in the picture I carry in my mind. It comforts me through all the days in the Arctic.' He kissed her tenderly on the cheek and turned away, heading for the gate.

Arabella's heart ached. She touched her cheek in the place where he had kissed her as she recalled his words. 'You are always in the picture I carry in my mind . . .' How she hoped that picture was of her and her alone.

She watched him walk away down the path. John Sharp was a handsome man who held himself upright, an air of natural authority about him that elicited respect rather than hostility. She knew his crew held him in high regard, even the older members who could chalk up many more whaling voyages than he. They admired the way John had not relied on his privileged upbringing to win him preferment, but instead at the age of twelve had taken on the lowliest crewman's position from which he had worked his way up, always willing to learn from the more experienced hands until he could match the best harpooner in Whitby.

John paused at the gate, raised his hand in farewell and called out, 'Take care of yourself, Arabella. Remember, your mother would want you to recall her with joy and not mourning.'

She nodded and raised her own hand, wishing their

years spent growing up together meant as much to him as they did to her; hoping that she sparked a quickening of his pulse as he did hers. How did he really see her? Whenever Arabella looked in the mirror she saw someone she regarded as plain. How she wished she was pretty like her sister Harriet!

Arabella walked slowly back into the house, wondering what the future held for them all without her mother to smooth their path.

'Reverend, I must . . .' Benjamin started, but was immediately stopped by the Vicar.

'Arthur, please, Benjamin. The formalities of today are over. We have been friends ever since I came to Whitby ten years ago. You gave me a wonderful welcome then, one I have never forgotten.'

'Immediately upon meeting you I recognised a God-fearing man, one after my own heart, so it was natural I should support you and your views.'

'You did indeed. I do not know if I could have forged bonds with my new parishioners without your taking up my cause.'

'Many of them needed prompting to follow the precepts of our church. You provided the moral guidance that was necessary.' Benjamin hesitated slightly then added, 'Arthur, I must thank you for that wonderful eulogy.'

'Nothing more than Jane deserved. She was a wonderful woman, a wonderful mother, and no doubt a wonderful wife.'

Benjamin's lips tightened as tears came into his eyes. 'She was indeed.'

'What will you do without her?' Arthur's voice was gentle, full of concern for his friend's future.

'I will immerse myself in my chandler's business and my merchant ventures. They will help to occupy my mind. I must put the business on a much firmer foundation for Charley; he's only fourteen but I will take him into the firm as soon as possible, enabling him to work his way up from the bottom so that he has learned every aspect of the trade by the time I wish him to take over from me.'

'And your daughters?'

'Daughters are for marrying, but Arabella will have to take Jane's place for now as head of the household. She is quite capable of doing so and will have the good Mrs Ainslie to help her. I will tell her what I expect of her tonight.'

'Wouldn't it be better to wait a while? Let her get over the shock of losing her mother first?'

Benjamin frowned as if such a consideration should never have been voiced. 'Life has to go on. The sooner Arabella gets a grip on her new responsibilities the better.'

His friend nodded but remained silent.

The evening meal in the Brook household was conducted almost in silence. Benjamin spoke only when absolutely necessary. His three daughters and son respected his wishes and resisted fidgeting. After they had finished they awaited grace and their father's permission for them to leave the table. Before he gave it, Benjamin issued his instructions for the weeks ahead.

'I was pleased with the way you conducted yourselves today and the respectful sobriety of your mourning clothes. Quite rightly they were without any adornment or frippery. I wish you to maintain a similar restraint until your six months of full mourning are over. Though you, Charley, could be excused, I believe you should not be favoured over your sisters so you will maintain the same level of observance as they will.' Charley, rubbing his face, scowled behind his hand. 'And you, Harriet,' their father continued, 'no strutting around as I saw you do on a couple of occasions today. There is no need for that. Respect your mother's memory at all times.'

Harriet looked contrite as she said quietly, 'Yes, Papa.'

'You all know what is expected of you so see that you follow my orders. I will know if you don't.' His severe gaze encompassed them. 'That is all.' As he rose from his chair he added, 'Arabella, come to my study in ten minutes.'

'Yes, Father.' She judged his serious tone merited a formal 'Father' rather than the more relaxed 'Papa'.

As soon as the dining-room door shut behind him, Harriet slid up to Arabella. 'What's he want?' she asked, her lively blue eyes sparkling with curiosity.

'I don't know.' Arabella gave a little shrug of her shoulders. 'But I soon will.'

A curious Harriet watched her sister hurry up the stairs then turned back to join Sarah and Charley in the drawing-room.

Arabella paused in front of the cheval glass in her room to appraise her mourning dress of black bombazine trimmed with crepe. She pulled a face at the thought of wearing similar dresses devoid of any ornamentation or colour for half a year more. Black made her look severe, she decided, especially as her hair was worn drawn tightly back at the sides under a centre parting. Satisfied that her dress was tidy, she sat down in front of her dressing table and looked into the mirror. She smoothed her hair and, seeing the pallor of her cheeks, pinched them to try to bring a bit of colour into them. Then she stared at herself in the mirror again. She did not know why her father had singled her out for attention. She looked at her fob watch. Better be on her way; he was a stickler for punctuality.

At precisely the right moment she knocked on his study door and answered the call of, 'Come in.'

'Ah, Arabella my dear, sit down.' Her father indicated the chair that had been placed on the opposite side of the desk from his. He waited for his daughter to be seated and then leaned forward, arms resting on the polished surface. 'This has been a sad, sad day.'

'Indeed it has, Papa.'

'But life has to go on. We cannot cease to strive because your mother is no longer here to help and guide us. There is now her place to fill, in as much as we can.'

Arabella's heart raced. What was her father getting at? Surely . . . No, that was impossible. Then she realised he was speaking again.

'Someone must take your mother's place as head of the household. It is your duty to do so.'

She stared at him in disbelief, all manner of thoughts racing through her mind. She uttered the one word that automatically came to her lips. 'But . . .'

Benjamin stepped in quickly. 'There can be no buts. You, as the eldest daughter, must take charge; look after me and your sisters and brother.' Seeing her colour fade and astonishment fill her eyes, he added with a firmness that brooked no opposition, 'It is your bounden duty!'

'Father, we do have Mrs Ainslie.' Arabella's words were only a weak protest because she knew he would not tolerate anyone going against his decision.

'Mrs Ainslie is a capable woman, the right sort of person for you to work with, but overall authority must rest with you. After the appropriate period of mourning is over, I intend our family life to return to what it was before your mother died. Obviously it will never be quite the same, but in outward appearance at any rate . . .' He saw she was going to say something but held up his hand to stop her. 'I intend to throw myself into my work; expand the business so that it is thriving when Charley takes over.'

Arabella's mind was racing even faster at his mention of Charley; her brother had his heart set on joining the whalers. Father clearly did not know this or else was ignoring his son's desire. She was about to say something but thought better of it; she would warn Charley instead.

Benjamin continued to speak. 'So, you see what extending the business will mean? Entertaining business acquaintances as well as friends. Your mother was always my able partner in that. You saw what she did . . . how she managed things. That is what I wish you to do in her place. I'm afraid this will inevitably mean you will not be able to take so many walks with your sisters and brother, nor with John when he is home from the sea. You must not neglect the charitable works your mother did either. They reflect well on the family. You must never forget the position we need to maintain.'

Arabella was speechless. She knew she was competent to do what her father was ordering her to do, after all she was her mother's daughter – but it would change the whole tenor of her life. Her youth could be lost; all her hopes and dreams vanish. If only John had proposed; if only they were already married! But her regret was swamped by the enormity of her father's demand. She could not oppose him; she had seen others cut off from family and security by defying a parent's authority.

'Very well, Father,' she answered meekly, though inwardly she was crying out to be released from the burden he was placing on her.

'Good. You will want for nothing. "Ask and you will receive," as the Good Lord said. Where are the others?'

'I think they will be in the drawing-room.'

'Then let us tell them now,' he said, rising from his chair.

As he entered the drawing-room, followed closely by Arabella, Harriet immediately recognised from her father's hard, solemn countenance and her sister's tight expression that what had passed between them had been serious. She had learned quickly as a child to read her father, recognise his moods and know how to manipulate them to her own advantage. She glanced quickly at Sarah and raised an eyebrow.

'Be seated,' said Benjamin, his authoritative tone making his children obey immediately. He took up position with his back to the fireplace, drew himself up and clasped his hands behind his back.

'I have just had a serious talk with Arabella . . . a necessary one on this sad day. I pointed out to her that, although life can never be exactly the same for us, we must endeavour to resume it as near as possible to the way it was when your mother was alive. She would want us to do that. It is necessary for someone to take over your mother's role. As you all know, that task always falls to the eldest daughter. I now call on you to acknowledge Arabella as head of the household and promise to support her in that capacity.' He paused and glanced

17

around. Seeing no acknowledgement in their expressions, he said, 'Is that understood?'

'Yes, Papa,' they answered in unison.

He gave a little nod. 'Arabella, we'll go and see Mrs Ainslie together.'

She rose quickly from her chair and followed him out of the room without a glance at her siblings.

'May we have a word, Mrs Ainslie?' Benjamin asked when the housekeeper answered his knock on the door of her private sitting-room.

'Of course, sir,' replied the middle-aged woman politely as she stepped aside to allow him to enter. She gave Arabella a smile of sympathy, guessing from her glum expression why she was accompanying her father to this interview.

Mrs Ainslie had come to the Brook household in 1810 at the age of twenty-five on the recommendation of Dr Fenby when Jane Brook had discovered she was expecting a child. 'Get yourself a competent housekeeper,' he had advised in a fatherly way. 'I know the commitments you already have through Benjamin's business. His growing ambition will bring you more. If you wish, I will have a word with him.'

Five days later the doctor had brought Vera Ainslie to the house in New Buildings and presented her to Mr and Mrs Brook. She impressed them as soon as she walked into the room. There was an air of competence about her that was emphasised by the forthright way she held herself. Her voice was firm but gentle and she answered all the questions put to her without hesitation. She had come from Lowestoft on the death of her parents to look after her only relation, an elderly aunt living in the town. After her aunt's death, she had been on the point of leaving

Whitby, even though she did not know what she would do, when Dr Fenby, knowing of her competence while living with her aunt, came up with the suggestion that she might like to think about becoming a housekeeper. She had accepted his suggestion and, while she came under scrutiny from Mr and Mrs Brook, herself subtly assessed what life would be like as their principal employee. Fortunately, both parties liked what they saw and Vera Ainslie moved into the Brook household the following week. She had been there ever since.

Now Mrs Ainslie indicated two chairs to her visitors and seated herself so she was facing them from the opposite side of the fireplace. The clock on the mantelpiece marked the seconds with a comforting tick. A gate-legged table stood in front of a large sash window covered by a white lace curtain. A small round table stood beside Mrs Ainslie's chair, holding a sewing-box and the knitting which had been occupying her nimble fingers when father and daughter had arrived.

'Mrs Ainslie, I must appoint someone to take on my wife's responsibilities and, as the eldest daughter, that person must be Arabella. I would like you to give her the same support and help as you gave Mrs Brook.'

'Yes, sir. And I am sure Arabella and I will get on very well. We will try and run everything here as Mrs Brook would have done.'

'Thank you, Mrs Ainslie. I know Mrs Brook thought extremely highly of you.' Thankful to have the interview over, Benjamin rose from his chair.

The housekeeper was on her feet immediately, ready to escort him from the room. Arabella spoke as she pushed herself from her seat. 'I'd like to stay and talk to Mrs Ainslie now, Papa.'

'Very well,' he approved.

As soon as the door clicked behind him, Mrs Ainslie spoke up. 'I think, miss, a cup of tea is called for.'

Arabella immediately felt relieved; the tone of the housekeeper's voice indicated her acceptance of the position that had been thrust upon her, one in which a younger woman with less experience would be her superior.

'It certainly would,' Arabella agreed.

'I won't be a moment,' replied Mrs Ainslie, and went into the small adjoining scullery especially installed for the housekeeper's use when the Brooks first employed her.

The swish of water, the rattle of cups and saucers, seemed to Arabella to set a seal on the new relationship between her and the housekeeper.

Mrs Ainslie appeared with a tray neatly set out with cups and saucers, milk and sugar. She moved her knitting aside and placed the tray on the table.

'My father has thrust this responsibility on me, Mrs Ainslie. I don't want you to think I asked for it,' Arabella explained.

'I thought nothing of the kind. Because you are his eldest daughter, I expected no less.'

'I don't want to change anything. It will be difficult to emulate Mama but . . .' the catch in Arabella's voice betrayed her feelings; she brushed away a tear that ran down her cheek. '. . . I will try to live up to Father's expectations. With your help.' The plea in the young woman's voice was not lost on Mrs Ainslie.

'I will do all I can to assist,' she promised. 'You need have no worries. I know you will cope very well.'

If she had been pressed to, she would have singled out

twenty-two-year old Arabella out as her favourite among the Brook children. Maybe it was because it was she who, indirectly, had brought Mrs Ainslie to this family and their house, a comfortable refuge when she had faced an uncertain future. But it was more than that, too.

She had watched the lovable first child grow into a charming, assured young woman, not as beautiful as the next child, Harriet, but with an air about her that attracted people. Keen of eye and mind, inquisitive and ready to learn, Arabella enjoyed life without being frivolous. She was respected and liked throughout Whitby. Mrs Ainslie knew of her feelings for John Sharp and hoped the young mistress would find the happiness she deserved.

Her favourite? Yes, but she loved all the children. Harriet was very pretty, and knew it. She loved beautiful clothes, which she wore with a panache that drew every eye. She could even bring life to the colour of mourning that convention dictated she must wear. Her smile and laughter were infectious, her vivid blue eyes could unashamedly tease and flirt, and she knew how to get round her father without his realising it. Mrs Ainslie hoped Harriet would always find life a joy and that it would never hurt her as it often did those who took their happiness for granted.

Sixteen-year-old Sarah, the quietest girl, naturally more serious than her sisters, knew how to enjoy the pleasures of family life and was close to all her siblings. In looks she fell between Arabella and Harriet, her hazel eyes matched by the subtle colouring of her hair, something that attracted attention of which she was aware. Mrs Ainslie knew that Sarah had begun to show an interest in a local boy, Jim Barbour, who had saved her from some teasing ruffians when she had wandered along the

21

quay one day, leaving Arabella to have a private word with John. At sixteen Jim was the youngest member of the crew of the *Sea King*.

Learning of Sarah's interest in Jim, her brother Charley had teased her with threats to tell their father; but he was a loyal boy, a trait Mrs Ainslie had seen developing in him as he grew up. And, oh, she saw how handsome he would become; many a broken heart would be cast at his feet. Evidence of keen determination and a strong will in one so young made her wonder who would triumph when the boy's desire to join the whalers was pitted against his father's resolve to mould him as his successor on land.

When she returned with the teapot, Mrs Ainslie was moved by Arabella's worried expression.

'Mrs Ainslie, do you really think I'll manage? I'm not my mother.'

'Of course you will.' The housekeeper hoped she sounded reassuring. 'I'll do all I can to help, you know that.'

'But Father wants so much.' Her voice choked with the thought of what that implied for her future, trapped in a role forced on her by paternal expectations and middle-class convention.

2

4 April 1832. We are hoping to persuade Father to let us see the Sea King *sail today. Ever since I can remember, we have always watched the whale-ships sail. It is an important day for Whitby. Everyone turns out to see them and wish them good hunting and a safe voyage. We will be disappointed if he won't let us. He can be strict about observing rules. We asked Arabella to seek his permission and she said she will try. She is keen because of John, I because of Jim, Charley because it's John's* Sea King *and Harriet because . . .*

Benjamin took his watch from his waistcoat pocket as his children filed into the dining-room for breakfast. He glanced at it, giving a little nod of satisfaction. They were on time but his curiosity was aroused; he sensed an air of tension as if, for some reason, they were presenting him with a united front. He noticed Charley's red-rimmed eyes but made no comment; his son would have to get over his mother's death, just as they all would.

'Good morning,' he greeted them, and received in reply a chorus of 'Good morning, Papa.'

Arabella headed for her usual place but stopped when she saw that it was not set. Her father caught her questioning glance and gestured to the seat her mother had always occupied. Arabella hesitated and then, embarrassed, took her place opposite him.

When they were all seated, with hands clasped in front of them and heads bowed, he said grace. After the final 'Amen' the usual outburst of conversation was missing and only necessary words were spoken during the meal. Benjamin judged this to be out of respect for their mother but became aware that his other three children kept glancing at their eldest sister, with what he took to be a degree of expectancy.

It was only when Arabella finally laid down her knife and fork that she seemed to gather her courage and allow herself to look directly at him.

'Father, we would like your permission to go and watch the *Sea King* sail this morning. It is the last whale-ship to leave Whitby this season and it is John's command. We know we are in mourning but the *Sea King* and John are special and . . .'

'Stop, young lady, stop!' Benjamin's words resounded round the room, making Sarah and Charley flinch. Harriet stiffened. Arabella's lips tightened. Her hands, hidden on her lap, clenched. Then she felt a surge of confidence; her mother's presence seemed to be with her. She eyed her father as he went on. 'We buried your mother only yesterday. There is an official period of mourning to be observed; you know you should all remain in the house.' His face darkened. 'No, you may not go. What would people think?'

Arabella dampened her lips. 'Father, this is a whale-ship that is sailing. The whalers deserve the special send-off Whitby folk always give them.'

'And this one is special to the family. We have never failed to see John go,' put in Harriet.

'What would he think if we weren't in our usual place on the cliffs?' added Arabella, thankful for Harriet's support.

'I will be at the quay to issue last-minute instructions to John,' returned Benjamin.

'While we sit at home twiddling our thumbs!' Harriet pouted, casting down her eyes when they momentarily met her father's smouldering gaze. 'What does it matter what people think?'

'You know full well that it matters to our standing in the community. And so soon after . . .'

'I think Mother would have wanted us to go,' said Arabella, quietly but with a conviction that revealed she truly believed what she was saying. 'I think you know what Mama's views of mourning were – that there is too much outward show for the sake of convention and appearance, especially where women are concerned.'

'And you men have it easy because you can escape by going out to work while *we* have to stay at home in the gloom of drawn curtains and lack of—' Harriet's boldness was cut short by her father.

'Stop!'

He let a charged silence fill the room, but Arabella and Harriet knew this tactic and were determined to have none of it.

'Father, you have put me in Mother's place in this household. Acting in my new capacity, and because of the special circumstances of this particular sailing, I ask you to relent and allow us, in the usual way, to wish our sailors good luck in facing the dangers that await them in the Arctic. We mean no disrespect to Mother's memory and I believe she would understand. We mean no disrespect to our friends or to the Whitby people either. In fact, I believe that, even if they threw up their hands in horror at our appearing in public so soon, they would appreciate our thoughts for local men who are, after all, helping to make your firm a thriving enterprise. Don't they deserve our visible support when they sail?'

Harriet felt like cheering her sister's eloquence and, seeing their father's anger ease a little, added her own support. 'We are not asking for mourning to be dropped altogether, just for a few hours while we see the *Sea King* sail. We will keep to ourselves, with no frivolity, and as soon as we return we will observe every mourning ritual.' She had put on her softest voice, one she had employed before to ease her father's obdurate attitudes; it was the voice that had won her most of her requests. 'I think those men will carry away something special with them when they see us waving from the cliff as usual.'

Seizing on this, Arabella added, 'You know Mother took a special interest in the whale-men's welfare. Allow us to be there in her memory.'

Benjamin swallowed hard. They were very persuasive, but he had to retain a semblance of authority so prolonged his consideration, letting it charge the atmosphere with the inference that he really did not condone their request. Then he said, with obvious regret, 'Very well. Your mother would have looked forward to being there with you, so for her sake I'll allow you to go. But it must be just this once that you abandon your mourning.'

Arabella and Harriet restrained their jubilation and desire to show their appreciation more openly. They knew their father preferred to keep outward displays of emotion in check. 'Thank you, Papa,' they said quietly.

He glanced at his other two children. Their eyes were

bright with pleasure but still held a touch of wariness. 'You two kept very quiet,' he said.

They gave him wan but appreciative smiles, then Charley burst out, 'But you'll let us see the whale-ships return?'

'I shall think about that at the appropriate time. I've said you may go today but there is a condition. I'll arrange for the carriage to be here for you in an hour and will issue instructions for you to be taken to the cliff-top. You must watch the *Sea King* from the carriage; you are not to leave it. Using the vehicle will ensure you do not mingle with people. As I told you, I will be on the quay so will not have time to get to the clifftop to be with you. When the *Sea King* has sailed, you must come straight home. Now, off with you.' He glanced at Arabella. 'See that you abide by all I say.'

'We will, Papa.'

The carriage arrived exactly at the time stated. The ruddy-faced coachman, Daniel Foster, was all attentiveness as he ushered his four charges into the coach after Benjamin had given him precise instructions.

He drove with care down the steep road to the bridge spanning the Esk in the heart of Whitby. Wives with babes-in-arms and others with young children holding on to their skirts jostled through the crowd to reach the quay and say goodbye to the husbands they would not see again for six months. Mothers gave their sons a blessing for a safe voyage; girls wanted a last hug from their sweetheart. Some folk made their way to the staithes and piers to be close to the ship when it sailed, while others chose to watch the *Sea King* from the cliffs to either side of the river. Whichever they chose, their numbers were constantly swelled by more and more people assembling to give these sailors the send-off deemed suitable for men around whom a certain reputation had grown. Men who hunted huge whales in treacherous Arctic seas from open boats with hand-held harpoons, bringing wealth to the town and good livings to their families.

The Brooks' coach travelled at a walking pace among the jostling crowd crossing the bridge. Conversations, shouts and the general hum of a working port rose in a cacophony of sound that was intensified by the cliffs rising above both sides of the river. Though some of them were saddened by the imminent parting, which would soon begin, signalled when the *Sea King* slipped her moorings, the prevailing atmosphere was one of gaiety.

The Brook children enjoyed the lifting of their spirits, but were reminded of their loss when they were recognised and sympathetic looks cast in their direction.

Daniel directed the horse along Church Street, passing the quays and the *Sea King*, around which the bustle in the final moments before sailing intensified. Arabella caught a glimpse of their father deep in conversation with John. How she wished she dare stop the coach and make her own goodbye, but she knew she must heed her father's instructions.

The coach rumbled on, gathering a little more pace as the crowds flocking towards the mouth of the river thinned. That pace slowed again when they turned into Green Lane and started to climb to the Abbey Plain. Driving past the ruined abbey, Daniel found a suitable place to park the carriage only a short distance from the assembled crowd.

'We can't see the *Sea King* come down the river,' grumbled Charley.

'We'll see her before she reaches the piers,' Arabella pointed out.

'But I want—' Charley cut short his protest. 'I'm off!' He flung open the carriage door, jumped to the ground and set off in the direction of the onlookers and the place from which they all generally watched the whale-ships sail.

'Charley!' Arabella's call went unheeded. She knew it was useless; her brother was devoted to the whale-ships and in particular the *Sea King*, where she knew all his future hopes lay.

'I'll go after him!' shouted the usually quiet Sarah, and was out of the coach at once.

Daniel appeared at the door, his face tight with anxiety. 'Miss Arabella! They shouldn't . . . Your father . . .'

'Don't worry, Daniel. You couldn't stop them.'

'But I received strict instructions that you were all to remain in the coach.' His face clouded over at the thought of the reprimand he would receive if Mr Brook heard that his children, supposedly in mourning, had been mingling with the crowd on the East Cliff. It was an encounter he would definitely not enjoy.

'It's all right, Daniel, I will take full responsibility,' Arabella reassured him. She knew her father was bound to find out and the thought of his reaction was already troubling her.

'Very well, miss.' He touched the peak of his hat and moved away.

'Where are they? Can you see them?' Arabella demanded of Harriet.

'Over to the left. Sarah's got him and is trying to bring him back. They are receiving some disapproving glances.'

Arabella felt a little relief when she saw Sarah's persuasive powers triumph. Charley, dragging his feet and glowering with disapproval, was heading for the coach.

'You shouldn't have done that, Charley. Father's sure to get to know and then we'll all be in trouble,' Arabella chided him.

Charley looked downcast. 'I'm sorry,' he mumbled. 'I just wanted to see . . .'

'I know,' cut in Arabella. 'You can see her from here. Just stand still.'

He shuffled nearer the carriage door and Sarah, after acknowledging Arabella's 'Thank you', stood with him, her arm around his shoulders.

Harriet's questioning look was acknowledged by Arabella, who gave her an approving nod. Both young women stepped out of the coach and went to stand beside Sarah and Charley.

'*Sea King!*' Someone in the throng had sighted the ship moving down the river. The name rippled through the crowd. Interest in the Brook family was diverted to the vessel and to giving the Whitby men the send-off they deserved.

Arabella's concentration on the ship as it was manoeuvred downstream became tinged with delight when she saw John standing near the helmsman. From his attitude and the way he gesticulated she knew he was intent on making sure his vessel reached the sea safely.

'Jim!' Sarah had spotted him among the men swarming up the rigging to loosen sails so as to catch a favourable wind. She saw him pause briefly and turn his head towards the East Cliff. Realising he would recognise the coach, she raised her hand and waved the handkerchief he had given her as a present. Her heart beat fast when she saw him wave back vigorously before resuming his climb.

'He's seen you! He's seen you!' cried Charley, jumping up and down beside her. 'There's John!' He glanced at Arabella and saw her attention was riveted on him.

God bless your voyage, John, and bring you safely home, she thought.

Ever since she was a little girl Harriet had always loved to see the whale-ships leave and return. Those days were special to her, and every time she waved the men off she renewed her vow that one day she would marry a ship's captain. Today that vow had become more prominent than ever in her mind. She recalled one day catching the glint in John's eye when she came downstairs in a new dress . . . Although she'd glimpsed a warning in Arabella's gaze, she knew he would not be averse to flirting with her. When John had initially hesitated before her more obvious ploys she had become more subtle in her approach.

The death of their mother had brought about a change of circumstances generally in the Brook household. Harriet wondered if John might have second thoughts about marrying the dutiful eldest daughter of a widower; the added responsibility that would bring, especially as the widower was his employer, could be oppressive. Harriet had seen a more serious side to Arabella emerge even though that duty had been thrust upon her only twenty-four hours ago. Already it was stifling her once attractive personality. Harriet thought this might well be the time to increase John's awareness of her.

She was not to be denied now in spite of their mourning. She took out the white scarf she had kept hidden in her black bag, holding it stretched between her hands

31

above her head in the certainty that John would know it signalled: 'Safe voyage. Remember me.'

'Harriet!' Arabella glared at her sister. 'Put that away!'

Any further exchange of words was precluded by a shout from Charley: 'He's seen us! He's seen us!'

John raised both arms and waved vigorously, then turned his attention back to taking the ship safely out of harbour.

Amidst shouts and cheers from both sides of the river the *Sea King* moved steadily towards the stone piers. The last whale-ship to sail this year received an enthusiastic send-off, to match that given to the rest of the fleet two weeks previously.

Leaving the protection of Whitby's sheltering cliffs, the *Sea King*'s sails filled with wind. She passed between the twin piers and took to her rightful place on the ocean. Her bow cut into the sea, leaving a foaming wake to mark her course.

'Hoist y'r main tops'l!'

'Hoist the top gallants!'

As the commands came they were instantly obeyed. The wind seemed to take joy from driving the ship through the undulating sea. The men who had been aloft swarmed down the shrouds, their job done, and resumed their allotted tasks on deck.

John looked back to the clifftop, picking out the two girls who waved to him there.

'We'd better go,' said Arabella at length.

'But we always wait until we can no longer see the *Sea King*,' protested Charley.

'I know, but this time it's different,' sympathised his

sister. She too would have loved to stay. She always felt especially in touch with John as the ship dwindled to a mere speck and then finally disappeared from sight, but today her father had placed a responsibility on her shoulders and she must see it was carried out. 'We only just managed to persuade Father to let us come today, we don't want to annoy him. If we do he may not let us come to see the whale-ships return.'

Grumpily, Charley kicked at the grass then climbed into the coach.

'Do you think the *Sea King* will manage to return with the others?' asked Sarah as they settled into their seats.

'It all depends how quickly John can find whales.'

It was going to be a long wait until they knew, but that time was far from Arabella's thoughts; first there was her father to face.

Reaching home, the Brook children settled uneasily in the drawing-room to await his return.

'I wish Mama were here,' said Charley, a catch in his voice.

'We all do,' said Harriet, tightening her lips to hold back the tears.

Sarah nodded and swallowed hard, but that did not prevent a tear from trickling down her cheek.

Arabella herself was too full of emotion to speak as the enormity of her loss hit home afresh. She dabbed at her eyes with her handkerchief.

Their thoughts were suddenly interrupted by the front door slamming shut and quick footsteps, determination in their tread, crossing the hall. The door was flung open. Their father glanced inside.

'Arabella, my study!' He turned and was gone, leaving the door open for her.

33

She rose from her seat. Her heart pounded; her mind was filled with apprehension. She paused and straightened her dress, giving herself a moment to compose herself. Then, feeling her siblings' sympathy, she walked briskly from the room.

Her father was standing with his back to the fireplace when she joined him, his face dark with anger. 'What's this I hear? My children, in mourning, seen among the crowd on the cliff?'

'I can explain, Father,' said Arabella, a tremor in her voice.

'You'd better! And it had better be good.' His piercing eyes bored into her.

'Charley jumped out of the coach and ran off. Sarah went after him and brought him back.'

'*That* is your explanation? It's not what I heard. I was told *you* were among the crowd watching the *Sea King* sail.'

'That's not strictly true!' protested Arabella. 'When Sarah and Charley returned, Harriet and I stepped down and stood beside them so we weren't among the crowd.'

Benjamin hesitated; his dissatisfaction with what he had heard was not salved one bit. 'All right, folk have a habit of embellishing tales and I take your word about what happened, but that does not alter the fact that you were in charge. You should not have let the boy misbehave. You are responsible for Charley's behaviour. If you are to take on your mother's role, you must be firmer with your siblings.'

'Yes, Papa. I'm sorry for what happened. Truly I am.'

Benjamin nodded. 'Very well. See that it does not happen again. Now send Charley to me.'

'Yes, Papa.'

Arabella left the room feeling hurt by the criticism and blame her father had heaped on her. He had not taken into account the demands he had made on her inexperience. How she longed for her mother, who had always acted as a buffer between her husband and children, ever-ready to soften their father's severity. And, John, why didn't you propose . . . no, why haven't you already married me? Then I would never have had this unlooked for responsibility meted out to me. Arabella's eyes welled with tears. She must escape, if only for a few moments, the stifling atmosphere of this house. First she poked her head round the drawing-room door.

'Charley, Papa wants you in the study.'

He froze in his seat; tears rose to his eyes and an awful sinking feeling gripped his stomach. He blanched and looked to his sister for help.

'Just tell him exactly what happened,' said Arabella. 'But I wouldn't keep him waiting if I were you.' She turned to head for the front door, pausing only to watch her brother walking reluctantly to his father's study.

Arabella stepped outside and drew in a deep breath of sea air. Then the tears flowed.

'Tell me what happened,' boomed Benjamin as soon as the door closed behind his son.

Charley hesitated nervously.

'Answer me, boy!'

'Er . . .' He bit his lip, fear in his eyes. 'Er . . . I jumped from the coach, no one could stop me, but Sarah came after me and took me back,' he replied, his voice barely above a whisper. 'I'm sorry, Father.'

'So you should be. You deliberately disobeyed me, and got your sister into trouble. That's nothing to be proud of.

35

You asked me if you would be able to see the whale-ships return. Well, I'll have to think very seriously about *that* and take your disobedience into full consideration.'

'Please, Father, punish me some other way, but let me see the whale-ships return!' Charley pleaded.

Benjamin grunted. 'I'll see. But it strikes me you are getting too caught up with the whale-ships; you ought to set your mind on other things. Now, go to your room and don't come out until you hear the dinner gong. I'm very disappointed in your behaviour today. It makes me wonder if I can trust you to be obedient in the future.'

Charley did not reply, only stared down at the carpet and for a moment saw the swirling pattern as the ripples of a beckoning sea.

'Off with you,' barked Benjamin.

Startled, the boy jerked his attention back to the present and scurried from the room, his father's final, 'Your room,' ringing in his ears.

Tears burst from his eyes as he ran up the stairs. He flung open his bedroom door, sent it crashing behind him and flung himself face down on the bed.

'Oh, Mama, why did you die?' he sobbed. 'You know how much I love the whale-ships, just as you did.'

3

8 April 1832. My thoughts are with Jim now; he should be in Shetland if the Sea King *has had favourable winds. It will be the last time he sees these shores, maybe even land, for six months. I hope the voyage is without danger and that he returns safely. He likes sailing with John and has every confidence in him as a captain . . .*

The smudge on the horizon gradually took on a more solid appearance as the *Sea King* edged closer to Shetland. John was thankful that the weather had remained fair and the sea calm throughout their run north. He knew he had not pleased the men when he had issued orders that no one was to be allowed ashore in Lerwick except for the necessity of taking on supplies. There had been mutterings, but no open hostility. On previous whaling voyages he had allowed the crew twenty-four hours ashore there – after all it was the last time they would be in touch with civilisation for some time – but he wanted to make up for their delayed sailing on this occasion.

They dropped anchor within close sight of the town, its grey buildings blending in with the unattractive hills that formed a dull backcloth. John, leaving the first mate in charge, chose a four-man crew to row him ashore to negotiate for fresh supplies. They passed several small boats already heading for the *Sea King*; their occupants, old and young, were aiming to carry out a brisk trade with the seamen, in eggs, chickens and fish in exchange for money, clothes or salt beef.

John negotiated for supplies for his ship and urged that delivery to the *Sea King* should be swift. Knowing the quality of Shetlanders as sailors, he then turned his attention to signing on six of them to make up his full complement.

The moment the *Sea King* dipped her bow into the sea on leaving Lerwick always made him feel that his striving and hard work, in moving from cabin boy to captain, had been worthwhile. Ahead lay the Arctic with its bounty that could bring wealth to him and to Whitby. He had never deluded himself that this life would be easy; the Arctic could be treacherous and would not yield its treasures lightly. Knowing that, John realised the responsibility he had towards his crew and the *Sea King*; every time he sailed out of Lerwick he firmed his resolve not to fail them.

With the weather still holding good and the ship under full sail, he let his thoughts stray to his home and those he had left behind there. He had always counted himself fortunate that when tragedy had struck his life, he had had the deep friendship and influence of the Brook family to help ease his pain and show him that life could still have a purpose. He would be ever grateful to Mr Brook for giving him the chance to achieve his desire of sailing to the Arctic.

Having no brothers or sisters of his own, John had become close to the Brook children and to none more so than Arabella. Of the same age and similar interests, they had shared much: walking on the cliffs; exploring the sacred stones of the ruined abbey; sharing the exhilaration of the wind-driven waves lashing the West Pier, and all the excitement of the sea-faring life as they strolled along Whitby's quays.

But then he recalled a Brook family outing to nearby Sandsend three years ago, shortly after he had returned from an Arctic voyage. They had seized the chance one fine autumn day to have a last picnic before he sailed again, to bring timber from the Baltic this time. The day had been filled with magic, creating the feeling that all was well with the world. He still recalled the moment when Arabella had suggested they should both walk by the sea. He had grasped this chance to be alone with her; to share a silence charged with a feeling that went beyond mere companionship. The gentle lapping of waves, sending fingers of white foam sliding up the beach, filled these moments with a music that haunted him when he was far away.

'I'll remember being here with you when I am alone in my cabin,' he'd said at the time, letting his fingers touch hers.

She'd sensed a change in the close friendship that had existed between them since childhood and let her fingers entwine with his. 'Only then?' she'd asked coyly, allowing the teasing twinkle in her eyes to betray her true feelings for him.

'You will always—' His words were interrupted.

'Wait for me!' A shrill cry broke the spell that was drawing them closer. They turned and saw Harriet running towards them, tugging at the ribbon that held her hair. Loose, caught by the movement and the breeze, it streamed out behind her in dark undulating waves. With one hand she held her pretty dress just high enough to clear the sand, revealing her ankles and white shoes. Two buttons at the top of her bodice had been unfastened, exposing a little more than her neck.

For one moment John felt shocked, but almost immediately sensed an upsurge of joy at the carefree aura surrounding Harriet. He glanced at Arabella and saw the look of displeasure cross her features. He knew she resented her sister's intrusion. His satisfaction on realising this was marred when he saw the dazzling light in the younger girl's eyes directed at him. He was aware, by the frown and hostile look she arrowed at Harriet, that Arabella believed her sister was openly flirting with him and did not like it. He recalled feeling flattered then but at the same time wondering, as he had done throughout the following years, if Harriet could ever take to the life of a sea captain with its inevitable long partings. He had more or less held her flirting at bay since, while at the same time admiring her restless heart, its spirit free as the ocean streaming away beneath the *Sea King*. He was heading for the treacherous waters of the North and the adventure he had always craved. Arabella would embrace this lifestyle with ease, Harriet with . . .? Was everything in life like that – a choice between safety and risk? he wondered. Arabella or Harriet?

John started at his own thoughts. They had never before become so clear in his mind; so demanding of a reply. They must always have been there but never before been acknowledged. Why now? Why was he suddenly seeing both girls in a different light, one that stirred his mind and body more strongly than ever? Was something inside trying to force him to make a momentous decision about his future? His lips tightened. Annoyed with himself, he shook his head as if to cast such thoughts back where they belonged. He was on a whaling voyage, one that would require all his concentration if he were to return safely to Whitby with a full ship.

'Barbour!' the first mate's voice boomed across the deck.

'Aye-aye, sir!' Jim left the rope he was coiling and, ever-eager to obey and please, sprinted across the deck.

'Remember when I showed you how to check a whale-boat and its gear last voyage . . .'

'Aye-aye, sir.'

'Off with you and do it now.'

'Aye-aye, sir.' Jim started to turn away.

'Hold on!' The mate suppressed a smile at the boy's over-eagerness. He levelled his eyes sternly on Jim. 'No mistakes, remember. Men's lives can depend on the way things are set out in a whale-boat. Everything needs to be in just the right place, ready at hand, when closing in on a whale.'

'Aye-aye, sir.' Jim ran off to the first whale-boat slung on its derricks and clambered on board. He still recalled vividly the instructions he had been given on his first voyage, and set about his task industriously. When he had finished, he paused before moving on to the next boat and looked around him. He was pleased to see the billowing sails above, carrying him within sight of the ice ocean that had thrilled him the first time he had seen it. He considered himself lucky to have been signed on as a member of *Sea King*'s crew and to be sailing under Captain Sharp's command. He was determined to make the most of this opportunity. And he was equally unwavering in his devotion to Sarah Brook whom, last year, he had saved from the teasing taunts of two hooligans on Whitby's East Side. Afterwards he had walked her home. At the gate to the grand house on the West Cliff, which had brought wonderment to his eyes, she had thanked him shyly, asked his name and then hurried up the path to the front door. As he had watched her go Jim had experienced a feeling he had never had before. He felt puzzled as he made his way thoughtfully back to the East Side and the office where he was to sign on as cabin boy to the *Sea King*.

That feeling returned the next day when he saw Sarah on the quay and sensed that she had come there on purpose to see him.

This proved to be true when she said, 'I've come to thank you properly, Jim,' as soon as she confronted him. 'I did not do so yesterday.'

Embarrassed, he stuttered, 'It was nothing, miss.'

'But it was, Jim. And my name is Sarah.'

'You want me to call you that?'

'Of course, if we are to be friends.'

He stared at her in surprise.

'Wouldn't you like that?' she asked.

His eyes widened. The daughter of the owner of the ship on which he was to sail wanted to be his friend! 'Of course I would,' he told her.

'Then it is settled,' said Sarah, her voice bright with pleasure. 'I'll be by to see you again tomorrow, and I'll be on the cliffs every time you sail and there again for all your homecomings.'

Young, innocent love had begun between them on that day.

It all came back to Jim vividly as he sat in a whaleboat on board the *Sea King*. Homesickness began to take hold of him until he chased the emotion from his mind. He had a job to do on board a ship he already loved on this his second voyage. There would be many more, and always with a sweetheart to come home to. He swung out of the whale-boat and went to the next, aware that he was a lucky man.

20 August 1832. Nearly five months since Mama died. It hasn't been an easy time. We have all missed her so much. Oh, why did she have to die? Papa keeps reminding us of the etiquette we have to follow. He expects us to remain indoors, but we do sneak outside occasionally for a breath of fresh air. I feel sorry for Arabella, trying to cope with Papa's heavy expectations. It has been a hard time for her, and Harriet hasn't been much help. I hope Papa relents a little now half mourning is close, and then with the Sea King *back Arabella will have John and I'll be seeing Jim again . . .*

Arabella sighed as she entered her room. Her shoulders drooped and she sank wearily into the armchair placed near the window. Her father reminded her constantly of her responsibilities, pointing out that she should not rely too much on Mrs Ainslie: 'Arabella, you wield the ultimate authority . . . exert it!' Tears rolled silently down her cheeks as heartfelt words escaped from her lips: 'Mama, how did you cope? Help me, wherever you are. Please help me!'

If only her father would relax his severity a little. She knew how much the loss of her mother had hit him, but hadn't the rest of the family been hit as hard? He didn't seem to recognise that they had lost the love of the mother they had adored. Nor did he appear to realise that Arabella had to comfort and support her sisters and brother in their loss while trying to cope with the pain of her own.

She recognised that Mrs Ainslie understood the situation, even though she made no adverse comment about Father's attitude. Arabella appreciated the way that the housekeeper emphasised to her employer that she was following the young mistress's orders.

They were thankful that he spent a great deal of his time at work. It was a balm to his loss, but that balm did not extend to his home-life, where he felt the absence of his beloved wife all the more and presented a severe front that they did not seem capable of breaching. With only a month of full mourning left, Harriet, Sarah and Charley were pestering Arabella to try and get their father to relax the half mourning observance and so give them more freedom. How she would like that too! It would mean she could freely see more of John on his return. She'd promised to try but knew she would have to judge carefully the right moment to make her request.

'Mr Meadows to see you, sir,' said Jake Carter, head clerk of the three employed by Benjamin Brook.

'Show him in.'

With the door to Benjamin's office open wide, Carter stood to one side as he indicated to Mr Meadows that Mr Brook would see him.

A big bluff character strode in. His round red face showed clear signs of good living; his eyes were bright with enjoyment of life. He was impeccably dressed in a grey frock coat and matching trousers. He passed his top hat and cane to Carter, who left the room as Benjamin rose quickly from his chair and came out from behind his desk to greet the newcomer.

'Henry! ' Their firm handshake spoke of a long-standing friendship. 'I haven't seen you for a while.'

'I've been away for a couple of months, Benjamin. I told you I was going.' He gave his friend a tap on the shoulder. 'You must have forgotten. Understandable, in the circumstances.'

Benjamin nodded. 'Sit down. A drink?'

Henry beamed. 'Never say no. You know what I like.'

Benjamin gave a small smile. 'That's something I haven't forgotten.' He moved to a table on which stood two decanters and some glasses. He poured two measures of whisky, bringing one to Henry, who took it with profuse thanks and an eye that spoke of anticipated enjoyment.

Benjamin returned to his chair behind the large oak desk, raised his glass and said, 'To friendship.'

Henry acknowledged the sentiment and added, 'Now, how are you settling down?'

'It's been hard. I miss Jane terribly. My business is my whole life now.'

'Don't let it take you over.' Henry fixed him with a serious expression. He had quickly summoned up a judgement born of their close relationship. 'Ben, we have known each other a long time. I know your two loves were always your wife and your work, but you also have a family. Don't forget that or them. They can be your great strength now.'

Henry knew very well Benjamin had never been quite comfortable with children, even his own. That had caused a distance between them that even Jane had not been able to break down; all she had been able to do was act as a wise go-between. Now that her influence was missing, Henry sensed that life for Benjamin's children would not be easy.

Benjamin did not reply to his observation; he merely nodded as if to say it had been noted. But Henry was determined not to see his friend fade away into a life of work and nothing more. He was a great believer that pleasure and work should be enjoyed in equal measure; that each was essential to and could enhance the other.

'Have you had any social life at all since Jane died?' he asked bluntly.

Benjamin looked shocked; his face darkened. 'Of course not! I'm still in mourning.'

'With all its outward trappings.' The tone of Henry's voice showed he strongly disapproved of them. 'They go on too long, darkening our lives when they were made for living, not prolonged mourning. We shut our women away at this time and that is not healthy, for them or for us.' Seeing that Benjamin was about to protest, he held up his hand to stop him and continued, 'I know you think I'm too liberal in my outlook but I believe we dwell too much on what is termed proper etiquette, the purely outward signs of our inner feelings. We observe these for too long. Of course we must observe some period of mourning, but the present ideas are too restricting – particularly to family life. Our loss should be mourned openly for only a short while, it seems to me, and after that privately, for as long as we like. Maybe forever.'

Without speaking, Benjamin stared at him in a way that Henry could not truly fathom. Then he said quietly, 'I've known your views of life for some time, Henry. How could I not in a friendship as close as ours? I know you mean well and are trying to make things easier for me.'

46

'I am. I have your interests at heart. There is only a little time left before you reach what etiquette dictates as the point of half mourning for your children. I think that moment is a good opportunity for you to lift restrictions altogether. Set them free from convention and let them get on with their lives.'

'And be frowned on by the rest of Whitby society?'

'Good grief, man, who sets any store on society's frowns? You have a life to live and so have your children. Let them live . . . they'll love you for it.'

Benjamin recoiled a little from Henry's final remark. The love of his children and his for them was something he had never truly considered before. That was Jane's sphere, her contribution to the stability and well-being of their lives; he was the provider, and to be that required time and energy devoted to work. The result had been that, while he was a loving and devoted husband, he had never been on intimate terms with his own children.

'Set them free? But I've never held them back,' he protested.

Henry gave a small smile. 'You think not? Unknowingly you did; it was Jane who made sure your attitude was not as destructive as it might have been. What worries me now is that without her, you may become estranged from your children. That would be a tragedy. They would not wish it to happen, and I have no doubt would try to avoid it, but with no mother to act as intermediary . . .'

He saw doubt tinged with hostility in Benjamin's eyes. Wanting no estrangement between them, he spoke up quickly. 'I am acting as your friend, offering good advice. You can take it or leave it; I will not be offended. I would not wish our friendship to be strained by these

47

words. You know Imelda and I will do anything we can to help.'

Benjamin relaxed. Henry was right; their continued friendship was important and he knew Imelda missed Jane's companionship. Remembering that softened his reaction. 'I take no offence, Henry, I know you mean well.'

'Good. Then I hope you will take kindly to my suggestion about this half mourning aspect.' He paused.

Benjamin looked curiously at him. What was coming now? 'Well?' he prompted.

'The whale-ships should be home in about three weeks' time and that, according to my calculations, should be about the time of the start of your half mourning period, if you continue to observe it. If, however, you don't, it will be easier for Arabella to fit in with my suggestion.'

'Arabella?'

'Yes. After all, she is fulfilling Jane's role, and I suppose you intend that role to extend beyond household duties?'

'It has not done so far because of mourning observance.'

'And rightly so. But hear what I have to say next. So far the six individual ship owners in Whitby have sent their whale-ships, after their return from the Arctic, to the Baltic ports for timber, making as many fast crossings as possible before the winter freeze there. That has always led to rivalry in purchasing the best timber. I propose that in future we should sail as a fleet and share all the timber, every grade, equally between us.'

Benjamin's eyes brightened as business replaced talk of family matters. 'That sounds like a good idea, but will the other owners agree?'

Henry smiled. 'I'm going to soften them up with a dinner party. In a fortnight's time.'

'Husbands and wives?'

'Of course.'

'But I . . .'

'You have Arabella to accompany you.'

'I know, but . . .'

'You told me she was taking Jane's place?'

'Yes, but . . .'

'Stop prevaricating. This is your opportunity to shed half mourning and step back into the world. Allow Arabella to become an asset now. She won't let you down.' Henry stood up briskly. He reckoned he had said enough to make the impression he wanted to and to force his friend to consider his and his children's future. Henry knew there was much he hadn't any influence over and that Benjamin would remain the strict father he always had been, but maybe, just maybe, he had made sufficient headway to ease his friend's strict regime a little. Back in company, with Arabella beside him, the pain of his recent loss may be eased.

'I must be going. Let me know if I should send you an invitation,' he told his friend.

Benjamin stared thoughtfully at the closed door. Henry's idea of an amalgamation of Whitby whale-ships operating together, instead of acting as rivals in the Baltic timber trade, was a good one and could be of great benefit to them all. He realised that if he were to join his fellow ship owners in this scheme, he would have to defy the accepted attitude to mourning. Would that be such a harmful thing? Half mourning was near. He could ease it for his children, and in so doing clear his own way to participating in Henry's venture. It was tempting, he realised, but he would prefer to seek a second opinion. Without saying where he was going, he left his offices. He strode purposefully to the Vicarage, where he was announced to the Vicar.

'I'm sorry to visit you without an appointment, Arthur,' he apologised as he took the Vicar's extended hand.

'There's never any need for you to make an appointment, you know that, Benjamin. Do sit down.' Arthur Bosworth indicated one of the armchairs set in his book-lined study and took another himself. 'What is it, Benjamin? I know from your expression that something is troubling you.'

He nodded. 'I have been invited to a social occasion which could have a beneficial outcome for my business, but it would mean that Arabella would have to accompany me and we would not yet be out of mourning . . . though very close to the start of the half mourning period.'

'And you want to know my opinion about accepting?'

'I would value it.'

The Vicar considered, his lips drawn tight, then he gave a small smile. 'Many see me as merely a fire and brimstone man, and maybe that is because I adopt an uncompromising attitude to matters of religion and our service to God. In all else I am, I hope, an understanding man. Regarding your query I have an open mind. Observing the general protocol of mourning is no bad thing; it keeps our minds fixed on our final destiny and brings to mind what we need to do to reach the heavenly rest that God holds out to us.

'There are times when I see families who would benefit from a relaxation of mourning attitudes, though.

Maybe this is the case in your dilemma. If a relaxation would be an advantage to you and your family . . . create better understanding between you, for example . . . then I would not frown on it. Ultimately it is up to the individual to decide. That decision may bring frowns and criticism from some, but no one should really stand in judgement over you. After all, "Who will cast the first stone?" Only you can judge what is right for you.'

4

27 August 1832. We should be going into half mourning in a couple of months. We need Papa to say when. We will then be able to wear the new dresses made for us six weeks ago. They are of deep mauve and very plain, but it will be a relief to be out of black. I do hope Papa will allow us more freedom then. The whale-ships should be arriving home soon. I hope they are all safe. These will be anxious days in the town. I am so looking forward to seeing Jim again.

Oh, I'll have to stop. Charley has just poked his head round the door. Papa wants us in his study NOW.

One by one Benjamin's children trooped into the room, casting anxious glances at their father sitting upright behind his large mahogany desk. They sat down without speaking; the girls prim and proper with hands placed together on their laps. Charley slumped, saw his father frown, and immediately straightened. Benjamin cast a glance at each child in turn, cleared his throat and started to speak.

'It will soon be time for you to go into half mourning. I know you still miss your mother, but I believe she would wish me to ease some of the restrictions placed on you by society.' He paused as if gathering his thoughts. His children waited in hopeful anticipation. 'You should still conduct yourselves with the utmost decorum and respect for her memory, especially while in company, but I am not going to impose any further restrictions on you. You may now move more freely and mix with your friends more openly. You girls have suitable dresses, I believe, and Charley has his new suit. You may also wear the appropriate jewellery, without being flamboyant. Use your commonsense in all these matters. That is all.'

Thankful for his decision, the girls knew better than to display their emotions so merely uttered a polite, 'Thank you.' But Charley's excited outburst startled them all. 'May we watch the *Sea King* when she arrives, Papa?'

Benjamin pursed his lips thoughtfully, eyes fixed on his son, who held his breath, hoping for the answer he wanted. 'Your behaviour when she sailed did not have much to commend it. However, I said I would consider the matter when she was due to return. Hopefully that will be soon. You have behaved well in the intervening period so I think I can say that you may.'

Charley's face lit up and he started to thank his father profusely, only for his words to die away when Benjamin held up a hand to stop him. He fixed his son with an expression that Charley knew well.

'Behave yourself when she arrives. There will be a lot of people about and some will be ever-ready to criticise your behaviour. Don't let me hear one word spoken against you.'

'Yes, sir.'

Benjamin nodded. 'That's that then.' His tone was dismissive but when they rose from their chairs he said, 'Arabella, I should like you to stay.'

'Yes, Papa.'

Knowing he liked to be face to face when taking her into his confidence, she moved her chair to a better position. Leaning forward on his desk, Benjamin eyed his eldest daughter intently. His voice was warmer than before when he told her: 'You have done very well since your mother died. I am pleased with you. Now, even though there are certain formalities we should observe, I think it is time to start inviting friends to visit us and to accept invitations.'

Arabella's heart fluttered and she felt a sinking feeling in her stomach. He was expecting her to take up the hostess's role her mother had filled with such panache.

'I know it will put more responsibility on you, but I have every confidence that you will manage. You will make a delightful hostess.'

Her father was not given to flattery, at least not that she was aware of; she had certainly never experienced it. It made Arabella a little suspicious about his motive.

'I'll do my best, Papa.'

'I know you will, so I have accepted an invitation to a small dinner party to be held by Mr Meadows. It will take place on the sixth of September. You already know him and Imelda well. You are also acquainted with the other guests – three whale-ship owners and their wives – so there'll only be ten of us. There's nothing to worry about. It's just a small dinner party. We'll be dining and talking.'

'But . . . Oh, Papa, what will I talk about?'

'Just take your lead from the others. They aren't ogres. You'll find it easy if you act sensibly and try to enjoy it. I know you will make a good impression on them all. That will help me establish a sound footing in the scheme Mr Meadows is going to put to them.'

Arabella's thoughts started to race. So that was what this was all about – the lifting of mourning restrictions had been instituted so that he could attend what was really a business meeting, disguised by the presence of wives and the promise of an excellent meal. No doubt the men planned to discuss this scheme, whatever it was, over their port and cigars. Her father could easily push other matters aside when business reared its head which, judging by the time he was spending away from the house recently, it was doing more and more frequently.

'I hope I am capable of doing whatever Mother would have done at such an occasion,' she said, quietly accepting what he wanted of her.

'I am sure you are. I have every faith in you.' Benjamin left a brief pause then added, 'Get yourself another dress, something special with the party in mind . . . something really attractive but not too ostentatious. Remember, we are still mourning your mother. As before, have the bill sent to me.'

Arabella quelled the excitement that coursed through her then. 'Thank you very much, Papa.' She had not expected such generosity. Another dress! Harriet would be jealous.

She started to rise from her chair.

'A moment more,' said her father.

She sank back, wondering what else was coming.

'I am going to Scarborough on the eighth on business, leaving soon after breakfast. I will be away for three days.'

'You may miss the return of the *Sea King*.'

'It can't be helped if I do. This is an important meeting. Jake Carter is capable of seeing to things if she does

55

dock before I'm back. There is nothing for you to worry about.'

Arabella subdued the urge to run up the stairs once she'd left the study. Safely on the landing, she raced to Harriet's room. When she burst in she found Sarah already there; both girls were holding their new dresses close and viewing themselves in the cheval glass. They swung round at her sudden intrusion.

'Won't it be nice to get into these?' cried Sarah.

Arabella laughed. 'It will, but I've something more to tell you and I'll need your help.'

Both girls were surprised by her exuberance. They knew the past six months had not been easy for her; her new responsibilities had weighed heavily on the eldest child. They were both pleased to see a new light shining in her eyes.

'It must be something good?' pressed Harriet.

The question made Arabella sober up. 'Well, part of it is. Papa has accepted an invitation to a small dinner party hosted by Mr and Mrs Meadows, and I am to accompany him.'

'You lucky thing!' cried Harriet.

'Am I?' said Arabella doubtfully. 'How will I fit in?'

'Of course you will,' said Sarah, confident of her sister's ability.

'Just go and enjoy it,' Harriet urged her.

Arabella still looked doubtful.

'You implied there was something good and something not so good . . . what is worrying you?' pressed Harriet.

'That I must attend the party.'

Harriet and Sarah cast questioning glances at each other. That didn't sound so dreadful to them.

'But Father has told me to get a new dress for it!'
Arabella pirouetted in the middle of the room, and her
sisters were pleased to see her look so joyful.

'Lucky you!' exclaimed Harriet, feeling a pang of jealousy.

'You deserve it,' said Sarah. 'I'm so pleased.'

'So am I,' Harriet added quickly.

'I'll want you two to help me choose.'

'That will be fun!' Sarah looked pleased to be asked.

'Of course it will,' agreed Harriet.

'Father said I must still observe half mourning, but it
can be a little more flamboyant.' Arabella gave herself a
little hug as she said, 'It will be so good to have something more attractive for when John gets back.'

Harriet froze inside at the expectations her sister's
words clearly implied. Those words echoed in her mind,
but secretly she determined not to be overshadowed when
John returned. She tightened her grip on her hurt feelings
and asked casually, 'Are you having Mrs Yates make it?'

'Yes. Mourning clothes are her speciality and we liked
the others she has made for us. There's not a lot of time
but I'm sure she'll cope. I'm off to tell Mrs Ainslie and
she'll send a message to Mrs Yates to visit the house
urgently.' With that she was out of the door.

Mrs Ainslie expressed delight at Arabella's news. 'You
have all observed full mourning impeccably and you
deserve some relaxation. It will be good for you to
accompany your father socially as well.'

'But how will I manage in front of all those ladies who
are older than me?' said Arabella, expressing her doubts.

'With great ease,' Mrs Ainslie told her. 'I'm sure they
will look for nothing more than that you be yourself. And
that, I'm sure, will charm them.'

When Arabella reached Harriet's room again she found that her sister had already donned her new dress and was helping her younger sister into hers.

'How do we look?' asked Sarah, tweaking the stuff at her shoulders, to set the dress more comfortably.

'Perfect,' Arabella replied enthusiastically. She eyed the style recommended for Sarah by Mrs Yates: a plain bodice with small shoulder cape attached, sleeves that puffed to the elbows then came tight to the wrists. The skirt was narrow at the waist and slim-cut, its only decoration being a band of black lace set a foot above the hem.

'I'm going to wear the brooch Mama gave me,' announced Harriet, picking up a cruciform silver brooch and pinning it below the clip that held her cape in position at her neck.

'So will I,' cried Sarah, racing from the room, calling over her shoulder as she did so, 'Get into your dress, Arabella!'

She laughed. 'You're both enjoying this, aren't you?'

'Why not? Mama wouldn't mind,' returned Harriet.

'I'm sure she wouldn't.'

'Go on then, get into your dress,' Harriet prompted.

Swept up in their enthusiasm, Arabella hurried to her bedroom. When she returned, Sarah was pinning her brooch to the front of her dress. The next few minutes were full of smiles and teasing as Arabella shrugged on her dress, ably assisted by her two sisters.

'That suits you,' commented Harriet, standing back to survey the dress with a knowledgeable eye. 'Mrs Yates certainly knows the cuts and fashion to suit. All three dresses are similar but each fits our own personality.'

'You see more in them than I do,' replied Arabella, 'but I'll take your word for it.'

'Wait and see what Mrs Yates suggests for your party dress, even if she does have to keep within the bounds of half mourning. I'll bet it will just suit you.'

A knock on the door stopped any further discussion. Harriet opened the door to find Mrs Ainslie there.

'I have word for Miss Arabella,' she said.

'Come in, Mrs Ainslie.'

The housekeeper stepped into the room.

'What do you think?' asked Harriet as she went to stand with her sisters.

'Truly charming,' replied Mrs Ainslie, casting an eye over them and revealing her approval in her tone of voice.

'You have had word from Mrs Yates?' queried Arabella hopefully.

'She'll be here at ten in the morning.'

At precisely ten o'clock the dressmaker was admitted to the house in New Buildings. A small but well-built woman with an ample bosom, she held herself firmly erect in a pose that gave her an air of authority. She was followed into the house by a young assistant who seemed to be struggling with her burden of material samples and patterns. They were shown into the drawing-room, where Arabella, Harriet and Sarah were waiting.

Brief greetings were exchanged then Mrs Yates, never one for wasting time over frivolous talk when business was to be done, got down to the matter at hand.

'I have brought along my new assistant, Miss Fairbrow, who has a good eye for colour and design. She is originally from Scarborough and is hoping to return there eventually and set up her own business.'

With greetings exchanged and the materials and patterns placed on the table, Mrs Yates continued, 'Mrs Ainslie's note said the dress was for you, Miss Brook.'

Arabella nodded.

'I concluded that, because Mrs Ainslie indicated there is some urgency, it is to be worn during the half mourning period?'

Again Arabella nodded. 'Quite correct.'

'And, because I have already made you a dress to cover this period, I take it the second is to be worn for a special occasion?' Mrs Yates tilted her head to one side and gave her a querying look that stated, 'I'm right, aren't I?'

'Indeed. You are very shrewd, Mrs Yates.'

'I pride myself on being able to anticipate my clients' needs. Because of that, I have brought with me the patterns I think may fit your requirements without being too frivolous. I have also brought samples of suitable materials in grey, mauve, and lavender. I have not brought black as I thought you would want to escape from that, though I should add that you wear it very well. Not many people do . . . certainly not your sisters, though I mean that as no criticism of them.' She shot an apologetic glance at Harriet and Sarah and saw they had not taken offence.

'Shall we take a look then?' said Arabella, rising from her chair.

As they all went to the table Mrs Yates added, 'May I ask, what is this special occasion? It will help with my suggestions.'

'My father has been invited to a small dinner party and I am to accompany him.'

Mrs Yates nodded. 'Let us choose the material and

colour first, while I think of some designs appropriate to the occasion.'

An hour later, after much discussion and exchanging of opinions and preferences, a decision had been made regarding the colour – it was to be lavender with mauve trimmings – but there were still differences about the design.

'It is more than likely that the other ladies will have their shoulders bare and carry lightweight shawls should they require additional covering.'

'I could do so, too,' replied Arabella.

'But I really think your shoulders should not be bare on this occasion, not at this particular time.'

'May I make a suggestion, Mrs Yates?' put in Miss Fairbrow, who had been standing looking very thoughtful.

'Of course, Miss Fairbrow, please do.'

'Why don't we attach to the top of the dress a closely patterned black lace? There would be just the suggestion of bare shoulders through the lace while they would still appear decently covered. You said Miss Brook wears black well. And if we chose a slightly deeper shade of lavender for the main dress, the black would be more compatible with it. I noticed you have such a shade in stock, Mrs Yates. Why not let me slip back to your workplace and bring the bolt while you discuss the pattern of the actual dress?'

'Off you go then,' said Mrs Yates, smiling as she visualised the effect.

A quarter of an hour later Miss Fairbrow returned. As she laid the materials on the table they all saw the potential in her idea and no one was more enthusiastic about it than Harriet. Buoyed by their enthusiasm, Arabella said, 'Let's go up to my room and we can see how it will look.'

Once she had draped the lace over her bare shoulders and the silk was held up in front of her, they all agreed it would look just right.

Two queries remained in Arabella's mind. She put the first to Mrs Yates. 'You will keep it reasonably plain?'

'Of course, my dear. Plain but elegant.'

'And it will be ready for the sixth?'

'It will. May we arrange a fitting here, at two o'clock the day before?'

'Yes, of course. Oh, I am looking forward to seeing it!'

When it was close to time for their evening meal that night and her father had not yet returned, Arabella sought out Mrs Ainslie.

'I think we should serve. It's unfair on Cook to have her preparations spoiled.'

'Very well, I'll tell her so and ask her to set something aside for Mr Brook.'

As it turned out that was not necessary because, just before the soup was brought into the dining-room, Benjamin arrived. He made no apologies or explanation for his late arrival but took only a few minutes to wash his hands before sitting down at the table with them.

'I've had Mrs Yates here today,' began Arabella tentatively.

'And?' he prompted.

'She is making me a dress for our visit to Mr and Mrs Meadows.'

Benjamin took a spoonful of soup, dabbed his mouth with his napkin and asked, 'Will it be ready on time?'

'She promised it would be.'

He nodded but made no further observation. Arabella felt a little hurt that he was showing no greater interest.

Harriet sensed this, so spoke up with some enthusiasm. 'Arabella's dress will be gorgeous. She'll look very elegant for your visit, Papa.'

'I hope it will be within the bounds of propriety in our present circumstances,' was his only comment.

His attitude annoyed Harriet. Arabella, sensing her sister was about say something she might regret, quickly asked her to pass the salt. As she took the silver container, Arabella caught Harriet's eye and gave a slight shake of her head, silently mouthing the word 'Don't.'

Sensing the tension, Sarah tried to ease it. 'I hope the *Sea King* is home soon and is a full ship, Papa?'

'I hope so too,' came his reply, but there was no advance on conversation from him for the rest of the meal.

It was a relief for his children when Benjamin rose from his chair. 'I won't take dessert, and I'll have coffee in my study. I will be there for the rest of the evening preparing for my visit to Scarborough.'

'What are you going there for?' the naturally curious Charley blurted out.

'For the moment that is none of your business,' replied his father sternly, 'but next year, when you start working as an office-boy in the firm that one day will be yours, you will know all my business.' Without another word he hurried from the room, leaving his son aghast at the implication.

As the door closed Charley looked plaintively at Arabella. 'I don't want to be an office-boy, I want to sail on the *Sea King*.'

'I know, Charley, but please don't provoke Father at

the present time. Wait and see how things turn out.' She regretted that this was the best advice she could offer him. Deep down she knew that some day there would be a clash of wills, and from what her father had just indicated that clash would come next year.

Arabella woke early. Was she anxious about John because no whale-ship had yet returned or excited because today she would have her new dress fitted? She expected to find her father in the dining-room but discovered he had already left for his office. It seemed he could not bear to be in the house for long; she could only think that it brought him too many reminders of her mother.

Harriet came hurrying into the room then and immediately asked, 'Are you excited, Arabella?'

Knowing her sister was referring to the final dress fitting, she smiled. 'Yes, I suppose so.'

'Suppose so? If it were me I would not be able to contain myself. And if you were worrying about Charley, don't. He'll look after himself.'

'I hope you are right.'

No more was said as Sarah and Charley appeared. Without their father at the table, breakfast was enjoyed in a pleasant atmosphere with the young ladies keenly anticipating Mrs Yates's visit, leaving Charley to wonder what the fuss was all about – after all, it was just a dress!

Mrs Yates and Miss Fairbrow were greeted warmly when they were shown into the drawing-room by one of the maids. Miss Fairbrow placed a large cardboard box on the table and carefully removed the lid while everyone stood around, eagerly anticipating what was about to be revealed. Miss Fairbrow's long delicate fingers unfolded the tissue paper and gently lifted the dress by its shoulders from the box, holding it up for all to see.

The gasp from the three girls said it all. The gown was exquisitely cut, the work of an expert, the lace top blending so well with the main body of the dress that Arabella's doubts about the combination were quickly disproved.

Mrs Yates, who had stood to one side observing, was pleased by their reactions. She gave a little nod of approval as she caught Miss Fairbrow's eye. 'Shall we see how it fits?' the dressmaker suggested.

'Oh, yes!' cried Arabella. 'Unhook me, Sarah.'

Within a matter of moments Miss Fairbrow was helping her into the dress. With the last button fastened at the back, the silk smoothed and the lace given one last pat, everyone stood back to assess the appeal of the finished article worn by the one for whom it was meant.

'Beautiful.' The word was drawn out in wonder from Harriet.

'You look so pretty!' said Sarah, clapping her hands together.

'I must see for myself,' cried Arabella, making for the door. 'There's a mirror in the hall.'

Everyone followed her and watched admiringly as she viewed herself. 'It's a perfect fit, Mrs Yates. It's so lovely . . . I couldn't have wished for anything better.' She turned to Miss Fairbrow then. 'Thank you, too. Your suggestion about the lace works very well while still observing half mourning. My father will be very pleased.'

The following evening, dressed in a black suit, white shirt, stiff collar and black bow tie, Benjamin stood waiting in the hall with Harriet, Sarah and Charley when Arabella came down the stairs. She kept her eyes fixed on her father. For one moment she thought she saw his eyes sparkle with approval, but then it was gone. She yearned for a comment that reflected what everyone else had thought about the dress, but all she received was a casual, 'Your new dress looks nice.'

'Nice, Father. Nice?' snapped Harriet, disgusted by his assessment. 'It's exquisite, and Arabella looks lovely in it.'

His lips set in a grim line and for a moment he glared at Harriet, but said nothing except, 'Shall we go?'

Harriet kissed Arabella on the cheek. 'Have a good time.'

'Enjoy it,' said Sarah.

Charley grinned and winked at his eldest sister, which made her smile and lightened her thoughts. Yes, she would try and enjoy herself, nervous though she felt at this moment.

Arabella felt her stomach tighten as she walked up the path to the imposing house Mr Meadows had had built on the edge of the new developments on Whitby's West Cliff. The door was opened by a maid who had clearly been instructed on how to greet the guests. She ushered them into the hall, and another maid came forward to take their outdoor clothes. Arabella glanced around uneasily but found the interior of the house was not as ostentatious as she had expected. The maid who had admitted them then led them to the drawing-room. As she opened the door, Arabella heard lively conversation all around and felt a return of her uneasiness, but as she stepped into the room Mrs Meadows immediately alleviated that feeling with a warm greeting.

'Miss Brook, how delightful to have you here. You are most welcome.' She held out both her hands to Arabella, who felt a comforting friendliness in her touch.

'Thank you, Mrs Meadows,' she said shyly, sensing she was coming under the scrutiny of the other guests who stood quietly conversing in twos and threes around the room.

Mrs Meadows glanced next at Arabella's father. 'You have a charming daughter, Benjamin. You go and talk with someone – I'll look after her.'

As Benjamin moved away, Imelda Meadows took hold of Arabella's arm and spoke quietly. 'This must have been a difficult time for you, trying to take your mother's place while still so young. Nevertheless, I have watched you grow up – and look at you now! A charming and delightful young lady who wears that wonderful dress exquisitely. The other ladies will certainly question you about it. You probably know them all to some degree or other, but I'll introduce you. I am sure you will find them all friendly.'

'Thank you, Mrs Meadows.'

'Well, for a start, my dear, we'll drop such formalities – I am Imelda.'

Arabella blushed at the idea of being on Christian name terms with ladies so much older than herself, but welcomed the ease it generated as Imelda introduced her around the room. She felt the other ladies accept her immediately into their circle, and the gentlemen made no attempt to disguise their admiration for her. This made her anticipate the effect she would have on John when he returned from his lonely voyage. Already her apprehensions about this evening were dwindling. Throughout the sumptuous meal the talk was pleasant and, acting the perfect host and hostess, Henry and Imelda kept the conversation flowing, making sure that no one was left out.

When the final course was finished, Imelda silenced the chatter with a nod and said, 'Ladies, shall we leave the gentlemen to their port and cigars?'

Once the door to the drawing-room closed behind them Arabella was bombarded with admiring questions about her dress.

'Such a perfect fit.'

'You wear it so elegantly.'

'Who made it?'

'Ah, Mrs Yates. Of course, it had to be. The creative flair is there.'

'The colour suits you so well.'

'What a brilliant idea to make the top of black lace . . . so appropriate for you at this time.'

'Who is Miss Fairbrow?'

'I don't know her. From Scarborough, you say?'

'If that was her idea then I can see she'll have a brilliant future.'

So the approving comments rolled on until other topics drifted into the conversation and Arabella was drawn into those too. She found herself really enjoying the evening. Curiosity about what the men could be talking about kept coming into her mind, but she knew better than to raise it as a talking point with the other ladies who undoubtedly knew no more than she did.

Benjamin leaned back in his chair, drawing on his Havana cigar, its flavour melding with the taste of the good port he had savoured with delight. Henry certainly knew where to obtain the best. He cast a glance around at the other men who seemed to be enjoying the evening as much as he; Joseph Simmons, an astute man in his fifties, already looking ahead to when he estimated the whaling trade would begin to run down; Cuthbert Peckitt, a flamboyant young man with a sharp mind who had served on the whale-ships himself once and had built up a successful business on the back of his knowledge; and Jock Norcliffe, a solid, seemingly easy-going personality but one nobody would ever get the better of. He was a Shetlander who had come in on a Whitby whaler, married a local girl and stayed. And last of all there was Harry, Ben's long-time friend. They had grown up together as boys, both gone to sea at the same time, then settled ashore and become friendly rivals. So far Henry had mentioned the reason for this dinner party only to his old friend. Benjamin waited for the general announcement.

Jocular laughter and conversation between the five men was silenced when Henry tapped the table and said, 'Gentlemen, may I have your attention? I have a proposition to put to you.'

Silence fell upon the room. They all recognised from his tone of voice that Henry wanted them to give this their serious consideration. All eyes turned to him.

'Our whale-ships should be home soon and we will then be sending them off to the Baltic as soon as possible, to take advantage of open water before winter descends and freezes it in its unyielding grip. It has always been a race between us to get the best timber; there has always been an element of luck in choosing the right port. We do not know beforehand where the best timber will be this year and inevitably some of us have to ship inferior, though still saleable, wares. I therefore propose we should sail as a fleet, each going to a specified port. We would then share all the timber when our ships return. After that, it would be up to each of us to sell his particular allocation as and where he wills.'

There was a moment of silent consideration before questions and opinions started to be aired about the merits and demerits of Henry's proposal. It took another cigar each and several glasses of port before agreement was reached. Handshakes sealed this and each man knew there was no need to draw up a paper contract; each trusted the others implicitly, and each was a witness to what had been discussed in this room.

After the final handshake, Henry said, 'Let us hope our ships are soon home from the Arctic. We'll turn them round quickly and send them off to the Baltic together.' He glanced around and received a nod of agreement from each man in turn. 'So, if there are no more questions, gentlemen, shall we join the ladies?'

From the conviviality that emanated from them when they entered the drawing-room, the ladies knew whatever had been discussed had reached a successful conclusion. Their men-folk would be in good humour for the rest of the evening.

So it proved.

On the way home, however, Benjamin was quiet and Arabella began to think she had not come up to the standard he had expected from her for this occasion. But, when they entered the house, he halted her as she was about to go upstairs. 'You did well this evening, Arabella. Everyone took to you. And your dress, apart from being impeccably made, showed the care you had taken to keep within the bounds of respectability at this time. Your mother would have been proud of you.' As if embarrassed by his own words, he turned away then and hurried towards his study.

With her heart racing, she watched him go. Praise indeed! Silently she mouthed the words 'Thank you' at the closed door and then walked thoughtfully up the stairs. Had a barrier been broken? Would her relationship with her father be easier now?

5

9 September 1832. Papa left for Scarborough yesterday. We have seen little of him this week; I expect he was preparing for the visit. Arabella has told us all a·out the party and made it sound very exciting. I'm d she enjoyed it. It is pleasant for us all to be into r half mourning clothes and have more freedom. I hope Jim likes my dress! Harriet seems quieter than usual. Maybe she's envious of Arabella for getting that second dress. I know Arabella is looking forward to seeing John again, as I am to having Jim home. I wish Harriet had someone. I hope the whale-ships return soon and then the crews will get a decent shore-leave before they sail to fetch timber from the Baltic. If they come as soon as I wish, Papa will miss their return . . .

'Whale-ships!'

The breeze swept the joyful cry from the West Cliff all across the town. It bounced off roofs, was taken up by different voices, and passed on and on with ever-increasing joy. It skimmed across the rippling river, reverberated from walls, floated in windows, knocked at doors and resounded in the minds of Whitby folk. It was soon followed by reports that all five vessels had been sighted. It was most unusual for the fleet to return together and everyone grasped at this stirring news with delight.

The regular daytime activities of the town ceased. Carpenters downed their tools; rope-makers made a last twist in their hemp; sail-makers put their needles aside; housewives rubbed the flour from their hands; jet workers stopped polishing; beer glasses were drained quickly or left half-empty; clerks laid down their pens; shops and offices were locked. People streamed on to the streets, exchanging joyous greetings as they made for the piers and clifftops. The cry swept along the quays, danced through ships' rigging, and finally penetrated the offices of Benjamin Brook.

'The *Sea King*'s back!' Jake Carter's voice was filled with relief and excitement. 'Come on, let's see her home.' He was on his feet and heading for the door with the other two clerks on his heels.

Though elated by the news, Jake felt the responsibility thrust upon him by the absence of Mr Brook. Not that he was incapable of carrying out his employer's orders; he had worked for Mr Brook for many years and could have followed the usual procedures in his sleep, but this time the situation was a little different. The *Sea King*'s cargo had to be unloaded quickly and the ship made ready immediately to sail to the Baltic with the other whale-ships, according to the arrangement Mr Brook had made with their owners. They were all to sail together to the Baltic after their quick turnaround. He knew the crews wouldn't like it; they would be expecting a few days ashore after the rigours of the Arctic before sailing again. The news of the sighting would bring the other owners down to the quays where their vessels would tie up. Jake should have time before the *Sea King* docked to agree with them the new sailing date for the Baltic.

'Whale-ships!'

The cry, passing along New Buildings, was heard by Sarah as she made an entry in her diary. She dropped her pen, sprang up from her chair and raced on to the landing, shouting, 'They're home! They're home!'

Charley burst from his room and was hard on her heels as they ran down the stairs. They reached the hall just as Harriet ran out of the drawing-room and Arabella appeared from the kitchen. They all grabbed their outdoor garments and ran from the house.

'Conduct yourselves properly!' Arabella reminded them as they hurried in the direction of the bridge.

They all wanted to be on the East Cliff, their preferred place for seeing the *Sea King* approach her home port. From there they hoped to be reassured that all was well with the ship and her crew; it was where John and Jim expected them to be. They hurried as best they could among the jostling crowd on Church Street, and by the time they had streamed up the one hundred and ninety-nine steps to the top of the East Cliff were all panting hard. They breathed deeply on the sea air, thankful to find an advantageous position from which to watch the vessels heading into Whitby.

Charley's eyes were bright and his mind filled with determination that the next time the *Sea King* sailed for the Arctic, he would be aboard. Nothing would stop him obtaining his father's permission to sign on. He loved that ship; she sailed the sea with a majesty that matched her name. He picked her out, in the lead, watching in silent admiration as she drew nearer and nearer.

Sarah's heart was racing – Jim was coming! How she longed to see him again.

Arabella watched in silence, her arms folded across her breast, as if holding safe the love she felt for John. She longed to know his true feelings for her; three words would do that. Only they could release her from the relentless expectations of her father. Benjamin may well object, but at least Arabella's restless yearning would be stilled.

Harriet watched the *Sea King*, thinking of the handsome features of the man who was now bringing the vessel home. As with all whale-men, there was a certain aura about him. The way he held himself and the authority he wielded suited him well. He was a captain but also a hunter, battling huge monsters from small boats, and an explorer, too, sailing unknown seas and charting unknown shores. Glamour stuck to these Greenlanders, as they were known, and in her eyes to none more so than Captain John Sharp.

The familiar sight of Yorkshire's cliffs and strands of sand never failed to thrill John whenever he brought his ship close to home. They were stirring sights indeed, heralding safety from the icy wastes and cold seas where danger was ever-present. The ruined abbey high on the cliff above Whitby welcomed him with its promise of peace, but today his heart was troubled; he had become aware during the past six months in the lonely Arctic that Harriet had stolen a place in his mind. She had bloomed there like an enticing flower, contesting his feelings towards her sister. Anxious to get home, where he hoped he would find a way to curb his turbulent mind, John had pressed hard in the hunt for whales and had filled his ship with blubber and whalebone.

75

Now he scanned the clifftop through his telescope. His gaze moved across the crowd, then stopped. They were there, all four of them; the girls in mauve – they were out of full mourning! That should make things easier. He felt a pull at his stomach; his problem loomed large. John lowered his telescope and turned his full attention to steering the *Sea King* towards the gap between Whitby's piers, stretching out into the sea like welcoming arms ready to embrace her sailors.

As the *Sea King* moved gracefully home and eased up the river towards the bridge, raised today to allow her passage upstream to her quay on the East Side, cheers rang out, filling the air with welcome, drowning out the cries of the seagulls that wheeled and swooped on the lively breeze.

The whole river seemed to fill with ships moving slowly to their berths; crews anticipating the joys of life ashore after the narrow confines of what had been their homes for six months. Welcoming arms would be waiting for them, and they would relish their embrace for a few days before embarking on the timber trade.

'He's seen us!' cried Charley, jumping up and down when he saw John waving. Arabella's face lit up with joy as she raised both arms above her head. John was safely home! Now there would be some time together for them before he sailed for the Baltic, and when that froze, which she hoped would be early, he would be home until late March. The reunion with him would bring her a measure of relief from the responsibilities her father expected her to shoulder. Maybe John would offer a solution to her future? Hope dwelt strong in her heart.

So concentrated was she on the commanding figure

bringing the ship home that she did not notice the light in Harriet's eyes, a light that was no longer the expression of a sister's admiration for a 'brother' but altogether sharper: it reflected her yearning for the captain of the *Sea King*. Harriet held her scarf high and waved it vigorously, feeling sure there had been a response from him just for her. She glanced at her elder sister and, seeing Arabella's attention fixed unmoving on the ship, Harriet slipped away through the crowd and ran down the steps to Church Street.

Sarah hadn't eyes for any of them; all her concentration was fixed on Jim, who was holding on to the ratlines with one hand and waving vigorously to her with the other. The gesture was filled with young love and she knew he definitely had not forgotten her while he had sailed the Arctic. She could sense, even from this distance, that he was happy to combine the two loves of his life, Sarah and the sea, and she was happy because he was happy, and their happiness united them.

Harriet's shoes barely touched the steps as her feet flew down and down to Church Street. Here, as on the Church Stairs, there were few people visible; the return of the whale-ships commanded the attention of so many. Even as she ran she was pleased she had worn this dress, though Arabella had frowned at her choice, declaring it a little too frivolous for half mourning but had ignored her sister Harriet. Now she knew she would impress John with the dress she had purchased especially with him in mind. From a high lace-trimmed neck, the pale mauve fabric came tight across her bosom to a small waist before flaring gracefully to the top of her black shoes. Its plainness accentuated its elegance. The only adornment she had allowed herself was a small matching cape clipped at her throat, a black leather belt, and black gloves.

Her haste was halted when she reached the quays; here were all the relations and friends of the crews, impatient to welcome their loved ones home, old sailors keen to hear about the Arctic they too had once sailed, and merchants needing to know the quality of the blubber contained in the ships. They already knew they were returning full by the whalebone they had seen tied at each masthead.

Harriet weaved her way among the people thronging the quay where the *Sea King* would tie up and waited close to where she thought the gangway would be run out, hoping that would happen before any of her siblings appeared. She gave herself a little hug of delight at the thought of how fortuitous it was that her father should be in Scarborough just when the *Sea King* arrived home.

'Where's Harriet?' Arabella's voice was filled with concern when she did not see her sister. 'If we don't go now the *Sea King* will be tied up before we reach the quay.'

'I don't know,' said Charley.

'Nor I,' replied Sarah. 'She was here when the ship passed between the piers.'

Arabella's lips tightened in exasperation. 'Where *has* she gone? She knew we should stay together.' Her eyes scanned the crowd but she saw no sign of Harriet. 'Have a quick look round,' she ordered sharply.

'I thought you said we should be off to the quay?' objected Charley, anxious to be there when the *Sea King* was manoeuvred to her berth.

'Have a quick look.'

Both he and Sarah hurried away but, anxious to be on the quay, were soon back with Arabella. 'We haven't seen her,' they reported.

'All right. We'll have to split up. Keep your eyes open for her on your way to the quay. If you see her, tell her I am annoyed that she left us and caused us to split up. You can find your own way home, but be there in two hours.'

They both realised Arabella had been generous with the time schedule and knew not to protest.

Arabella herself searched the crowd as she made her way down the Church Stairs and along Church Street. It slowed her progress and she began to realise she may not see her sister until she arrived home again; after all, Harriet professed little interest in the *Sea King* except that it was a Whitby ship returning from the Arctic.

Excited murmurs ran through the crowd as the *Sea King* manoeuvred her way past the bridge and was brought to the quay. John was ever watchful, but Harriet saw his glance rove quickly across the other onlookers then stop on her with a expression of surprise and delight. She smiled with a matching air of pleasure and raised her arm, to which he responded before turning his attention back to the final moments that saw the *Sea King* safely home.

The gangway was run out and Captain John Sharp walked down it with a confident stride.

'Harriet! I didn't expect . . .'

His words were stifled as her arms came up around his neck and her lips met his. For a moment he was taken aback by this outward expression of her feelings, then he allowed them to overwhelm him when he realised that many of his crew were being greeted in a similar way. Embarrassment fled from him and he returned kiss for kiss as he held her tight. Then he broke off to cast a quick glance around him. 'Your father?' he queried with a touch of apprehension in his tone.

'Away in Scarborough,' she replied reassuringly, then pulled him back closer and kissed him hard again. Out of the corner of her eye she had seen Arabella reach the quay.

The smile vanished from Arabella's face. A moment ago she had been eagerly anticipating her reunion with John. She pulled up sharp, a terrible feeling gripping her. What she had just witnessed were no ordinary kisses; they were not the sort of kisses she had seen exchanged between Harriet and John previously. Those had been sister and brother kisses; these held passion and said much more about the two people who embraced each other. Arabella stood frozen with shock. What she did next would shape the course of their lives. She felt a sudden pang of jealousy for these two people who had once meant so much to her. Would that ever be the same again? Could she ever forgive them for placing her future in jeopardy, stripping her of hope, leaving her destined to be a spinster tied to her widowed father until she was old enough for an independent future? Tears started. Was she feeling sorry for herself, angry with John and Harriet, or merely frustrated? She began to turn away then stopped. It was no good shying away from what would have to be faced sooner or later. Better sooner. Maybe the initial confrontation would be better achieved while her father was away.

She took a grip on herself, using the opportunity to

dab away the dampness in her eyes, turning around as if looking for someone. Charley was pressing unattached sailors from the *Sea King* with questions about the Arctic and they were ever-ready to indulge the owner's son. Sarah had found Jim and their absorption in each other blinded them to the events on the quay. Arabella drew herself up and walked briskly towards John and Harriet.

'Hello, John,' she said coldly. 'I hope the voyage was successful.'

Her businesslike tone was a deliberate ploy. 'Arabella!' He flushed deeply, bent as if to kiss her but she turned her cheek away. Her movement gave her eye contact with Harriet and she was shocked to see the look of triumph in her sister's eyes. It was as if this was something she had plotted and she was clearly elated that she had succeeded. 'John and I plan to marry,' she announced.

The words were like ice around Arabella's heart. With her eyes fixed on her sister, she did not notice his reaction.

'I think it might be wise if John dined with us tonight.' Arabella directed this statement at her sister as an order. John had no say in the matter. She turned and walked away, but once she knew she was out of their sight she could not hold back the tears. She reached home in a daze, quickening her steps in her haste to find, within the four walls of her home, protection from the hurt tearing her heart out.

On reaching the house in New Buildings she ran upstairs to her room. As the door closed behind her, she leaned against it. The significance of what she had witnessed on the quay hit her again and this time she could not withstand the shock. Her legs only just managed to drag her to the bed. She sank down on to it and lay staring at the ceiling, unable to hold back the tears.

Slowly they subsided and cold reasoning took over, posing questions to which she as yet had no answers. How long had the understanding between John and Harriet been going on? Why had she not been aware of it? Why had they kept it a secret until now? Why had they allowed her to discover it this way? Hadn't John realised that she loved him? And then – why, oh, why, hadn't she made her own love known to him? Why had she concluded he knew? Why had she expected and waited for him to make the first move? A lifetime without John would be a lifetime without joy or hope in it. If only . . .

The sound of a door closing below, followed by voices, startled her, alerting her to the present. Sarah and Charley! She sat up on the edge of the bed. Oh, God! She had invited John to dine this evening. When she had done so she had thought it best if the three of them got this matter straightened out before Father returned; Arabella needed to know if they were truly committed to each other. It would not be easy and certainly couldn't be discussed in front of Charley and Sarah. The evening ahead was going to be strained.

For a moment John watched Arabella thread her way among the crowd then turned to face Harriet. 'Marriage?' His query was pointed.

'After a kiss like that, what other conclusion am I expected to reach?'

Before he could reply she kissed him again, with unmistakable passion. 'That should seal it, John!'

Harriet had noted shock in her sister's eyes but had

also seen jealousy, and with that had come a feeling of triumph. She had snatched one of the most eligible men in Whitby from under Arabella's nose! She had grabbed at life and it felt good. There had only been glances between them before today, but the kiss that had followed John's initial surprise had told her all she wanted to know. He felt as she did. Why hadn't he come to her? She knew the reason – Arabella. But she had judged right; his feelings for her sister were not as strong as others had believed. Now he was Harriet's!

John's heart was beating fast. What had he done to Arabella? But Harriet's kiss had salved the troubles that had beset him in the Arctic. Love was revealed in that kiss and in the way she hugged him. He felt joyous, as if his whole future lay like a dreamland before him. It was there for him to take, to make his own and enjoy. But there was a little pang in his heart as well. He had seen shock in Arabella's eyes. He'd had no wish to hurt her but knew that he had, deeply. He felt a strong urge to put things right between them, but how could he? Arabella's invitation? If only . . . It was no good putting it off; better that everything was brought into the open now, then maybe life could go on as if this awkwardness had never arisen. But he knew that was only wishful thinking.

'How long before you can leave the ship?' Harriet's voice broke into his thoughts.

'It will be a while. You'd better go home. I'll join you there.' He saw doubt in her eyes. 'I'm not trying to avoid what we must do. It's better to . . .'

'I know,' she interrupted. 'But I don't want to go alone.'

He nodded. 'I'll be as quick as I can. I'll walk you to

your father's office; you can wait there until I'm ready.'

'Captain Sharp, I'm sorry to interrupt,' Jake Carter broke in. 'Mr Brook is in Scarborough but he left instructions to pass on to you if you docked before his return.'

John looked askance at him.

'The *Sea King* is to be unloaded and made ready for the Baltic as quickly as possible. It is fortuitous that all the whale-ships arrived together. Mr Brook has made an agreement with their owners that all the ships will sail as a fleet, each to a designated port to pick up timber there. They will then return together and the timber be divided equally.'

John's nimble brain readily grasped the implication. 'It will cut out rivalry. No one will get all the superior timber.' He nodded approvingly. 'Can you see to the unloading?'

'I've got men ready to start.' Jake indicated a group gathering near the gangway. 'They will get some done this evening and the rest tomorrow.'

'Good. And our supplies for the Baltic voyage?'

'All in hand.'

'So when do you reckon we'll be ready to sail?'

'In the evening, three days hence.'

'Very well. I'll check with the other owners and captains.'

'When the whale-ships were sighted I contacted the other owners immediately. They have agreed that schedule.'

'Excellent. I'll confirm it with the captains then. Good work, Carter.'

As Jake hurried away, John turned to Harriet. 'We can't do anything about our situation until your father returns, and that may not be until after I've sailed. I'm not going to have much time . . . maybe you should excuse me from dinner this evening?'

Her eyes flashed. 'No, John! You are not leaving me alone with Arabella this evening until explanations have been made.'

'But I'll have a lot to see to.'

'Do the bare minimum now and the rest will have to wait until tomorrow.' Her tone was commanding.

He nodded. 'Very well, I'll be as quick as I can.'

Half an hour later they were crossing the bridge to the West Side. Though neither of them voiced their feelings they were both filled with apprehension, wishing the forthcoming confrontation with Arabella didn't have to take place.

She meanwhile had composed herself, removed the evidence of her tears, pinched colour into her cheeks, made her hair less severe, straightened her dress and attached to it a piece of jewellery that John had given her last birthday. She had resisted the temptation to wear her special occasion dress. The everyday dress she wore instead was equally attractive and of a deeper mauve that emphasised the beauty of the brooch pinned above her right breast.

She heard the front door open and rose from her chair. 'Wait here, you two,' she said with a quiet authority which made Sarah and Charley remain in their chairs without a word. In the hall, she closed the door behind her. She saw Harriet's embarrassment and felt some degree of satisfaction in that, but held her reaction under control.

'Where's John?' she asked coldly.

'He's gone home to wash and change for dinner,' answered Harriet, then added with a touch of defiance in her voice, 'I'm going to do the same.' She was up the stairs before Arabella could answer.

She returned to the drawing-room. 'Harriet and John will be with us shortly,' was the only explanation she gave, and they all returned to the books that they had been reading, though Arabella was not seeing any of the words in front of her.

Half an hour later, hearing footsteps crossing the hall, she rose from her chair again and hurried from the room. She signalled to the maid that she would take over and glanced in the direction of the stairs. Harriet was coming down; it seemed obvious that she too had been listening for John's arrival.

'We are all in the drawing-room. Sarah and Charley know nothing of what has happened. I ask you not to mention it until we three are alone after the meal,' Arabella said evenly.

'Very well, Arabella, if that's the way you want it,' John got in first in case Harriet felt like defying her sister, but he need not have worried; Harriet had had her triumph and was not prepared to mar it with open disagreement now. She nodded her approval of his words.

They followed Arabella into the drawing-room. Immediately Charley was on his feet, plying John with questions about the voyage, while Sarah managed surreptitiously to glean information about Jim. Outwardly it appeared a happy domestic scene and for a brief moment Harriet's guilt, and hope that John was not having second thoughts about their relationship, sprang to the surface. It was swiftly curtailed when Arabella rose from her chair, saying, 'We can dine now.'

As they walked into the dining-room and sat down,

Sarah felt uneasy. Something here was not quite right. Arabella was too cautious, as if she were afraid of saying something she shouldn't. And there was a coldness in her attitude that Sarah had never seen before. Harriet's words were forced and the light-heartedness in her voice that was usually there, no matter how serious the conversation, was missing. Besides, tonight there wasn't anything resembling conversation between them. John had little to offer to the stilted exchanges, it seemed, and even his answers to Charley's questions about the voyage were curt.

Sarah was puzzled. What should have been the happy return of the *Sea King* had gone sour. Only Jim's homecoming remained as a bright light in her life. It had brought joy to them both and only been marred when Jim had been told he would be sailing again so soon. Was that what was blighting this evening too? Even as she raised the question in her mind she dismissed it. The atmosphere around this table spoke of something more serious than that and it seemed to weigh heaviest on John and her sisters. It worried Sarah; she did not like trouble.

Her suspicions that all was not well heightened when Arabella, after saying the final grace and rising from her chair, addressed Sarah and Charley. 'You two . . . take a game or some books to the small sitting-room. I want to talk to Harriet and John.'

She went quickly into the hall, leaving in her wake an air of authority that would not tolerate any objection from the other four. Arabella crossed the hall briskly and went into the drawing-room, leaving the door open. She went to stand behind the wing-chair she usually occupied, knowing that there she could conceal her clenched fists as she fought to hold strong and not to break down in a show of emotion that would reveal her true feelings. She would not let Harriet and John see how deeply she was hurt; that would only add to the triumph she had seen in her sister's eyes. Rising above that in a dignified manner would only intensify their embarrassment and guilt.

'Sit down,' she said quietly when they had entered the room and John had closed the door.

'I will remain standing,' said Harriet, seeing this as an act of defiance against what she was expecting to hear from her sister.

Arabella made a gesture that said, 'Suit yourself.'

John spoke quickly, not wanting Harriet to say something that would further hurt her sister. 'Arabella, I'm sorry,' he began.

'Sorry?' she returned as if puzzled. 'Sorry I came across you unexpectedly and saw the way you were kissing Harriet? Sorry that you let your guard slip and allowed your secret to be displayed for all to see? Sorry you were not honest with me? And what did it all mean: all the things we shared, the happy times we had together?'

Embarrassment and bewilderment clouded his face.

'You jumped to conclusions.' Even as he put this up as his defence he felt guilt in his heart. He'd never had any intention of hurting Arabella. Had admired her too much for that. What had happened on the quay seemed to clarify the thoughts that had haunted him on his Arctic voyage. Had he been a fool to nurture them in the first place – and to be overwhelmed by Harriet's kisses and the words she had whispered in his ear? But what had happened had happened.

Arabella gave a little shrug of her shoulders. 'I was

wrong,' she said, without disguising her sadness. 'So be it.' She turned to Harriet next. 'Have you nothing to say?'

The question hurt Harriet. She could have coped better if Arabella had stormed at her, lashed her with her tongue, said what she really felt. This cold candour disarmed her, leaving her with nothing to say in her own defence. It was victory for her sister and nullified her own triumph, leaving her feeling empty.

'What is there to say?' she attempted lamely.

'Sorry?' Arabella held up her hand. 'No. Don't use that word. It is meaningless. Ask me to give you my blessing instead.'

Harriet was taken aback but she saw her sister's eyes fixed meaningfully on her, almost defying her not to, and so the words came out quietly: 'Give me your blessing, please, Arabella.' Harriet knew she had been humiliated and realised Arabella knew it, too. Her sister had triumphed today, not she.

Arabella, her hands unclenched, came from behind the chair and went to her sister. She placed her hands on her shoulders and looked hard into her eyes. 'Be happy, dear sister.' The last two words sounded so cold! Arabella kissed her on both cheeks. As she made the final gesture she whispered in her sister's ear: 'If you ever make him unhappy, you'll have me to answer to.' Then she turned to John and embraced him. 'Have a happy life, John.' As she kissed him on both cheeks and stepped away, a shudder ran though him. For one moment he was afraid, then shook it off, annoyed with himself for allowing his mind to entertain dark thoughts on what should be a happy day.

Arabella was at the door. 'I am pleased this has been cleared up before Father returns. No doubt you will approach him when he does.'

She fled upstairs and sank on to her bed, her emotions drained by the tension of keeping them under control; from not allowing herself to vent her true feelings which would have exposed her dignity to ridicule. Tears flowed for what she had lost and her sister gained. John, whom she loved, was lost to her now. He would not be there to support her while she looked after her father like a dutiful daughter. The life that lay ahead was not one she had ever anticipated or expected. All hope was lost, submerged in the sands of what she saw as a cruel betrayal.

6

11 September 1832. Papa will be back today. The weather looks good for his journey. Oh, Arabella has just called for me and I hear her calling for Charley too. I wonder what she wants . . .

'I've something to tell you. Sit down.' Arabella stood in front of the drawing-room fireplace. She waited under the gaze of Sarah and Charley, who were wondering if Harriet was going to join them. They soon had their answer when Arabella imparted her news. 'Harriet and John have told me they wish to marry.'

It seemed an eternity before the words sank in. Their exchange of glances showed astonishment and disbelief.

'But I thought you and John . . .?' Sarah's voice faded away on the question. She got to her feet and came to her sister. There was no need for words as she hugged Arabella. They wept together, then, as Charley came to them and took Arabella's hand in sympathy, she straightened up and said, 'Ah, well, it seems I was unaware that his affection was directed elsewhere.' She forced herself to control the catch in her voice that threatened to betray her devastation. 'Obviously they will want to seek Papa's permission so I wish you to keep this to yourselves until after they have seen him. Don't breathe a word to anyone.'

11 September 1832. I wonder what Papa will think about Harriet and John. What a surprise Charley and I got. Arabella must have had a shock. How can I comfort her? She's generally so strong . . .

Pedestrians on Church Street scattered out of the way of the coach from Scarborough as it swung into the White Horse yard on Whitby's East Side. The clatter of hooves and rumble of wheels brought a stable-man and two boys from their late-afternoon tasks to attend to its arrival.

'Good run, Zac?' the stableman called to the driver, red-faced from the wind and the exertion of controlling the horses.

'Aye, Rick,' came the reply. Zac cast a sharp glance at the two boys. 'Calm 'em! Calm 'em!'

The boys grinned at each other; it was always the same when Zac arrived, even though the steaming horses stood calmly awaiting the reviving attention they would receive in the comparative comfort of the stable. Watered, fed and brushed, they would be stood down until they hauled the coach back to Scarborough tomorrow.

'You've made good time,' commented Rick.

'Ever known Zac Busby be late?' returned the coach-man as he swung down to the ground.

Two boys wearing aprons tied at the waist had run from the building to welcome and help the five passengers. The yard buzzed with activity, everyone thankful that the day was dry if not sunny.

Benjamin Brook thanked the coachman and had a quick word with the landlord, who had come out to see that everything was in order. 'I'm leaving my case here for a few minutes. I see the *Sea King* is at her berth. I'll pay her a visit.'

'Very good, sir,' the man replied, ever-ready to oblige.

Benjamin strode briskly from the yard and headed for the *Sea King*. He had derived great satisfaction from his Scarborough visit and been equally pleased to see the *Sea King* at her berth on his return, her cargo of barrels of blubber, wrested from the icy Arctic seas, being stacked on the quay.

'A good cargo, Carter?' Benjamin's question brought Jake spinning round on his high seat.

'Good morning, sir. You've had an early start.'

'No sense in hanging around. Business was concluded satisfactorily late last night so I caught the first coach this morning. The cargo?'

'Excellent.'

'Good. What are the arrangements for the Baltic?'

'I've agreed with the other owners to sail on the evening tide in two days' time.'

'Captain Sharp?'

'Is meeting the other captains, arranging sailing procedures. I'm not sure when he'll be back.'

'Good. When you do see him, tell him I'll be at home and will await him there.'

'Yes, sir.'

Benjamin started to move away, then stopped and looked back. 'Carter, good work.'

'Thank you, sir.'

Jake Carter's efficiency had put Benjamin in a good mood. Charley would learn a lot, working alongside a good clerk like Jake Carter.

'Welcome, Papa!' Arabella greeted Benjamin when he walked into the drawing-room before even shedding his outdoor clothes.

'Thank you. It is good to be back.' His matter-of-fact greeting was just as she'd expected.

'I trust your visit was worthwhile?'

'Indeed it was.'

'You would have seen the *Sea King* safely back?'

'I did, but I didn't see John. Carter told me he was conferring with the other captains.'

'You'll see him this evening. He dined with us last night and I have invited him again this evening. I thought it easier for him because of sailing again so soon.'

'Excellent. He can bring me up to date about the Arctic and the cargo, and will reveal to him some further plans.' Benjamin started for the door. 'No doubt it suits you too.'

His final comment was like an arrow to Arabella's heart but she fought down any visible reaction.

Her father paused with his hand on the door knob. 'Is Harriet at home?'

'She is visiting Melissa Hartburn, who is indisposed, but she'll be back to dine this evening.'

He nodded, and left Arabella pondering what her father's attitude would be when confronted with John's proposal, for surely he must bring his relationship with Harriet into the open before he sailed again.

'Is everything in hand, Jake?' asked John as he strode on to the deck of the *Sea King*, highly satisfied with the sailing plans he had made with the captains of the other ships bound for the Baltic.

'Aye, Captain. Blubber, whalebone and all whaling equipment cleared. Provisions for the Baltic voyage will be brought on board in the morning.'

'Good.'

'Crew happy, Captain?'

'Reasonably so. Although some are grumbling at the quick turnaround.'

Jake nodded. He had been aware of the crew's objections but none of them had been hostile; it wouldn't have paid them to be that way. 'By the way, Mr Brook is back from Scarborough; came in on the first coach. He was sorry you weren't available but understood. Said he expected to see you later at the house.'

John made no comment, merely nodded and went to his cabin. This news had set his thoughts racing. He had half-hoped he would have sailed again before Mr Brook returned; it would have given him more time to consider how best to approach him. But that was not to be and he decided to arrive at the Brook house early so he could get the matter out of the way before dining. He hated to see Arabella hurt but knew now his relationship with her was irrevocably soured. He recalled how, in the Arctic, the two sisters had contested in his mind; although Arabella came strongly to the fore at times, her presence was always clouded by her changed domestic circumstances. And finally it was Harriet who had won.

Nevertheless, as determined as he was to approach Mr Brook immediately, John was feeling more uneasy with every step he took towards the house later that day.

'Good evening, sir.' The maid who opened the door greeted him brightly and took his captain's cap to hang in the closet in the hall. 'They are all in the drawing-room.'

'Thank you.'

He hesitated momentarily at the door, gathering himself for what lay ahead. Then he walked in. 'Good evening, everyone.'

All returned his greeting. Only Arabella hid hurt and hostility.

'Ah, John. Jake Carter told me you had a good voyage.'

'Yes, sir.'

'Splendid!'

'Sir, there is something I would like to talk to you about.' Though he had grasped at the chance and held his voice firm, John felt queasy.

'Is it the whaling or the Baltic expedition?' asked Benjamin, rising from his chair. 'Come, we'll go to my study. We have time before our meal. The family won't wish to be bored by business.' He was already on his way out.

John avoided looking at anyone, though he could feel Harriet's and Arabella's eyes on him. He experienced a measure of relief when the drawing-room door closed behind him but renewed apprehension when they were closeted together in the study.

'Sit down, sit down.' Benjamin waved his hand in the direction of a chair as he went to another behind his desk. 'What is it, whales or timber?'

'Neither, sir.' John sat bolt upright, hands gripping the arms of his chair.

Seeing his serious expression and posture, Benjamin frowned and waited for him to go on.

'Sir, I would like to ask for your daughter's hand in marriage.' The words were out; the question posed. Mr Brook did not look shocked.

'I expected this some time ago, my boy,' he replied lightly, 'though it does raise a problem about Arabella's position in this household. Have you discussed it with her?'

The words were thundering in John's mind and he cursed himself for a fool; he had said 'daughter' and not mentioned Harriet's name. 'Sir,' he hastened to quash Mr Brook's impression, 'it is not Arabella I mean but Harriet.'

For a moment Benjamin was taken aback but, quickly realising that this would in fact suit his own convenience rather more, he felt relieved. Nevertheless he automatically said, 'I thought you and Arabella . . .'

'Just very good friends, sir.' John was quick to stop him from saying anything which might lead to further embarrassment.

'Have you asked Harriet?'

'We have reached an understanding.'

Benjamin gave a little nod. 'Well, you have been part of this family for a long time and it would give me pleasure to see you more closely allied to it so the answer is, yes, you may ask Harriet formally.'

'Thank you, sir.'

'However, there is one thing you must understand . . .' Benjamin rose from his chair as he was speaking and went to the bell-pull. 'I think it would be wisest at this point to have Harriet here too.'

A maid appeared a few moments later and Benjamin told her to ask Harriet to come to his study.

'Sit down,' her father instructed when she arrived, uneasily twisting her fingers. As she went to the chair next to John's she cast him an anxious glance but learned nothing from his expression. 'John has asked for your hand in marriage and I have approved,' her father informed her.

All the nervous tension drained from her. The world was suddenly flooded with sunshine. A broad smile drove all trace of apprehension from Harriet's face. 'Oh, thank you, Papa.' She turned to John then and saw relief and joy in his eyes. He held out his hand to her and she took it gratefully.

'There are some things you should both understand, though, and I shall disclose them now because they will affect any plans you may be thinking of making. John is bound for the Baltic in two days' time and will continue to sail there until the sea freezes over. Normally I would then have laid the ship up for a period before the next whaling season. However, this time I won't be doing so.' He glanced at John. 'No one else knows this yet. The reason I went to Scarborough was to close a deal with two merchants seeking to ship wine and lace from Spain. I saw it as an opportunity to keep the ship employed throughout the winter. I don't think the crew will object as it will put more money into their pockets at a time when previously they were unemployed.

'Now, as you will both realise, this means John will only be in Whitby for a very short time between sailings. You may ask why I cannot secure another captain to handle the wine trade, but I would rather send John on this initial venture. I have every faith that he will put it on a sound footing, then someone else can take it over the following year. This means I would like you to postpone your marriage until after the next whaling season.'

'Papa . . .' Harriet's tone signalled her objection, but John, knowing she would try to charm her father round, squeezed her hand warningly. He wanted to appear willing to comply with Mr Brook's suggestion, seeing it as his opportunity to establish a stronger position within the firm. Charley would be the heir, but John believed he could still make himself indispensable.

'That will be perfectly in order, sir, and I thank you for the opportunity you are giving me to establish the wine trade for you.'

'Good.' Benjamin looked at his daughter for her approval.

Harriet pouted disappointedly. She had hoped her father would agree to an early wedding. She wanted a ship's captain for a husband and John was exactly that, as well as a handsome man, a fine figure who drew everyone's attention. He had done well for his age and, with her father's approval, she saw him one day working alongside her brother, taking the firm to new heights and power within Whitby; maybe even beyond. She would have wealth and position then. She did not wish to see it slip through her fingers. Arabella could be a danger; John could change his mind . . . but her father had made up his mind. She could do nothing but agree.

'You won't ever regret it,' promised Benjamin. 'Now let us rejoin the others.'

When they re-entered the drawing-room Benjamin went straight to the bell-pull and tugged it four times – Mrs Ainslie's special signal.

She appeared a few moments later. 'You rang, sir?'

'Mrs Ainslie, I have a special announcement to make and I think it only right, because of your devoted service, that you should join the family to hear it.'

12 September 1832. Mrs Ainslie was shocked; I saw it in her eyes. If I hadn't been watching her, I would have missed it. Harriet marrying John was not what she had expected at all. The rest of the evening passed off pleasantly. Father produced champagne. Harriet was excited. John, too, though I saw him look at Arabella with concern more than once. Poor Arabella was hurt, though she tried not to show it. What will things be like between her and Harriet now?

'I should like to see John sail. Will anyone come with me?' Harriet put the question at breakfast after her father had left the dining-room to take last-minute instructions to John. Sarah, knowing Harriet would not want their father to see her alone on the quay, read the tentative note in her voice but also saw this as a challenge to Arabella; after all, their elder sister had been in the habit of being on the quay whenever John sailed.

Sarah cast a sharp glance at Arabella. She could see her sister straining to be impassive but caught a glimpse in her eyes of sharp regret. The tone she adopted for her reply, however, was charged with contempt that such a question had even been put. 'He is only going to the Baltic,' she commented, quite contrary to her own previous attitude, and went on to level criticism at Harriet for being maudlin – something she had certainly never considered herself to be.

Sarah saw Harriet bristle and feared a fiery response instead of her more usual subtle coyness. Arabella and Harriet's relationship, which up to now had been sisterly and loving, was close to being damaged forever. Harriet's response here could tip it in that direction. Sarah did not want that; she loved both her sisters but in different ways. What had happened was challenging her to take sides; she wanted to avoid that, or at least not be forced into a more open allegiance. Harriet's attitude at this moment could force her to decide with whom her support lay. Sarah held her breath. She could see Harriet desperately holding back the sarcastic reply she wanted to make.

Before a word more was uttered the door burst open and Charley, attired in redingote and cap, stood on the threshold. 'I'm off to see the *Sea King* sail.'

Sarah smiled to herself. In all innocence, their brother had broken the mounting tension and had provided an answer to Harriet's question.

'Wait, I'll come with you.' Harriet was swiftly out of her chair and left the dining-room without another word.

As the door closed, Sarah felt uncomfortable to find herself alone with Arabella. 'I'm sorry,' she said quietly.

'Don't be,' replied her sister.

'But you and John . . .'

'You can't do anything about it.'

'I wish I could.'

The reply brought a wistful smile to Arabella's lips. 'So do I. You can go with them, Sarah. Don't you want to see your young man sail?'

'You know about Jim?' Sarah's eyes widened in surprise

and at the same time expressed her hope that her sister was not going to disapprove.

Arabella smiled. 'It was obvious to me.'

'But I never . . .'

'Women's intuition. And the signs of love for a special person are not easy to disguise, though you may believe you are giving nothing away.'

Alarm surfaced in Sarah. 'Does Father know?'

Arabella laughed. 'He wouldn't recognise it if you paraded it in front of him! He's too full of his work – no bad thing at this time. You needn't worry. Off you go to see Jim sail.'

'No, I'll stay here with you. I made no particular arrangements with him and, as you said, it isn't as if he's on a whaling voyage.'

'I know, but . . .'

'I'll stay with you,' insisted Sarah.

'Thank you. It would have been hard for me to be alone today.'

As time passed and the subject of John was avoided, Sarah was pleased to see her eldest sister relax, though not in the way she had known her do in the past. Sarah realised that Arabella still suffered deeply from what she must see as a joint betrayal.

Strength of will carried her through the sensitive moments when Harriet returned. She sensed her sister had not been looking forward to returning to the house in New Buildings, but inevitably it had to be faced. Arabella knew that, by her outward recognition of the situation, she had disarmed Harriet and saw it as a triumph over herself and her true feelings also.

During the succeeding days Harriet was thankful for

the easing tension and what she saw as Arabella's magnanimous acceptance of the situation. John was relieved to hear this from her when he returned from the Baltic. His conscience had troubled him throughout the voyage when, recalling that kiss they had exchanged after her mother's funeral, he had been forced to recognise how close he and Arabella had once been. Then Harriet had vanquished him with her irresistible vivacity, and he had convinced himself that Arabella had been just a friend. He was conscious he had not behaved well to her.

Her pretence of acceptance was dropped in the privacy of her own room where she wept for the love she had lost. She was frequently reminded of her obligations to her father, whose demands on her increased at this time, with invitations accepted and others made in return. During the first two or three of these she was forced to endure enthusiastic comments about Harriet's engagement, a situation that was only salved by her father's public praise for the way she had slipped into the role so capably filled by her mother.

It was thoughts of her mother that made her resolve that Christmas should be celebrated without any outward display of feeling from her.

Sarah was pleased that Arabella brought her into the discussions with Mrs Ainslie about the festivities and did not bar Harriet from them either. When the arrangements appeared to be falling into place, it seemed that Christmas would pass without any worsening of the undercurrents of tension that ran between the two older girls. Sarah wished it would in any case, and hoped that the tradition of John's sharing Christmas Day with them, as he had done since he had been left alone, would not spoil the outward peace.

*

Two days before Christmas, with Whitby in sight, John prepared to take the *Sea King* into port. His voyages to Spain, since the Baltic had been cut off to them, had been successful, bringing wine and lace to be sold on quickly from the Brook warehouses. The crew were in a good mood, heightened by the knowledge that their next departure would be on 2 January. With money in their pockets, they would enjoy Christmas all the more.

With the ship safely at her quay and the cargo being handled by the port's stevedores, John stood his crew down. After attending to paperwork he was preparing to leave his cabin when there was a knock at his door.

'Come in,' he called.

The door opened tentatively and Jim Barbour stepped inside, nervously twisting his woollen cap in his hand.

'Well, what is it, Barbour?' prompted John when the youngster did not speak.

'Er . . . I'm sorry to disturb you, sir.' As he spoke he fished a small package from his pocket. 'You may be visiting the Brook family, sir. If you are, would you give this to Miss Sarah, please, sir?' Jim blushed a deep red and looked extremely embarrassed.

Though he was surprised by the request, John recognised the courage Jim Barbour must have conjured up to approach his captain this way. He could only guess at what he would be carrying but, with an inkling that it had something to do with young love, could not bring himself to refuse the unusual request. After all it was Christmas, and that was a time of goodwill to all.

'Very well, Barbour.' He held out his hand for the package.

Jim hesitated. 'And this letter, sir?'

John nodded and took the items.

'Thank you, sir.'

He expected Jim to turn and leave but the youngster stood his ground. 'Sir, please would you give them to Miss Sarah on Christmas morning without anyone else knowing?'

John smiled. 'I will, Barbour. Your secret will be mine.'

Jim's face lit up with a broad smile. 'Thank you, sir, thank you.' All shyness had disappeared in the knowledge that his plan had been achieved successfully.

As the door of his cabin closed behind Jim, John felt good, not only because he was helping two young lovers but because he felt the boy's request said much for the way he himself was viewed as a captain. And he was pleased for Sarah; Jim may be from humble origins but John had seen that his capabilities would take him far and was keen to see them develop. And he liked the courage of the boy.

It was only after John had accompanied the Brook family to church that he was able to speak to Sarah on her own. She was flabbergasted when he said, 'Jim Barbour asked me to give you these when no one else was about.'

'Oh, my goodness!' she gasped as she took the package and envelope. Her cheeks reddened when she met his knowing smile.

'I'm sworn to tell no one,' he said reassuringly and turned away, missing her quiet though appreciative 'Thank you.'

Sarah gazed at the items in her hand for a moment, then, with her heart pounding and her mind full of joy, she raced upstairs. She flung herself on to her bed, gazing up at the package and letter which she held above

105

her head. Her lips mouthed one word, 'Jim!', and with it came an overwhelming desire to see him again. Sitting up, she tore open the package and unravelled a piece of tissue-paper to reveal a jet brooch.

'Oh, Jim, it's lovely,' she whispered with tears welling in her eyes. She sat gazing at it for a few minutes and then opened the envelope. Unfolding a sheet of paper, she was confronted by a bold hand that read, 'Happy Christmas, Love, Jim'. Underneath was written in smaller script, 'Meet me at 2 o'clock at the west side of the bridge.'

Sarah's heart raced. Could she . . .? She would! She sat for a few moments working things out, then she placed the brooch and note in a drawer of her dressing table. Returning downstairs, she sought out her brother.

'Charley, I want a favour.'

He looked at her suspiciously. 'What are you up to?'

'I want you to be my chaperon.'

He looked surprised. 'Where are you going?'

'To see Laura Gibbons.'

He pulled a face.

'It will only be for a few minutes, just to take her a little present.'

He looked reluctant.

'Please, Charley, please. It's important.'

'When? Now?'

'No. Two o'clock. We'll leave here at a quarter to.'

'That's all right then. Things will be a bit dull here this afternoon. I'll walk you there, and then go off to look at the ships and call back for you.'

'Thanks, Charley. I'll tell Arabella, but you keep this to yourself.' She saw a suspicious gleam come into his eyes and added, 'Say no more, Charley.'

*

106

Tradition was followed when the Brook family served their staff Christmas dinner at lunchtime so that the family could have their own meal in the evening. After the staff had enjoyed themselves, Benjamin retired to his study, where everyone knew he would stay until the evening. Harriet and John settled in the small sitting-room, and Sarah approached Arabella. 'I'd like to go and see Laura Gibbons just for a short while. Charley will escort me.'

'Very well.' Because their celebrations this year had been subdued, Arabella gave her approval. 'But don't be late back.'

'We won't be long,' Sarah reassured her.

It was only when she'd closed the door after seeing them out that Arabella realised she had no one to talk to; she was completely alone. She could hardly join Harriet and John, and her father would no doubt be dozing. She supposed she needed to consult Mrs Ainslie and see that everything was taken care of for the evening meal, but it was hardly a festive occupation. Arabella sighed, regret and hurt filling her heart once more. She had thought she was beginning to bring such feelings under control, but here they were, rearing their ugly heads again. Would she never be free from them?

Sarah bustled Charley along. Suddenly he stopped in his tracks. 'Come on, I don't want to be late,' she urged.

'You're going the wrong way,' he pointed out.

'No, I'm not. I'm going where I want to go. Come on!' She started off again and he was obliged to run to catch up and fall in step with her.

'Where are we going? What are you up to?'

'You'll see in a few minutes.'

They came down beside the river a few yards from the bridge. There were people about; some heading to make Christmas calls on family or friends, others ready to stop off at one of the many hostelries. Sarah strained to catch a first glimpse of Jim. When she saw him her heart missed a beat, and she automatically waved.

'Who are you waving at?' queried Charley.

'Jim Barbour.'

'Jim Barbour? I thought we were going to see Laura Gibbons?'

'It was an excuse, Charley. And you'll say nothing of this.'

He smiled knowingly. 'I could blackmail you.'

'You wouldn't!'

He laughed and shook his head. 'No, who knows what I may want in return one day?'

Jim heard the last remark and said, 'Anything, any time, Charley. Thanks for bringing Sarah.'

'Charley, we are near the ships,' she pointed out.

'I suppose I could get a bit nearer.' Her brother grinned.

'You do that. Jim and I will walk out on the West Pier and back. Meet you here in an hour.'

There was no more to be said.

As soon as they had set off, Sarah slipped her hand into Jim's. 'Thank you for that beautiful present. I will treasure and wear it all my life.' She unbuttoned the top of her redingote to reveal the brooch pinned at her throat

'And I will picture you with it there wherever I sail.' Jim glanced to right and left; there was no one nearby on this section of St Ann's Staith; quickly he bent forward and pecked her on the cheek. Sarah read it as a declaration of his love for her, so, when he would have walked on, tightened her grip to prevent him. She raised herself on her toes and kissed him on the mouth. She held the kiss for a moment but, remembering where they were, released him reluctantly. They walked slowly on. No word passed between them but each knew the shared silence was creating a new bond. They impressed this time on their minds, he to take with him wherever he sailed, and she to hold him near in his absence.

They reached the West Pier, its stone arm reaching out to defy the sea's onslaught, and offering, along with its counterpart on the East Side, protection to ships and those who sailed in them.

'Want to walk further?' asked Jim, concerned that the freshening wind was sending huge waves pounding over the pier.

'I love it like this,' said Sarah. 'I imagine it's the deck of a ship and we are together on it, sailing the world.'

Jim stopped and turned her to him. Looking down at her, he drank in the picture of a girl with her hair blowing loose and eyes sparkling with the excitement and enjoyment of being caught up in the wildness of the wind and the sea while sharing it with him.

Charley was not waiting for them when they returned to the bridge and they took advantage of a few more minutes alone together.

'I'll be thinking of you,' said Jim, seeing the boy come hurrying down Bridge Street.

'And I you,' returned Sarah. 'You'll be sailing again after New Year. I hope I can see you again before then.'

'So do I.' He turned to Charley. 'Thanks for making this possible.'

Pleased to see his sister so happy, he said, 'Any time.'

In this brief exchange, a liking and trust had been forged between the two lads.

'Thanks, Charley,' said Sarah as they hurried home.

'You like him then?'

'A lot. No, it's more than that.'

'I like him too, Sarah. Be happy.' She had not buttoned up her redingote. 'Did he give you that?' Charley asked, indicating the jet brooch.

'Yes.' She nodded with obvious pleasure.

'How are you going to explain it?'

'All in good time, Charley.'

When they arrived at the house in New Buildings, Sarah went straight upstairs and placed the brooch lovingly in a silk scarf in one of the drawers of her dressing table.

Arabella made no more than a passing enquiry about Sarah's visit to Laura, but her empathy with her youngest sister and womanly intuition made her a little suspicious that something more than a call to a friend had taken place. She knew better than to press the subject, though, realising that more than likely Sarah would reveal the real reason for her absence in good time. Meanwhile there was the rest of Christmas Day to be faced.

When they gathered in the drawing-room prior to the evening meal, Arabella fought hard to subdue her jealousy as she saw a conversation developing between her father, Harriet and John from which she was excluded. It was as if she was destined forever to live within the restrictions placed on her as mistress of the household. The thought of such a bleak future scared her.

Benjamin had kept his mind fully attuned to the timber trade and he, along with the other whale-ship owners, was highly satisfied with the higher profits brought by the new arrangements for trading in the Baltic. Once those ports were frozen in, he had switched the *Sea King* to the Spanish wine trade and been pleased with the result and the way that John's enquiries, made on his own initiative, had also found them new business in that country.

'As I indicated when you arrived in port, John, I wish you to resume the wine trade during the first week in New Year and keep it going until we bring it to a halt for the whaling season.'

'Father, it's Christmas Day. No more business talk,' Harriet scolded him gently.

Benjamin gave a small smile of contrition when he felt his daughter pat his arm. 'Sorry, my dear. It's just that John is doing so well, I see him as a great asset to the firm. I intend to give him more authority after your marriage. It will be beneficial for all concerned and he can be a big influence on Charley, whom I intend to take into the firm in June.'

Harriet's face lit up. The warmth of her smile embraced her father as she kissed him on the cheek. 'Thank you, Papa. That is wonderful news. To tell us now is a most generous Christmas present. I know John won't let you down.'

'Thank you, sir, but I hope you aren't going to pen me behind a desk too soon?' said John.

'You are too valuable in your present role to move just yet.'

Arabella had been aware of the good mood among the group and wondered what was being said. At one point she had caught Harriet glance in her direction and thought she had detected a tinge of satisfaction there, at her expense. Arabella bristled and her lips set in a tight line. Immediately she was annoyed with herself for letting her façade slip; Harriet had caught her reaction and allowed her triumphant smirk to penetrate Arabella's defences once more.

The moment was broken by the sound of the gong in the hall.

Led by Benjamin, who escorted Arabella, they took their places in the dining-room, Arabella at the opposite end of the table from her father, Harriet and John on one side and Sarah and Charley on the other. Though she fought the emotion, Arabella felt left out again, the odd one out. Harriet sensed this and played on it, making her sister feel more and more uncomfortable with remarks and comments that only she could feel hurt by.

'Father's going to give John more authority once we are married.'

'John and I are so looking forward to widening our social circle.'

'Have you more dinner parties planned, Father?'

'Isn't it time you were entertaining ladies to tea, Arabella?'

That brought a sharp reply. 'Yes, it is, and you can help me,' snapped Arabella, knowing her sister abhorred what she called 'these boring and prissy occasions'.

'I'll think of some excuse,' hissed Harriet.

But her father caught the words. 'Harriet, you must help your sister.'

Arabella gave her a look filled with satisfaction at their father's intervention. It also gave her pleasure to see her sister pout, knowing she had detected in her father's tone that it would be no good turning coy to get her own way as she had done so often in the past. He set great store by such occasions, seeing them as a necessary adjunct to helping the firm prosper.

The rest of the meal and evening, though subdued,

passed off pleasantly enough with games and carols at the piano, in spite of the undercurrent of resentment between the two sisters.

As she prepared for bed Arabella reflected on this and wondered if she should make an extra effort to accept that John was lost to her and get on with her own life. A tear trickled down her cheek when she considered once again what it held for her as the eldest unmarried daughter, tied to a widower who expected her to run his household and look after him.

16 February 1833. Jim loves his life on the Sea King. *I am sure he will do well in the future . . .*

'The *Sea King*'s sighted, sir,' Jake Carter informed Benjamin.

'Good,' he replied, looking up from the document he was perusing. 'Let me know when she's nearing the piers.'

'Yes, sir.'

'Is everything ready for her fitting out for the whaling?'

'Yes, sir. Everyone concerned has been engaged under the usual terms. The shipwrights have been informed that she's been sighted, and the new ropes are ready. The whaling tools removed for the winter trading are now repaired and ready to be put back on board at the appropriate time. If there is nothing new to be done we should achieve a quick turnaround.'

'Good, the sooner we can dispatch the *Sea King* to the Arctic the better. We need a good return this year. Judging by weather conditions here and reports I've had from ships sailing south from the Shetlands, the weather could favour an early sailing. I'll arrange it with Captain Sharp. We need 1833 to be even better than 1832.'

Charley raced on to the quay but slowed abruptly when he saw his father. He started to turn towards a pile of boxes behind which he could watch the *Sea King* come to her berth without being seen but realised his father had noticed him. Easing his breathing, he sauntered over to his father.

'Hello, sir, come to see the *Sea King*?'

Benjamin did not answer the question; the reason for his being on the quay was obvious. 'Where have you been?' he asked, eyeing his son with a grave expression.

'I heard the *Sea King* had been sighted, sir, and went on to the East Cliff to watch her come in.' Charley feared what his father's reaction might be to that so was relieved when Benjamin answered amiably.

'Hmm, very commendable to show such interest. One day she'll be yours.'

Charley was taken aback. 'Really, sir? Really?' His bright eyes widened with excitement.

'Of course. As my only son, you'll take over the whole firm one day.'

'If I'm to do that, sir, I should sail on her. Can I go when she sails for the Arctic next month?' Charley had seen his chance and took it.

Benjamin scowled back at him. 'Of course not!' he snapped. 'I can't have my son and heir risking his life on a whaling voyage.'

'But, sir, that's what I want to be – a whaling captain.'

'Enough! Get those stupid ideas out of your head. You

have to learn all about the running of the firm. I've arranged for you to join it at the end of June.'

'But . . .'

'No buts!' barked his father. 'That is what I have planned for you and that is what you will do. There's no more to be said.'

Angry tears started to well in Charley's eyes but he fought them back. It wouldn't do to be seen crying. Instead he walked away, shoulders hunched in a sign of protest. He'd watch the *Sea King* dock from elsewhere. As he sought his new position he decided to ask John to put in a word for him with his father, but even as that thought came to him he realised it would carry no weight. From the 'I won't be challenged' tone of his father's voice, and from the look he had just given Charley, he knew it would be to no avail. It was with a heavy heart that he watched the *Sea King* approach the bridge, open already to allow her to move into the inner harbour.

Charley loved that ship and only wished his father would realise it. He knew Benjamin admired the skill of the craftsmen who had built her, and appreciated the men who sailed her, but she was nothing more to him than a means to bring him more wealth. But Charley saw her as a thing of grace and beauty even though there were more attractive ships. To other eyes the *Sea King* was sturdy rather than graceful, built to withstand the Arctic ice. His disappointment was subdued as he watched her man-oeuvred safely to her quay. He thrilled to the activity on board, wishing all the time that he was part of it. That in turn heightened his determination to overcome his father's opposition. He had no out and out objection to taking over the firm one day, as his father wished, but must first defy him and realise his own ambition to become the captain of a whale-ship. And, because of what he had just heard of his father's plans for him in June, he was going to have to act soon.

As he observed the bustle aboard the *Sea King* an idea began to evolve in Charley's mind. While considering its possibilities, he came to the conclusion that although he could carry it out alone, it would be wiser to enlist some help. But where could he find it? Whom could he trust?

He saw his father deep in conversation with John on the deck of the *Sea King*. He could not hear their words but could tell his father was issuing instructions and John was raising objections. His father's gesticulations displayed an uncompromising attitude and John's shrug of the shoulders and nod signified acceptance of what he had been told. As his father left the ship, Charley heard John issue orders for the crew to assemble on deck immediately. Anticipating an announcement, Charley's curiosity took him closer to the ship to catch the words.

With the crew gathered on deck, John announced, 'Mr Brook wants us to sail to the Arctic earlier than usual. We will depart in mid-March.' The murmurings that ran through the crew signified their disapproval of having their usual time ashore, before leaving on a six-month voyage, cut short. John had expected this and had already pointed it out to Benjamin, but he would not compromise.

'If you don't want to sail, say so before you leave this ship today. Mr Brook has said he will not hold a refusal against you when it comes to future voyages, but of course there will be no wages if you don't go.' John paused, letting that implication seep in. No wages would mean no allowances for dependants during their absence

116

in the Arctic and they and their families would face hard times next winter. John knew, as no doubt did Mr Brook, that places for sailors were not easy to come by at the present time and the chance of signing on again presented a big incentive.

'I have been assured by Jake Carter that all is in hand to unload and refit the *Sea King* quickly and will therefore relieve you from all duties as of now, so you can get as much time as possible with your families and friends before we sail. Those who do sign on, I expect on board by nine the day before we sail. Final preparations will be made then. I will allow you ashore that night and expect you to be back on board by nine the next day. Now, I will be in my cabin ready to sign on those of you who wish to sail on the *Sea King*'s whaling voyage.'

Charley heard it all. He hadn't much time to persuade his father . . . Even as that thought came into his mind it was dismissed. He continued to watch the ship. He saw some of the crew talking among themselves, seeking opinions as to what they should do. Should they sign on here and now, to be certain of wages? Or should they leave whaling and try a merchant ship? But the money from whaling, with a proportionate share of the catch depending on their crew rank, could be a lot better . . . Or maybe try another whale-ship that would not be leaving Whitby so soon? Charley saw them begin to make their way to the captain's cabin, and then, signed on, collect their belongings from their bunks in the fo'c'sle and leave the ship.

He tensed, his heart racing faster as he watched each man go down the gangway to the quay and in ones and twos head for home. Most of the crew had left when a lone figure walked briskly down the gangway, left the quay and hurried along Church Street. Charley broke cover and followed. Frightened of losing sight of him among the sea of shoppers and others pursuing their trades, Charley closed the gap. When the sailor turned into Henrietta Street, Charley glanced up at the towering cliff behind, its overhanging rocks seemingly poised to fall and destroy the houses below. The sight sent a chill through him. Was it a visual omen that tragedy hovered over his scheme? His step faltered but only for a moment. If he did not act now his plan would be harder to take to its desired conclusion. Wanting to catch the sailor before he reached his home at the poorer end of the street, Charley broke into a run.

'Jim! Jim Barbour!' he called.

Wondering who called his name, Jim stopped and turned round. He was surprised to see Charley Brook running towards him.

'Jim, may I have a word?' he panted, coming to a stop in front of the youngster who at sixteen stood an inch or two taller than fifteen-year-old Charley. Jim was wider in the shoulders, too, his hands broader and with strong fingers. His rugged features were tanned by the wind and the sun; his brown eyes lit up with curiosity when he recognised Charley.

'Have you a message from Sarah?' he asked eagerly.

Charley shook his head. 'No. I want your help.'

'My help?' Jim was curious. What could his employer's son want with him?

'Yes. I want you to help me stow away on the *Sea King*.'

'What?' Jim stared at him in astonishment. 'It's more than my job's worth. No! I can't and won't.' He started to turn away but Charley grasped his arm.

118

'Wait! Please hear me out.'

'Why should I?'

Charley levelled his eyes at him. 'You owe me, Jim. Remember?'

Jim's lips tightened. He recalled the words that had passed between them at Christmas and was not one to renege on a promise. 'Aye, I remember, but why do you want to be a stowaway? Your father owns the ship.'

'I want to be a sailor and he won't let me. He told me, just before the *Sea King* docked, that he plans for me to go into his firm in June – sitting behind a desk. I don't want that, not yet. I love that ship and I want to sail on her. If I don't seize my chance now, I'm doomed to an office life before I want it. Please help me. We have time to plan it.'

Jim saw that the genuine desire in Charley's eyes was coupled with determination. He stood there thoughtfully and Charley realised it would not be wise to interrupt the debate that must be going on in his mind.

'Does Sarah know about this?' asked Jim.

'No, no one does. But if that's a condition of your helping me, I'll tell her. I know I can trust her.'

'I think it might be a good idea for her to know.'

Charley nodded.

'You want me to find a place for you to hide?' Jim asked.

'No. I've explored that ship thoroughly and know it like the back of my hand. I could stow away without you or anyone else knowing.'

'And where might that be?'

'In the bow-locker.'

'Good grief! It's only a storeroom with no light, no porthole. You'll be fierce cramped. How do you expect to survive?'

119

'I will.'

'But . . .'

'It's a good place because at the start of the voyage nothing is likely to be wanted from there.'

'And if it is, what then?'

'I'll have to take my chances with Captain Sharp's understanding.'

'How long do you plan to remain in hiding?'

'Two days' sailing to Shetland, one day in port there, then I appear when it's too late for Captain Sharp to return and put me ashore for a ship bound for England.'

'You have it all worked out.'

'Yes, but I need the help of someone on board. Someone has to know I am there and supply me with water. Food I'll bring with me.' Charley gave Jim an appealing look.

'It's risky,' he objected, 'especially if you're found and it becomes evident that I helped you.'

'No blame will be attached to you. Captain Sharp realises I know the *Sea King* inside out. He won't think of me having had any inside help, and even if he does I'll deny it. Please, Jim, do this for me? I'll never forget it.' Then Charley added the one thing he thought would finally win Jim's agreement. 'I know Sarah will approve of your helping me and repaying your debt. She'll thank you for this.'

Jim could see no harm in the plan once Charley had sworn to keep quiet. He did owe the boy, and if it would please Sarah he was committed. He stuck out his hand and Charley shook it firmly. Giving a broad smile he said, 'You're a pal.' With those words and the handshake, Jim felt his relationship with Sarah had moved on to an even more solid foundation.

Charley's footsteps were light as he walked back along Church Street, but while his emotions were high he grappled with a difficult decision. When should he tell Sarah . . . now or nearer sailing time? He crossed the river still undecided but by the time he entered his home had reached a resolution that, no matter what happened, from then on his future course in life was shaped. That thought sent his mind and heart racing.

He looked in the drawing-room. Sarah was not there; nor was she in the small sitting-room. He didn't want to give himself time to think any more so took the stairs two at a time, raced along the corridor, gave a sharp knock on Sarah's door and hurried in, sending the door to behind him.

She looked up from the book she was reading while sitting on the window-seat. 'Charley?'

'Sarah, I need your help!' he gasped before she could say any more.

'Help? What's the matter?' Her words were filled with concern, brow furrowed in query.

He flopped on to the window-seat beside her. 'I've just seen Jim and he . . .'

'Jim?' Alarm filled her; her eyes widened with dismay.

'He's all right.' Charley emphasised the words to reassure her. 'He's agreed to help me but only on condition I tell you . . .' The words were coming out too fast.

'Charley, slow down!' she put in sharply. 'What's this all about? Tell me, slowly.'

He began his story and, as he proceeded, Sarah's eyes widened in disbelief. 'You won't get away with it,' she cautioned.

'I will. I must. Otherwise I'll be condemned to that office long before I wish to be.'

'I have no doubt you'll get aboard and hide away, but you'll be missed here.'

'That will only be after the *Sea King* has sailed and nobody but you will know I'm on board. Just as I thought it wise for someone to know I was on board, and enlisted Jim's help for that, he thought it best if someone here knew where I was.'

'He was right,' said Sarah.

'And that's you, but you must not reveal the truth until I have left Shetland. I will write a letter to Father there and get it to a ship leaving for England. That will clear you of any blame should it become apparent that you knew I had stowed away, and it will help ease your conscience about keeping quiet. You must agree, Sarah, please? Otherwise Jim won't play his part and then I'll never achieve my ambition.'

Sarah hesitated, her mind doubting that Charley's plan would succeed, but she could not deny the pleading look in her brother's eyes. If she did, she knew it would haunt her for the rest of her life. She reached out and took his hand. 'All right, Charley, your secret's safe with me and you can tell Jim I know about it.'

'Oh, thanks, Sarah.' Elated, he kissed her on the cheek. 'I'll make sure I see him tomorrow.'

'And while you are about it, you can make arrangements for Jim and me to meet and *you* can be our chaperon again.'

'Anything for you and Jim, Sarah.'

8

18 March 1833. Sailing day. I expect Charley is aboard
the Sea King. *I did not want to be a part of his plans but
it is done now. I hope he isn't found before they leave
Shetland and that it is never discovered Jim helped him.
I dread to think of what will happen here when he is
missed. And again when the letter comes. Father will be
furious. I hope the voyage is successful and Charley
works like a good crew member. Then Father may be
more lenient, may even agree to Charley's taking part in
other voyages before he has to sit behind a desk . . .*

'She's a fine ship!'

The *Sea King* had slipped her moorings and passed
beyond the bridge.

Benjamin turned to see who, among the crowd now
hurrying from the quay to get to a better vantage point,
had made the comment. He saw a well-dressed man
whom he judged to be about thirty. He was tall, maybe
an inch or two over six feet, with bright eyes that
enhanced his sharp features and made him appear handsome.

'Indeed it is,' replied Benjamin. The pride in his voice
was unmistakable.

'Ah, from that tone I detect you may have a vested interest in her?'

'I have. She is my vessel. And, I must say, you have an eye to appraise a ship's worth.'

'Now you are embarrassing me, sir, though I must admit to an interest in ships.' He paused, then held out his hand. 'Stephen Waite, at your service, sir.' The warmth in his smile and his pleasant demeanour impressed Benjamin. His grip was strong and firm, something Benjamin liked in a man.

'Benjamin Brook,' he replied briskly.

'Pleased to know you, sir, and meeting you may be fortuitous for me.'

'Oh? Why should that be?'

But Benjamin held up a hand to stem his reply. 'Before you answer, sir, the bridge has just closed. The remaining two whale-ships are sailing in three days' time. I must go to the West Pier to bid my vessel farewell. If you wish to answer my questions, you'll have to walk with me.'

Stephen had been prepared for the authority in Benjamin's voice; he had recognised a man with power and influence and was up to matching them. 'It would be my privilege to accompany you, sir.'

'Then let's go.'

'Sir, please tell me, do so many Whitby people turn out whenever a ship sails?'

Benjamin smiled knowingly. 'Ah, that tells me you are a stranger to these parts?'

'I am, sir.'

'Yes, everyone comes out to see a whale-ship sail. They'll do so again in three days' time. You see, the whale-ships and the men who sail them are vital to Whitby's economy.'

124

'But surely other vessels are just as important?'

'Of course, but the whale-ships sail dangerous seas; the men risk their lives in icy conditions in what are often unknown waters, so there is an aura around them. They are regarded as special. And, don't forget, it can be six months before they see their home port again. For all these reasons, Whitby folk want to give them a good send-off.'

Stephen nodded. 'Interesting.'

'Now those answers?'

They had crossed the bridge and were heading for the West Pier, Benjamin keeping a wary eye on the *Sea King* all the time.

'Well, sir, as you correctly surmised I am not from these parts. I was born in Bristol and lived there until two years ago. Father was a sea captain sailing out of there.'

'So that's where you inherited your interest in ships?'

'Precisely. I might have followed him but Mother was adamant that she didn't want another son going to sea after my brother was lost overboard in a violent storm off the Irish coast.'

'I'm sorry to hear that. Your father?'

'He too went down with his ship, a year later, wrecked off the Scillies.'

'Tragic,' sympathised Benjamin with a shake of his head.

They had reached the West Pier.

'We'll continue in a few minutes,' said Benjamin, weaving his way among the onlookers until he'd reached the best position from which to watch the *Sea King* take to the open sea. He raised an acknowledging hand to John and turned it into their sign signifying 'Safe voyage'.

Stephen respected Mr Brook's desire to watch the *Sea King* sail. He let his own thoughts roam over what had happened since leaving Bristol, events he had never anticipated but which he had seized upon when he saw the opportunities they presented; opportunities like the present one, which had necessitated his using the name Stephen Waite instead of his real name of Stephen Boulton . . .

With nothing to hold him in Bristol after his mother's death, he'd left for London, determined to prove that he could face the world and use the talent he had to secure himself a fortune in the mercantile world. He was not short of money, but knowing that it could run out one day, he'd sought employment in the world he already knew – shipping and its ancillary trades. After two weeks in the capital he approached a firm of ship's chandlers about the possibility of employment there. Smartly dressed and well groomed, he presented himself with confidence, only to be told that there were no vacancies at present.

Disappointed, he walked from the building and paused outside the front door, deciding whether to turn right or left. Decision made, he tapped the top of his hat and tripped lightly down the four steps to the pavement. There were other fish to fry.

He heard the sound of quick-moving feet behind him but took little notice until he felt a tight grasp on his arm and voice say, 'Hold on.' Annoyed at the intrusion, he swung round, anger mounting in his face as he glared at the man restraining him. He saw a young man of about his own age, well dressed and with an open friendly face.

'Geoffrey Hardcastle,' the young man said as he released his hold and held out his hand.

After only a slight hesitation, Stephen took it and felt a firm, friendly grip. 'Didn't I see you inside?'

'Yes, I sat in on the interview. Something Father insists on . . . my getting to know every aspect of the trade.'

Stephen glanced back at the brass plaque next to the door of the building he had just left then turned a quizzical eye on the young man.

'That's right,' Geoffrey smiled. 'My father's firm.'

'So what might the owner's son want of me?'

'There's a coffee house just down the street. I'll bet you'll admit it's the best coffee you've ever tasted. We can talk there. I've something to say that might interest you, Stephen Boulton.'

Stephen could not even guess what this was about, but what matter? It would be interesting to hear what Hardcastle had to say.

Ten minutes later, with a table between them and coffee at hand, Geoffrey began: 'I liked your demeanour and attitude during that interview. You are a very personable man. I know someone who may be able to help you. She has some influence in London's maritime circles.'

'She?'

'Oh, don't look so surprised. London's full of enigmas, and Pamela Seaton is one of them.'

Standing on the pier in Whitby beside Benjamin Brook, Stephen smiled to himself, recalling how that chance encounter in London had led him to this tiny port on the Yorkshire coast.

Two evenings after the encounter with Geoffrey Hardcastle, Stephen was shown into a small, elegant house in a quiet London street. He felt it had an air of opulence and saw that it was decorated and furnished with consummate taste. He immediately wondered what new world he had had the good fortune to walk into. He watched the servant who had admitted him to the house cross the hall, knock on a door and then turn away to disappear down a passage. It had obviously been a prearranged signal for a few moments later Geoffrey appeared and greeted him profusely.

'Slip your coat off for a few minutes and have a glass of Madeira, we've time,' he suggested as he ushered Stephen into a drawing-room in which the furnishings and walls were subtle shades of pale blue, all blending harmoniously.

Once they were sitting comfortably with glasses charged, Geoffrey raised his and said, 'To an enjoyable evening, and a profitable one for you.'

Stephen acknowledged the toast and then said, 'You indicated this was a small gathering of Mrs Seaton's friends. Are you sure I'll be welcome?'

'Of course. I told her I would like to bring a guest and she agreed. You'll be arriving with me which will indicate to Pamela that I vouch for you; she will accept that and make you most welcome.'

'Then prepare me. Tell me something about her?'

'I will tell you only a little. It will be best for you to form your own judgement. She is a very able lady, a widow who inherited her husband's business.'

'And that was?'

'A ship's chandler, the same as my father. He and Pamela's husband, though there was an age gap of ten years, were great friends as well as rivals. Since Pamela took over, she has expanded and moved into shipping.'

Stephen nodded thoughtfully. 'Geoffrey, are you sure about taking me?'

'Now don't be thinking like that. From what I heard at

that interview your knowledge of the mercantile world, though based largely on Bristol trade, showed a keen desire to look ahead. And I think Pamela will be able to give you that chance.'

'Well, if you are happy to introduce me then I am grateful to you. If nothing comes of it, there will be nothing lost, I suppose.'

'We haven't far to go – walking distance.' Geoffrey took a hunting-watch from the pocket of his waistcoat, flicked it open and said, 'I think we should go.'

Both men drained their glasses, donned their redingotes and hats, and left the house. They walked a few streets away.

'Third house on the left,' said Geoffrey in a quiet tone, as if in deference to the smart terrace of bow-fronted, three-storeyed houses ahead of them. He tugged at a highly polished bell-pull and a few moments later the heavy door swung silently open.

'Good evening, sir,' said a liveried manservant, obviously recognising him.

'Good evening, Fenton. This is Mr Boulton.'

'Good evening to you, sir,' said Fenton with an inclination of his head to Stephen. He turned back to Geoffrey. 'Mrs Seaton told me you would be accompanied by a friend. May I take your coats?'

A few minutes later he was escorting them across the hall towards a door through which could be heard the buzz of conversation. He knocked on it then stood back to allow the two new arrivals to enter a large elegant room which was wide enough to accommodate four windows on the street-facing wall.

A quick glance told Stephen that there were fourteen guests, seven of each sex, already in the room. He deduced the fifteenth was their hostess, for she was the centre of attention. But his quick assessment stopped there. He took in nothing else within the room because his whole attention became focused on Mrs Seaton. She glanced in their direction and then, after a quiet apologetic word to the others, moved gracefully towards them.

This was not the elderly widow he had expected to see! He was captivated by her porcelain beauty, the slim lines of a body that a close-fitting cream silk dress did nothing to hide. He started, chiding himself for staring like a country bumpkin.

'Geoffrey, how delightful to see you.' She held out her hand to him and he raised it towards his lips. 'And this must be the young man you told me about?'

'Yes, this is Stephen Boulton.'

'I am pleased to meet you, Stephen.' She held out her hand to him and he took it as Geoffrey had done.

'And I to meet you, Mrs Seaton.'

She threw back her head and laughed, 'Ah, I see Geoffrey has not instructed you, so I will. When in my house, my friends do not address me as Mrs Seaton . . . I am Pamela.' She raised her finger in reproof. 'Remember that.'

Her eyes had never left him. He was drawn by their boldness, the way they scrutinised him as if searching for his very soul. With that observation he realised he was surrendering to her, to a woman whose age he put at no more than thirty-one or -two. He felt flattered that she should want to bewitch him, and so soon after their meeting.

Pamela turned to Geoffrey. 'You did not tell me he was so handsome. That was sly of you.'

'I thought it best to give you no preconceived idea of

whom I was bringing. I wanted you to make up your own mind.'

She turned to Stephen then. 'All he told me was that he thought you may be an asset to my firm. We shall see, but no more of that this evening. We are here to enjoy ourselves, business can be discussed another day. So, Stephen, you are welcome to my home.'

'I thank you.'

'Now come along and meet my other guests.'

He soon realised he was in select company; people of wealth, who had obtained it by hard work and shrewd decisions. They all enjoyed the good things in life and were sparkling companions who had an easy manner with each other. Throughout the evening, during which the conversation flowed over many topics and they enjoyed an excellent meal, Stephen was aware he had stepped over a boundary, and resolved to keep the right side of it henceforth. But he realised that it would not be a one-sided affair; he would have to contribute too. Though Pamela had said no business talk, and there wasn't, he was aware she had subtly held him under scrutiny for most of the evening. She was making her appraisal of him as a man so as to be forearmed when the talk turned to business on a day of her choosing. Anxious as he was to meet her again, drawn by the desire to be in the presence of such a beautiful woman, he knew it would not be wise to make the first move. He would be called at the appropriate time; when the call came he would be ready.

Within twelve weeks Stephen had answered the summons, displayed a knowledge of the maritime world that he knew Pamela could not ignore, shown an enthusiasm to contribute to her company's wealth but no desire to take it over; he allowed all his ideas to appear to have come from her. He exuded charm. So much so that he became her regular companion at various social events across London. Stephen took to his new life with zest, not least for sharing Pamela's bed from the moment she invited him into it, six weeks after their first meeting.

Pamela for her part had found what she had craved after the mourning period for her husband was over and she had moved back into London society. She had many admirers but recognised that most of them only wanted to marry a rich widow for her money so held them at arm's length; the rest she dismissed as too unattractive to meet her needs. Then Stephen Boulton had walked into her life. From the moment he came into the room with Geoffrey, she was drawn to him. If he could serve her business interests, as well as her more personal ones, then Stephen Boulton had to be hers. She made it her business to check that he could, in every respect.

When they finally came to terms with each other, Pamela laid down some rules. 'Stephen, you are an attractive man; many women will want you. I will overlook any infidelity so long as you always come back to me. If you don't, I will cut you off completely. You will leave me with nothing, and I'll see to it that your name is so sullied you'll never get another job anywhere in the mercantile world. You know full well that I have that power. You are mine, Stephen Boulton, and don't you forget it.'

That night he thought about the consequences if he strayed from her conditions, and decided to live with them. He lived in luxury, he had money, and he enjoyed his work because it offered him scope to develop new ideas, which pleased Pamela because they worked for the good of her firm. She was particularly enthusiastic concerning the plan he would put to Benjamin Brook, if his first sounding hooked that gentleman. One thing he must not let slip was that his real name was Boulton and not Waite. Pamela had insisted that he should not be seen to be linked with her firm because vultures might anticipate rich pickings. So as Stephen Boulton was known to be involved with the Seaton firm, it was decided that he would become Stephen Waite for this venture. There was a firm of that name trading from Bristol.

'Mr Waite, thank you for being so patient.' The voice startled Stephen and brought him back to the West Pier in Whitby, with the *Sea King* heading for the Arctic.

'I suspect you have a special feeling for that ship, sir,' he commented. 'Have you sailed in her?'

Benjamin started. 'Not that ship, no. My sailing days are behind me now. Had a bad experience as a young man. In fact, I hate the sea. It can be vicious and, as I'm sure you know, can easily kill.' He started to retrace their steps.

Stephen matched his pace. 'Then why . . .?'

'I admire a ship's lines, and of course I like them for the wealth they bring me. As for anything else – no. And that's why I do not wish my son to go to sea, especially as he's the only boy and there's a good solid business waiting for him on land.' Benjamin paused and then said quickly, 'You were telling me about yourself.'

'To continue, sir. I've built up a good business trading out of Bristol, it's well established there, but at present I'm looking at the possibility of moving some of my endeavours elsewhere. I had an idea it might be worthwhile looking at some of the ports on the East Coast.'

133

'And that's why you are in Whitby?'

'Yes. And why I suggested it was fortuitous for me to have met you. As a respected and successful trader here in Whitby, I wondered – if it is not intruding on your time – if you could advise me on the prospects of establishing a business here, as a subsidiary of my firm in Bristol?'

'Well, I would need to know a little more about which trade you are thinking of concentrating on if you decide to use Whitby.'

'That can be easily done, sir. Dine with me at the Angel this evening? I would be most grateful if you would. Your advice could save me much valuable time, no matter which way your information and advice lead me.'

Benjamin considered for a moment. This young man had an air of confidence about him, someone who could easily make a decision in the knowledge that he was right or if not live with the consequences. A solid business in Bristol? Well, Benjamin could soon check on that. It could be beneficial to have this young man trading through Whitby. Ships sailing from Bristol plied different seas, visited different lands, from those sailing out of Whitby, and who knew what advantage a link between the two ports could bring to Benjamin Brook?

'Very well,' he agreed.

'Splendid, sir, splendid,' cried Stephen with apparent pleasure. 'Shall we say seven o'clock?'

'Ideal,' agreed Benjamin.

When they parted he headed for home in a thoughtful mood. As he had expected, he found none of his family there. He knew his daughters would have been on the West Cliff to see the *Sea King* sail and had no doubt afterwards taken advantage of the outing to see what was on display in the shop windows. Charley, of course, would still be along the quays somewhere, probably viewing ships preparing for their next voyage.

Benjamin went straight to his room and made ready for his visit to the Angel. He heard someone come into the house, and when he finally came downstairs found his daughters in the drawing-room.

'I am going out now and will not be back until late. I am dining at the Angel this evening,' he announced.

'Very well, Papa,' answered Arabella.

'With anyone interesting, Papa?' asked Harriet brightly.

'Someone I met while watching the *Sea King* sail.'

'Anyone we know?'

He shook his head. 'A stranger from far away. We got talking and he asked me to dine with him.'

'Have a good evening, Papa,' said Sarah, hoping that would hasten her father's departure; she didn't want him asking where Charley might be. That question would come soon enough.

'Thank you, Sarah,' he said. 'I'll be on my way. I have a call to make before I go to the Angel.'

She breathed a sigh of relief when the drawing-room door closed behind him.

Benjamin, his mind on Stephen Waite, walked briskly to a house in Bagdale. Recognising him when she answered the door and made his request to see Mr Peckitt, the maid invited him to step inside. 'I'll see if he is available, sir.' She crossed the hall and entered a room that Benjamin knew was Cuthbert Peckitt's study. She reappeared a few moments later. 'Mr Peckitt will see you, sir.'

Benjamin nodded his thanks as he passed her to enter the room.

'Benjamin! This is a pleasant surprise.' The young man was already coming from behind his desk as his visitor entered the room.

'I'm sorry to intrude on your time, Cuthbert.'

'You aren't doing that. If I can't stop what I'm doing when a friend calls, it is time to give up working. Please sit down.' He indicated a comfortable chair. 'You'll take a drop of whisky?'

'You tempt me, Cuthbert.'

'Then give way to temptation,' he laughed as he went to a decanter and glasses set on a tray beneath an oil painting entitled 'Whalers in the Arctic'. He poured whisky into two glasses and, knowing Benjamin's preference, added a mere dash of water. He handed one glass to Benjamin and took a comfortable seat facing his friend. Cuthbert raised his glass. 'Your good health.' Benjamin nodded and reciprocated.

'Cuthbert, if I remember rightly, two years ago you spent about six months in Bristol with an uncle there?'

He nodded. 'Yes, I did. Father thought it would do me good to see another side of the shipping business.' Wondering why Benjamin should bring this up now, he cast an enquiring glance at him.

'Did you come across a firm by the name of Waite?'

'Yes,' replied Cuthbert without hesitation. 'A small firm but, as I remember, with the potential to expand.'

Benjamin nodded thoughtfully.

'Why this interest in Bristol and in Waite's?'

'I got into a casual conversation with a Stephen Waite today while watching the *Sea King* sail. He told me he had an established business in Bristol and was looking to expand elsewhere, with the result that he's here in Whitby.'

Cuthbert smiled knowingly. 'And you, ever open to opportunity, are tempted to exploit his interest?'

'Why not? I knew you had been in Bristol and thought you might shed some light on this firm. And I also knew you would not be interested yourself because of your whaling commitments in Hull as well as here in Whitby. And, equally aware of your integrity, I knew that what I revealed would not pass beyond these four walls.'

'I appreciate your trust and assure you that our discussion will go no further. I've told you the little I know about the firm. I can't say that I've ever met a Stephen Waite.'

'He's young and exudes enthusiasm for the mercantile trade. Has an appreciative eye for ships as well.'

'I said the firm had potential for expansion; if what you tell me is true then it seems this Stephen has fulfilled that and wants more. I don't think I can tell you anything else.'

'What you have done already is a help. We are always suspicious of such information until we can verify it.'

'True. I think you should know more than what I have told you, though. I'm only sorry I can't enlighten you further.'

'It has given me a foundation on which I can build this evening. I am dining with him, at his invitation, at the Angel.'

Cuthbert smiled. 'I think you've seen an opportunity already.'

'Well,' Benjamin drew the word out, 'I thought if he was seeking expansion outside Bristol, why not look at the possibilities he can offer me? I'm heavily dependent on whaling, though not as much as you. I know you won't agree, but I can see the day when we will have to realign our sights on the commodities in which we trade. This may be an opportunity for me to do that.'

They fell into a discussion about the future of the whaling trade, of Whitby's development as a port and the potential for expansion and diversification. Cuthbert, heavily committed to whaling in Whitby and in Hull, saw his future as bound to that industry, whereas Benjamin, with thoughts of making the firm sound for Charley, saw greater diversification as his goal. They were enjoying their discussion, unaware of how quickly time was passing, until Bristol was mentioned again.

Benjamin was on his feet in an instant after draining his glass of its second refill. 'I must be off! Can't have Mr Waite thinking I'm a bad timekeeper. Thank you for the information and the pleasant discussion.'

'I'll be interested in the outcome,' said Cuthbert as he escorted his friend to the door.

'I'll keep you informed.'

'Has either of you seen Charley?' Arabella asked as she accompanied her sisters into the dining-room for their evening meal.

'Last time I saw him was when I came into breakfast this morning,' said Harriet. 'He'd had his and was in a hurry to be out.'

'Typical of him on a day when any whale-ship is leaving,' commented Sarah.

'But he should have been back by now,' said Arabella as she reached her place at the table.

'It's a good thing Father is not here for this meal or Charley would have felt his tongue,' said Harriet.

Sarah, wondering how her brother was faring, made no further comment; she did not want to be drawn into speculation about his whereabouts. She was saved from any further discussion of his absence when a maid entered the room with a letter in her hand.

'Mrs Ainslie's just received this, miss. It's addressed to you.'

Arabella took the letter and immediately recognised the writing. 'It's from Charley,' she said, glancing at her sisters before turning to the maid. 'Who brought it, Lucy?'

'A boy none of us knew. He said he was told to bring it here.'

'Who by? Did the boy say?'

'No, miss. He was gone in a flash.'

Arabella nodded. 'Thank you, Lucy.'

By the time the maid reached the door Arabella was slitting the envelope open. She read the few words quickly, then looked up at her sisters. They registered the relief on her face as they waited for an explanation.

'He's gone to Toby Munroe's and has been invited to stay the night.'

'So we'll see him tomorrow?' commented Harriet.

'I expect so,' said Arabella.

Sarah was thankful for Charley's thoughtfulness. This had not been part of his original plan, so far as she knew. Staying at Toby Munroe's was not a regular occurrence but it was not unknown to happen on the spur of the moment. With this note her brother was making sure he would not be missed for at least another twenty-four hours, maybe even more.

*

Charley stretched his aching legs as much as he could in the cramped space of the bow-locker. The creak of the timbers was music to his ears; he was sailing north on the *Sea King*! He had had no qualms about finding his sea legs. The rolling and plunging motions had had no effect on him and that confirmed his belief that he was born for the sea and even made his self-imposed confinement tolerable. Nevertheless Jim's visit, short though it was, after two hours' sailing, had aided his resolve. He must remain hidden here until he could no longer be returned to Whitby.

His recollections of the tales he'd heard of hunting whales in the vast frozen Arctic, from the lips of men who had been there and enjoyed telling their stories to a wide-eyed boy, brought keen anticipation of what lay ahead. His thoughts also embraced his family; he hoped the letter he had written pretending he had stayed at Toby Munroe's would delay the discovery that he was missing. He shuffled on his bed of ropes, seeking more comfort, and finally fell asleep; there was little else to do.

'I'm sorry I'm late,' Benjamin apologised to Stephen Waite as he entered the comfortable saloon bar in the Angel.

'Think nothing of it,' came the reply as Stephen rose from his chair at a round table positioned so that he had a view of the door. The occupants of other tables glanced at the new arrival. Some, familiar with one of the leading merchants in Whitby, acknowledged Benjamin with a nod or raised hand, extending their curiosity to the stranger who had welcomed him.

'I visited a friend on the way here and we got carried away. The time flew by,' explained Benjamin, exchanging a firm handshake with his host.

'It is of no account. Come, sit down.'

As soon as they were seated a waiter appeared and placed a small tray holding a tumbler and a small jug of water in front of Benjamin.

Stephen nodded his thanks at the waiter and said to Benjamin, 'I took the liberty of enquiring what you usually drank when you visited the Angel.'

'That's very civil of you,' he replied, in his mind already adding to his assessment of this young man, who was not losing an opportunity to impress by disclosing an enterprising mind. 'I trust it has not extended to the food?' he added with a wry smile.

Stephen laughed, amusement dancing in his eyes. 'Ah, that would not be as wise. I should not anticipate your tastes there, nor should I inflict mine on you.' He picked up his glass and raised it to Benjamin. 'To you, sir, and to a pleasant evening.'

Benjamin lifted his glass and acknowledged the salutation.

They settled down comfortably to enjoy their drinks. Their talk was general until after the waiter had taken their orders. They both chose soup, and on Benjamin's recommendation, Stephen ordered the steak and kidney pie made to the Angel's special recipe while Benjamin chose cod.

'You indicated earlier today that you were looking to extend your Bristol business to another port. Why?' Benjamin initiated the real discussion.

'As you will no doubt know, Bristol was very heavily committed to the slave trade. With the Abolition Bill in 1807 the city suffered, though there were still certain captains who pursued the trade in spite of heavy fines if caught. Generally Bristol was forced to look elsewhere for a mainstay. It suffers from the lack of any industry of its own, though ship-building is increasing. There are no industrial centres close by and the rivalry of Liverpool as a major port in the West does not help. However, there is potential to develop other imports, some of which are already trading through Bristol. And I see the possibilities of extending those further through another port.'

'What had you in mind?'

The answer to that question was delayed because the waiter came to tell them that their meal was ready. It was only when they were settled with their oxtail soup that Benjamin raised the question again.

'I'm in the exploratory stage at the moment, looking at possibilities, and not necessarily here in Whitby,' Stephen explained. 'I need somewhere with untapped potential . . . a place where the facilities of a good harbour, warehousing and available markets would help make for a successful enterprise.'

Benjamin nodded. 'And you intend this to be a completely new firm, but affiliated to your Bristol company?'

'That is what I have in mind at the moment, but if there were other possibilities, such as a link with a local firm or even forming a partnership with one that already exists . . . I'd consider them.'

'Wherever you set up this project, what would be special about your trading?'

'I would base it on the commodities we bring into Bristol and on local products, acting as a forwarding agency to other ports around the country and using the sea because transporting by land over long distances is totally inadequate.'

'I agree with your assessment. Access to the hinterland

142

is not easy from Whitby. Most of the trade conducted round here is by sea.'

'I visualise the possibility of a chain of ships working from port to port around Britain,' Stephen enthused.

Benjamin raised his eyebrows in an expression of surprise. 'A bold idea, if I may say so, and one that will need careful thought.' He paused a moment then added, 'You would establish agents in each port to act on your behalf, receiving goods that merchants needed to transport onwards?'

'It is an idea that could well tempt them, because it would make it possible for them to widen their markets.'

'You would need reliable and trustworthy agents on the ground,' pointed out Benjamin.

'Very true, sir. I would plan to pay them a percentage of the profits from the deals they instigated so that it would be in their interest to keep every deal honest and above board. Or I would come to agreements with people like yourself, established merchants who would gain nothing from trying to outsmart me. Their own reputation would be at stake.'

'And the ships?' queried Benjamin.

'That is something I need to look into further. I have three vessels sailing out of Bristol, engaged in the West Indies and American trade. The latter, I can see, has great potential. It is a vibrant, expanding country. They would continue to ply those seas. As regards the ships required to move goods around this country, I see the possibility of hiring those and their crews locally. But, as I say, that is something that needs careful setting up and I have not as yet gone into it deeply. It will take time to do so. I am in the early stages of my idea. Whitby ships and sailors have a high reputation. That is why I came here.'

'I should think it would be essential to include London in your calculations.'

'Too much competition there. It is ports like Whitby where I can see the wider possibilities.'

'Once again, I must point out that there are traders already doing just what you are proposing.'

'Ah, yes, there are. But I believe that they operate within the confines of a particular locality, whereas I propose to encompass ports all around Britain and Ireland.'

'Well, I must say, this is a grandiose scheme, but one which I can see has merit and promises a great deal.'

'I'm pleased to hear that, sir. So you think Whitby may fit well with my ideas?'

Benjamin nodded thoughtfully. 'Yes, I do. Your trade here would be in handling the goods that Whitby exports by sea and importing goods that are required very locally. Because of the relatively inaccessible hinterland here, I believe that anything requiring onward movement inland – for example, goods connected with the West Yorkshire woollen trade – would be better handled through Hull. There is no reason why the trade through those two ports can't be kept separate.' He paused and nodded. 'No, I can't see any reason why your idea shouldn't work. It will need a great deal of setting up but I can see that, established along the right lines, it could bring in a very nice profit.'

'It is reassuring to hear you say so, sir. That gives me much to think about.' Stephen's voice assumed a lighter tone. 'Now, if I may suggest, let us leave business aside, relax and talk of other things.'

Benjamin bowed to his host's suggestion, though he would have enjoyed talking business all night. By the time he was walking home, his opinion of Stephen Waite had soared. The young man's conversation had been entertaining and brisk, embracing a wide range of topics without ever dominating the evening. Nor did it distract from the pleasure of the food and wine they had shared, and about which he had exhibited a keen knowledge – an asset in the wine trade should that enter into his calculations. Benjamin had much to think about.

Stephen Waite also had much to ponder as he settled in his room with a nightcap of whisky. He congratulated himself on what he believed had been a successful talk with Benjamin Brook. Seeds had been sown and he had a feeling they would bear fruit. He was sure Pamela would agree with what he envisaged for her firm in Whitby. The future looked bright. He only wished she was here to share his bed tonight.

'I'm going to bed, I've a bit of a headache,' said Sarah, pushing herself out of her armchair after closing the book she had been reading. The printed words had meant nothing to her with her mind focused entirely on Charley.

'Can I get you a drink?' Arabella showed concern and prepared to lay down the tablecloth she was embroidering.

'No, no,' replied Sarah hastily. She wanted no fuss, only desiring to escape the fraught atmosphere that lay heavily on the elder two girls. 'Are you waiting up for Father?' she asked in an attempt to create some communication between them before she departed.

'No,' replied Arabella. 'He said he was likely to be late.'

'Good night then,' offered Sarah.

Harriet did not speak, allowing the fact that she was closing her book to do it for her and her action in following Sarah from the room to show that she had no desire to be left alone with Arabella.

Arabella's lips tightened as she gazed unseeingly through dampening eyes at the closed door. Her heart was still filled with love for the man whose betrayal she tried to erase from her mind and regard as only a temporary lapse on his part. Surely in time he would realise the strength of her love for him, and that it was she with whom his future should be shared?

Harriet knew Sarah's sympathies lay with Arabella so did not attempt to catch her up on the stairs or to speak to her. They went their separate ways on the landing.

Sarah sat down heavily on the edge of her bed, feeling the enormity of what she had done pressing down on her. She hoped Charley was all right. Though she did not know the detailed lay-out of the *Sea King*, she knew sufficient to realise he would be hidden where no one was likely to find him, and that meant in discomfort and darkness. 'Oh, Charley, be safe,' she whispered.

When she closed the door to her room, Harriet leaned back against it and once again allowed the pleasure of her triumph to seep through her. She had ensnared one of the most eligible bachelors in Whitby – a ship's captain with a rich future before him – and she had snatched him from her sister! She danced across the room, flopped down on to her bed and gazed up at the ceiling with laughter in her eyes and on her lips. She would want for nothing when John made her his wife.

9

19 March 1833. I'm not going down to breakfast until Papa has left the house. I don't want to be there if he queries Charley's absence, though the note pretending he's at Toby Munroe's may delay any such action.

I wish Arabella and Harriet were reconciled. They hardly speak nowadays. Father doesn't notice, obsessed with work and memories of Mama. I wish I could heal the rift. If they were still on good terms it might ease the trouble that will erupt when Father eventually queries Charley's non-appearance . . .

Sarah heard something bang and recognised it as the front door. She dropped her pen and rushed to the window which gave her a view of the path to the front gate. Her father was departing! She breathed a sigh of relief. Now questions would not begin until this evening at the earliest. She watched him for a few moments and frowned. He was not walking with his usual briskness – feeling off colour or else preoccupied about his business? The latter, more likely than not. She turned away from the window and went to the door. As she neared the bottom of the stairs she heard footsteps on the landing above. She stopped, looked up, saw Arabella approaching the top of the stairs and waited for her.

About to mention the *Sea King*, Sarah held her tongue for fear of making a slip and giving away Charley's secret. Besides, she knew any such mention would only revive Arabella's memories of John and reopen a wound. Instead she asked, 'Have you any plans for today?'

Arabella gave a sad smile. 'The usual meeting with Mrs Ainslie, then I'll have to have the household accounts ready for Father, and later I'm visiting seamen's widows as Mother used to.'

They had reached the dining-room. When they went in they found Harriet already having breakfast.

'Good morning, Harriet,' said Sarah brightly, hoping to ease the tension between them.

'Good morning, Sarah,' she replied.

Sarah's lips tightened in annoyance that she did not offer the same greeting to her other sister.

Arabella noted the slight; she offered no reconciling words, merely asked, 'Did you see Father?'

'He was at the front door when I came down. We did not speak,' Harriet replied coldly.

Relief overcame Sarah. Her father obviously did not know that Charley wasn't at home.

'I wonder when we will see our dearly beloved brother?' said Harriet skittishly.

'No doubt this evening,' said Sarah, and almost immediately was annoyed with herself – she realised she had spoken rather too quickly. She saw Harriet cast her a sharp glance so quickly added, 'If he's with Toby already he may as well spend the day with him.' She dismissed any further comment on that subject by going to help herself to some porridge and posing a new question. 'I wonder who Papa dined with yesterday evening?'

'No doubt someone connected with business,' said Harriet. 'If he is going to return the favour, I'll suggest he invites him to dine here.'

'You do that and you can help,' snapped Arabella. 'No excuses about having another appointment, as you're so apt to do.'

Harriet made a gesture that indicated she was shrugging off the responsibility.

Seeing Arabella's eyes spark fire, Sarah stepped in. 'Harriet, if inviting this person helps to further Father's business then you should help. You'll benefit in the long run.'

Harriet cocked her head. 'I suppose so. After all, John is involved in it too, isn't he?' The barb struck home and silenced her sisters. She seized her opportunity. 'It could make for an interesting evening. A chance for you, Arabella. After all, it's better to be a bewhiskered old fuddy-duddy's darling than be left on the shelf!' The second barb sank even deeper. With a smirk of satisfaction Harriet stood up, dropped her napkin on the table and swept from the room.

Sarah, seeing Arabella had been hurt again, went to hug her and said, 'Take no notice. I know it's hard not to, but she's not worth your tears. And *never* cry for yourself.'

Arabella gave her a tremulous smile as she whispered feelingly, 'A wise head on young shoulders.'

'Jake, bring me the trading ledgers for the last two years,' ordered Benjamin when he arrived at his office, glad to be out of the freshening wind which was driving

149

threatening clouds from the south-west. He had eyed them suspiciously as he had crossed the bridge but decided they were no threat to the *Sea King*. He shrugged himself out of his redingote, hung it on the coat-stand in the corner of his office, placed his hat on the small table beside the stand, smoothed his jacket and was about to sit down at his desk when he was halted by a knock on the door.

Jake came in with the ledgers.

'Thanks,' said Benjamin, indicating to his chief clerk to place them on his desk. 'You remember, a couple of years ago we analysed the commodities we were handling at the time?'

'Yes, sir.'

'Do you still have the information we compiled?'

'Yes, sir. I never throw anything away that might come in useful.'

'Just as I expected,' said Benjamin. 'Very good.'

'You'd like it, sir?'

'Please. But before you bring it, add any up-to-date figures you think appropriate.'

'Yes, sir.'

Jake left the room wondering what his employer had in mind. An hour later he returned. 'Here is the information you want, sir.'

'Thank you, Jake. I'll call you if I need anything else. See I'm not disturbed unless it is vital and something you cannot handle yourself.'

'Very good, sir.' Jake left the room, once again wondering what Mr Brook was up to. He knew his employer well and judged that he must be looking into some new scheme that had caught his imagination.

Benjamin's concentration was intense, extracting from

the ledgers the information he deemed relevant to deciding if he should involve himself with Stephen Waite's scheme. After three hours he leaned back in his chair, satisfied with what he had gleaned. He sat thinking for a few minutes then rose from his chair, donned his coat and hat, left the building and headed across the bridge for the Angel.

'Good day, sir,' greeted the landlord.

'Good day, Giles,' Benjamin returned. 'Is Mr Waite around?'

'No, sir, he left mid-morning by the coach for York.'

Surprised that Waite had not mentioned his departure was imminent, Benjamin's lips tightened in annoyance. 'Did he say where he was going?' he asked, his voice sharp.

'Yes, sir. He was going to look at the new facilities along the banks of the River Tees and then on to Newcastle.' Sensing Mr Brook's displeasure at this, the landlord tried to pour balm on troubling news. 'He seemed a very competent young man.'

Benjamin gave a non-committal grunt. Did this mean that Waite had dismissed any idea of trading through Whitby? He frowned. 'And that was all?' he snapped.

'Oh, no, sir. He has booked the same rooms here for the last two weeks in September.'

This was another surprise; but Benjamin saw in it the possibility that Waite still had Whitby very much in mind. However, he would not raise his own hopes too high yet. After all, the young man had informed him he would be looking at other ports, and Benjamin could not blame him for that. He could do nothing to bring matters forward but would just have to wait patiently for Stephen's return. And at least he would have more time to ensure this venture would be viable and profit-making.

'Where is that boy?' Arabella expressed her concern in strong tones. 'I hope he gets back before Father arrives, otherwise there'll be ructions. And he'll feel my tongue when he gets home.'

'You know what it's like when he and Toby get together. They don't notice the time,' offered Sarah, who had taken up position on the window-seat in the drawing-room from which she could see the return of their father and try to judge his temper from the expression on his face and the way he walked up the path. Whatever sort of day he had had it was about to turn bad, she decided uneasily.

Harriet entered the room but did not speak; she went straight to the book she had abandoned earlier in the day and started reading.

Arabella ignored her and picked up the needlework she had allowed to rest on her lap while speaking with Sarah.

Sarah contented herself with looking out of the window. Ten minutes later she stiffened and announced: 'Papa.'

'Have you seen anything of Charley, Harriet?' asked Arabella, reluctant even to speak to her.

'No, I'm not his nursemaid,' she snapped without looking up from her book.

'He's not been home today. I only wondered . . .'

'He'll feel Papa's anger if he isn't here for the evening meal.'

'And we'll feel the aftermath,' said Arabella, irritated by the lack of concern in Harriet's voice.

'You will, you mean. You're in charge, after all,' said Harriet smugly.

Arabella seethed inwardly but kept her desire to retaliate under control. She would not let her sister see that she was unsettled by the inference.

The tension heightened when they heard the front door open and close. They all experienced some relief when they heard their father's footsteps cross the hall and the pattern of noise change to one indicating he was going upstairs. They all knew the moment of confrontation was only being postponed, though Arabella and Harriet still hoped it would be prevented by Charley's late appearance. Sarah, knowing otherwise, prepared herself to be on guard against a slip of the tongue or any revealing reaction.

Half an hour later they heard the gong sound, signifying the evening meal was ready to be served. They rose from their chairs and paused, listening to their father's advancing footsteps.

'This won't go away,' commented Arabella, starting for the door.

Their father was sitting in his place at the head of the table when they entered the dining-room. They went to their seats and sat down. One place remained empty.

Benjamin said nothing but sat perfectly still, hands resting lightly on the edge of the table. The wall clock marked five long minutes. Then . . .

'Why isn't the boy with us?' Benjamin's eyes were fixed on Arabella at the opposite end of the table.

'I don't know, Papa.'

He swung his gaze towards Sarah. 'Go and fetch him,' he ordered.

'Yes, Papa.' She sprang to her feet knowing she faced an impossible task. Nevertheless she hurried from the room and went through the motions of visiting Charley's room before returning. 'He's not there, Papa,' she announced.

'What?' thundered Benjamin, 'He knows what time we dine and that I won't tolerate lateness. Where has he been today?'

'We don't know, Papa,' replied Arabella. 'We haven't seen him since he went to see the *Sea King* depart yesterday.'

'What?' Benjamin roared again before Arabella went on.

'We received a note from him yesterday saying he was staying at Toby Munroe's. We did not see you last night to tell you, and you were gone early this morning. We expected to see him today but we haven't.'

Benjamin's lips tightened; his eyes smouldered with annoyance. 'Was there any sign he had been in his room, Sarah?'

'I think we would have known if he had been home,' put in Arabella.

Benjamin cast her a hostile look. 'I asked Sarah a question,' he snapped.

'No. Papa, there was nothing to indicate he had been there,' she replied quickly, desiring to divert her father's wrath from Arabella.

Benjamin snapped his fingers at one of the maids standing by the door to the kitchen quarters, ready to serve the meal when instructed. She stepped forward.

'Tell Mrs Ainslie I wish to see her immediately,' he ordered, emphasising the last word.

'Yes, sir.' The maid scurried away, eager to be out of the room. A few minutes later the housekeeper, her expression serious after the maid had told her of Mr Brook's mood, entered the dining-room.

'My son appears not to have been here all day, Mrs

154

Ainslie. Have you seen him?' he asked before she had time to utter a word.

'No, sir.'

'Apparently he sent a note saying he was staying at the Munroes' last night.'

'Yes, sir. So Miss Arabella informed me.'

'And he's not been home today?'

'Not to my knowledge. May I suggest, sir, he could be staying another night at the Munroes'?'

'If so, why hasn't he let me know?' Benjamin turned his eyes back to Arabella. 'Did his note stipulate one or two nights?'

'It just said, "Staying the night".'

He grunted. 'Mrs Ainslie, you will accompany Sarah to the Munroes'.' He glanced at his youngest daughter. 'Find out if Charley is there, and if he is tell him to return immediately.'

'Yes, Papa.' She rose from her chair.

'Mrs Ainslie, tell Cook to delay the meal until you return.'

'Yes, sir.' The housekeeper then hurried after Sarah who was already at the dining-room door.

As the door closed, Benjamin looked hard at Harriet. 'You've not said a word.'

'There was nothing for me to say, Papa,' she replied. 'I know nothing. The note was addressed to Arabella. It was her responsibility.'

He made no comment to this but said, 'We may as well sit more comfortably until they return.' He rose from his chair and led the way to the drawing-room.

As they hurried through Whitby's streets, Sarah's mind was trying to deal with the quandary in which she found

155

herself: tell what she knew or remain silent? Take Mrs Ainslie into her confidence or not? Could the house-keeper, who was close to them all, present a solution to her present difficulty?

'Mrs Ainslie, Charley is not at the Munroes',' she said, quietly but firmly.

The statement brought the housekeeper to a sudden halt. She stared at Sarah with disbelief, but even as the thought crossed her mind that this couldn't be true she knew that it was. Sarah would not lie or try to cloud the issue.

'You know something?'

Sarah bit her lip then nodded. 'Yes, I do.'

'Then tell me – and tell me quickly,' Mrs Ainslie urged, her eyes wide with curiosity and enquiry.

Sarah told her what she knew.

'Oh, my goodness!' gasped the housekeeper. 'What will your father say?'

'Do we have to tell him?' There was a pleading note in the girl's voice.

The housekeeper considered the situation for a few minutes then said, 'I don't see what else you can do.'

'But I don't want to wreck Charley's plan! If I tell Papa now he'll send word to Shetland, by the whale-ships due to leave Whitby, ordering Captain Sharp to find and return Charley.'

'That's just what I've been thinking about.'

'And?' prompted Sarah.

'Captain Sharp left early. I have a friend whose hus-band, Aaron, is second mate on the *Sea King*. He told her that Captain Sharp was anxious to be in the whaling grounds first and it was likely he wouldn't linger in Shetland. Two days' sailing to Shetland and the others not due to leave here until three days after the *Sea King* . . . that means she is more than likely to have left Shetland before they arrive. You say Charlie would not reveal his presence until after Shetland was behind them?'

Sarah's frown and the doubt in her eyes were vanishing. 'So Papa can do nothing to get Charley back?'

'Provided that the *Sea King* has not been delayed.'

'I do hope she has not.'

'You'll have to tell your father.'

'I don't mind that so long as I know he can't fetch Charley back. He has his heart set on this voyage. It's his one chance to prove his point . . . something he won't be able to do once Father has him installed in the office.'

Mrs Ainslie admired Sarah's loyalty to her brother. 'Come on then, we'd best go home to face the music . . . maybe it won't be as loud as we expect. Be sure to emphasise the fact that Charley is sending a letter from Shetland. It will show your father that the lad is at least thinking of him, and maybe help ease the blow of a son's defiance.'

On hearing the front door open, Benjamin eyed Harriet. 'Tell them we are in here.'

Harriet hastened out to fetch them, surprised when she saw only Sarah and Mrs Ainslie. 'Father wants you in the drawing room.'

They passed her, ignoring the question in her eyes. She would know the answer soon enough.

Benjamin was on his feet, back to the fire, when they walked in. He stared in disbelief when Mrs Ainslie closed the door behind her. 'Where is he?'

Harriet scurried to her seat. Sarah stood up so she

could view them all. Mrs Ainslie stood two steps behind her.

Sarah had decided that the only approach was to plunge straight in with her story; it would not ease matters to hold back or try to talk round the situation. 'Father, Charley is on board the *Sea King*,' she announced.

The immediate impact of that bold statement was a palpable silence that was broken by Benjamin's exclamation of shocked disbelief. 'What?' His voice bounced off the walls.

Sarah's response was to repeat her statement.

'I heard you the first time!' snapped her father. He swung to face Harriet. 'Did you know of this?'

Her eyes widened. 'No.'

'John never said anything?'

'No!'

Benjamin's eyes narrowed. He believed his daughter, but said, 'My God, if John has colluded in this, I'll break him!'

Harriet's mind reeled under the impact of what that would mean – she knew if her father's ruthless streak surfaced it could be the end of John's career. Marriage? Even as the question arose in her mind she knew what the answer would be. As all this spun quickly through her thoughts she was answering him in a strident voice, 'He wouldn't, Father. He wouldn't and you know it!'

Benjamin turned his eyes to his eldest daughter but left the question unspoken; he already knew from Arabella's bewildered expression that she knew nothing about this.

Sarah realised it was time for her to speak. 'Father, I have a confession to make. I knew Charley was going to stow away on the *Sea King*.'

'What?' His thunderous voice and penetrating gaze condemned her. 'You—'

Sarah knew it was no use holding back so boldly interrupted him. 'Let me explain everything, Father.' Then she went on quickly to recount all that had happened, without mentioning Jim's name.

Benjamin scowled and fumed as the story unfolded. 'He had all this planned, told you, and even though you went through the charade of looking in his room earlier, you never said a word to me?'

'I couldn't, Papa, I couldn't. Charley had his heart set on it. I couldn't betray him.'

'He must have had help. Who was it?'

Sarah tightened her lips.

'Who was it? I demand that you tell me.'

'I will not betray anyone,' she replied firmly, settling her stance into a more defiant posture.

'You deserve a thrashing, young lady. Be thankful that I have never raised a hand to any of my daughters. But you will be punished – no new dresses or shoes for you this year.' He looked hard at Arabella. 'See that it is carried out. Now, all this concealment will have been for nothing – I shall send word to Shetland by the other whale-ships to inform Captain Sharp that he has a stowaway aboard and must send Charley home.'

'I think that may be too late, Father,' said Sarah.

'What do you mean?' Benjamin frowned.

'As Mrs Ainslie and I were going to the Munroes' I was trying to decide what to do. I thought it best to explain to Mrs Ainslie before we got there. She advised me to confess to you.'

'Quite right,' Benjamin approved.

'I didn't want to betray Charley and have him sent

home when he has such a desire to sail on the *Sea King*. Mrs Ainslie pointed out that it would be unlikely that would happen because the *Sea King* would have sailed from Shetland before the other whale-ships arrived.' She glanced round at the housekeeper, who caught her plea and then explained her theory to Mr Brook.

He gave a little nod, agreeing with her, and said slowly, 'It all hinges on whether the *Sea King* leaves Shetland on time.'

10

24 March 1833. I hope the Sea King *wasn't delayed in Shetland. I know Father is hoping she will have been. These last few days have been so fraught. Nothing will settle down here until we know . . .*

The door of the bow-locker squeaked, startling Charley out of a fitful dose. He rubbed his eyes against the weak light that filtered in.

'Charley, are you all right?'

'Aye, Jim.' He started to struggle to his feet.

'We're a day's sailing out of Shetland. I reckon Captain Sharp won't turn back from here.'

'Good,' replied Charley with obvious relief. 'I'll be glad to be in the fresh air.'

'Follow me.'

'Hold on, Jim.'

He looked back, wondering why Charley was delaying.

'Thanks, Jim, for all you've done, but let me face Captain Sharp alone, then you need not be connected.'

Jim shook his head. 'No, that would mean an investigation of all the crew, which would not be a good idea. It could breed resentment towards you later. It must be just you and me.'

Charley pondered this for a moment then nodded. 'All

right, if you say so. I'll make sure no blame is attached to you, though. Did you manage to send that letter to my father?'

'Yes. Found a ship that is calling in at Whitby on her way to London. You can be sure it will be delivered – it's sailors' trust.'

'Thanks.'

'Come on. Let's face Captain Sharp. There's a good sea running so he'll be in a fair mood.'

'I hope so.' Charley's nerves were taking hold as he followed Jim across the deck. He noticed the curiosity in the eyes of sailors they passed. They would recognise him as their employer's son, and there was only one way he could have got on board: as a stowaway. How would the captain deal with him?

John Sharp was 'at home', standing beside the helmsman, enjoying the pitch and roll of the ship beneath him, listening to the hiss of the sea as the bow cut through the water, and thrilling to the sight of the wind-filled sails driving them on towards the beckoning Arctic. His delight was rudely shaken when he saw Charley Brook and Jim Barbour crossing the deck towards him. Charley! Here! All manner of thoughts rushed through his mind. He knew of Charley's desire to go to sea; knew Mr Brook opposed it. Now he was faced with a dilemma – turn back and put the lad ashore to appease his father while losing valuable time in the whaling grounds . . . or carry on and try for a good catch, a full ship and optimum profits?

He drew himself up, exuding authority. Anger with Charley for putting him in this predicament rose within him. The intense fury in his eyes bored into the two youths who came to a halt in front of him.

'Sir, I—' started Jim.

'To my cabin!' John's order cut in, promising a severe roasting later. Or worse.

'John, I am . . .' Charley wanted to make his explanation quickly but was silenced.

'I said, to my cabin!' He glared at Charley, who knew he would be given no quarter because he was his father's son or Harriet's brother. John looked beyond them. 'Mr Chapman!'

'Aye-aye, sir!' The first mate hurried over to his captain.

'Take charge, Mr Chapman, while I deal with these two.'

'Aye-aye, sir.'

John turned away and strode to his cabin with the two youths, dreading what was to come, following in his wake.

As soon as the door of his cabin closed, John erupted. 'What is the meaning of this? A stowaway on my ship!'

'I can explain, John, I'm—'

His look darkened as he interrupted harshly. 'It's "sir" on board this ship!'

'Yes, sir,' muttered Charley blushing with humiliation.

'And don't mutter! Speak up so you can be heard and there can be no misunderstanding.'

'Yes, sir.' Charley's tone was stronger.

'A stowaway.' John's eyes swung to Jim. 'I suppose you helped him, Barbour?'

'Yes, sir,' replied Jim firmly.

'I'm to blame, sir,' put in Charley, and went on quickly to add, 'I persuaded him . . . well, you might say black-mailed him.'

John cast his gaze upwards. 'What am I hearing?

Maybe it would be better if I learned no more of that. All that concerns me is what has happened on board my ship. The simple facts are that you stowed away and Barbour helped you. I should turn about and put both of you ashore in Shetland and find a ship to take you to Whitby. That would lose me good whaling time . . . either way I risk incurring your father's wrath.'

Charley seized on this. 'Let me stay, sir. I wrote a letter to my father . . .'

'I got it to a sailor in Shetland, sir,' put in Jim.

'And Sarah knew all about what I intended to do so my father will probably already know,' said Charley. 'Please don't turn back, sir. I wanted to sail on the *Sea King* and this was the only way I could do so. Father would never have allowed me to sign on.'

John set his lips in a grim line. Charley was here now, and it was plain it was to satisfy his heart's desire. Hadn't John himself experienced such a desire? Wouldn't it be better for all concerned to sign the boy on and continue with the voyage?

'You both know that what you have done is wrong and deserves punishment. If I return, it will be up to your father to administer it. If I carry on, it will be up to me. Do you understand?'

'Yes, sir,' they chorused sheepishly.

John let them stew in uncertainty for a few minutes while he went to sit behind the small table he used for a multitude of purposes. He steepled his hands thoughtfully in front of his lips and allowed unease to linger in the two boys whose contrite faces were turned towards the knotted floorboards.

'I'll carry on with the voyage,' said John, eyes fixed on them. He could almost hear the relief singing through

164

them. 'Mind you don't let me down on this voyage . . . or any other, for that matter.'

'Yes, sir. Thank you, sir,' they both said, one after the other.

'Brook, you will have to sign on as a crew member. We'll do that right away. Barbour, send Mr Chapman to me.'

'Yes, sir.' Jim, pleased that he had got off so lightly, hurried from the cabin.

As soon as he had gone, John eyed Charley. 'You will be treated no differently from any of the crew; you will be ready to do whatever you are told without question. Every task, no matter how insignificant it appears, is important to the success of this voyage. Learn quickly and you'll be given more responsible work. For your own sake, and if you're to have any hope of your father's eventual approval, do not fail.'

'Yes, sir.'

John was pleased to see the bright enthusiasm in Charley's eyes but added another warning. 'Expect no special favours from me.'

'I don't, sir.'

There was a knock on the door. In answer to John's summons it opened and the first mate came in.

'Mr Chapman, as you will have guessed we have a stowaway.'

'Yes, sir.'

'Sign him on. From this moment he is a crew member of the *Sea King*.'

'Aye-aye, sir.'

'You no doubt know he is Mr Brook's son?'

The first mate nodded.

'He is to be treated no differently from anyone else.'

'Aye-aye, sir.'

John found some paper and a pen. Mr Chapman made out a form that would suffice as a signing-on document; then the captain and first mate witnessed Charley's signature.

'Wait outside, Brook,' ordered his captain then.

'Aye-aye, sir,' replied Charley. He left the cabin walking tall – he was finally a member of the crew of the *Sea King*, bound for the Arctic to hunt whales!

As soon as the door had closed John relaxed his severe expression as he looked at his first mate. He and Mose Chapman had joined the *Sea King* together and worked their way rapidly to the positions they now held. They had a deep faith in one another's ability and that had made for a well-run ship, one on which sailors were eager to serve. They knew where they stood with the captain and first mate of the *Sea King*, two men who were strict but fair, who could handle the rough with the smooth, and would tolerate 'horseplay' among the crew only so long as it did not get out of hand.

'Work him hard, Mose. No easing up because of who he is. I know Charley would not thank you if you did. He wants to prove something, so no quarter. Get him on to hard and responsible jobs as soon as he knows the running of the ship and all that's required in the whaling grounds. The crew will be suspicious until he proves himself. I reckon he'll want to be accepted quickly. See to it, Mose.'

Chapman gave a small smile. 'I will. By the time this voyage is over, he'll be a man. From the look in his eyes, I reckon he's keen enough. Must be to have been in the bow-locker since leaving Whitby.'

'Thank goodness he had Barbour's help and didn't do it on his own! He could have died down there.'

A week later, Benjamin and his daughters were sitting in the drawing-room, awaiting the sound of the gong, when they heard the distant sound of the doorbell. A maid entered the room.

'Sir, Mr Jake Carter is asking to see you.'

Surprised that Jake should be calling at his private residence, Benjamin immediately told the maid to show Mr Carter in.

'I'm sorry to disturb you at home, sir, but shortly after you left the office a sailor came in. He said he had just arrived from Shetland where he had been given a letter and asked to deliver it in Whitby. His ship was delayed in Newcastle otherwise you would have had it sooner.'

Benjamin was out of his chair in a flash and taking the letter from Jake, saying, 'You did right to bring it here.'

'I thought you would want it right away, sir.'

'That's very thoughtful. Thank you.'

Jake made a courtesy nod and, sensing the charged atmosphere the arrival of the letter had brought, knew this was no time to linger and left the room.

Recognising the writing, Benjamin announced quietly, 'It's from Charley.' There was disappointment in his voice; the arrival of the letter signified that the *Sea King* had left Shetland before the arrival of the Whitby ships. His attempt to stop his son had been in vain. With a deep-felt sigh, he sank back on to his chair. His hands were shaking as he tore the letter open, eager to see what his son had to say for himself. He read Charley's words of explanation, the expressions craving forgiveness for his disobedience and his hope that on his return his father would be proud of his son's achievements.

Benjamin coughed. He could not let his daughters see the dampness he felt rising in his eyes and was thankful that at that moment the gong sounded.

'Let us go to the dining-room. Charley is well and has explained himself,' he said, rising from his chair and making for the door. His daughters, filled with relief, none more so than Sarah, followed him, unaware that their father was busily offering up a silent prayer for the safety of his son on a first voyage into dangerous waters.

'Barbour!' The first mate's voice boomed through the sharp air.

'Aye-aye, sir!' Jim yelled, left the rope he was coiling and ran to report.

'A day since Brook was discovered, a day since I told you to show him the running of the ship. Report.'

'Sir! He knew the ship better than me. Officially and unofficially, he's spent a lot of time on board whenever the *Sea King* was in Whitby.'

'Sea legs?'

'No trouble, sir.'

'Fo'c'sle?'

'He had no gripes, sir.'

'Reactions of the crew?'

'They were a bit suspicious at first but he mucked in, which showed he did not want or expect any special privileges because of who he is. They accepted that and have treated him no differently from any new member of the crew. The tricks on a greenhorn have all been tried.'

Chapman smiled. 'And how did he react? There are some roughnecks aboard . . . good sailors, good hunters, skilled in the ways of the ship, but they'll not tolerate a greenhorn for long and will give him a good going over.'

Jim grinned. 'He hasn't flinched yet, sir, and I don't think he will. He'll do any job that's put to him. Didn't shirk at scrubbing the deck nor cleaning out the galley.'

'Good. Tomorrow I'll be allocating boat-crews and we'll do a launch. You'll be with me.'

'Yes, sir!' Jim's delight was evident; Mr Chapman was considered the best harpooner in Whitby.

'Brook will be a reserve for my boat-crew.'

'Sir, I don't think he will have . . .'

'I don't suppose he has,' Chapman interrupted, 'but he's got to learn. We'll do a launch tomorrow and he'll have to learn fast; no good having a weak peg when he may be wanted at an oar if someone is ill or hurt.'

'Yes, sir.'

'Right, you've time before you both go on watch to familiarise him with the contents and lay-out of a whale-boat. You know how essential that is. Lives can be dependent on a man's knowledge of and familiarity with it.'

'Yes, sir.'

As he left the first mate to find Charley, Jim realised that his friend was being thrown in at the deep end but was sure he would not shrink from any responsibility or challenge.

'Charley, come on, Mr Chapman's told me to familiarise you with the whale-boat.' As they crossed the deck Jim went on, 'Be sure to remember everything I tell you, 'cos it'll be your job to check everything in it is in place – vital when we're hunting whales.'

'That sounds as if I'm going to be allocated to a boat-crew,' commented Charley, excitement shining in his eyes.

'Aye, you'll be with the same one as me – Mr Chapman's.'

'Jim, that's grand! He has quite a reputation . . .'

'He has, so you'll not be permitted to make one mistake.'

'I've rowed on the river at home, but this . . .'

'Hold on, Charley, you'll only be on stand-by for now. If there's an emergency, someone not well or injured or whatever, *then* you'll be called on. You'll get your turn at the oars before that – tomorrow probably if the sea's reasonably calm, Mr Chapman informed me. Here's his boat. Up into it.'

They shinned up into the whale-boat hanging on its davits. Jim explained the lay-out of the equipment – one harpoon at hand in a wooden rest with its point on the bow so that it was ready for the harpooner. The fore-ganger – a rope spliced carefully to the harpoon so that the throw was not affected – lay coiled beneath. Another harpoon was positioned close at hand should a second be needed. Stowed near the bow were six lances.

'After the harpoon has struck and held, those are used to kill the whale once we can get alongside it,' explained Jim. He saw Charley already knew this, so, thinking his friend no doubt knew what everything was for, contented himself with directing Charley's attention to where the equipment was placed in the whale-boat. 'I can't stress enough that everything must be in the right place,' he concluded. 'That's vital.'

'Who's in Mr Chapman's crew?' Charley asked.

'We won't really know until the crews are allocated,

but I'll make a very good guess that Bob Whitehouse will be his boat-steerer. He's responsible for getting us on to the whale, so, as the rowers are facing him, they follow his orders. Mr Chapman will be rowing bow oar, but once we're nearing the whale he'll ship his oar and take up his role as harpooner. When he makes his hit all hell will be let loose and the boat-crew must take orders directly from him. If a kill is made, the whale, as you know, will be towed back to the ship for flensing. Any questions?'

'Who sets the rhythm of the rowing?'

'Mr Chapman will probably have Zeth Glaisdale. He rows stroke oar and takes his stroke speed from Bob. The other rowers match Zeth.'

Charley nodded, picturing himself rowing in unison with the rest of the crew.

'Any more questions?' Jim asked.

'No,' replied Charley.

'So now all that stands between you and some real action is more practice in the boat and a place becoming vacant. One piece of advice: obey Mr Chapman instantly and without question, no matter what his order is. If by any chance you are switched to another crew, be as attentive to the harpooner's orders as you would to Mr Chapman's.'

'Understood,' rapped Charley in mock deference to Jim's authority.

With a favourable sea running the next morning all hands were mustered and the crews allocated to the whale-boats. Only Mr Chapman's was launched, with Charley as one of the crew. He settled in his allocated place. Once everyone was ready, Bob Whitehouse's order of 'Shove off!' rang out and the boat was pushed away from the side of the *Sea King*. Clear of the ship, Bob called, 'Out oars!' Charley, as he had been shown, eased his oar into its rowlock. As his hands closed round the loom of the oar he sensed a thrill run through him. On Whitehouse's command the crew dipped their oars in unison. Anxious not to make an error, Charley was a fraction of a moment behind the others but he righted himself quickly. Bob set a gentle rhythm. The oar was heavy, the water seemingly bent on creating problems for Charley, but with determination he settled to it and was thrilled by the way the whale-boat cut easily through the sea. But he soon realised this was no easy boat-trip when Bob increased the stroke speed and he had to match Zeth's tempo. His muscles ached, he sweated in spite of the cold air, and gasped in air to ease his aching lungs.

By the time they returned to the *Sea King* he was almost spent, but sheer determination not to be seen to be weakening allowed him to ship his oar without trouble and clamber back aboard ship. When his feet touched the deck his legs almost gave way but he straightened up to see Jim grinning at him. He also read admiration in his friend's eyes.

'Well done,' said Jim, giving him a slap on the back.

'Aye, lad, you did well,' praised Mr Chapman. 'A few slips that can be ironed out in the next couple of days, at the end of which we'll be nearing the whaling grounds. Then you'll take your place as stand-by oar.' The first mate nodded his approval and strode away to make his report to the captain.

Charley, feeling muscles he never knew he had aching, raised his eyes skywards as if to say, 'Oh, no, not more of this?' He peeled the gloves from his hands and saw they had not given him a lot of protection.

'They'll harden,' said Jim sympathetically. 'We've all been the same; now we don't notice any soreness.'

Three days later, when Charley clambered aboard after his fourth session of rowing, he did so much more easily; the aches were still there but he knew they would disappear as his body grew used to working with the heavy oar. He was hoping that when they sighted whales he would be called on to man an oar as a regular crewman.

With his daily chores over and time to spare in the evening before going on watch, he left the fo'c'sle and went on deck. Though it was late it was still light. The wind had dropped to a gentle breeze but it was still sufficient to let the *Sea King* part the placid sea. Charley leaned on the rail and was soon lost in the tranquil atmosphere that hung across the seascape, enticing the ship ever onwards. The North shone with a white, beckoning light that poured magic into the unknown. It brought an overwhelming silence that struck deep into his being; the gentle flap of the sails, the soft purr of creaking ropes and the swish of the sea along the ship's hull did nothing to mar that bigger silence but seemed to enhance it. Charley was lost in the enchantment that drew him ever deeper into the very soul of this vast, cold ocean.

Lost in its irresistible allure, he was unaware of someone coming to stand beside him until a softly spoken word broke, yet did not spoil, the spell he was under.

'You've felt it, Charley.'

Captain Sharp! Charley straightened up. 'Sir!'

'Relax, Charley, for a few moments.'

He felt that John's tone was for once reflecting the friendship they had shared in Whitby. 'Felt it?' queried Charley, with a puzzled frown.

'Yes, the "Call of the North". I could tell as I came across the deck that you had fallen under its spell. It isn't everyone who feels it, but I can tell you have.'

Charley glanced to the light due north. 'That's what it is?' he said quietly, as if the sound of his own voice would shatter the mystique. From that moment he felt he was part of a completely new and utterly beguiling world.

'Yes,' said John. 'It has captured you. You'll want to return time after time. And even if that becomes impossible, the lure of the North will never leave you.'

They stood there in silence, lost in a world familiar to one, new to the other, caught up in the 'Call of the North'.

John broke it by becoming the captain of the *Sea King* again. 'I hear you've done well at the oars. Keep it up, Brook. You may be needed when we sight whales.' He turned and walked away.

Charley gazed out across the sea and thought of home. No one there would ever know who had helped him; Sarah would keep his secret, he was sure.

'I hope Charley is fitting in with the crew,' said Arabella, somewhat concerned, as she and Sarah left the house in New Buildings to go shopping. 'I don't think John would give him any special privileges . . . and rightly so.'

'Jim will look after him.' Sarah bit her tongue; the words had slipped out automatically, but they had betrayed a deep secret.

'So that's who helped him?' Arabella picked up the inference quickly.

Sarah, annoyed with herself, reddened. 'Arabella, please, please, don't say anything! Jim will be in deep trouble if it becomes known. I'm hoping John will over-look his involvement.'

Arabella stopped walking and placed a comforting hand on her sister's arm. 'I'm sure John will be tolerant, and your secret is safe with me.'

'Thank you.'

11

30 April 1833. These have not been the best of times. I still miss Mama very much. Papa is quiet, brooding over the loss of her and his concern for Charley. He talks to us only when it is essential, but we still suffer from his strict attitude. He has never again mentioned the stranger with whom he dined in March. If it was a business proposition, it must have fallen through. So Harriet's taunting of Arabella was all for nothing. Arabella was hurt. I know she regards John's interest in Harriet as a betrayal, but I believe she loves him still. I think of Jim every day and pray that they are all safe . . .

The *Sea King*, driven by a gentle wind, sailed steadily north for three days under almost cloud-free skies. Charley felt all the excitement of being where he had always wanted to be – on the deck of a ship sailing the Arctic Ocean.

'Don't expect it always to be like this,' Jim warned him. 'That sea can be the devil. The wind will roar and make the rigging sing like a banshee to haunt your dreams. The decks will be awash and the heaving ship will try to toss you overboard. You'll have to cling to the guide ropes or anything else you can get hold of. Beating rain can turn to freezing darts, and you'll be certain the pounding sea will split the ship in two. You'll wish you were tucked up in bed in Whitby then.'

Two days later Jim's predictions came true and, for a further two days, Charley saw the truth in his friend's last observation. There were times when he was sure they would perish, but he saw how Captain Sharp's skill, in handling the vessel and in directing his crew, who obeyed his orders instantly, brought the *Sea King* safely through the tumult and into calmer waters. Now they all hoped that before long, with the lashing rain driven away by the wind and visibility rapidly extending, they would sight whales.

'Mr Chapman!' John's shout brought the first mate hurrying across the deck. But before he reached his captain an order came, 'Get a man aloft!'

'Aye-aye, sir.' Mose stopped and yelled, 'Varley, get aloft!'

'Aye-aye, sir.' Dick Varley, the man with the sharpest eyes on the ship, knew what was wanted of him. He swung on to the bulwark with the agility of a man used to following this order, grasped the shroud lines and, ignoring the sway of the ship, climbed to the masthead. He settled there as best he could and began to scan the ocean.

'Ice to the north!' was his first shout. 'Five miles.'

'North, five miles,' shouted John. Seeing Varley raise his hand he knew he had heard correctly. Immediately he rapped out orders that brought the *Sea King* on to a westerly course, keeping the ice to starboard.

The hunt was on. The crew hoped whales would soon be sighted and they could start filling the ship with blubber. Once the first strike was made the work would become hard and exhausting and, if they could get among the whales with all their boats, it would be non-stop. The men would work with a will; they knew Captain Sharp did not like to set course for home until he had a full ship.

Minutes passed into hours and the men were beginning to despair. Still no shout from the masthead. Where were the whales?

Varley had been aloft four hours; John was considering replacing him when 'Thar she blows! Thar she blows!' rang out from the masthead.

Immediately despondency was swept away and every man was alert and eager to know more about the sighting.

'Whither away?' yelled John.

'Ahead, two miles!'

Immediately John sprang on to the bulwark and climbed a few rungs of the rigging for a better view. He focused on the spouts rising in the distance. His heart beat faster. Whales! Maybe twelve! Work this right and it could be the best of starts to their season.

'Hold her steady, Mr Chapman!'

'Aye-aye, sir!' The first mate moved closer to the helmsman so that he could be sure his captain's directions were followed correctly.

John guided the ship closer until he deemed it wise to stand off. When he was satisfied he called, 'Away all boats!'

Charley watched with rising excitement as the boat-crews went instantly into action. Through experience and practice, each man, eager to hunt, carried out his job meticulously so that all the boats hit the water without mishap. The men were quickly into position and the rowers on the side nearest the *Sea King* pushed their boat away from the ship. Oars were dipped. Boat-steerers called out as they used their long steering oars to set each craft heading for the whales.

Charley's eyes were on Mr Chapman's boat in which Jim was one of the rowers. He heard Bob Whitehouse call out, 'Heave, lads, heave! Bend ya backs!'

Muscles rippled, backs bent in unison, oars pulled on the water, propelling their boat through the undulating sea.

'Heave! Heave! Faster! Faster!'

Zeth Glaisdale, at stroke oar, taking in the order, increased the rate and Mr Chapman's boat surged ahead of the others.

Charley, caught up in the excitement, felt like cheering. His attention was fixed on every facet of the hunt, absorbing it so he knew what to expect when, as he hoped, he too was a member of a boat-crew. He wished the ship was nearer the action so he could see in more detail what was happening now the boats had got among the whales. The sea became a cauldron of heaving water, flukes came high in the air, boats backed quickly to escape the crash that could turn them to matchwood, harpoons struck, whales churned the sea, lances flashed in deadly precision, successful boats headed back for the *Sea King* with their kills. Now activity burst out aboard the ship, ready to receive the prizes wrested from the sea that would bring money into Whitby and make the winter months easier for the men of the *Sea King*.

Under the eyes of their captain the first whale was positioned alongside the ship, flensers were ordered on to it, blubber was peeled from the body, hauled on to the deck and cut up to be stored in casks in the hold, leaving the deck running with grease and blood. In spite of the nauseating smell, Charley was glad he had been assigned to working on the deck rather than filling barrels below decks; at least he was out in the fresh air where the speed of the constant activity kept the cold at bay. It continued as three other whales were positioned alongside to be dealt with in turn.

As the last piece of blubber disappeared below decks, Charley, breathing heavily, leaned against a bulwark and stared at the carcass that had been cast adrift.

'Your first whale hunt,' said Jim, giving him a slap on the shoulder as he came up beside him. 'Tired?'

Charley glanced over his shoulder at his friend. 'Aye, I am that. Lucky you, being in the boat.'

Jim grinned. 'Wait until you get a taste. It's back-breaking towing them last whales back,' he pointed out, referring to the additional job of helping other boat-crews to get their kills back to the ship after they had taken their own kill alongside.

'Barbour! Brook! Get that deck cleaned!' yelled Mose. They straightened up and put as much enthusiasm into their reply as they could but it was obvious they were not keen.

'Move!' rapped the first mate.

'Aye-aye, sir.' They both knew they would get a lash-ing from his tongue if they did not show more spirit. They hurried to join the others who had also been assigned to the job.

'Wonder what Sarah would say if she could see us now?' said Jim as he flung the first bucket of sea water across the slippery deck.

'Probably have a good laugh,' commented Charley. With the bristles of his brush scraping across the planking, he thought of home and how his sisters would never have had cause to brush a floor.

7 May 1833. I wonder if Charley has seen his first whale. I hope life aboard the Sea King *is not too hard for him, but I know Jim will look after him. What a different world for them while here we are living in comfort. Thankfully the hostility between Arabella and Harriet is far less evident; in fact, almost non-existent. Arabella seems to have accepted the situation, giving way because of her love for John, which I am sure still remains in her heart. I only hope that holding on to it does not ruin her life . . .*

Benjamin, feeling well satisfied after a meal of Cook's splendid roast beef, cooked exactly to his liking, followed by custard accompanying a treacle tart, ran his napkin across his lips and laid it on the table. His glance settled on his eldest daughter.

'Arabella, I have issued invitations to the Meadows and Northcliffes to dine with us two weeks from today. You will arrange it with Mrs Ainslie and Cook.'

'Yes, Father,' she replied. 'Will Mr and Mrs Northcliffe's family be accompanying them?'

'No. Mary and Roger are staying with their aunt and uncle and, as you know, Kate and Peter Meadows are visiting some friends in Durham. But I expect you three to dine with us. Your punishment is lifted, Sarah, but do not keep secrets from me again.'

'Oh, thank you, Papa,' she enthused, with fingers

crossed behind her back making the secret she still held about Jim secure.

'Harriet, I want you to help Arabella with all the arrangements; it is time you did more. After all, when you are married to John, you will have to do it then, so the more you learn now, the better it will be when you are on your own.'

'Yes, Papa,' Harriet replied meekly, realising there was wisdom in her father's instruction.

Sarah, comprehending that, unknown to him, the reference to the forthcoming marriage would likely distress Arabella, gave her other sister a sympathetic look and was rewarded with a smile of thanks.

Benjamin heard footsteps on the stairs just as he reached the front door after breakfast the following morning. He turned and, seeing his eldest daughter coming down, retraced a few steps. 'Arabella, I'm glad I've seen you. The dinner party . . . make it something special.'

'Very good, Papa. I'll see to it.'

'And don't forget, involve Harriet.'

'I won't forget.'

With a brief nod he left the house.

A few minutes after Arabella was seated at the table in the dining-room, her sisters came in and went to help themselves to porridge.

'I've just seen Papa. He wants the dinner party to be special but didn't say why. Just because they're good friends, I suppose.'

'Special?' Harriet's eyes lit up. 'A new dress then!' she added, sitting down at the table.

'He didn't say that,' replied Arabella quickly, knowing how easily her sister could get carried away.

'Not in so many words,' Harriet flashed back. 'But that *is* what he would mean.'

'No,' said Arabella, 'it's how you are interpreting his words.'

Harriet gave a shrug of her shoulders. Before she could comment, Arabella continued, 'We have plenty of dresses already but I don't think he will object if we buy some new accessories. I'll ask his permission and we'll go shopping tomorrow.'

'That's better than nothing,' said Harriet, then added a bit of advice. 'Let's all choose the dresses we'll wear and then we can get the accessories to suit.'

'It'll be fun,' laughed Sarah, looking forward to a shopping expedition with her sisters.

That evening Benjamin approved their request when Arabella put it to him.

The three women set out in a light-hearted mood to find accessories to complement the dresses they had chosen to wear for the dinner party.

They did not rush their decisions, making the most of the time they had at their disposal, each helping the others to make their choice. Sarah was pleased not only for the advice Arabella and Harriet offered her but also because her sisters seemed to have set aside the ill feeling created by Harriet's betrothal to John.

As they walked home she commented with great pleasure, 'Oh, that was just like the shopping expeditions we shared with Mama. They were such happy occasions.'

Arabella and Harriet agreed, for once.

Bearing in mind her father's observation about what would face her in this respect after she was married to

John, Harriet paid particular attention to Arabella's role in the preparations for the party. She was struck by the way her sister controlled the staff, especially Mrs Ainslie and Cook, noting her authority in dealing with them even though she was so much younger. She realised that Arabella made it appear her decisions were coming from them. It was a subtle form of managing others that she only now realised had been used by their mother also. When Harriet pointed this out to Sarah, she admitted that she too admired Arabella's delicacy in this matter. Sarah was pleased to see Harriet giving Arabella due credit, for it augured well for a harmonious future, something she hoped would be cemented by the party.

The guests were given a warm welcome when they arrived and, with everyone in a light-hearted mood, the tone was set for a pleasant evening. The queries from the guests about Charley's absence were neatly side-stepped by Benjamin. Conversation flowed across many topics and interests, the men careful to avoid business talk in mixed company. Cook had excelled herself, and Mrs Ainslie supervised the service so that the meal was leisurely without being slow. Arabella kept a watchful eye on the whole proceedings without interfering, knowing that her trusted housekeeper would have everything behind the scenes under control.

Observing that everyone had finished the final course, Arabella said, 'Ladies, shall we leave the gentlemen to their cigars and port?' Anticipating their agreement, she rose gracefully from her chair.

The three men sprang to their feet and escorted the ladies to the door, then returned to the table.

When they reached the drawing-room, Arabella offered the ladies coffee. She led the conversation into talk of fashion and the latest magazines that were devoting more and more space to this fascinating topic, to attract a wider readership.

Mrs Northcliffe and Mrs Meadows took the opportunity to reiterate their admiration for the accessories Arabella, Harriet and Sarah were wearing, taking the opportunity now to examine them more closely. Sarah was particularly pleased at the comments on Jim's brooch, which was a delicately shaped whale.

'A reminder of a special friend . . . someone serving on a whale-ship perhaps?' asked Mrs Meadows, a teasing twinkle in her eye.

Sarah said nothing but her blushes answered the question for her. She would not be drawn by the subtle probing that followed and was thankful when Arabella diverted the conversation on to the latest gossip about the arrival in Whitby of a new dress-maker from Hull.

Half an hour later, when the three men came into the drawing-room, Henry Meadows' first words were addressed to Arabella. 'May I say what an excellent meal that was?'

'It is kind of you to say so, but the triumph really belongs to Cook,' she replied graciously.

'Of course it does, and praise is due to Mrs Ainslie also. She has the duties of the staff at her finger-tips and they are all a credit to her. But you, Arabella, have the overall responsibility for making an evening such as this truly pleasurable.'

'Mr Meadows, you flatter me. But I must add that my sisters, Harriet and Sarah, should share in your praise since they were a great help to me. I know they will wish to be included in my thanks for your appreciation of all our efforts.'

Benjamin injected a serious note into the conversation then. 'I did not mention this earlier but I think I must do so now because I would rather you heard it from me than from others when the *Sea King* reaches Whitby.' The sober tone to his voice raised their guests' curiosity. 'You asked about Charley when you arrived and I skated over your enquiries. The truth is, he's on board the *Sea King*.'

The guests were flabbergasted because they all knew that Benjamin had been set against his son going to sea.

'You gave in to him then?' said Henry.

'I did not!' replied Benjamin emphatically.

'Then . . .?'

'He stowed away.'

'What?' Jock Northcliffe gasped.

'Good grief! Wasn't he found?' asked Henry.

'No, and didn't make himself known until they were a day's sailing from Shetland. He indicated that was his intention in a letter he sent me from there. He knew it would jeopardise the voyage if John Sharp ordered a return to Shetland to put him ashore.'

'It seems he had it all thought out, but how did he exist from Whitby to a day's sailing out of Shetland?' asked Jock.

'He must have had help, but of course I don't know from whom.'

'And if I know Charley, you never will,' observed Henry.

Throughout these exchanges Sarah had been most anxious in case her part in Charley's plot was mentioned. It wasn't, and she was grateful for that.

'So what will you do when he gets back?' asked Imelda Meadows.

'Stowaways have to be dealt with.' Benjamin cut his words off sharply so that everyone knew that was the end of the matter for this evening. It was now a private matter between father and son.

1 June 1833. Father has not been well this last week but it is nothing serious. The doctor has given him a potion which has controlled the fever and he has been told to stay in bed another week. I have been helping Arabella in the sick-room; Harriet hates being there, it makes her really bad-tempered . . .

'Harriet, where are you going now?' asked Arabella. 'Can't you sit with Father for a while?'

'I have done.'

'But only once in the last week.' In spite of the truce that had been called between the two sisters since the initial hostilities, Arabella felt she had to speak out.

'Twice.'

'What? Once was only for couple of minutes when you looked in and he was sleeping.'

'So it was no use stopping.'

'You could have been there when he woke up. I think you should go and give Sarah a break now, instead of gallivanting.'

'I hate sick-rooms.' Harriet screwed up her nose at the thought and started across the hall.

'You'd better get used to them. You won't be able to escape them all your life.'

'I'm not like you.'

'I never wanted to be in this position but . . .'

'Oh, yes, the ever-dutiful daughter! Carry on with that and see where it gets you.'

Anger at this veiled prediction of her dull future sprang to Arabella's lips but she held it back. After all, Harriet was her sister and they had been close once. She turned away and walked slowly up the stairs.

She had reached the door of her room when she heard a bell tinkle and knew immediately that the sound came from the handbell she had placed on the table beside her father's bed. She sighed and tightened her lips in exasperation as the sound recalled Harriet's attitude. She stiffened, drew a deep breath, and chastised herself for allowing unkind thoughts towards her father to seep into her mind. She smoothed her dress, patted her hair and walked purposefully to his door.

'What is it, Papa?' she asked, making her tone light and soothing.

'My glass is empty,' he replied, a touch of rebuke in his voice, implying that she should have known.

He was lying with his face turned away from her so she allowed herself an exasperated expression but said amiably, as she rounded the bed, 'I'll pour you some more.'

'A tot,' he grunted.

'Now, Papa, you know the doctor said no to that until you are up and about again.'

'Old fool,' he snapped.

'That's no way to speak about someone you are prepared to call a friend. Besides, Dr Fenby has your best interests at heart.'

Benjamin grunted with contempt. 'Where's Harriet? She knows where the bottle is.'

The inference hit Arabella. Connecting it with her sister's earlier hint that she had visited their father more frequently than Arabella had supposed, she realised there was truth in it.

'She should *not* have been giving you whisky; it isn't good for you in your present state.'

'Don't be mawkish!'

'Mawkish or not, there's your water, Papa.'

He made a sound of disgust.

'Seems to me you are getting better,' she shot back as she reached the door.

'Doctor said I would be next week. You've just said I should take notice of him!'

Arabella closed the door behind her, sighed and let her shoulders droop. She could not do right for doing wrong. The sooner he was up and back to work the easier it would be; he was not a good patient, and Harriet certainly hadn't helped.

Sarah tried to introduce what she had heard about the latest proceedings of the Whitby Society into the conversation during the evening meal. She received little reaction from Harriet and only lukewarm curiosity from Arabella, who, before her mother's death, had been much more interested in the Society. Sarah detected an undercurrent of dissatisfaction between the two elder girls. It was no surprise to her that it came to a head once they were in the drawing-room away from the servants' ears.

'Harriet, you had no right to give Papa whisky!' Arabella's authoritative tone stung her sister to an angry retort.

'Don't you dare criticise me.' She glared at Arabella. 'It comforted him.'

'Comfort him or not, it went against the doctor's orders.'

'Good gracious! A little drop of whisky would do no harm.'

'How do you know? You don't understand the underlying causes of Father's illness.'

'Goodness me, you *are* taking a serious view of it. There's nothing drastically wrong with him. Just a mild sickness attack, if I'm right.'

Arabella seized on that last remark. '*If* you're right . . . exactly! You could be wrong, and going against the doctor's orders may have serious repercussions. So don't give him any more.'

'Arabella's right, Harriet,' put in Sarah.

'Oh, you would side with her,' snapped Harriet, giving her youngest sister a withering look.

'With what's right,' replied Sarah pointedly.

'Always the goody-goody,' sneered Harriet.

'Leave her out of this,' rapped Arabella.

'She stuck her nose in,' said Harriet, quick to respond.

'No more whisky until Father is back at work!' said Arabella in a tone that indicated it was an end to the subject.

Indignant at this, Harriet stood up, grabbed her book and said, 'It's no good my sitting here with you two, I'll read in bed.' Her voice softened but still held a sting when she added, 'Then I'll dream of John and our future together.' A mocking smile curved her mouth as she glanced across at Arabella and drew satisfaction from seeing the taunt strike home.

Arabella picked up her tapestry and gave vent to her feelings by stabbing the canvas viciously with every stroke of the needle.

'Don't let her rile you,' said Sarah softly.

Arabella gave her younger sister a weak smile. 'I thought things were getting better between us.'

'I'm sure they are,' soothed Sarah.

Arabella frowned, dismay in her eyes. 'We never used to be at such loggerheads. Maybe it's my fault. Maybe it's my jealousy that has brought out this hostility between us. I'm sorry if it sometimes comes back on you, Sarah.'

'Don't be. I'm sure it's not all your fault and I'm certain it will resolve itself. Let me help all I can. Ask for anything.'

'Just be there if I need you.'

12

12 August 1833. Time is passing. All of Whitby looks for the return of the whale-ships. I hope they are all safe and have full loads. I long to see Jim and Charley again! I hope he has done well so that Father will not be too hard on him for his disobedience. Father recovered well from his indisposition and is now immersed in his work again. I'm pleased Harriet is much more amiable and less prone to taunt Arabella. Maybe she's in better spirits because John will soon be home. I know their reunion will hurt Arabella but I believe she is strong enough to deal with it without any unpleasantness. If that is so and Harriet's present mood continues, all will be well. In the meantime we pray for the safe return of all the ships . . .

'Get aloft, Varley!' Mr Chapman's voice thundered across the deck as it had done each day for the past month, but there was never a shout of 'Thar she blows! Thar she blows!' to send men's minds soaring with relief. Two more whales would see the *Sea King* a full ship and then it would be 'Hoist all sails!' to catch the wind and speed them away from the ice that was appearing further south than usual at this time of year.

September arrived but still no sighting. John was worried. He knew he would soon be faced with a decision that he did not want to make – leave, or try for those last two whales? Maybe he could risk staying another two weeks. During the next four days five ships were sighted, and each time Varley from aloft reported they were heading south – leaving; heading for home. John knew this made his crew uneasy. He knew they talked among themselves, questioning his decision to remain a little longer when other vessels were departing. They were restless. A whole week passed. Still no whales.

'When will we head home?' Charley asked one evening as, their watch finished, he and Jim stood at the rail. The breeze was gentle, the sea smooth. Thoughts turned easily to the south and home.

'Soon, I hope. We ain't seen whales for long enough and that's not a good sign. The crew don't like it.'

'I've heard them grumbling, wanting the captain to set course for home.' Charley frowned. 'I didn't like what they were saying, Jim.'

'Don't concern yourself, Charley. I know it must rile you when you hear them complaining and moaning about the captain, but it's only crew talk; they'll do nothing about it. They really do trust Captain Sharp. If we don't sight whales soon he'll head for Whitby, I'm sure he will.'

Charley felt relieved by Jim's assurances.

'Mr Chapman, do you find this weather unusually calm?' Captain Sharp asked, observing the glass-like sea.

'Aye, sir, it's uncanny. I've never experienced anything like it in all my twenty years' sailing the Arctic. The whales have disappeared; they know something unpleasant is brewing. The crew sense it too, sir.' The first mate held back from expanding further; he couldn't make it more obvious that his opinion and that of the crew was that they should run south now.

'Two more days, Mr Chapman, two more days,' said John thoughtfully. 'The whales are somewhere close, I feel it in my bones.'

Twenty-four hours passed. No whales were sighted. John was uneasy. He felt he should accept that he was not going to sail into Whitby with a full ship, but the instinct that had served him well in the past told him to wait. He had posted three more men high on the rigging; four sets of eyes were better than one. Intuition told him to hold the ship on a westerly course, whereas reason was trying to make him steer east, allowing him a quicker passage away from the ice. It was not threatening at the moment but conditions could change rapidly. The *Sea King* sailed on.

'Ice!' The shout came from aloft, where Varley had been keeping an eye on the distant ice fields as well as searching for a tell-tale spout.

Mr Chapman, knowing instinctively from his lookout's shout that the ice was moving, yelled, 'Whither away?'

'Starboard quarter! Three miles!'

A slight motion broke the calm air. Sails stretched, rigging moaned, timbers creaked. Concern crept into everyone's mind. If the strengthening breeze caught the ice it could present a greater threat. The first mate glanced at his captain. This was surely the time to turn away from what was proving to be a barren sea? He saw a gleam in his captain's eyes that he had seen before, but under present conditions did not like.

Captain Sharp made no comment on the lookout's information. Instead, he strode across the deck, swung on to the bulwark and climbed the rigging until he achieved the height he knew would give him the perspective he wanted. Holding on by one hand, he shielded his eyes with the other and assessed the ice conditions. He did not like the direction of its movement, or the curling arm of ice that he could see on the starboard side aft of the ship. He was going to have to call off the hunt and forgo returning with the prize he wanted. He hesitated and scanned the ocean one more time: only sea and ice. His lips set in a grim line of frustration. He started for the deck and was three rungs down when the air was split by a cry.

'Thar she blows! Thar she blows!'

Excitement surged up in John.

'Whither away?' came from the first mate.

'Ahead, one mile!'

As he scrambled down to the deck, John shouted, 'Launch one and two, Mr Chapman! I'll take one!'

'Aye-aye, sir!' Although disappointed, Mr Chapman knew he had been left with the responsible job of manoeuvring the *Sea King* to keep as close as possible to the two boats and deal with the catch they hoped to make.

John hit the deck at a run. The crew for boat number one were already racing across the deck. The man in front of John lost his footing and crashed to the deck. A scream of pain told him the sailor would be useless to the crew. The second boat had already hit the water. John did not want to miss the chance of filling his ship so yelled at the first person he saw standing by to help with the launching. 'Brook, get aboard!' Taken aback by the unexpected command, Charley seemed frozen for a moment. 'Move, Brook! Move!'

'Aye-aye, sir!' He was into the boat, had dropped on to the vacant thwart immediately in front of his captain and was in position by the time the boat hit the water. Jim, already at his oar, caught his eye and winked encouragement to his friend, who was about to experience his first true action as a member of a boat-crew. Eagerly they pushed away from the ship and, as oars dipped and drove the vessel through the sea, Bob Whitehouse steered towards the spouts.

'Heave, lads, heave!' Whitehouse encouraged them.

Knowing that there was no time to be lost, men bent their backs willingly. Charley, now thankful for the practice he had had in a boat, fell into the rhythm, determined to match the rest of the crew. The boat cleaved through the undulations, deepening under the influence of the strengthening wind.

'Faster! Faster!' called their captain.

Zeth increased his stroke. The men matched him. Charley's muscles strained and burned with each pull on the oar. He set his mind to the task and with concentration came oblivion to what was happening around him until a swing brought about by Bob's control of the steering-oar jerked him back to the immediacy of the moment. He was aware that they had nearly collided with the other boat which seemed to have made a sudden appearance from a trough in the sea. The manoeuvre separated the two boats but John had noted that boat number two had headed for a spout on their port side.

'Hold her straight, Bob!' he yelled.

'Aye-aye, sir!'

The boat sped on. Charley was tempted to look over his shoulder to see if their quarry was ahead of them but knew this could upset not only his rhythm but that of the whole crew. Another ten minutes, during which they lost sight of the other boat, passed. Charley was breathing hard from the exertion, his whole body bathed in sweat in spite of the cold, but there was no let-up. Was this never going to end?

Then Bob made the signal they had all been waiting for. Rowing stopped instantly, leaving momentum to carry the boat on. The rowers quelled the urge to look round, none more so than Charley who wanted to have his first live close-up view of this huge creature of the sea. He was aware of the movement behind him – Captain Sharp standing up; they must be close to the whale. Charley tensed, waiting for the upheaval he knew would come. In that moment he recalled Mr Chapman's instructions in training – the man who occupied the thwart he was now occupying had to be ready to assist the harpooner in any way he demanded.

Charley watched the boat-steerer scull the boat gently through the water, taking them ever nearer the mountainous whale he sensed towering over them. He glimpsed boat two attached to a whale riding a wave as they towed it towards the *Sea King*. Another signal. He knew they were very close. He could not resist a quick glance over his shoulder. He saw John, harpoon in hand, arch his back, then uncoil himself and release his hold on the harpoon, to send it arcing over the sea. His judgement, born of long experience, was perfect; the harpoon plunged into the whale; the barbs gripped and held.

'Stern all!'

The crew bent their backs willingly to drive the boat away from the whale, knowing that they were in grave danger as its flukes churned the sea when they came out of the water. A maelstrom broke out around them. The men drove hard to avoid what they knew was coming. The flukes towered high, then flashed down into the sea, slashing the water into a turbulence that threatened to swamp them. Oars still dipped and drove the boat through the churning sea. Even in their exertions men breathed a sigh of relief that they had escaped the full force of the pounding flukes.

'Bail!'

Two men who had been allocated the job if it became necessary shipped their oars, grabbed the buckets near at hand and bailed as fast as they could.

'She's sounding!' John's voice cut through the cold air.

Almost at the same instant the whale disappeared. John speedily made two turns around the boat's bollard of the rope attached to the harpoon. The line ran out as the whale sounded, faster and faster, so fast that John called, 'Brook, bucket!' Charley grabbed one, scooped water and flung it over the bollard to prevent it catching fire from the friction. He kept at it until a signal from John told him to stop. The rope had gone slack.

John read its meaning. 'She's rising!'

Men tensed. Where would the whale surface? They could be thrown out of the boat and that might mean death in the cold, cold sea. They were held in limbo as they waited. Suddenly the sea was blasted into heaving waves when the whale surfaced, thankfully at sufficient distance from the boat to prevent an immediate catastrophe, but the danger was not yet over. This whale was not about to give up. It had an immense desire and will to escape. It ran, dragging the boat with it. There was nothing the crew could do but hang on. They gripped anything they could to stabilise themselves as the boat skimmed over the sea, bouncing behind the whale, cutting through the waves. John was alert to every possible manoeuvre by the mammal he was determined to conquer but, at the same time, aware of the danger of being towed too far from the *Sea King*. Five more interminable minutes. The whale altered the direction of its run. It was heading for the ice! John fought down a rising panic. Dare he stay fast to it any longer? But he wanted a full ship! It must turn away or tire . . . He held on.

Two minutes later his stomach tightened. The whale was slowing. This might give them a chance. 'Haul!' he called.

Men grabbed the slackening rope and pulled with renewed energy. Slowly the boat was brought nearer and nearer to the whale, towards a position where John could use the lances and make the kill.

'Steady, lads, steady,' he warned. He gauged the distance carefully. Most of the rope was back in the boat. A few more yards . . . He picked up a lance, his movements careful so as not to disturb his quarry. Every man in the boat was tense – they wanted to go home. This, the final kill, must succeed. Even as they entertained the thought the whale moved, then ran. The unexpected action caused John to lose his balance. By the time he'd regained it the rope was running out fast. It went taut; still the whale ran; the crew could do nothing but hold tight and let their vessel bounce across the heaving sea in the wake of the whale.

Gathering himself as best he could in the swaying

boat, John tried to assess their circumstances and find a way to conquer this monster so that he could fill his hold. But he realised they were at the mercy of the whale's behaviour and all they could do was to run with it until it was exhausted. Then he saw ice ahead. The whale must turn! It must! Then the ice seemed to be upon them and he was yelling, 'She's going under!' The whale dived while maintaining a course directly for the ice.

'Axe!' yelled John, holding his hand out behind him, expecting Charley to put the axe there. 'Axe, Brook! Axe!'

Nothing. He looked round, furious anger darkening his face. No axe nestled in its clamp on the inside of the boat!

'Brook! Axe!' Charley was scrambling in the bottom of the boat. 'Brook!' No axe, only a forlorn look from Charley.

The rope attached to the harpoon could not be cut! They were fastened to a whale that was heading for the ice! Disaster faced them!

The whale went under the ice. The boat followed with a shattering crash against the frozen water. Three men were flung out, the others dragged under and down with no chance of escape. One figure soared through the air to crash down among the shattered timber falling around him. An oar smashed into his head. He went under and knew no more.

John's shoulder felt as though it had been pounded with a heavy hammer but he was safely on the ice. Although his mind was numb, his senses reeling, he was aware of a figure sprawled a few yards away. He pushed himself round and slid across the ice. He reached the figure, pushed back the hood of the jacket which had fallen across the man's face. 'My God!' he whispered. 'Charley!' He stared at the silent figure. He shook off his right mitten, scrabbled a gap in Charley's clothing and felt for a pulse in his neck. 'He's alive!' Joy soared in his mind before shock set in and he began to shake, tears bursting from his eyes as he realised they were doomed; isolated on the ice where, with no possible shelter, they would soon freeze to death. Better if they had gone down with the boat!

13

14 September 1833. Where is the Sea King*? All Whitby's other whale-ships are back. The only news we could get from one of the ships was that she had last been seen heading west in a favourable sea. That was some comfort. I'm sure we'll soon be giving the* Sea King *her own rapturous welcome. I hope Jim and Charley are safe! We had Father with us for the evening meal . . .*

'Do you think the *Sea King* will be safe, Papa?' Harriet asked as they settled at the dining table after he had said grace and ended with, 'Remember your mother.'

Benjamin hesitated a moment before answering, 'You should never entertain doubt.'

'Then you think we'll see her soon?' Harriet pressed.

'Of course. There are any number of reasons why she could have been delayed,' he replied. 'She's in John's safe hands.'

His words were meant to be reassuring but each of them around the table still harboured anxiety. Benjamin for the son he had never wanted to go to sea; Sarah for her first love, Jim, whom she was determined would be her only love ever; Harriet for her betrothed and the opulent life he could give her; Arabella, confused in her loyalties, singled out her brother, Charley, but knew there would be a void in her life if John ever succumbed to the sea.

'I'm sure she'll soon be home,' Benjamin added. 'She's a stout ship. Now I've something to tell you and ask of you.'

He hesitated, took a sip of wine then continued, 'You remember earlier this year . . . in fact, it was the evening the *Sea King* sailed . . . I dined at the Angel with a gentleman I had met by chance on the quay that day?' They nodded. 'We talked business that evening and he went further north to explore other possibilities. On Monday last I received a letter from him saying that he would be back in Whitby next week and would like to meet me again. He indicated he would be staying at the Angel as before and would like me to dine with him. I take this to be an indication he has given serious thought to what we discussed and would like to carry it further. I think, under the circumstances, it would be more appropriate if he dined with us here.' His glance encompassed his family. He saw no adverse reaction to this suggestion.

'Very well, Papa,' said Arabella quickly.

'Excellent. Will you arrange it with Mrs Ainslie and Cook? I will leave the invitation at the Angel, to be given to him on his arrival.'

Benjamin retreated to his study.

Harriet raised her eyebrows as the dining-room door closed behind him. 'So we are to meet the nameless fuddy-duddy,' she said, recalling her previous comment when her father's meeting with the stranger had been mentioned.

Arabella pursed her lips into a small smile at the observation but made no mention of how she had felt that day. Though she still regarded John's switching of affections as betrayal, she had determined not to let it blight her life; maybe she could one day gain joy from the role her father had appointed her to.

'It's possible he isn't,' commented Sarah.

'More than likely he is, if he's a business acquaintance,' said Arabella.

'He must be a fuddy-duddy,' Harriet emphasised. 'Ah, well, let's make the most of it. Who knows? He may enjoy a bit of flirting?'

'Don't overdo it,' warned Sarah, 'we don't want to antagonise Papa. He's on edge worrying about Charley because the *Sea King* hasn't made port yet.'

'Oh, the *Sea King* is sure to be back before the stranger comes to dine,' said Harriet with conviction.

'Varley, what do you see?' Anxiety filled Mr Chapman's call to the man at the masthead.

'Captain's still running with the whale!'

The first mate faced a dilemma. Number two boat had returned with its catch. The whale was tied alongside. Flensing should begin, but that meant he would have to forgo taking the *Sea King* nearer number one boat.

'Any danger, Varley?'

'No, sir. Ice is moving. It could swing astern but it's no threat yet.'

Chapman raised his arm in acknowledgement. He moved to the rail to view the whale tied to the ship. The flensers were ready, irritably awaiting his command to go over the side and start their skilled job that would put blubber into the empty barrels waiting below decks. But something held him back from giving the final order.

'Whale's running again!' The cry from the masthead stunned everyone; this whale was putting up a fight.

'My God!' The alarm in Varley's voice reached everyone on deck. 'It's running for the ice!'

Chapman knew the dire consequences if it chose to dive under, but that presupposed the captain took no action. He must surely cut the rope!

'It's going under!' yelled Varley. Then his shouts chilled every heart on board the *Sea King*. 'Cut the line! Cut the line!' Such instinctive instructions from the lookout were of no use to the boat-crew. They were too far away.

The first mate knew from the pleading in the lookout's voice that the life-saving action had not been taken. There was only one thing he could do. His orders rapped across the deck to the flensers. 'Cut the whale adrift.' In an instant ropes were cut and the dead whale was allowed to drift away as sails were brought up to catch the rising wind. The helmsman needed no order to head the ship in the direction pointed out by Varley.

Mr Chapman was about to call for a report when he got it.

'They've gone under! Boat smashed! There's three flung out, two of them on the ice.'

'Stand by to launch number three boat!' The boat-crew ran to their positions, all eager to get the boat away on the first mate's order. But as eager as he was, there was nothing he could do until the *Sea King* was in the right position, as near as possible to the men on the ice.

John brushed at the tears before they froze. The action was mechanical but it sharpened his thoughts. Charley was alive! That realisation forced the need for action into

John's numbed mind. But what could he do, isolated on the ice with nothing to help them survive? Automatically his eyes turned in the direction in which he knew the *Sea King* lay. He saw nothing but undulating waves in a lonely sea. Despair threatened but he allowed himself a glimmer of hope. Varley would have been at the masthead to observe and report on the hunt; maybe, just maybe, he had seen the fate of boat number one. John had to cling to that hope. He shook Charley's shoulder. He must try and rouse the boy. Awake, he could resist the cold that waited to take him from this world. Charley moaned. The sound heartened John.

'Charley! Charley!' he pressed. 'Can you hear me? Charley!'

The youngster stirred.

John called his name over and over again. Relief came into his voice when he saw the lad's eyelids flicker.

'Charley!' He put more urgency into his tone. 'It's . . .' About to say 'John', he paused. Deeming a tone of authority might be more effective, he said, 'It's your captain!'

Charley's eyes flickered again and then, responding to John's voice, opened wide. 'Sir!'

'Brook, pay attention.'

'Sir.' Charley struggled to sit up but succumbed to a pain in his side. He winced. 'What happened, sir?' The question brought everything flooding back. 'Oh, God! The axe . . .'

His eyes widened with horror at the recollection that the axe had not been where he should have secured it, and with that came the memory of the boat hitting the ice then going under. He stared wildly around. 'Where's Jim?' He saw only his captain. 'Jim! Jim!' Then realisation struck. 'It was my fault! *Mine!*' He grasped John's arm. 'I killed them!' His voice rose hysterically and dry sobs racked his body. 'Jim! I killed Jim!'

John knew the truth behind this self-accusation. Charley's carelessness had led to the deaths, but blame barely mattered when they too were about to die. That thought made him glance across the waves as if his desperation could cull salvation out of the vast and desolate sea. His glance froze, fixed on . . .

'Charley, a sail!' It must be. What else could that speck be? John shaded his eyes, keeping them fixed on what might be their saviour. And it could only be the *Sea King*! Thank goodness for the exceptional eyes of Varley and Chapman's prompt action. 'We're saved, Charley! We're going home!'

Charley bit his lip. 'I'll have to face everyone . . . They'll know it was me who killed them . . .' Fighting the pain, he rolled over, nearer the edge of the ice. 'It would have been better for me to die.'

'Charley, no!' John screamed and grabbed him. 'That's not the answer.'

'Let me go!' Charley struggled to free himself but John's determination was stronger.

His thoughts were racing. He pressed himself closer to Charley so that he was looking straight into his eyes. 'Listen to me. This is your captain speaking. Say nothing about the axe.'

'But . . .'

'*Nothing!* That's an order.'

Charley did not speak.

'Understood, Brook?' John's eyes demanded the proper response to the captain of the *Sea King*.

'Aye-aye, sir!'

John saw the query in Charley's eyes so made his

explanation firm and clear. 'Only you and I know the truth about the axe, and there is no need for anyone else to share it. The question of my cutting the rope is bound to arise. I will say that as I was about to do it, the whale's action caused me to lose my balance. Before I recovered it we hit the ice. You understand, Brook? *That* is what happened. No one was to blame.'

For a moment Charley was about to protest but he thought better of it.

'Yes, sir!'

'Good. Cast the incident from your mind. Don't let it blight your life. You will cause more hurt and pain for those who have lost someone if the truth comes out, and it would cause your father untold anguish. Don't let that happen.'

'Yes, sir.'

They fell silent, watching the *Sea King* come nearer and nearer, her billowing sails giving them at least hope of a tomorrow.

'Ice on the move!' The cry from the masthead was one Mr Chapman did not want to hear.

To effect a rescue he would have to heave to, lower a boat and watch the boat-crew row with a vigour to match that employed when close to whales. He must then stand by while they took the two men into the boat, which would not be easy now the ice had started to move, and then returned to the ship with all haste to be manoeuvred aboard. There would not be a moment to spare.

Mr Chapman's orders rang out to bring the *Sea King* into position half a mile from the ice. The boat was lowered under the expertise of a man who had done this many times. It had hardly touched the water before it was pushed away from the ship. Oars were dipped and the crew immediately fell into a fast rhythm, propelling the boat towards the two men on the ice.

The first mate watched, taut with anxiety, urging the boat-crew on. There was nothing he could do but keep the *Sea King* as close as possible to the rescue site – a rescue that must succeed. His faith lay in the boat-steerer, whom he knew would never hold back from a mission that involved saving lives.

'Ice to the east!' The unease underlying these words from Varley was not lost on Mr Chapman. He sought a better view from the rigging. What he saw sent a frisson of fear through him. The area of ice to their east had widened and was moving south, threatening to swing astern of the *Sea King*.

'West!'

The one word hurled from the masthead turned Mr Chapman's gaze in that direction. Ice was curling south from the main area on which the two crew members were stranded. He cursed. The *Sea King* was now threatened from both east and west. If the ice continued to swing in from two directions she would face being caught between it.

'Row! Row!' the first mate found himself shouting even though he knew the boat-crew were too far away to hear his urging and, not having his advantage of height, would be unaware of how the ice was threatening them.

Dare he take the *Sea King* nearer the ice? He made a quick assessment. It could be the only way they would escape being trapped. Decision made, he stayed where he was and rapped out his orders loud and clear to the second mate, who brought the ship nearer the ice to facilitate a quicker rescue once the boat-crew had the two men on board.

The boat-steerer noted the directional change in the *Sea King*'s passage and realised its implication. The first mate wanted his boat with the two stranded men back at the ship sooner than was humanly possible.

'Bend ya backs, lads, bend 'em!' The boat-steerer's words lashed at the crew. They knew from his tone that they were in danger. Every man responded. The boat cut through the water towards the ice. 'Faster! Faster!' Every muscle strained. Then, 'Ship oars!' The men responded immediately. The boat continued to glide over calmer water. The boat-steerer leaned on his long oar and with a skill learned and honed over the years brought the boat swinging round alongside the ice, close to the two men.

'Captain!' There was some relief in the boat-steerer's voice as the crew reached out and assisted the efforts of their captain and Charley in scrambling into the boat. They were barely aboard when it was shoved away from the ice and oars were flashing again, propelling the boat back towards the *Sea King*.

The men took in ice they had not seen previously, closing in on the *Sea King* from both sides! There was no need for any order for them to row faster, they did so automatically. They reached the ship with the ice close behind them. Ropes were thrown and men scrambled aboard, helping the two whom they had rescued.

The first mate sized up the situation quickly. His captain and Charley Brook were all in. He took full authority on himself. 'Captain's cabin, immediately!' He signalled to two crew members standing by. 'Get them warm clothes and drinks.'

'Aye-aye, sir!'

The two rescued men were hurried away. Mr Chapman called all hands on deck but even as he did so heard the ominous scraping of ice on either side of the vessel. The ice was closing fast around them. Could he force a way out, find open water, head for safety and home?

'Mr Varley, report!'

'Open water to the south but ice bars our way!'

Mr Chapman's orders flew thick and fast. They brought fresh hope as a lookout posted in the bow reported a lane opening up, but joy was short-lived when it closed again with thickening ice. The movement of the *Sea King* gradually surrendered to the might of the ice, which had by now developed a determination to hold the ship in its unrelenting grip. The vessel made one last timber-grinding shudder before an ominous silence enfolded it, and with that silence depression descended over her crew.

The September sun shone bright, sending its warming rays bouncing off Whitby's red roofs. It was one of those days that usually brought a sense of well-being, but today a shade of doubt hung over the minds of the town's inhabitants whose lives were so intricately entwined with the sea. None more so than the minds of the families whose men-folk had left Whitby aboard the *Sea King* six months ago.

21 September 1833. There is no news of the Sea King. *We try to keep up hope. Arabella is quieter than usual. Harriet is restless. We want Charley back. Oh, Jim, where are you? I'm praying you are safe. Please, please, come back.*

The Brook family, each in their own way, feared the terrible consequences of losing Charley, John and Jim, losses that could have lasting repercussions on their lives.

14

24 September 1833. I wish we had news of the Sea King. *We are growing anxious but live in hope that nothing serious has happened. This evening we have Father's 'fuddy-duddy', as we have christened him, dining with us. I wish he were young; he might be attracted to Arabella. She deserves to be happy . . .*

Knowing that their father would want them to create a good impression on their visitor, the three sisters had chosen to wear attractive evening dresses, but each had in mind the hope of pleasing someone else when they took them from their wardrobes.

Arabella held her pale blue broché silk dress against herself as she viewed it in the mirror. 'Beautiful,' had been John's comment when he first saw it eighteen months before. Remembering brought dampness to her eyes but she stiffened herself against the return of tears. That time for those had passed. She lived in a new world, though still in the same surroundings.

Harriet slipped a moiré antique pink dress over her shoulders. Laughter curved her lips as she imagined John being tempted by the pose she struck as she admired herself in the mirror. She spun round to send the skirt

213

swirling, imagining the joy she would feel in his arms at his homecoming.

Sarah adjusted the fall of her skirt, looked up and cast her eye over the image in the mirror. Cream suited her. She wondered what Jim might say if he could see her now. She expected he would feel he was stepping into an unfamiliar world and would be embarrassed, but she was confident she could cure him of that and then they would walk hand in hand through a long and happy life.

Each in her own room, they listened for the arrival of the guest. The front-door bell rang; they heard the door open and close; the voices of their father and his guest as they entered the drawing-room. As planned the girls came out of their rooms together, met on the landing, and took the steps in unison. They made the briefest of pauses in front of the double doors to the drawing-room which they opened together so as to make a grand entrance, planning to take the fuddy-duddy by surprise.

But it was they who received the surprise. The image they had formed in their minds was completely erased by the sight of the man who rose politely to greet them.

He was tall, his every movement graceful and unhurried. His smile was warm, embracing them all but making each of them decide it was meant for her and her alone. 'Ladies,' he said, in a voice as smooth as velvet, while he made a small bow that offered his respects.

'Mr Waite, my daughters, Arabella, Harriet and Sarah,' said Benjamin with an unusual touch of pride in his voice that astonished and pleased them.

Again he bowed and said, 'This is indeed a pleasure,' while skilfully hiding his surprise. Meeting three charming young ladies was something he had not expected.

'Mr Waite,' they chorused politely.

He smiled. 'Oh, please, let us dispense with formality. I am Stephen.' He glanced quickly at Benjamin; seeing no immediate objection he held his host's gaze and said, 'If you approve, sir?'

Benjamin did.

'I think it would make for a pleasanter and more relaxing evening.' Benjamin saw distinct possibilities in being on good terms with Stephen Waite.

'The pleasure is all mine, sir.'

Stephen's smile sent a glow through each of the sisters. This certainly was no fuddy-duddy! In fact, he was just the opposite. This evening was not going to be as boring and prolonged as they had anticipated.

Arabella, recalling without any malice Harriet's barb about her marrying a fuddy-duddy, smiled to herself as she sat down opposite Stephen Waite. Oh, those eyes! A possibility? Ah, well, who knew? But even as these questions moved swiftly through her mind, she thought of John.

Harriet repressed the excitement that had set her heart racing on first sight of this handsome man. How would those perfectly shaped lips feel against hers? She felt a tremor of shock at the thought, but drove it away with a recollection of John, her betrothed.

Sarah was enchanted; she had never experienced such a sensation in the presence of a man before and it troubled her for a few moments until she recalled Jim and knew instantly that she would be his and only his. She may enjoy Stephen's company but that would never replace the love she felt for Jim.

When they were seated Benjamin dispensed Madeira for his guest, eldest daughter and himself, and cider for his other daughters. Stephen informed them, 'I have requested your father not to talk business this evening. That can wait until tomorrow.'

'I heartily concurred,' put in Benjamin, 'and also added that we should not allow the *Sea King*'s absence to spoil our evening. I am sure that all is well and John will bring her safely home.'

Stephen nodded and added in a convincing tone, 'I have experienced the late arrival of vessels and the worry that can bring. Then the ship is home and you wonder why on earth you were troubled. I feel certain that will be the case here as well.' He went on to set the tone for the evening by raising his glass and making a toast: 'To three charming young ladies.'

Stephen exuded charm without being overbearing; he drew everyone into the conversation; was attentive to their needs at the table; and showed his gratitude to Mrs Ainslie and her staff, with special appreciation of Cook's culinary skills.

'Where is your home, Mr W—?'

Arabella's question was stopped by him raising his hand and smiling at her, a teasing twinkle in his eyes as he said, 'Christian names, please, Arabella.'

She blushed at the correction.

'My home is in Bristol. I have lived there all my life,' he informed her.

'Does your wife come from Bristol too?'

He smiled at the question; no beating about the bush with this young lady. 'I am not married, Arabella.'

'You've never been married?' queried Benjamin, somewhat surprised.

'No, never.'

As Stephen's attention switched from Arabella to Benjamin, Harriet raised an eyebrow at her sister as much as to say, 'Now's your chance!' but all she received in reply was a frown and an almost imperceptible shake of the head.

The sound of ice grinding at the *Sea King*'s timbers struck a presentiment in John's mind. He should be on deck; he must learn the true situation to be able to assess their chances of escaping the Arctic. Pushing aside the blankets that had been heaped on him for warmth, he swung himself tentatively from the bunk. Thankful that he had suffered nothing worse than bruising, he reached for the dry clothes that had been laid out for him. He shrugged himself into them, pulled on thick woollen socks and hauled on his sea boots. He grabbed his leather cap and started for the door before he remembered Charley. He guessed Mr Chapman must have put the boy in his own cabin. That assumption was confirmed when he looked into the first mate's cabin and saw the boy lying staring wide-eyed at the ceiling, an expression of terror on his face. John had no doubt what was occupying the youngster's mind. He entered the cabin and closed the door behind him.

Charley started at his appearance. 'Sir!'

'How are you feeling?' asked John gently.

'Horrible, sir. It was my fault!' His eyes, filled with guilt, widened at the thought of what that would mean.

'Charley, it was not!' John's voice was sharp, pitched to penetrate the youngster's state of shock. 'You hear me?'

Charley gave a slight nod. 'But I killed . . .'

'You did not!' broke in John fiercely. 'Don't ever think that and never express it to anyone. Do you remember what I told you on the ice?'

'Yes, sir,' replied Charley weakly.

'Convince me,' thundered John, eyes smouldering with anger at Charley's weakness.

Startled, he put more feeling into his words. 'I do remember, sir.'

'Then you will recall that I gave you an order. See that you obey it!' John knew he had said enough. He hurried from the cabin. Reaching the deck, he took in the situation at a glance.

'Should you be up, sir?' asked the first mate in concern.

'I'm all right, Mose,' replied John, believing the familiar form of address would be more appropriate under the circumstances. 'I was lucky . . . only a few aches and pains. Thank you for your prompt action in getting the *Sea King* to us, and also for putting Charley in your bunk.'

'You looked in on him?'

'Aye. He'll get over his ordeal.' John left a slight pause and then asked, 'What's the situation here?'

'Not good, sir.' His first mate quickly apprised the captain of the facts.

'Varley! What chance?' The lookout heard the concern in the captain's voice but also recognised it was tinged with hope. How he wished he could give even the slightest hint that the ice showed signs of relenting, but his experienced eyes saw nothing to bring gladness to the hearts of the crew.

'None, sir! The ice is spreading south. There are no lanes opening.'

A grinding sound against the stern confirmed his judgement, mocking any hope they had retained of escaping.

'Can we break our way out?' yelled John. Though he

knew the answer he had to put the question; explore every possibility.

'Not possible, sir! The ice is thickening as it's moving south.'

John turned to his first mate. 'Looks grim, Mr Chapman.'

'Aye, sir, it does. Do you want Varley down?'

'Leave him until he confirms there's no change in the ice that we can exploit.'

'Aye-aye, sir.' Chapman turned his gaze to the mast-head. 'Varley!'

'Aye-aye, sir.'

'Stay a while. Report any favourable change immediately.'

'Aye-aye, sir.' Varley knew exactly what he would be looking for and that the crew would still be hoping to hear good news before long.

'Mr Chapman, we'll prepare for a long wait.' John's voice was matter-of-fact, as if this was something they had done before.

'Aye-aye, sir,' replied Chapman staunchly, exuding confidence that they could face a long, hard winter, beat it and survive. It was a situation that none of them had had to face before but they knew their efforts would all have to be geared to the ultimate goal – survival.

'First, Mr Chapman, muster the crew on deck now.'

'Aye-aye, sir.' He took a deep breath, feeling the cold air sharp in his lungs. 'All hands on deck! All hands on deck!'

His command was passed on and within a few minutes all the crew, with the exception of Varley, were standing before the captain and first mate.

'Men, I'll not try to conceal our position. Unless the

weather changes in our favour very quickly we are trapped. Varley reports thickening ice, especially to the south, our escape route.'

Murmurings ran through the crew. They had half expected this but had hung on to the hope that Varley, with his more extensive view from the masthead, could see an escape route. Now that hope was all but dashed. Fear gripped them all.

As he walked back to the Angel, Stephen was pleased with himself. He was more than sure he had made a good impression on them all, and that was to the good. He had soon realised that Benjamin, while not adroit at showing his affection for his daughters, nevertheless had a deep concern and love for them; Stephen had therefore displayed a genuine interest in them while showing them all the respect their father would expect a gentleman to observe.

His thoughts dwelt on all three girls but it was Harriet whom he found had really captured his attention. He judge her to be pretty, lively, someone who enjoyed life and wanted to get as much out of it as she could: riches, comfort and enjoyment. With the determination he had detected in her, he knew she would stop at nothing to realise her desires. He was doubtful that this aspect of her character was fully known to the rest of her family. Maybe he could . . .? But even as his thoughts took him down a tempting path, Pamela's warning words came sharply back to mind. Would Harriet be worth the risk of losing everything he had gained by his association with Pamela? Dare he risk her finding out? But how could she? Whitby was far away from London . . .

15

27 September 1833. I'm worried. There is no news yet of the Sea King. *A ship on her way to London from Shetland called at Whitby today but it had no news of her. The last information of a whale-ship arriving in Shetland was on the 14th. This has created a feeling of unease amongst us. We daren't voice our thoughts. Please God, bring the ship home . . .*

Stephen Boulton crossed the bridge briskly to the East Side. He had made enquiries as to where the *Sea King* would tie up on her return, but as he viewed that position from the bridge was disturbed to find that particular quay unoccupied. His lips tightened. If she was lost it might affect his plans. Maybe he could determine Benjamin's attitude at their prearranged meeting this morning.

As he entered the offices of Brook and Son he put on a smile and greeted Benjamin with a warm handshake.

'That was a most pleasant evening, Mr Brook, and an added pleasure to meet your delightful daughters.'

'I enjoyed it too, as I'm sure they did.' Benjamin paused then said, 'Please, do sit down.' He indicated a chair on the opposite side of the large oak desk. His serious expression was intensified by the shadow of doubt in his eyes.

Stephen sensed that this meeting was not going to turn out the way he had wished.

'A ship arrived from Shetland this morning on its way to London. It brought no news of the *Sea King*.'

'I'm sorry to hear that. I hope it will not influence your reaction to the scheme I have in mind.'

'Well, I think it only fair to say, here and now, that the *Sea King*'s cargo would have had a significant effect on my future plans.'

'But there is still the possibility she will return,' pressed Stephen.

'True, but I do not wish to pursue any future business until I know she is safely home. If, God forbid, she does not return, I will have to reassess my position then. But let me hasten to add, it is not beyond the realms of possibility that I could still go ahead with a venture agreeable to us both. Therefore I would ask you to wait a while, though I fully understand if you wish to move on and take your scheme elsewhere.'

'Let us not anticipate the worst. The *Sea King* may still return. I will wait. I like Whitby and a break from business matters would do me good. I have competent managers who can look after things in Bristol. So, if it presents no inconvenience to you, I will stay.'

'I appreciate your response. Your decision will give me a chance to look into the assets I can turn towards the new venture, should it suit my needs.'

'Admirable,' returned Stephen. He rose from his chair. 'I won't disturb you any longer.'

Benjamin stood up to accompany him from the offices. 'If you are going to spend some time in Whitby, do drop in here any time. And you will always be welcome in my home.'

'That is most gracious of you, sir. I may take advantage of your generosity.' Stephen left a slight pause and added, 'Maybe I can repay that in some small way by escorting your daughters to a musical concert, or possibly a carriage ride on a pleasant day?'

'By all means. They would appreciate that. They sometimes enjoyed such outings with their mother, but I don't seem to be able to find the time.'

John sat alone in his cabin, tormented by the problem which would not leave him. He ran a hand over his face as if that would wipe it away and present him with the answer. The horror of what his crew might have to face kept pushing into his mind. Despair was very close behind.

John started and cursed himself. This was no way for a captain to be thinking. He had to lead his men, give them hope that they could and would survive a long dark winter trapped in the ice. He had to keep their confidence high. Each man was different and each would tackle the future in a different way; he had to understand the crew as individuals and see that the attitude of each contributed positively to their survival. Any doubt that this was possible must be banished. Constructive plans had to be made. He pushed himself to his feet, strode to the door and yelled, 'Mr Chapman!'

As he turned back inside he heard, 'Aye-aye, sir.' A few moments later the first mate appeared. 'Sir?'

'Sit down, Mose,' said John. As the first mate did so, he went on, 'We've come through a lot since we sailed on our first voyage together as boys, but we've never had to face a situation like this.' He left a short pause. Knowing his captain and friend well, Mose recognised that this was not the moment to make a comment. 'Have you had Varley aloft again?' John continued.

'Aye. There's ice as far as he could see. I don't like to say it, but I don't think there's a chance of our breaking out.'

'I agree. Therefore we must suppose we are here all winter and had better make preparations for that. Three things need immediate attention: food, warmth and morale.'

The two men spent the next few hours making plans; the cook would make a list of food supplies and a rationing system be enforced. There was plenty of timber that could be used for warmth, but care would have to be taken about which parts of the ship's structure could be used without imperilling her more. Extra clothing would be doled out if required, though it was expected each man would have provided plenty for himself.

'It won't be easy to keep the men fully occupied,' went on John, 'but it is essential to do so, to avoid despondency creeping in. Some will succumb and their attitude may insidiously affect the whole crew. We must be alert to combat this. Thoughts of home, family and friends must not be allowed to let melancholy creep in. We must emphasise the joy we will all experience when we see them again. Not *if*, Mose, but *when*!'

Left in the quiet of his cabin, John himself thought of home. He remembered the passion in Harriet's kisses. Would that always be there, even after their marriage? Now things had gone this far he couldn't change his circumstances. He must face the fact that Arabella hated him.

7 October 1833. Still no news of the Sea King. *Our fears for the safety of her crew had been growing but we were shocked when Father announced this evening that we must regard the ship as lost. My heart sank. Jim! Oh, Jim! And Charley – you can't be lost on your first voyage! Please God, no! I was so numbed by the blow I hardly heard what Arabella said . . .*

'This is dreadful, Papa. No, it's worse than that.' The note in Arabella's voice matched the horror in her eyes. 'Is there no hope?'

Though his own heart and mind were being torn apart, Benjamin tried to be strong but knew he was not succeeding very well.

'I suppose there is always hope,' he replied quietly. 'If the *Sea King* is caught in the ice without suffering damage there may still be a chance for her, but the Arctic winter will be setting in now, the weather will worsen, and the crew, even if they still have their ship, will be faced with severe cold and possible hunger.' His voice broke and his face went ashen at the thought of the consequences that could arise from the picture he had painted.

Arabella felt drained by despair but tried to muster a glimmer of hope even though her eyes were brimming with tears. 'But men have survived a winter in the Arctic?'

Benjamin nodded. 'You are thinking of Barents and one or two others, but they were explorers, able to adapt to their particular situation. I know of no whale-ship crew that has survived. The men are really just sailors.'

'But special,' put in Sarah.

Benjamin gave a wan smile. 'Yes, Sarah, they are; they are whale-men, but that does not give them any special aptitude for survival in a frozen, unforgiving world. I think we must try to come to terms with the distinct possibility that the *Sea King* and her crew are lost, including . . .' His voice faltered and he choked on one whispered word: 'Charley!' He pushed himself sharply from his chair and strode to the door.

Sarah started to go after him; she wanted to give him comfort, and in return hoped for a glimmer of the parental fortitude for which at this moment she yearned. She knew she would have received it from her mother. But she caught Arabella's eye and saw that her eldest sister had read her intention and deemed it wisest for Sarah to leave their father to his private mourning. Arabella knew he would want to come to terms with the loss of his son in his own way.

She struggled to keep her own feelings under control but was finding it extremely difficult. Though she felt weak inside she had to make a show of strength, not only for herself but for her sisters. 'We should not give up hope. They may survive,' she said in a distant manner that carried, unintentionally, a trace of doubt.

Harriet, who had sat staring at the table since her father's announcement, looked up sharply. 'Don't be stupid,' she ranted. 'They're gone! Gone! We'll never see any of them again! Never!'

Even though shocked by the sudden outburst and the alarm it had brought to Sarah's face, Arabella had to utter one word, 'Hope . . .'

'Hope?' shouted Harriet. 'Don't you mean hopeless?'

'Don't take that attitude, Harriet. There may be—' said Arabella, only to be cut off.

'Stupid! You're stupid to cling to hope that isn't there!' With eyes blazing, Harriet sprang to her feet and swept the vase from the occasional table beside her. It shattered

226

on the floor, leaving flowers strewn in a widening stain from the spreading water. 'You can mourn Charley but not John. He's mine, and I know his last thoughts will be of me!'

Though Arabella reeled from this hysterical outburst she was on her feet, reaching out to her sister, wanting to calm her, but Harriet shoved her away. Caught unawares by her sister's reaction, she staggered and fell back into her chair. Sarah, taken completely aback, tried to help her eldest sister while Harriet stormed from the room, slamming the door behind her.

The two sisters sought comfort in each other's arms. Arabella sagged. John, my love! Charley! This shouldn't be! Sarah shuddered. Jim! Oh, Jim! And Charley! They held each other tight while silent tears flowed at the thought that they may never see their loved ones again.

Charley wiped the dampness from his eyes as he lay on his bunk, to which he had been ordered several days before. It helped his recovery from the aching and bruising but did nothing to ease the torment in his mind. He had killed four men, one of them his friend Jim. How could he face Sarah if ever they saw Whitby again? Maybe it would be better for him if they didn't? He wouldn't have to confront her day after day with a terrible secret locked in his heart, one kept from others too who had lost loved ones. If he disclosed that secret he would be disobeying his captain, something that would stain his character in the eyes of seafaring men forever. He would be shunned on two counts after that. No, he must obey his captain and that implied keeping his secret, which in turn meant occupying his mind with other things.

He swung from his bunk, bent on resuming an active

life on board the ship, facing with the rest of her crew the long, dark winter ahead.

Arabella stirred in her bed. Had she heard something or had she been dreaming? No, there it was again; a tap on her door, gentle so as not to awaken anyone else. There was another tap.

'Come in,' she called quietly. Raising herself on her elbows, she watched the door open and was surprised to see Harriet slip inside the room and close the door quietly behind her. She glided across the floor in typical Harriet fashion but this time there was a touch of hesitation in the graceful movement. She reached the bed before she spoke.

'Arabella, I'm sorry for my outburst yesterday evening. I shouldn't have acted like that.' She sounded penitent and sincere.

Arabella pulled back the bedclothes and held out her arms to her sister. Harriet fell into them gratefully and Arabella pulled the covering over them both. As they hugged each other, one seeking forgiveness, the other forgiving, they drew comfort from the warmth of their closeness.

'This is what we used to do when we were little,' said Arabella.

'Yes, when we had Mother to comfort us,' recalled Harriet, drawing confidence from the memories. 'Forgive me, Arabella?'

'Of course. You were under a terrible strain. You couldn't help reacting that way.'

'You're so kind.'

'No kinder than you would have been under the same circumstances.'

'But do you really believe they may still survive?'

'We have to hope.'

'That doesn't answer my question.'

Arabella hesitated. Though she did not like admitting it, even to herself, she had to say, 'I think it is very unlikely, but I will try to keep a glimmer of hope alive.'

'I don't think I can even do that. I'm not as strong as you. It would mean living in prolonged mourning, though it would be without the outward trappings while we await confirmation that they have been lost, then mourning again when we knew they were lost. No, Arabella, I'm going to face my loss now. Life's too short not to get on with it.'

'If that's what you want to do, who am I to say you are wrong? It's not my way but I won't criticise you.' Arabella had resolved in these last few minutes that the important thing was to mend the rift between Harriet and herself, now that John was lost to them both.

The days passed. The gloom that had settled over Whitby with the loss of the *Sea King* and its crew gradually lifted and the town resumed its normal life. It was not quite so readily resumed in the Brook household.

Harriet tried to be cheerful with her friends but sub-dued her attitude at home. Her father was still devastated by the loss of Charley. He saw the once glowing future of the firm now submerged in impenetrable blackness. He remained at home, shut in his study day after day, ignoring the hints from his daughters that he should try to resume working at his office so that he could be at the hub of the activity there and fully occupy his mind, taking it away from thoughts of the tragedy.

Arabella's own thoughts were torn. Maybe a new

friendship with Stephen could help ease the pain of loss, but could he ever match up to John? She would not give up hope of seeing him again.

Sarah tried to take up her life where it had been so heartbreakingly interrupted. She clung to hope but at the same time admitted the loss to herself by resolving never to marry; she would always only be Jim's.

As the rising sun was just beginning to replace the darkness over Whitby with a pale light, Sarah stirred, uncertain what had caused her to do so. She raised her head off the pillow to hear better. Had she really heard correctly? Silence. About to lower her head and seek sleep again, she stiffened. She was right; the heavy silence was broken by sobs.

This time she was convinced that the sound she had heard every morning since the loss of the *Sea King* was reality and not a dream. This morning the sobs seemed louder and were coming from the next bedroom. Arabella's. Wide awake, Sarah slipped from her bed, chiding herself for her previous neglect. Slipping a robe around her shoulders, she stole quietly from her room.

She glanced along the landing in both directions but they were shrouded in darkness; the early-morning light filtered through the stair window. She detected no movement anywhere. The house was still. Sarah shivered. Though she knew this as a friendly house, its friendliness had recently taken on the mantle of mourning, as if trying to tell her that her hope should be abandoned. She shuddered and chided herself for her thoughts.

In Arabella's room the curtains were not drawn together; the pale morning light cast an eerie glow over the figure sitting on the window-seat, looking out. She was slumped in despair and the sound of her quiet sobbing was heartbreaking.

Sarah softly closed the door and stood still for a moment. Her eldest sister, whom she had always regarded as the one strong enough to hold the family together, looked utterly spent. Sarah knew, in spite of the rawness of her own feelings for Jim, that she must be strong for Arabella now.

She glided across the room, only speaking in a hushed tone when she was close to her sister. 'Arabella?'

If she was startled she did not show it. She glanced at Sarah as her sister sat down beside her and put her arm round her shoulders. Arabella sank against her in an attitude that begged for the warmth of human contact. Sarah did not speak for a while but held her until she was sure she was bringing succour to her sister.

'You weep every morning at this time, don't you?' she asked finally.

Arabella looked surprised by this. She frowned, eyes filling with concern. 'Oh, Sarah, I'm so sorry. Have I been waking you?'

'That's all right,' she replied, rubbing her sister's shoulder with a comforting touch. 'I was uncertain, but this morning convinced me I had not been dreaming. Realising that I had been hearing the sounds every morning bothered me, so I came . . .'

'I'm glad you did. You are a comfort to me, Sarah. I know it must be hard for you too.'

'We all grieve in our own way but you sob every morning when daylight is just beginning to show. Arabella, it is not good for you, you must . . .'

Arabella sat up, giving a wan smile as she touched Sarah's lips to stop her from saying more.

Sarah took her hands in hers and looked deep into her sister's eyes. What she saw there were pools of unfathomable love. 'You must love John very much,' she whispered.

Arabella nodded. 'I do. I know I shouldn't. I thought I was beginning to forget any thoughts of love, but I feel it more and more as the days bring no news of the *Sea King*. It seems the dreaded possibility just makes me love him more and more. But, Sarah, I mourn not just for John, but also Charley and Jim and all the men on the *Sea King*.' Still holding her sister's hands, she turned to look out of the window. With her gaze fixed on the fiery disc appearing over the horizon, she said quietly, 'I weep for the morning sun.'

For a moment, her own thoughts turning to Jim and eyes filling with tears, Sarah was lost in a puzzled silence. Then she said, 'I don't understand?'

'I weep so that the morning sun may dispel the Arctic darkness, and give light and warmth to the men on the *Sea King*.'

'Then I'll come and weep with you,' Sarah told her, glad in the bitterness of loss to be able to do this much for the men so cruelly lost to them.

16

7 October 1833. I think we all now accept that the Sea King *is lost. Even if she were trapped in the ice, it would be impossible for anyone to survive. We don't voice these thoughts but I can tell the last glimmer of hope is almost extinguished. We try to go about our lives as normally as possible and received a boost today when Mr Waite called. He lightened the atmosphere and gave us something different to think about . . .*

'You seem to be enjoying that book, Harriet,' commented Arabella, glancing up from her embroidery.

'I am. It's *The Settlers in the Woods* by John Galt.' She paused for a moment, eyes fixed on the tablecloth in Arabella's hands. 'You remind me so much of Mother when I see you doing such exquisite embroidery.'

'That's kind of you, but I'm sure I'm not as talented as Mama.'

'I think you are,' put in Sarah, laying down her pencil and holding her drawing at arm's length, the better to assess it.

'Show!' urged Harriet.

A little reluctantly, Sarah turned the drawing so both of them could see.

'That's splendid!' cried Harriet on seeing Sarah's interpretation of Whitby Abbey in relation to the cliffs and the sea. She had not drawn a true representation but had skilfully evoked the atmosphere of the ruin.

'Truly wonderful,' agreed Arabella. 'You must never let your talent fade. I have no doubt that one day you will sell your drawings.'

Sarah smiled, delighted with their praises; she was finding that drawing helped to ease the pain of Jim's disappearance. 'If you think that of me, you must surely recognise your own dexterity with the needle.' She glanced at Harriet then. 'With all the reading you do, you should be able to emulate some of those writers. You ought to try.'

Harriet laughed. 'What? So we'd become known as Whitby's talented trio?'

'Why not?' grinned Arabella.

'Mother would have encouraged us,' said Sarah. 'Papa won't, except to comment, "Very nice" and turn back to his paper.'

'He'd be right so far as I'm concerned,' returned Harriet.

'What do you mean?' asked Sarah with querying frown.

'Women writers aren't accepted.'

'Well, it's time they were,' said Arabella indignantly. 'Maybe you can make that happen.'

Any further speculation was prevented by a knock on the drawing-room door. A maid came in carrying a small round tray on which there lay a calling card.

'A gentleman wishes to know if Mr Brook is at home. I told him he was not, so he asked if any of the Misses Brook was here?' As she was speaking she crossed the room to hold out the tray to Arabella.

She took the card, glanced at it and said, 'Please show him in, Lucy.'

'Yes, miss.'

Harriet and Sarah looked at their sister expectantly.

'Who is it?' asked Harriet, her voice low.

'Tell us,' urged Sarah.

'Mr Waite . . . Stephen,' Arabella revealed.

Both girls gasped and Arabella recognised a touch of pleasure in their reactions, but more so in Harriet's. She couldn't have denied the lift in her own spirits too; the change of company would do them good.

The door opened and Stephen came in with a brisk step. 'My dear young ladies, I hope I am not intruding on your leisure?' His query was tempered by an expression of pleasure to see them.

'Not at all,' replied Arabella. 'We are delighted you called. Father told us you might do so.'

'Good.'

'Please, do sit down. Did you want to see Father? I'm afraid he is out. We have at last managed to persuade him to leave his study.'

'I thought that might be the case – confining himself here, I mean. I have called at his office several times only to be told he was not there. I did not wish to intrude, but after the open invitation he made I thought it would be impolite of me not to call. I waited until I thought a suitable time had passed.'

'Very thoughtful,' said Harriet.

'You'll take tea?' Sarah asked.

'That would be delightful,' he replied with an inclination of the head.

Sarah rose from her chair and went to the bell-pull to order tea. Conversation flowed, with everyone avoiding any mention of the tragedy that had taken place in the Arctic, but everyone could sense the underlying tension that came with this purposeful avoidance until finally Arabella could bear it no longer.

'Stephen, it seems we are all being careful to avoid mentioning the *Sea King*. I think it would be better to get that topic out of the way so that at least on a conversational level there need be no fear of distressing anyone.'

Stephen's pause before answering was accompanied by a small nod of agreement. The sisters fixed him with their eyes as if what he was about to say would be an important announcement. 'I entirely agree with you, Arabella. The subject cannot be completely avoided. To be open about it in conversation is the best way to deal with it.'

'Then give us your opinion, Stephen,' entreated Harriet. 'Do you think there is any hope that the men of the *Sea King* will survive?'

He looked serious. 'There is still hope, I suppose. Survival, if at all possible, must depend on the Arctic conditions, obviously, but also on whether the ship is still habitable, and how the captain organises life aboard to combat the isolation and mind-destroying circumstances in which they find themselves.' He pulled himself up short. 'My dear young ladies, I should not be pursuing such avenues of conjecture. My sincere apologies.'

'Stephen, it was I who brought the subject up,' Arabella pointed out. 'I take it that you do not retain any hope?'

'There must always be room for that.'

'Rubbish!' snapped Harriet. 'There is no chance of our seeing any of the *Sea King*'s crew again.'

Stephen was taken aback by the vehemence of her

words. He began to regret the picture he had painted. 'I agree it is extremely unlikely,' he said quietly, 'and think we must get on with our lives until we receive news one way or another, and that is not likely until the whaling season next year. So, my dear young ladies, I present you with an invitation – allow me to take you to Robin Hood's Bay. I will order a carriage and arrange with the landlord of the Angel to supply us with a picnic. We must do it soon. We are in an excellent spell of October weather at the moment. I put a lot of trust in the local fishermen wherever I am; their weather-eyes are second to none. The men I have spoken to here predict the mild spell will last another week. So may I suggest two days' time?'

'That is most kind of you, Stephen,' Arabella replied for them all. 'We will look forward to it. I know from what Father told me about your visiting that he will approve your invitation.'

'Mr Chapman, what do you have to report this morning?' John had instigated a report from the first mate at nine o'clock each day.

'Morale is high at the moment. Some men still believe we may get the chance of a breakout but others are beginning to think that is wishful thinking. However, I've sent Varley aloft this morning. I don't expect anything positive from him but for the time being it keeps the crew's hopes alive; with the ice shifting as it does, he may spot some open water.'

'A good thought, Mose, anything to keep morale high. Though I think you and I realise the full gravity of our situation. We are likely to experience the full harshness of the Arctic winter. Keep a particular eye on those who have the highest hopes; they are the ones most likely to crack when they realise their expectations are deceived.'

Any hopes that the crew still held were destroyed four hours later by Varley's shout of 'Heavy ice! Heavy ice!'

'Whither away?' yelled John, heart beating faster at this news; something that could herald the ultimate disaster.

'Ahead, and closing from port and starboard!'

John cursed. Trouble was too mild a word for what might happen next. The ship could be crushed. There was nothing they could do, no manoeuvre they could make to lessen the risk, gripped as they were in the pack ice. He was thankful he had had the water pumped from the ballast to meet just such a situation as this; with the ship lightened she could ride the pressure of the ice more easily, but that did not negate the possibility of her being stoved in.

'Keep reporting, Varley!'

'Aye-aye, sir!'

The lookout kept his assessments of the ice's progress clear and precise.

Mose delegated tasks to keep the men's minds occupied but they were trivial, with no power to alleviate their situation and the terror of being crushed to splinters. He knew it was useless and, like the crew, gave up in order to watch the ice closing in. The heavy ice moved closer and closer, pushing the pack ice before it, piling it up in ever-growing mounds that grew then imploded into jagged, lethal precipices of ice. Slowly, slowly, nearer and nearer, the ice sought to be united around the *Sea King*.

Men lined her rails, watching, fearing and praying.

Charley was among them, conscious that it was he who had brought them to this fate.

The ship shuddered under the first onslaught of the heavy ice on her port side. Then came the second tremor. John felt the deck tremble beneath his feet; the movement caused by the pressure of the heavy ice on the starboard side. The grinding of the ice and the moaning creak of timbers sent alarm coursing through every man. Then the pressure on the ship eased.

'Report, Mr Varley!' John yelled.

'Heavy ice ahead has ceased to move. Port and starboard are filled with heavy ice as far as the eye can see. We are trapped, sir, well and truly trapped!'

John glanced at Chapman. 'The *Sea King* rode the ice well. She's settled firmly with only a slight list to starboard. Held like this we might . . .'

But the length and gravity of Varley's report spelled doom in the minds of the crew. The atmosphere on board had changed completely; now it bowed to their inevitable fate.

The predictions that Stephen had received from the fishermen along the quay proved to be true. The day of the planned picnic dawned with the promise of pleasant early-autumn weather. He arrived with the carriage complete with rugs and a mouth-watering picnic.

There had been no opposition from their father when the sisters had informed him of Stephen's invitation. Benjamin saw it as a good way of keeping alive in Stephen's mind the likelihood of a business deal between them, something that was looking more and more appealing as he summed up what the loss of the *Sea King* would mean. Though it did not present a total disaster, as far as his business was concerned, he would need to recoup that loss in some way and maybe Stephen offered his best chance.

'Is your father not here?' Stephen enquired when he arrived at the Brook residence.

'He left his apologies,' replied Arabella as they rose from their chairs in the drawing-room.

'Tell him I'm sorry to have missed him. I'll catch him one day soon at his office. I must say, I'm glad that he is showing interest in work again. The situation is not eased for him by not knowing for sure the *Sea King*'s fate.'

'True,' agreed Arabella. 'He hinted one evening at dinner, most unusually for him, that there was the possibility of a business deal with you. If that is so, I must say we are grateful to you.'

'I think it may be of mutual benefit to us both,' concluded Stephen as they neared the front door. 'But enough of business! It's a fine day, let us enjoy it.'

'It looks as though we are going to have to go on our own,' laughed Arabella. 'Where are my sisters?'

'Does it really matter?' said Stephen, with a twinkle in his eye.

'I think we would be in deep trouble if we left them behind,' she responded with a smile.

As if on cue Harriet and Sarah appeared on the landing. Seeing Arabella and Stephen in the hall, they raced down the stairs, laughter in their eyes and apologies on their lips.

'Good day to you both.' Stephen's smile encompassed the two of them. 'I was about to compliment your sister on her dress, but now I will offer a general encomium.'

They felt slightly embarrassed about their individual

feelings as his eyes swept from one to the other, appearing not to linger but imparting the information that everything he saw was very much to his liking.

Arabella, smoothing the front of her pale blue ankle-length dress, looked shyly at the patterned carpet. It seemed to her that Stephen knew she had picked a dress that emphasised her small waist just to impress him. As she looked up she caught a twitch of his eyebrow but could not read its meaning. Was that done on purpose to make her wonder? She shook the puzzle from her mind, chiding the thoughts brought on by this man's searching eyes. Wasn't it only about three hours ago that she had sat on the window-seat in her bedroom and wept for the morning sun?

'That is a charming dress, Harriet,' he commented, letting his gaze dwell on it.

She was delighted by his observation; she had taken special care in making her choice and was glad that the colours obviously appealed to him.

'The dark green suits you, but your choosing to mingle it with pale pink shows a bold belief in opposing colours. I believe that reveals you have a similar bravery about many other things in life.'

She read the twinkle in his eyes, directed just at her, as a hidden suggestion that might be fulfilled in the future. She blushed as she turned to Arabella and said, 'Capes?'

'It looks like a beautiful morning but I think it wise to take them,' replied her sister, bringing the conversation back to everyday matters.

'And you, Sarah, have chosen a dress that suits your personality perfectly,' Stephen told her.

'And what might that be?' she asked coyly, though bereft of any real desire to know.

Stephen was not only taken aback by this but puzzled, too. He sensed he was not having any effect on this girl in the way he had on her sisters, especially Harriet. He weighed up his answer quickly. 'That shade of pale grey, a most charming colour in my humble opinion, indicates you like a quiet life.'

'I do,' she replied.

'No young man in it?'

She hesitated. Her eyes dimmed as thoughts of what might be happening in the Arctic flooded her mind, and she recalled the tears she had shared with Arabella but a short while ago.

'Ah, I see there is,' put in Stephen quickly, his voice laced with apology. He went on in a gentle tone, 'You obviously do not want to talk about him. I apologise. I do not wish to probe.'

Sarah smiled wanly and with an inclination of her head accepted his apology. 'The matter is closed, Stephen.'

He bowed his acceptance.

'Now, let us enjoy the day!' she suggested brightly.

Stephen swept his right arm in front of him as he made an exaggerated bow to them and said, 'Young ladies, your carriage awaits you.'

As he escorted them to the carriage and saw them comfortably seated he was pleased with the start to the day. In these few moments he felt he had learned much more about them to add to the impressions previously gained at the dinner party, all of which could be helpful in expanding his dealings with their father. He was particularly pleased that the sombre attitude he might have expected after the loss of the *Sea King* was not being allowed to surface, especially in Harriet who, so far as he

242

knew, had suffered the loss of her betrothed. She appeared to have accepted that loss. He sensed in her a desire to get on with life – the same trait he so admired in Pamela.

Stephen took the reins and guided the horse out of Whitby. He kept the conversation flowing easily, learning more about the town and this family in particular as he did so.

Nearing Robin Hood's Bay, he found a track that took them closer to the cliff edge. Negotiating it at a walking pace, he found a hollow that gave them a view across the bay to the high cliffs at Ravenscar.

'Are you happy to picnic here?' he asked.

'Yes,' answered Sarah.

Arabella and Harriet nodded in agreement.

'Then here we will stay,' cried Stephen. He jumped from the carriage and helped each girl to the ground with a smile on his face.

'Let me help you,' Harriet offered when she saw him taking some spare rugs from the carriage.

With everyone taking something, they soon had the rugs spread on the ground and then hauled out the picnic baskets.

'Be careful with that one, it sounds as though it contains bottles,' warned Arabella.

'This one's heavy enough to feed an army!' Harriet could not wait to see what it contained. 'Come and look at this,' she called. The others crowded round and stared in amazement at the quantity of food.

'If we are going to unpack it to see what the good landlord has provided, we may as well start eating now,' said Stephen with a chuckle.

'It's earlier than we usually eat,' Arabella pointed out.

'Well then, we can eat again later,' said Sarah.

'A good idea,' agreed Stephen, happy to go along with this. 'Then we won't offend those who have prepared such a feast.'

'Let's open the other baskets first,' suggested Arabella.

One contained plates of various sizes, another glasses and cups, and a third held four bottles of wine, a bottle of champagne, and four bottles of cordials. Laughing over this largesse, they set about revealing the contents of the food basket and placing them on plates: beef and ham beautifully sliced, tongue, individual meat pies, salad and pickles. For dessert, stewed fruit, a blancmange, a fruit pie, biscuits, cheese and butter, and cakes.

'The good landlord has done us well,' commented Stephen.

Harriet and Sarah were speechless.

'My goodness!' exclaimed Arabella. 'We'll never eat all this!'

.

'Timpkins, if my calculations about our drift are correct we shan't be near any land for a considerable time, so our chances of using that old gun of yours to help supplement the rations have gone.'

'Aye, sir,' replied the cook miserably. 'The few birds we shot soon after getting fast were scrawny things, but they helped.'

'So what have we left now?'

'As you know, sir, we were nearing the end of our voyage so stocks aboard had run low. Very low really. We never expected this.' He gave a gesture of resignation. 'We have biscuit and salt meat; they aren't in the best of condition but they'll have to do. I also have flour and dried fruit, but not a lot.'

'We'll have to put the men on hard rations. We could be frozen in for nearly six months unless this severe cold relents sooner. With that in mind, instigate an allowance per man immediately; no exceptions.' He saw a query come into the cook's eyes and pointed a finger at him. 'I mean *no* exceptions.'

Timpkins knew exactly what this meant, and that he should not dare to slip an extra biscuit into the captain's rations. 'Aye-aye, sir.'

When the door of his cabin had closed behind the cook, John looked at his first mate, who had been witness to this order. 'The men may grumble at starting a rationing system right away, but I think it best.'

'I agree, sir. Timpkins will be scrupulous.' Mose paused then mused, 'I wonder what they'll be having . . .'

John saw the wistful look in his eyes and cut him short. 'Don't think about it, Mose!' His lips twitched. 'Biscuits and salt meat, with fruit pudding for a treat? It could be worse.'

Arabella gave a long contented sigh as she lay back on the rug along with the others, the remains of their picnic spread around them. 'I enjoyed that. I won't want to eat again for a week!'

'I'll bet you won't resist the cakes later,' said Sarah, staring up into a blue sky. The autumn sun warmed them, adding to the mood of contentment that had settled over the group. Two empty bottles lay on the grass beside them. Arabella closed her eyes, just for a moment . . .

17

9 October 1833. It has been a splendid day. The weather was good for our picnic near Robin Hood's Bay. But I feel guilty now. I was enjoying myself while Jim was far away. Oh, where are you, Jim? Are you all right?

Stephen, propped on one elbow, gazed across the bay where the sea lapped lazily against a long sweep of sand. The picnic had been more than satisfying, particularly the bottle of excellent wine he had shared with Harriet. Aware of her sitting a few feet away, he moved his head to bring her into his line of sight. She sat with her feet drawn up, her arms around her knees. Her pretty dress splayed out around her, a pool of green and pink. Her gaze was far away and he wondered where it had taken her. Maybe to the beau she had last seen on the *Sea King*, leaving Whitby for the Arctic. But he would not probe.

He was beside her now, glancing at her sisters. They were both asleep, no doubt replete after the more than satisfying meal and warm sunshine. Catching Harriet's eye as she turned her head, he could not resist whispering, 'Would you accompany me on a stroll along the cliff?'

She nodded. He put one finger to his lips and glanced

at Arabella and Sarah. Harriet smiled. He rose to his feet beside her, paused to survey the sleeping forms and gave a nod of satisfaction. He took Harriet's hand, helping her to her feet, and started along the path that ran beside the edge of the cliff.

There was something reassuring about his touch, firm, supportive, yet gentle and caressing.

Harriet realised that this was the first time she had been completely alone with a stranger. Well, almost a stranger. John was far from her mind now; he was lost and she was free to shape a new future. A handsome young man was walking beside her, holding her hand.

But where would her thoughts have taken her had she known that at this very moment Stephen was recalling the attractive, vivacious woman he had left in London?

Arabella's eyes flickered open. Where was she? Then realisation flooded back. The cliffs near Robin Hood's Bay. She relaxed in the sweet ambrosia of contentment. The blue sky above remained unmarred. The sun had moved but still it warmed her. She lay wrapped in a feeling of peace. She did not want to move; wanted to remain like this forever. But lost as she was in an unreal world, she nevertheless became aware of someone beside her. She turned her head slowly and saw Sarah still fast asleep. Arabella looked lazily around then. Harriet? Stephen? They weren't there. They must have gone off together. Why did Harriet have to be so flirtatious? Did she want Stephen now? For the briefest of moments alarm bells rang, but they were quickly supplanted by memories of John. Arabella sank down again and let her mind wander back to the days when she and John had shared picnics.

As children they had run, played, and helped set out the food. Recalling one occasion when John had fallen and sat down in the blancmange, Arabella smiled to herself and revisited more of her favourite memories.

There had been a picnic on the beach when he had found an old box floating in the water. He had jumped on it, yelling, 'I'm captain of the *Star*,' only for the wood to break and pitch him into the water . . .

Arabella jumped in alarm as the box materialised into the *Sea King*, breaking up among the ice with her men thrown into the icy water: gaunt, haunted faces filled with fear and John gasping for air as he sank to his cold grave. With her heart racing, she sat up and looked around, fearing what she might see, but it was still a sunny day on the cliffs near Robin Hood's Bay.

'This bloody cold!' The muttering came from one of the bunks in the forecastle of the *Sea King*.

'Makes my feet bloody well ache,' said someone else.

'Put more socks on.'

'Can't, used 'em all.'

Charley listened to the moaning banter that seemed to be used to try to keep the men's spirits up. Then the subject changed as he knew it would; he had heard it all before.

'Why the hell didn't the captain run with the other ships when we saw them heading south?'

'A full ship. Wanted a full ship, to impress . . .'

Charley clamped his gloved hands over his ears. He knew what was going to be said and did not want to hear it. A wave of guilt swept over him; he was to blame for all of this. They could still have escaped if they hadn't had a rescue to stage; they could still have escaped if he had stowed the axe correctly. But he hadn't, and now . . .

Harriet and Stephen walked in silence for a few minutes, getting used to being alone together. They admired the scenery, the colours of the grasses and the rocks, the seabirds screeching as they sought purchase on tiny ledges on the cliffs, the gentleness of the sea below . . . not allowing themselves to think about the power it could exert over men's lives in other moods. Harriet found her attempts at conversation about Stephen's life skirted around, as if he did not want to talk about it. While a little peeved by this she accepted his reserved attitude, believing she would gain more knowledge in time.

They had walked about a mile along the path that twisted and turned, dipped and rose, making the walk full of interesting variations. When they came upon a hollow with an invitingly smooth swathe of grass, Stephen enquired if she would like to rest a while.

She felt there was a challenge in his eyes. 'Yes, that would be pleasant.' Then she added, 'It will make the walk back easier,' but her tone implied she suspected there was more than that behind his suggestion.

This did not go unnoticed by Stephen who assisted her to the ground. When he sat down close to her, his fingers found hers again. She did not draw away. Their eyes met boldly. He drew her close and, lips meeting, they sank back on the grass.

Sarah stirred, and then came wide awake immediately. She sat up and looked around, taking in everything instantly: the remains of the picnic, no Harriet, no Stephen. Arabella?

There she was! Sarah jumped to her feet and ran silently over the springy turf. She resisted the urge to shout for fear of what it might provoke. She stopped beside the rigid figure of her sister, standing at the edge of the cliff, staring down at the sea breaking at the foot of the cliffs far below. Sarah grasped her arm. 'Come away,' she whispered.

Arabella started, looked at her with a slight smile and said, 'I had decided not to.'

Shocked that she had even considered the possibility, Sarah turned her gently away from the cliff edge.

Reading concern in her sister's actions, Arabella said in a firm voice, 'I'm all right.'

'Don't ever think about it again. You scared me. Arabella, you are needed. I need you.'

Arm in arm, they walked slowly back to the rugs without uttering another word; the bonds of sisterly love, which had strengthened between them while they wept in the mornings together, had grown even stronger in these last few minutes.

'I suppose we had best be getting back,' said Harriet, somewhat reluctantly. 'If Arabella and Sarah have woken, they will be wondering where we are.'

'You are right,' agreed Stephen grudgingly. 'We'll meet again soon, I hope.' He brushed her lips tantalisingly with his.

Her arms came swiftly round his neck and she put all the passion she felt for him into her kiss. As she let go she whispered, 'Make it sooner.'

He jumped to his feet, held out his hand and pulled her up from the ground. Harriet brushed the grass from her dress and straightened it. 'Can you brush the back,

Stephen?' she asked. He swept the grass away and then she made sure that none was left visible on his smart suit.

'There they are!' Sarah pointed to the two figures appearing in the distance.

'Good,' said Arabella. 'Let's get the cakes ready. I'm dying to try them.'

'I thought you said you'd never want another bite?' teased Sarah.

'Sleeping makes you hungry!' pronounced Arabella.

'Did you enjoy your walk?' Sarah queried when Harriet and Stephen arrived.

'Yes,' replied Harriet. 'It has given us an appetite, hasn't it, Stephen?'

'It certainly has,' he replied. 'In spite of the lovely lunch, I'm ready to do justice to that spread,' he added, eyeing the cakes Arabella and Sarah had set out.

'Why didn't you wake us?' Arabella asked. 'We could have walked with you.'

'You both looked so peaceful, we thought the sleep would do you good,' explained Harriet with a smile.

John bit into one of his daily ration of biscuits. It was hard but in a way he was thankful for that; it would last longer in his mouth.

'Did you have a pleasant day with Stephen?' Benjamin asked when he saw his daughters at breakfast the next morning.

'We did, Papa,' replied Arabella. 'The day was reasonably warm for autumn, so we were able to picnic.'

'Picnic? I didn't know it was to be a picnic.' Benjamin frowned.

'Nor did we, Papa,' put in Arabella quickly, recognising her father's displeasure. 'It was a surprise for us.'

Benjamin, still tight-lipped, nodded. 'Don't get carried away by that young man's good nature. People notice and talk, you know.' He frowned, wondering if he was becoming too lenient.

'The Angel provided a wonderful array of food,' put in Sarah with undisguised delight, wanting to temper her father's attitude.

'And Stephen was so attentive and considerate,' continued Harriet.

'And interested in everything we could tell him about Whitby and Robin Hood's Bay,' added Arabella.

'I'm pleased to hear that,' said Benjamin. Maybe it signified he was thinking seriously about establishing himself in Whitby, possibly involving the firm of Brook and Son. Benjamin's study of his own accounts and trading statistics were leading him to believe that a new connection with Stephen was highly desirable, now that there would no longer be an income from the *Sea King*.

16 October 1833. This evening Stephen took us to a concert. It was very enjoyable. I particularly liked the piano solos. I'm glad Mama made us study the piano, but it must take a lot of practice to play as well as the pianist this evening.

20 October 1833. Stephen was very attentive this evening, especially to Harriet, when he took us to see As You Like It. *It was put on by the local thespians in the large room at the Freemasons' Tavern, which they have used since the theatre burned down in 1823. We had a splendid evening, the laughter and jollification through-out the play raising our spirits. I wish Papa had accompanied us, though, it would have done him good.*

'Lucy, get yourself ready, I'm going shopping in five minutes,' said Harriet, from the stool on which she was sitting in front of her dressing table.

'Yes, miss,' replied Lucy. She left the room and made haste to get ready and be waiting in the hall.

Harriet made one last survey of herself in the mirror, secured her small bonnet with its ribbon beneath her chin and left her room. She moved gracefully down the stairs, and joined the maid waiting at the front door. Lucy opened it and Harriet sailed smoothly along the path to the Iron Gate, with her maid in her wake.

They continued in this manner to Baxtergate where Harriet slowed her pace so as to look in shop windows. She had recently received her allowance from her father. Though she had no particular purchase in mind, she wondered what might catch her eye. She enjoyed pur-chasing what she described as 'the nice things in life'. She stopped in front of a window with colourful shawls arranged in such a way as to attract customers' eyes.

Harriet pondered. 'I think that yellow one with the red border would suit me, Lucy, don't you?'

Lucy was not going to disagree with her mistress's appraisal, so merely said, 'Yes, miss.'

'Come along then,' said Harriet, and led the way into the shop. Half an hour later they left the shop with the shawl she had seen in the window and also another that had attracted Harriet with its vivid scarlet. As she'd swung it round her shoulders and viewed herself in the long mirror, with the shop-keeper and Lucy looking on, she'd felt swathed in unbridled flirtation. Stephen had come to mind then and she'd smiled at her own thoughts.

Harriet left the shop in a buoyant mood. Closer to the bridge she stopped at a shop that she knew made excellent leather attire for wearing on horseback, and also produced a fine array of gloves. It took little time to persuade herself to make a purchase there; her present four pairs were all quite worn, she decided. After trying on several pairs, she found the perfect fit and left the shop feeling delighted with her purchase.

They crossed the bridge, Lucy carrying the packages, thankful there was nothing heavy in them. Mistress and maid turned into Church Street and sauntered slowly in the direction of the Market Place. As she moved away from a shop window, Harriet stopped short. Her pulse was racing. Stephen was coming along Church Street! Immediately her mind was on that crimson shawl and the thought it had invoked. She blushed but quickly forced herself under control. She took a few steps forward, her eyes fixed on Stephen, hoping he would see her. He must; the street was too narrow for him not to, even among the flow of people moving both ways.

Then their eyes met.

'Ah, Miss Brook.' He raised his hat and smiled, wiping away the thoughtful look she had noticed previously. 'How delightful to see you.'

'Mr Waite.' Harriet inclined her head in acknowledgement.

Aware of Lucy's presence, even though she had discreetly moved a few steps away, he said, 'A shopping expedition, Miss Brook?'

'A few purchases, but I think I have bought all I want.

254

I am just window shopping now, to see if anything new is on display. And you, Mr Waite, what brought such a serious expression to your face in Church Street?'

'Thoughts, Miss Brook, just thoughts,' he replied. He showed no inclination to impart any further information, but said, 'The charm of your presence has driven them away.'

She read the teasing flicker in his eyes. 'You flirt, Mr Waite.'

'Could there be anyone more delightful than you to flirt with? Miss Brook, you said you had finished your shopping; I have no engagement; would you care to walk with me?'

Harriet, about to make an immediate acceptance, pulled herself up; she should not appear too eager in front of Lucy. It was not becoming for a young lady to seem too eager, and particularly not after his open attentions to her at the play. 'Mr Waite, I should not intrude on your time . . .'

'You would not be doing that, Miss Brook. As I said, I have no engagement looming. It would be a privilege and a delight if you would accompany me. Shall I turn round or will you?'

'To answer that implies acceptance.' She hesitated just sufficiently to make him wonder, then said, 'Very well, Mr Waite, I will. We can walk as far as Green Lane before we turn back.'

'It would be my pleasure, Miss Brook.' He bowed in acceptance of her terms.

Harriet turned to her maid. 'Lucy,' she called.

'Miss?' The girl came to her.

'Take the parcels home, Lucy. Mr Waite will escort me.'

'Yes, miss.' After only a brief glance at Stephen, Lucy hurried in the direction of the bridge.

Stephen matched his stride to Harriet's, which she carefully held to no more than a stroll, taking his arm when he offered it to her.

'I did enjoy the play and must thank you again for the outing, Mr Waite.'

'The pleasure was mine.' He held up his finger in a gesture that would brook no opposition when he said, 'I thought we were on more intimate terms than "Mr Waite".'

She pursed her lips, suppressing a smile. 'So we were.'

'And your maid is out of earshot now.'

Harriet chuckled. 'So she is, Stephen, so she is.'

Their conversation continued in this light-hearted manner. They became lost in it and in each other, almost oblivious to the activity upon the quays around them. Whitby life flowed on unabated, unaffected by two young people forging a new alliance.

Outside the house in New Buildings, Harriet invited him in but Stephen politely refused, tempering the disappointment he saw come over her face by saying, 'I enjoyed our stroll. Maybe we can do it again sometime.'

'I enjoyed it too,' she replied. 'And the answer is yes, I would love to.'

'Three days from now?' he queried.

'Most suitable,' she agreed.

'You'll be shopping again, no doubt, and dismissing your maid in the same manner?' There was a note of seriousness in his question beneath that teasing smile.

'Of course,' she replied. 'Should we meet in Church Street again?'

'Make it the west end of the bridge. I'll have you for longer if we meet there.'

She nodded her agreement and said, 'Longer still if we meet half an hour earlier.'

'Then it shall be half an hour earlier,' he replied with obvious delight. He raised his hat to her and walked away.

Harriet watched him go for a few moments, admiring the upright, athletic figure, and set her mind to wondering.

Entering the Angel, Stephen ordered a tankard of ale and requested a pen and paper. He took these to his room, refreshed himself then sat down in a chair near the window to sip thoughtfully at his ale. Was his liaison with Harriet worth the pricking of his conscience when he recalled his life with Pamela? His lips tightened. He stood up, went to the table and took up the pen . . .

Dear Pamela,
I continue to be optimistic about the possibilities
here. It is a pity that Mr Brook's decision is
delayed, but understandable. He is clinging to the
hope that the Sea King *will return. I doubt that. I*
have made discreet enquiries about his firm and
assets and am almost certain that, though he
would not now bring the same resources he would
have done had the Sea King *returned a full ship,*
he will still take up the offer of amalgamation
when I make it. I am working to that end, and
hope that when it happens you will agree the wait
was worthwhile. I am sure the partnership you
and I enjoy will prosper even more on the strength
of it.

*I hope life in London is still providing you with
opportunities for enjoyment. I am sure you will
not be short of beaux to escort you. I miss your
company, and have your wonderful alluring smile
always before me. The young women of Whitby
pale by comparison to you.*

With my deepest affection.

Ever your humble servant . . .

He sat back, re-read the letter, then signed it with a
flourish.

John was seated in his cabin, quill in hand, several sheets
of paper before him. He went to the door, opened it and
called, 'Mr Chapman!'

'Sir?' Mose spoke cheerfully as he came into the
cabin. John was thankful for a first mate who could
always present a positive appearance, even in the most
extreme circumstances. He hoped that side of his friend's
character would not be tested to the limit by what might
lie ahead.

'According to my calculations, we have drifted something like one hundred and seventy-five miles since we
became fast. Fortunately it is in the right direction – south.'

'Giving us a chance of escape sooner than might have
been expected?'

'Yes, but don't pin high hopes on that. Nevertheless,
you may relay the fact to the crew; it could brighten their
hopes.'

'Yes, sir.'

'Fortunately the drift has little effect on the stability of
the ship, and the sea has been reasonably good to us;
very little swell, though I fear it will not remain so.'

Four days later, on 12 November, John's fear became reality; the weather changed for the worse. The sun disappeared in a thick enveloping shroud of fog that sent tentacles of freezing damp on to the frozen ship. After the initial report no man ventured on deck. In the shelter that below decks offered, they experienced no upturn in morale. Contemplating their situation, they saw the fog as a portent of doom. With time on their hands, and little to do but try to respond to the captain and first mate's attempts to occupy them, they were slipping into lethargic despondency.

Anxiety was aroused more deeply in their minds when the ship shuddered and lurched. Alarm sprang to every face. Every man knew his safety depended on the strength and stability of the ship. If she foundered their lives were forfeit.

Everyone scrambled up on deck, and gasped at what they saw. The fog had completely disappeared, dispersed by a keen wind. The *Sea King* was thankfully still held fast in heavy ice, but they stared in awe at the huge iceberg that loomed ahead on the starboard side, thankfully still some distance away. The pressure of the wind was forcing it against the sheet ice, causing it to send ridges before it. One of these ridges had been driven against the ship, with the effect they had all felt. The men stood as if frozen along with the ice that covered the ship, staring at the massive berg, hoping that something would make it release its pressure. Ice ground ominously against her side but the *Sea King* held fast, resisting the attempt to crush her.

Not a word was spoken; the men watched as if in a trance, their own fate visible in front of them. How long for, no one knew. Then: 'The berg's moving!' Who had shouted? No one noticed. But everyone heard and hung on the words, realising they carried the hope of release. Seeing the berg caught by the current and the changing direction of the wind, a cheer rang out from every man on board. They saw safety for the moment and ignored the long-term possibilities. They cheered and cheered, clasped each other's hands, and some even danced a little jig.

A cry of pain cut through the cheers. A seaman lay sprawled on the deck. In a moment the captain and first mate were beside him.

'Hollis?' John queried.

'Ankle, sir,' gasped Hollis, his face wreathed in pain. 'Slipped and went over on it.'

'All right. We'll get you to your bunk.' John delegated three men to do that, and within minutes Hollis was in his bunk with his swollen ankle made as comfortable as possible.

'The first real casualty,' commented John when he and Mose went to the captain's cabin.

'Aye, sir, but . . .'

'Let's not think of what may be upon us in the future,' cut in John. 'See that Hollis gets all the attention he requires.'

Three days later, when they met for their daily review of the situation, Mose reported on Hollis's situation. 'He is doing well, thanks particularly to Charley Brook.'

'Brook?' John looked askance.

'Aye. Charley has kept constant watch on him, and has made Hollis do as he is told. Seems Charley suffered a similar sprain to an ankle. He recalled what Miss Arabella did, and has applied it to Hollis.'

John gave a grimace of surprise and added the question, 'Frostbite?'

'Charley's watching out for that too after I told him the symptoms; so far, so good.'

When the door closed behind Mose, John sat back in his chair looking thoughtful. Arabella. That mention of her name had not only stirred memories in him but brought a picture of her vividly to mind. It was almost as if she was there, wanting to tell him something, but because of something he had done was unable to do so. What was she going to say, and what had he done to prevent her? He frowned. The nagging questions faded from his mind but he was left with that picture of Arabella. He wondered again, why her and not Harriet? Finally he tightened his lips in exasperation and told himself it was only because Arabella had been mentioned and she and Charley were close.

Arabella shot up in bed, wide awake immediately. A dream? No, a reality, but far away from here. She slipped quickly from the bed, automatically swept her wrap around her, went to the window-seat and, seeing the light rising in the East, wept for John and for the morning sun to warm him.

18

23 October 1833. I'm looking forward to my day in Ruswarp with Laura's friends tomorrow. Their house overlooks the river and if this exceptional weather continues we shall have a pleasant day outside. I wouldn't worry about the weather if Jim were here; he would be my sunshine . . .

Sarah wasn't the only one who looked eagerly out of her bedroom window the following morning.

Harriet drew back her curtains and breathed a sigh of relief. The sky looked settled, with every sign that it would remain so. She hugged herself and pirouetted across the room to the mahogany wardrobe. She plucked out a dress, held it against herself, looked in the full-length mirror, pulled a face and threw the dress on to her bed. She chose another, hesitated in critical assessment, then, satisfied that this would capture Stephen's attention, went about making sure that the rest of her attire would too, not a hair out of place and fingers perfectly manicured.

She stopped at the door to her room, her hand on the knob. Realising that an outward display of exuberance might attract questions, she took a deep breath and composed herself. With that came a prick to her conscience.

Maybe John was still alive; maybe he would survive and return to Whitby and claim her as his betrothed. What then? She stiffened. Such thoughts were absurd; there was no chance that anyone could survive an Arctic winter. And she was certainly not going to miss the chance of cultivating a man like Stephen. She already felt sure he liked her and would make quite certain she was right.

'Where's Papa?' she asked, sweeping her glance across her sisters as she went to her place at the table.

'He left ten minutes ago. He's going to Scarborough on business.'

'And I'm off now,' said Sarah, placing her napkin beside her dirty plate. 'Laura invited me to go with her and her mother to visit friends in Ruswarp.' She headed for the door calling, 'Goodbye,' over her shoulder

Harriet smiled to herself. She now knew where everyone would be, inwardly certain that Arabella would be seeing to the household duties in collaboration with Mrs Ainslie, as she did every morning, preferring to get them out of the way so that she had the rest of the day free.

'I'm going to collect some items that were being ordered for me,' Harriet informed her sister.

'Ah, yes, you said, wedding presents for Josephine.'

An hour later Harriet was walking briskly in the direction of the bridge with Lucy having to trot to keep up with her. Becoming aware of this and not wanting to appear too eager to meet Stephen when they 'accidentally' came face to face, she slowed her pace. Lucy breathed a sigh of relief and drew deeply on the fresh sea air.

They crossed the bridge and entered a shop in Church Street where Harriet found her order ready. She passed a few minutes in conversation with the owner of the business, who was always ready to oblige and cultivate the Brook girls; they were good customers and conducted their shopping in the considerate manner of their late mother.

Lucy picked up the parcels and followed Harriet from the shop, hoping the rest of the morning would be spent at this more leisurely pace. Her wish was fulfilled. Harriet sauntered along, pausing to look in shop windows or to pass the time of day with friends, but always moving in the direction of the bridge. Reaching it, she was careful not to let Lucy see the way she scrutinised the people crossing the bridge in their direction . . . and especially those at the far side.

Harriet's heart began to flutter with anxiety. She could not see Stephen. He should be close by now. She was sure she had timed her arrival correctly. She reached the West Side; she would have to keep walking. If she hung about Lucy would become suspicious.

'Good morning, Miss Brook!'

Harriet was so lost in her dilemma that she jumped and. She swung round. 'Oh, Mr Waite!'

'I'm sorry if I startled you, Miss Brook, I did not mean to,' he said with a polite bow as he raised his hat.

'Apologies are not necessary, Mr Waite,' she replied, stepping to one side so that the flow of people off the bridge was not impeded.

He moved with her and said, 'This is no place to carry on a conversation. If you would like to continue, may I suggest that you walk with me?'

'That would be most pleasant, Mr Waite.' She turned to Lucy who had remained within earshot due to the pressure of passersby. 'Lucy, you may go now. I'm sure Mr Waite will see me home?'

Lucy cast a quick glance at him.

'Of course, Miss Brook, it will be my pleasure,' returned Stephen with a polite inclination of his head.

Lucy caught Harriet's eye and knew she was dismissed.

With the girl swallowed up in the crowd, Stephen said, 'That was very neatly done. Now I suggest we return to the East Side.'

'That sounds as though you have something in mind?' asked Harriet coyly.

Stephen made no reply but guided her through the throng of people on the bridge and, once they reached Church Street, turned her in the direction of the quays. Twenty yards farther on he stopped her beside a carriage that was attended by a driver.

'Your carriage awaits you,' Stephen told Harriet with a sweeping bow.

'Oh!' She could only gasp at this unexpected development and turned wide, enquiring eyes on him.

'Let me help you.' He offered his hand; she took it and climbed gracefully into the carriage. Once he had seen she was comfortable Stephen settled beside her. He turned to her. 'Ready?'

'Yes,' she nodded. 'This is so unexpected.'

'And approved of, I hope.'

'Of course,' she replied, but left a query in her eyes.

'I thought a little privacy might be acceptable,' he explained.

'Approved once more,' she returned. 'And where are we going?'

'I've told the driver to take us to the clifftop near the ruined abbey, and then maybe . . . well, we can decide as we go.'

The driver did not hurry the horse but let it make its own

time, climbing to the top of the cliff. There he turned it along the track that led away from the ruins. He kept the pace leisurely, giving Harriet and Stephen time to enjoy the spectrum of colours dancing in the waves far below, changing with every undulation of the restless sea.

'That's a view I would never tire of,' Stephen commented.

'You'll be able to see it often if you settle in Whitby,' said Harriet. 'Is that your intention?' she added quickly, intent on supplementing the little she knew of Stephen Waite.

'I have not decided yet. So much depends on your father so far as my business plans are concerned, and he is waiting until he has definite news of the *Sea King*.' He saw her frown at this and added, 'I'm inclined to agree with you but I must respect his wishes.'

'And if what we both know to be the truth is confirmed, does that mean you will forget the possibilities you now see in Whitby?'

'No. I think the town offers great trading potential and, if at all possible, I want to be part of that.' He allowed a slight pause to fall but before she could speak went on, his eyes firmly on hers, 'There are other incentives for me to stay, of course.' As he was speaking he reached out and took Harriet's hands in his, drawing her slowly towards him. Their eyes and hands were locked together until their lips met; then Harriet released her hold and slid her arms round his neck. She felt his arms at her waist, and they met kiss with kiss.

On their slow drive back to Whitby, a charged silence that neither of them appeared to want to break settled between them.

Harriet felt flattered that this handsome man beside her

should find her attractive; that a man of the world such as he should desire the company of someone whose life experience centred round this Yorkshire port. She felt easy with him, protected, and at the same time yearned to know him better. His kisses had told her he wanted more of her, too.

Stephen had been attracted to Harriet from the first moment he had seen her but knew that he should be cautious. She was betrothed, though now he knew she regarded herself as free from any obligation because she firmly believed she would never see John Sharp again. He liked the effervescent personality of this girl who knew she was pretty and would unashamedly use all her wiles if she set her mind and heart on someone; from her kisses Stephen sensed he was that someone. He knew she was Benjamin's favourite daughter. Maybe he could turn that to his advantage, though he would have to tread carefully; Benjamin still retained the hope that somehow the *Sea King* would have survived, and if it had there could be another problem – John. In the meantime . . . Stephen let his mind race ahead.

After the horse and carriage returned to the White Horse in Church Street, he walked Harriet back to the house in New Buildings. When they were parting at the garden gate, he kissed her lightly but found himself trembling with a passion that communicated itself to the girl whose hand he held. 'Same time, same place, next week?' he asked, eyes narrowing with challenge.

Harriet tossed her head. 'I can't wait that long. We'll meet the day after tomorrow.'

'Captain, the men are showing more and more signs of despondency. We haven't enough tasks to keep their minds occupied.'

'Yes, the signs have been worrying me too. I reckon we can start laying in a supply of wood from the ship's timbers to keep the fire going, but it will have to be done carefully, so as to maintain the ship's stability.'

'Yes, sir. I have been giving that some thought.'

The two men formed plans for this course which they expected to have to put into operation within the next two weeks.

'So that is settled, Mose. Now what about improving their minds – are the Bible classes we started going down well?'

'Yes, sir, though they aren't to everyone's taste, and even the most ardently religious get tired of the Good Book being pushed down their throats.'

'Then we'll alternate the classes with reading sessions . . . find out who brought books with them . . . but we'll continue with our morning prayers. We must pray that God in His wisdom will bless us with the miracle of survival.'

'Amen to that, sir.'

'And we must see that the men are not overworked – with food rationed they will begin to lack stamina. Have they made any complaints?'

'Only the usual curses against this terrible land. Everyone swearing they'll never come whaling again, and wondering why they ever did in the first place.'

'It's in the blood, Mose.'

'Aye, it is, otherwise you and I would never have set foot on a whale-ship again after our first voyage.'

'Any other complaints?'

'Some men, the weaker ones, are complaining of dizziness. Most of those don't want to make an effort.'

'Lack of food, Mose. Any chance of an increase in

rations?' Even as he said it, John knew it was a stupid question. He shook his head. 'Of course there isn't.'

He was about to stand up when the ship shuddered and an ominous grinding against the starboard side brought prolonged expressions of alarm from the two men. They hurried on deck to size up the situation. Nearly all the crew were there, drawn by the alarming sound. John saw terror in many faces. The unearthly noise that could spell their doom played on everyone's emotions.

He and Mose felt some measure of relief when they saw that the situation was not as bad as it had sounded below deck. A quick assessment told them the movement had been caused by an increase in the strength of the wind and a change in its direction, but that the ship was maintaining its position in the ice.

'We're holding,' said John. 'Reassure them.'

'Aye-aye, sir.' Carefully keeping his balance on the ice-covered deck, Mose moved among the crew, endeavouring to settle everyone's fears.

'Varley!' John's call rang through the icy air.

'Aye-aye, sir.' The sailor was quickly beside him.

'Aloft. The change in the wind might have opened up some lanes.'

'Aye-aye, sir.' Varley moved to the bulwark.

'Careful how you go.'

The sailor appreciated his captain's concern, knowing he had seen how treacherous the frozen ratlines could be.

John waited, watching his best lookout climb steadily until he reached position at the masthead.

Varley's sharp eyes searched the frozen seascape, thankful that the atmosphere was wonderfully clear, but he saw nothing that gave him hope.

'A frozen world, sir,' he yelled.

'Any signs of a break-up, a lane, a glimpse of water?'

'None, sir. But ice is piling to starboard . . . could be trouble if it moves this way.'

'Keep your eye on it for a short while.'

The sound of the ice grinding upon itself sent a chill through every man, and when it moved against the ship that chill turned to fear.

It was to haunt them for days, draining them of sleep and hope.

John, alone in his cabin, succumbed to the same despondency as his men. Their chances of survival were diminishing with every passing moment. He tried to focus his mind; imagine the worst scenario and plan his survival. Then returning to Whitby and marriage to Harriet . . . If the *Sea King* fell victim to the ice and they all perished in this, the loneliest part of the world, what would become of Harriet? Would all that vivacious, sparkling promise be snuffed out too? No, a flame such as she should not be dimmed, let alone extinguished. His vision of her was still bright in his mind as he fell into a doze.

Ten minutes later he felt a touch on his shoulder and came wide awake. He was alone in his cabin. He must have been dreaming. Yet he felt certain . . . his mind spoke one word then: Arabella. It should have been Harriet. Why her sister? The query loomed large in John's mind and bothered him; it was almost as if he was being unfaithful to Harriet, and yet he felt no guilt that thoughts of Arabella occupied his mind. Had she really been there, trying to tell him something, giving him hope for the future? He would not have been surprised. That had always been Arabella's way.

Far away, two sisters awoke with very different thoughts on their mind.

Harriet's were concentrated on the day ahead, viewing it with excitement; she was meeting Stephen Waite, the handsome man any girl would be proud to have as her escort. His prospects in Whitby looked good, especially if he could link his business with her father's – she would want for nothing then. Stephen was here, alive and seductive; John lay frozen in the icy wastes far, far away or else in a deep watery grave. She had mourned him briefly, and then convinced herself that he wouldn't want her to be miserable. Harriet slipped out of bed and went to choose a dress that would flatter her figure.

The early-morning light awoke Arabella as it had been doing every day since the loss of the *Sea King* had seemed inevitable, and with it the loss of the man she loved. She turned back the bedclothes, draped a robe around her shoulders and walked slowly to the window-seat, sending her thoughts far to the north. She sighed, watching the pale eastern light filter through the high, thin clouds, bringing a new day to Whitby. It was just another day to her – monotonous; unfulfilling; not the future she had dreamed about.

Arabella brought herself up short then. She should not think like that. The poor unfortunate men of the *Sea King* would have given anything to be in her position! Her eyes dampened and tears started to trickle down her cheeks; concentrating her mind on the crew, she prayed for the morning sun to shine on them and drive away the Arctic night.

'No maid to escort you?' commented Stephen when Harriet greeted him beside the carriage; he had the driver conveniently positioned near the bridge.

She smiled coyly. 'Easier to tell Arabella that I was

going to visit Lavinia, a friend who lives not far away, and needed no chaperone. I also told her that I wouldn't be back until this afternoon.'

Stephen raised a questioning eyebrow. 'So I shall have your company for longer today?' he said as he helped her into the carriage and then climbed in beside her.

'And I yours,' she said quietly, revealing her pleasure at the prospect nevertheless.

The driver, as instructed by Stephen, sent the horse along the road that was flanked by busy quays. Once they were clear of all the activity and were starting up the carriage road that led to the top of the cliff, Stephen relaxed. 'You're not due home until this afternoon?'

'That is what I said,' she answered coyly, but with a hint that she had contrived to put them in this position.

He liked that. 'Then we shall have to think about having some luncheon. I can't send you home again hungry.'

Though Harriet did not query this, she believed he had anticipated the possibility of such a situation arising. Well, she had put the bait in his way and he had taken it. Her whole body felt suffused with pleasure.

'I have found an inn just south of Robin Hood's Bay. I have cultivated the innkeeper and he will do us well.'

'So you have explored the area since coming here?'

'Of course. I like to know the full potential of any location of interest to my business.'

'But taverns aren't your business.'

'True, but I also like to know the facilities for relaxation locally. One cannot be tied to business all the time.'

'And you are finding them satisfactory in and around Whitby?'

'Yes, especially when enhanced by the company of someone like you.' He turned on the seat to face her and took hold of her hands. 'Harriet, I'm falling in love with you,' he declared.

'Stephen!' Her one word reply was laced with surprise. Even though she had been angling to hear those words, she had not expected this reaction quite so soon.

'Say you love me too? Make this a day I . . . no, we . . . will always remember?'

'Stephen, I do! I do!' She flung her arms round his neck and kissed him. He held her tight while they prolonged the embrace.

When they eventually broke apart, Harriet murmuring, 'You have made me so happy,' he suggested that they should walk a while and luxuriate in their declarations of love for each other.

They walked along the clifftop, hand in hand.

'Will you be telling your family?' he asked.

'Of course. They must be told that I'm in love.'

'I think it would be wiser to keep this to ourselves for a while.'

'Why?'

'We can't talk of marriage yet. You are betrothed to another man and your father has approved that.'

'Fiddlesticks! John won't be coming back. You know that.'

'I don't for sure, and nor do you.'

'They won't survive . . . can't survive.' Even as she spoke Harriet felt guilt creeping into her mind. She had declared her love for John by accepting his proposal. Everyone would see that as binding. But had she not accepted primarily so as to secure a future life of ease, as well as to show her power by stealing John from Arabella? But now Stephen had come into her life; he too offered her a life of ease and luxury, and stirred in her

273

feelings she had never experienced with John. She could not deny them. Harriet shook her head and repeated, to convince herself and dismiss her troubled conscience, 'They can't.'

'There is always that possibility. We should wait until we know something definite, and until then should keep our love for each other a secret. If John comes back, then you and he . . .'

'. . . would still be finished. Arabella can have him! She'll jump at the chance.'

'Arabella?'

'Yes. She and John have been close ever since his mother and father died. I think most of us and our friends thought they would marry, only John proposed to me.'

'Then all the more reason for us to wait. For your father to know now might make him less amenable to what I hope will be a very sound commercial proposition between us. He may not take kindly to my pre-empting a situation that could well resolve itself.'

'As it will.'

'Then there is no harm in waiting. We'll know by the end of March. It's not far away. So, Harriet, please, let us keep our love for each other to ourselves for now. It will be better that way.'

'What if you walk away from me before we know . . .' She let her voice trail away, and her eyes fill with tears.

He put a finger under her chin and raised her head so he could stare earnestly into her eyes. 'I would never do that, Harriet.' He kissed her lightly on the lips. At that moment she felt something was missing from his response and doubted the sincerity of his words. That couldn't be right, could it? Doubting the man you were in love with. Oh, but he was so handsome, such a catch . . .

When they were back in the carriage, he kissed her again. 'Don't let anything spoil today, Harriet. You'll see, I'll be proved right and then you'll thank me for waiting.'

But, privately, she wondered about that.

With a contented sigh, Harriet leaned back against the high-backed settle and eyed Stephen across the table. 'That was simply delicious,' she said. 'Your choice of food and wine has been impeccable . . . a credit to your planning.'

'Planning?' He looked at her with apparent surprise.

She laughed, eyes sparkling as she said, 'Don't tell me you didn't, once I had agreed to meet you again? This table was already set when we arrived, and is in a discreet part of the room as well as being made more private by these two high-backed settles.' He smiled at her without denying it. She added, 'I thank you for your consideration.'

'It has been my pleasure.'

'And long may that continue.'

He picked up the wine bottle and topped up their glasses.

'Oh, dear, the day is not so good now,' remarked Stephen as he helped Harriet into the carriage later and saw her comfortably settled. The wind had strengthened, driving grey clouds inland from a sea now flecked with white-caps. 'I'd better get you home.'

Just then the ruined abbey came into sight. Harriet gripped his hand and called out, 'I want to walk in the wind. Stop, Stephen, do! Dismiss the driver!'

Springing to the ground with an athleticism that Harriet admired, he ordered the driver to return to the

White Horse. He came round the back of the carriage, eyes taking in the graceful sweep of her back that her coat could not hide. Then he saw her, in what appeared to be one movement, untie the ribbon of her bonnet and sweep it from her head, at the same time plucking the pins from her hair and letting it flow free. He reached up to take her hands and help her to the ground. Once there she released her grip and laughed aloud.

'This is wonderful, Stephen. I love to be on the cliffs on a day like this.' She took his hand and began to walk. 'And it's even better today, sharing it with you.'

He fell into step beside her and let her set the pace. He was content enough to have her in his life but caution prompted him to watch his step. He could easily become carried away, and that might destroy his relationship with Pamela. But she was far away . . . need never know!

'Stephen, are we really going to have to wait until Father finally accepts that there is no hope for the *Sea King*?'

He stopped and turned her to face him. Placing both hands on her shoulders, he made her look into his eyes. 'That is what I think best. We have to keep on the right side of your father; he has given his approval to your betrothal to John. To break that would only antagonise his attitude towards me, which would not augur well for our future.'

Harriet stamped her foot in irritation. 'Oh, why did I ensnare John? If I hadn't, things would have been very different now.' The words were out before she realised it.

'You deliberately set out to ensnare him?' Stephen allowed his laughter to ring out into the wind.

'I had to.'

'*Had to*? I don't believe that for a moment.'

She pouted. 'Arabella was always the focus of John's

276

attention and it annoyed me. I had to do something about it.'

'But there were others who would have jumped at the chance of marrying you.'

'Oh, there were, but none could match up to him.'

'So you used your wiles to steal him from your sister?' Stephen threw back his head and laughed again. 'Maybe you'll throw me aside if someone else . . .'

'Never! No one could ever be better than you.'

He pulled her closer and stared down at her upturned face. 'You are a vixen, Harriet. A vixen. But I love you for it.'

She clung to him as his lips crushed hers, and held him tight when he would have stepped away. 'And I love you too, Stephen.'

They walked on again in a charged silence. The wind howled an accompaniment to the mysterious impulses that surged through them.

'I think we had better be getting back,' suggested Stephen. 'You don't want to be missed. And those clouds are looking a bit ominous.' So lost had they been in one another that it was only now that they noticed how the sky had darkened.

'You are right,' Harriet reluctantly agreed.

They had taken a track that ran away from the edge of the cliffs and into rough pasture. They had only covered a hundred yards of this when the first spots of rain began to fall. They quickened their pace, but it was not enough for them to evade the downpour from the sky. Within a matter of moments they were soaked.

'Quick, over there!' Stephen gripped Harriet's hand tighter as they ran towards a dilapidated stone building that had once provided shelter for grazing animals.

Panting from the exertion, with water dripping from their hair, they ran undercover. Their eyes met and immediately laughter rang out.

'You should see yourself,' said Harriet.

'You don't look any better.'

'I don't suppose I do. I'd better do something about it.' She shed her coat and glanced around their shelter. A partition the height of a man, its wood rotting, still protruded from one wall, offering some degree of privacy. Without a word Harriet crossed the dirt floor. Stephen watched until she had disappeared behind the woodwork.

Her fingers flew over buttons, hooks and ribbons until, without support, the soaked dress fell around her feet. She picked it up and flung it across the partition. Her hands moved faster, more clothes fell to the ground, and then she stepped into the open, facing Stephen. He stood bare-foot, his shirt half off, staring as Harriet appeared. She did not speak; her nakedness said more than words. Despite his earlier words of caution, the sensation that ran through his whole body then was overpowering. He tore his shirt from his shoulder, flung it aside and strode towards her.

Harriet did not move but drank in the power that emanated from his bare torso, this unbridled desire, revelling in the knowledge that she had aroused it.

He closed his arms around her, knowing she wanted to be crushed by them and by his lips.

After a few moments, still intensifying their kiss, she let her hands slide downward towards the waistband of his trousers. He stepped out of them and pulled her down with him to the cold, bare ground.

19

18 November 1833. The year draws on. Christmas will soon be upon us, but this year it will not be the same for us nor for the families of the lost crew. Their loss will blight what should be a joyful time. Dare we still hope that God may yet be merciful and the following Christmas be one of joy? I know Arabella still weeps when the sun comes up. When I hear her, I sometimes join her, hoping I bring her a little comfort, though it can never be enough. I think there are times when she wants to be on her own, and I have my own thoughts of Jim . . .

'Mr Chapman, if we weren't in such a precarious position, we would be admiring the beauty that is being revealed to us at this moment.'

'Aye, we would that, sir,' replied the first mate.

The two men had been standing together silently for ten minutes watching the light slowly disappearing from the sky, knowing that not many days hence this was something they would be unable to do. Then darkness would reign for twenty-four hours a day, until the sun once again peeped above the horizon for the first time in its new cycle of providing the Arctic with light and warmth.

'I'll do my rounds, sir. I think they appreciate seeing me.' Mose gave a half-smile. 'They like to have someone to grumble at. It keeps their peckers up a bit.'

'You're a good man, Mose.'

'We'll pull through, sir.'

John made no answer to that but fished a key from his pocket and handed it to his first mate. 'We've not a lot left but give them another plug of tobacco.'

'They'll appreciate that, sir.' He gave a little nod and left to negotiate the icy deck.

John turned his attention back to the sky and the little light that remained. What was left of the sun tinged the light clouds with a vast array of colours: red, orange, carmine, fading to saffron and lighter yellow. The sun dropped below the horizon, the colours faded, but still the sky held an intense white light that set the ice glowing as far as the eye could see, as if touched with a magical brush. John was almost overwhelmed by the beauty of the scene and thankful that he could appreciate it in spite of the precarious position they were in . . . He stiffened then, prompted by shame for entertaining such a thought. Arabella would not want him to think like that . . . He started and automatically straightened up, glancing around him . . . There was no one; only an empty frozen deck over which the white light was fading into an eerie glow. An unusual stillness surrounded him.

His lips moved without making a sound. 'Arabella.'

Her name again. He experienced an intense desire to be able to share with her the wonders he had just witnessed. His lips still formed her name and now it troubled him. Why had she come to mind and not Harriet? He realised Harriet would not have appreciated this startling natural beauty in the same way as Arabella. If only he could have combined the two sisters into one! He smiled at the thought and walked back to his cabin.

7 December 1833. Life is settling down to its usual routine except, of course, that we do not have Charley and John here, nor Jim. I miss him terribly; I had planned to tell Papa about my feelings for him and ask his permission to invite Jim to visit us at some time over Christmas. Now that will remain only a dream.

15 December 1833. The second Christmas without Mama. Hopes for the Sea King *are very low. This Christmas is going to be rather sombre. Papa, although still sad, has tried to encourage us to treat it as normally as possible but that is not going to be easy. I especially wonder about Jim and Charley. If they are still alive, what must their Christmas be like? I went shopping for presents and even bought one for each of them, just in case . . . I got Papa some tobacco, Arabella some embroidery silks and a set of needles, and Harriet a beautiful belt with a large clasp that will look so well on her slim waist. I had just reached home when Stephen arrived to say goodbye. He is going home for Christmas; will be back in Whitby in the New Year . . .*

Harriet woke on Christmas Day feeling sickly. She sat on the edge of the bed but felt the room whirl around her. She held her head and, after a few minutes, walked unsteadily to the dressing table where she sat down and viewed herself in the mirror. 'I can't go down looking like this,' she muttered to herself. 'Maybe I'll look better after I've washed and dressed.'

As she pinched her cheeks one final time she wondered how Stephen would be spending Christmas. With that thought she remembered the passion and urgency they had felt in each other's arms on that rainy day in October, and how her love for him had developed since. Her smile faded as she realised what the possible consequences could be. Dread filled her; she needed Stephen now but he would not be back until next year. She would have to face the next few weeks alone, carrying on as if there was no shadow hovering over her. She looked at the presents she had wrapped so carefully a week ago. As she picked them up she knew she would receive some in return and would have to display excitement and joy, when all the time her mind would be crying out to Stephen to help her. She drew in a deep breath, determined to keep her true emotions hidden, and strode from her room, going to the drawing-room to place her gifts on the pile under the window.

'Something exciting for me?' queried Sarah with a smile.

'Wait and see,' replied Harriet. She shuddered inwardly when she realised that these three simple words held a different connotation for her.

The day went well. After the family had served Christmas dinner to the staff at noon, they spent a lazy afternoon before dressing for their own Christmas dinner in the evening. About to leave her room, Harriet experienced a surge of nausea but fought it down and went to join the others. When they were seated at the table she managed to hide her true feelings at the sight of all the food. No one noticed her feeble appetite. With everyone singing the praises of Cook, they returned to the draw-ing-room and, with no patience to wait any longer, started to exchange presents. Expressions of delight and thanks filled the room. None were more heartfelt than Harriet's when she opened her present from Sarah. A beautiful belt, embroidered in a multitude of vivid colours, lay in her hands.

'You made this, Sarah?' she asked with surprise.

'Yes.'

'It's beautiful. I will always treasure it.'

'Try it on . . . see if it fits comfortably,' urged Sarah.

Knowing she could do nothing else, Harriet stood up and fastened it round her waist.

'Perfect,' approved Arabella.

Harriet's thoughts were racing. Maybe . . . but what about in a few months' time?

That thought was made more pressing when Benjamin gave each of his daughters a note authorising the pur-chase of a new dress of their choosing. Harriet thought hers would have to be something rather special if it were to cover up the condition she dreaded to find herself in.

John, sitting in his cabin, pictured what might be hap-pening in that same house. He singled no one out for his special attention but rather drew on the familiar; a leisurely meal with pleasant conversation which would be carried on afterwards in the drawing-room. The fire would be burning brightly, the room warm, the atmo-sphere cosy. Mr Brook would return to his study, the others would play cards, read, sing around the piano or maybe just listen to Arabella playing . . . he thought she was the most accomplished pianist. Arabella! There, he had thought of her again. He criticised himself for that.

Harriet, if she clung to the hope that he could survive, may even now be planning their wedding. Marriage? He tried to stop the little niggling doubt that came into his mind then. Annoyed with himself, he got to his feet, put on an extra layer of clothing and went outside.

He was thankful that the wind had dropped somewhat but it still had the strength to unite with the sea and cause the ice to move, something that seemed unceasing in this desolation. The sound of the grinding of ice on ice, or ice on ship's timbers, was disconcerting. He had to keep the men constantly alert to the dangers that could result from their perilous position. Careful watch had to be kept for any damage to the ship's seams; the pumps had to be manned continually, not only to pump out water that if left aboard could hasten the ship's end, but in order to keep the pumps from freezing up and becoming useless.

The first mate appeared beside him. 'I've been for'ard. I don't like the way ice is piling up on the fore-quarter. It's as high as the rails . . .'

'All right, let's call the men out. We must push it away when it threatens to come over the bulwarks. If any spills over and accumulates on deck, we are doomed. I know the men are weak from lack of food, exhausted with all they have to do to try to keep this ship intact and stable, but . . . There's no need for me to say it, Mose. Come on, let's rouse 'em.'

A few minutes later grumbling men, resentful of their captain's and first mate's cajoling, came on deck and slithered and slid to the bulwark and the offending ice. They knew what to do; they had done it before, but that made it no easier this time. John and Mose worked beside them, knowing that the men appreciated this.

After an hour the ship's groans grew louder. 'She's moving!' someone shouted.

'Hold hard!' yelled John.

Men stopped pushing at the threatening ice, thankful for the relief.

The ship swung slowly under a different pressure from the encroaching ice. Men held their breath, fearful of break-up but hopeful of more stability. For some awful moments the ice, sea currents and strengthening wind seemed undecided what to do. Then they relented and ceased to contest the invasion by humans of the natural world. The ice held the *Sea King* firmly, the sea eased its drift and the wind no longer threatened.

'Well done, men!' called John. 'An extra dram of grog tonight. Just a drop . . . we must keep some for Christmas Day.'

'Aye, if we're still here,' muttered someone under his breath so that no one heard what might be considered a prophecy of doom.

20

7 January 1834. Stephen is back in Whitby. He arrived late yesterday and visited us today. It was good to see him again and I certainly noticed a lifting of spirits after the quiet Christmas and New Year we experienced . . .

'Harriet, Sarah and I are going to visit old Mary Dwyer. I've heard that she is ill so we thought we'd take her a basket of food that she can manage. Do you want to come along?'

Harriet screwed up her face. 'Do I have to? You know I'm not very good at that sort of thing.'

'No, no.' Arabella raised her hands to stem any further objections. 'You just please yourself.' She turned to Sarah. 'Shall we go now?'

'Why not? Mid-morning should be a good time.'

The two sisters left the drawing-room where they had just finished their mid-morning chocolate. As the door closed behind them Harriet pursed her lips thoughtfully. This could be just the opportunity she wanted. She sat for a few minutes, pondering what she would say, and then rose from her chair and headed for the stairs. Arabella and Sarah were crossing the hall to the front door. When it closed behind them, Harriet hurried to her room, grabbed her outdoor coat and bonnet, and a few minutes later was heading for the Angel Inn.

'Good day, Miss Brook,' said the landlord. 'May I help you?'

'Is Mr Waite here, by any chance?' she asked calmly, as if it were a matter of course that she should want to see him.

'Yes, miss. I've just seen him go into the smoking room. Would you like to wait in the small parlour and I'll tell him you are there?' He indicated a door to her right.

'Thank you.' Harriet went into the room. It held a small, round dark oak table with four matching chairs in the middle of the floor, and fixed seats along three of the walls which were of dark panelling. Harriet found the whole effect depressing. It seemed to weigh heavily on her. The door opened then and Stephen came in.

'This is a surprise, Harriet. I didn't expect to see you so soon.' He kissed her on the cheek and was surprised to feel how tense she was.

'I have something I want to ask you.'

'Go ahead then.'

'Not here. This room is too depressing.'

'Then wait. Three days from now we will be able to have our usual room near Robin Hood's Bay. That inn has happy memories for us . . .'

'No, I need to ask you before then. Can we walk?'

'If that is what you wish. I'll get my coat and hat.'

She nodded.

He was soon back, dressed to combat the sharp air and the breeze blowing from the sea. There were a few breaks in the grey clouds overhead and no rain.

'Where would you like to walk?' Stephen asked.

'The West Pier,' she replied quickly.

'The breeze will be fresher there.'

'Let's find out.' Harriet stepped out and he matched his stride to hers.

The walk beside the quays, sheltered by the cliff, was pleasant, but once they left the protection of the land the breeze tugged at them more strongly. Stephen made no comment. He respected Harriet's desire to remain silent. He was curious but knew he would hear soon enough what she wanted to ask him.

As they moved on to the pier she removed her bonnet, ran her hands through her hair and let the wind catch it up behind her. How impulsive she was, always seeking freedom, but the next moment he found that he was wrong.

Harriet placed one hand on his arm and turned him to face her. He found himself looking down into a very solemn face.

'Stephen, can we make our love known to the family?' she asked, leaving him in no doubt that she meant it.

He looked astounded. This certainly wasn't what he had expected to hear. He frowned. 'I thought we had talked about this? We decided to wait until March, when Whitby's whale-ships are in Shetland on their way to the Arctic. They may glean some news of the *Sea King*, if there is any, and send it back to us.'

'I know we did, but . . .'

'No, Harriet, we should stick to our plan. It is only fair on your father. In fact, on all of us.'

'But . . .'

'It's no use looking so distressed.'

Tears started to her eyes.

'And crying won't make me change my mind.'

'I'm pregnant!'

For one moment he did not seem to hear her. The whole future for Harriet hung upon his answer. The sea stilled, seagulls hung in flight, boats were held fast in the water, people frozen at whatever they were doing.

'*What?*' Stephen's voice lashed at her, his shock and disbelief betraying that he understood exactly what she had said. Anger boiled beneath the surface but he had enough presence of mind to control his feelings. Giving way to them here would not help resolve the situation. This demanded calmness. He must reason with Harriet or she might reveal the truth without his approval.

He gripped her arms and stared earnestly into her eyes. 'Are you sure?'

'Well, as sure as I can be at this stage. I thought you ought to know.'

'Yes, yes.' he nodded. 'You did right,' he added, trying to sound both approving and tender. He knew it was no good suggesting she rid herself of the child; Harriet was not a person who would approve of that course and was looking to him to do the right thing. He needed time. But first he must make sure she remained on his side and did as they had already agreed.

'Shouldn't we tell someone?' she pressed him.

'Not until you are certain . . . not until it becomes evident. Then we shall. Something may yet happen to negate any move we make now, and then we would look foolish. Far better to wait.' He took her in his arms. As they held each other he whispered in her ear, 'Trust me, Harriet,' and felt her nod.

As they walked back neither of them appeared to want to speak, but when they parted Stephen said in all seriousness, 'Tell no one, Harriet. Not yet.'

'All right,' she replied meekly, inwardly disappointed

by his reaction to her announcement. She had hoped it would be one of joy.

Reaching home, she was relieved to discover that Arabella and Sarah had not yet returned. Harriet went straight to her room and primed herself for what, to all outward appearances, would be an evening like any other in the Brook household.

Grim-faced, Stephen slammed the door behind him when he entered his room at the Angel and cursed the problems now ahead of him. Infatuation had betrayed him. Should he do the right thing and marry Harriet? But that would mean losing Pamela and a life in which he wanted for nothing. True, there were prospects in Whitby, but not guaranteed as they were in London. He knew Benjamin would be furious when he learned of Harriet's condition and could easily cut them both off to fend for themselves . . . and that he could not face, accustomed as he was to the luxury of London. Stephen's agile mind turned over every possibility of a way out of this dilemma. His hopes soared when he realised no one in Whitby knew of his London con-nections; they only knew about Bristol, and did not even know his true name, Stephen Boulton. He could return to his London life and Stephen Waite would then be lost to the rest of the world. The sooner he left Whitby the better.

The following morning, sitting in front of her dressing-table mirror, Harriet stared into her own eyes. Her lips tightened and she cursed both herself and Stephen for being careless. But after a while, her anger abating, she became more resigned. It had happened; she couldn't alter that. Stephen had said they must wait; she recalled his last words: 'Trust me.' She would have to. There was nothing else she could do.

About that same time Stephen was in his room in the Angel, putting pen to paper:

Dear Pamela,
I am sorry to have to tell you that the commercial opportunity here in Whitby has not turned out as I had hoped. It is with regret, therefore, that I inform you I will no longer be pursuing our planned venture here but will be leaving the town today. As I still believe we may be able to implement our scheme elsewhere, I will make it my business to look into further possibilities in the next couple of weeks. Wherever this takes me, rest assured I will be back in London before too long.
I hope you will approve my decision when I explain the reasons fully upon seeing you, though I will say now that I believe we would have lost money here in the long run, and that would not have satisfied either of us.
Yours affectionately . . .

Stephen sat back in his chair, re-read the letter then signed it. Having sealed it, he picked up another sheet of paper and wrote:

Dear Harriet,
I regret that I have been called away on business and will be leaving Whitby today. I am not sure when I will be back, but hopefully before long. I

will be in contact as soon as I know.
    Till then, I remain, yours affectionately . . .

He signed himself 'Stephen', sealed the letter and sat back, satisfied with the choice he had made. Then he went downstairs to see the landlord and take breakfast for the last time.

'I'm sorry to see you go, Mr Waite, but I hope you will be back again soon,' said the landlord as Stephen settled his account.

'Yes, I hope to be, Giles. I shall certainly hope to take advantage of your hospitality again, you have made me most comfortable.'

'It has been our pleasure, sir.'

In the coach bound for York, Stephen contributed little to the conversation between the other three passengers but remained thoughtful. He had only partially burned his boats. Now he must consider his future actions. He fingered the two letters in his pocket.

Arriving in York, he marvelled at the coachman's skill in guiding his four bays through the narrow streets to the York Tavern in St Helen's Square. Stephen rapidly ascertained that the coach would be returning to Whitby the following morning. 'Coachman, be a good fellow. On your return, would you please see that this letter is delivered?'

The coachman took the letter, glanced at the address, noticed Stephen handling some coins and said, 'Certainly, sir. It will be delivered tomorrow afternoon.'

'Splendid. And thank you for a good journey today.'

'Thank you, sir.'

Stephen entered the tavern, paid for his letter to

Pamela to be taken to London on the next mail coach, booked himself a room for the night and reserved a seat as far as Durham on the Edinburgh coach leaving the following day.

Harriet was coming down the stairs when Lucy turned away from the front door, which she had just closed.

'Oh, miss, this has arrived. It's addressed to you.'

'Thank you, Lucy.' Harriet took the letter and, recognising Stephen's writing, returned to her room.

She sat on the edge of her bed and opened the letter, eagerly anticipating his reassurances and expressions of love for her. The anticipation drained from her face as his brief, uninformative words cut deep. He had left Whitby, did not say where he was going nor give her a definite date when he would be back. The one small comfort she could draw from his words was that he hoped to be back before long. Now she could do nothing else but wait.

A week later, on arriving home for his evening meal, Benjamin informed them that he had received a letter from Mr Waite. 'He tells me he has been called away on business, apologises for his sudden departure and hopes we can resume our friendship when he returns to Whitby.'

'Does he say where he has gone, Papa?' asked Harriet tentatively.

'No, but his letter bears a Durham mark. However, he indicates he will be moving on from his present location. I have no idea where.'

John pulled on his jacket, crammed his cap on his head, then, finding the effort hard, paused a few moments to recover his strength. He left his cabin to go on deck, thankful there was now a little more daylight each day. It brought hope with it. Soft snow was falling but he sensed a touch of warmth in the air, though did not allow this to raise his spirits too much; he knew it could be a false herald.

Then came the news he had been dreading.

'Sir.' The first mate came alongside his captain. 'I regret to inform you there are signs of scurvy in three men.'

'Oh, no.' John raised his eyes heavenward. 'Are you sure?'

Chapman nodded. 'They are complaining of sore gums. I've seen them – swollen, tender and bleeding, and in one case some of the teeth are loose. The men are all speculating. I've tried to calm them, saying it could be the lack of food.'

John shook his head. 'Sadly, there is nothing we can do about it,' he said, his voice filled with misery and frustration. 'If it gets hold, the inevitable will happen. But, please, try and stop the men from speculating on that, otherwise their will to battle on will be undermined. Do anything you can to keep their minds off the awful consequences of scurvy.'

Chapman added a piece of more encouraging news. 'I'll boost their hopes with something: we are taking on less water and the pumps will only need to be manned once or twice every half-hour.'

'That's some relief. The men are getting weaker and physical effort is becoming more draining. I'll do my daily round now.'

John went among the crew with encouraging words, sympathy and advice. He discussed the food situation with the cook, and the fuel stock with the two men he had put in charge of the supply.

'You have controlled this very well,' he praised them. 'Keep it up and don't forget what I told you at the start: take the ship's timber with care. Remember, when we escape the ice, I want to take the *Sea King* back into Whitby. I'm sure all the crew will want me to do that.'

'Aye, sir,' they both replied.

When he went into the fo'c'sle the men sprawled on their bunks struggled to their feet. He saw the effort was getting to be too much for them and waved them to stay where they were. He and Mose spoke to each man.

About to leave the fo'c'sle, he was halted by a tremulous voice. 'Sir, may I say how thankful we are for Charley Brook's efforts?'

'Thank you for saying so,' John replied, keeping his curiosity capped until he and Mose were outside. 'What was he referring to?' he asked, eyeing the first mate.

'Charley asked me not to draw your attention to it . . . I've honoured his wishes but I knew it would get out eventually.'

'What has he been doing?'

'He's here, there and everywhere, looking to the men's needs, especially those who are least able to do things for themselves, even though his own strength is being sapped by it. He takes on anything, the most unpleasant jobs that come with sickness, and always has an encouraging word for everyone, trying to keep their spirits up.'

John felt a touch of pride in Charley. 'I'll have a word with him. Tell him he's doing a good job.'

'Sir,' Mose put on his official tone to make his request, 'please don't do that. He doesn't want you to know.'

About to ask why that should be, John halted himself when he realised. Charley was salving his own conscience for what had happened in the whale-boat.

21

14 January 1834. I've noticed this last week that Harriet has not been her usual self. Maybe she's feeling under the weather; the days have not been bright, but they'll be worse in the Arctic for the crew of the Sea King *if they are still alive. I cling to a strand of hope . . .*

'Sir, two deaths last night,' the first mate reported to his captain. 'Harvey and Coburn.'

John, his face drawn and haggard, his cheeks hollow, sighed with dismay. 'It's hard to lose crew members even though we were expecting it.' He thumped the table in irritation. 'If only we had had more food and . . .' He clamped his lips tight in exasperation. Then words exploded from him again. 'If only! If only! Oh, what's the use?' He jumped up from his chair, angry with his own attitude. This was no way to be thinking. Succumb to the despair behind those words and all hope would be gone from him. And it was still there . . . maybe only a flicker, but sometimes the smallest flame could be fanned into a fire. 'Mr Chapman, we must give those men a proper burial. Muster the crew!'

'Aye-aye, sir!'

The call to muster on deck was answered by moaning,

grumbling and cursing. The pale light cast an eerie glow across the gaunt-faced, heavily clad men gathering together on deck.

'Men!' Chapman put as much strength into his voice as he could. It cut through the cold air and brought silence to the group. 'Captain Sharp has something to say.'

'Some of you will already know that Harvey and Coburn died during the night.'

'Was it scurvy, sir?' someone shouted.

John hesitated. Should he tell the truth or not? He couldn't conceal the facts forever. Better they knew now and heard it from him. 'Yes.'

Men's hearts chilled, matching the penetrating cold that now seemed to bore into their very souls. Scurvy . . . the dreaded word! The disease all sailors feared.

'We will give them a Christian burial.' John knew he had to lead by example so added, 'I will sew them in blankets; I'll need help.' His bald statement called for volunteers. He could have delegated men to the unpleasant job but chose to put it to them on a voluntary basis, in order to make the men feel they were all there to help one other.

'I'll help, sir.' As expected it was Mose beside him who spoke.

'So will I, sir.' He saw Charley step forward then. About to say the boy was too young for this job, he remembered what Mose had reported. In that moment he knew that Charley was man enough, maybe before his time but circumstances had seen to that.

'Thank you, Brook.'

In the next few minutes John had all the men he needed.

One hour later John mustered his crew on deck again and said prayers over the two bodies which had been placed towards the bow of the ship, to wait there until there was open water for their last resting place.

It was a scene that was to be repeated twice more in the following two weeks until John felt his own strength and resolve weakening.

Stephen smoothed the collar of his chamois-coloured redingote while he waited in the entrance hall of a Durham hotel. In a convenient mirror he eyed the set of the black satin neck-cloth tied around the high collar of his white shirt. About to turn away, he paused to adjust his wide-brimmed brown beaver hat to a more rakish angle.

'Sir.' The voice beside him drew his attention away from his hat. 'The London mail came in half an hour ago. There is a letter for you.'

Stephen nodded as he took the letter from a youngster in the livery of the hotel. 'Thank you.'

'A good job it arrived before your coach is due to leave, sir.'

'Indeed it is, young man.' Stephen drew a coin from his pocket and flipped it in the air to be caught by the youngster.

'Thank you, sir. Have a good journey. And may the snow hold off.'

'I hope it does.' Stephen glanced at the clock. Twenty minutes more and he would board the coach, having reserved a seat for the full journey to London. He found a chair in the bar and ordered a whisky. Must be fortified against the cold, he justified the purchase to himself.

When he was settled, he opened his letter:

Dear Stephen,

I was pleased to receive your follow-up letter to the one you sent prior to leaving Whitby. I must say again that I was surprised you had come to the conclusion the town was not for us. Previously you had spoken so highly of the prospect of acquiring a foothold there. However, I stand by your judgement and look forward to hearing all your reasons when you reach London. I thank you also for your recent letter from Durham. I gather you are not inclined to move our business so far north. So be it. I could write more, but there is no point since I am expecting you soon. We will talk then.

I hope this letter reaches you before you leave Durham, and look forward to having you with me again.

Yours affectionately,
Pamela

Stephen smiled thinly and put the letter into his pocket, his thoughts dwelling on what might have been had he stayed in the North. As it was, his future hopes were all bound up with Pamela and London. He did not give one further thought to what might lie in store for Harriet.

That same day Harriet too received a letter. Thankful that it had arrived when everyone else was out of the house, she took it to her room, eagerly anticipating news of when Stephen would be returning to Whitby.

She sat on the edge of her bed and unfolded the paper. Her eyes started to skim the words, looking for those that would tell her when he would take her in his arms again, but after only a few seconds she froze. Shock over-whelmed her. This could not be true! Then she read on more slowly, her face turning ashen.

> *Harriet,*
> *I will never be in Whitby again. Our relationship*
> *can go no further. Do not try to find me; your*
> *search will be futile.*
> *Stephen*

*

Arabella entered the house in better spirits. Afternoon tea with a friend had been comforting; she had drawn strength from advice to cling on to hope, even though it was growing more slender with each passing day. In some ways she wished she had reached Harriet's accept-ance that the *Sea King* and her crew were lost; it would have made life easier in spite of the tragedy. But Arabella was not made that way. Without any definite news she clung to hope.

As she mounted the stairs and walked along the land-ing to her room, her thoughts dwelt on John, Charley and Jim as usual. Then she stood still. Was someone crying? She inclined her head, listening intently. She was right; the sobs were coming from Harriet's room. Her sister crying? Harriet wasn't one to give way to her feelings in that way, not unless it was something catastrophic. She would pout, sulk, appear hurt and produce an expression that was on the verge of tears, but very rarely did they flow. Something must be terribly wrong.

Arabella moved towards Harriet's door but hesitated with her hand poised to knock. Would her sister thank her for interfering? She brushed that question aside and knocked lightly on the door. There was no answer. The sobs seemed to become more muffled. Arabella pushed the door slowly open.

'Harriet,' she called quietly. 'Harriet, are you all right?' She stepped inside. Alarm surged through her when she saw that her sister lay sprawled across the bed, her head buried in a pillow and her whole body heaving with sobs. 'Harriet,' she called again as she crossed the room to the bed. Arabella sat down and placed a comforting hand on her sister's shoulder. 'What is it?' she asked soothingly. 'What's the matter?' She pressed gently on Harriet's shoulder, trying to ease her over so they could be face to face.

Harriet's hand, holding a piece of paper, flapped in front of her. Arabella took it, but before looking closer at it asked, 'You want me to read this?'

Still sobbing, Harriet nodded and twisted over on her back, staring up at Arabella to get her sister's reaction to those telling words.

Arabella read. Puzzled, she stared back at Harriet. 'What does this mean?'

'He's not coming back!' There was irritation in the voice that forced out these words.

'But what does that matter . . .' Arabella's voice trailed away. The words were self-explanatory. 'You and Stephen Waite . . .?' She looked aghast.

Harriet nodded.

'How could you?' Arabella scolded. 'It's just as well he isn't coming back.'

'But I'm carrying his child!'

The statement was like a thunderclap.

'What?' gasped Arabella.

'I'm pregnant.'

Arabella paled. She could find no words.

'Please help me, Arabella, please!' Harriet flung her arms round her sister and buried her head in her shoulder as sobs racked her body once more.

Arabella held her tight, thoughts racing. The consequences would be very serious: their father would be devastated; a family regarded as upright pillars of the community would be disgraced; fingers would be pointed accusingly; questions asked. Who is the father? Where is he? Even though many trials lay ahead of them, however, Arabella fought to bring reasoning to the situation; one of them had to, and Harriet was in no fit state.

Her whole body was shaking. 'He told me he loved me,' she wailed. 'Loved me? He used me! Used me!'

Arabella tightened her hold. 'Hush now, Harriet. Recriminations will get us nowhere. What's done is done. We have to think this through. Am I the only one who knows?'

Harriet gave a nod. 'And Stephen.'

'Then we have time on our side.' She eased her sister away so that she could look into her eyes. Arabella's heart ached to see the red rims around Harriet's eyes and their expression, pleading for help. 'It will mean you have to act as if nothing has happened. There is no visible evidence that you are carrying a child and nor will there be for a few weeks yet. You are going to have to tell Father, though.'

Harriet clutched at her sister. 'Must I?' she cried, her face creasing with terror at the thought of their father's reaction. 'He'll have me locked away somewhere.'

'I'll do my best to stop that, but I don't see how we can do anything else but tell him. In the meantime something may occur to us, and we can plan how best to approach Father. The important thing now is that you act normally so that no one queries your behaviour. It won't be easy but you must carry it off.'

Harriet looked devastated but managed to say, 'I'll try, but please be there for me, Arabella. Please.'

'I will be.'

The day that Harriet had been dreading arrived with a knock on her door. It seemed to her to herald her own doom.

Harriet opened the door and, seeing her sister's expression, stepped to one side without a word. Arabella closed the door behind her.

'I think you know we can't put it off much longer,' she said in a sympathetic tone.

'Oh, Arabella, must we tell Father?' But Harriet knew there was no other course open to them.

'We can't do anything else.'

Tears started to flow then. Arabella stepped forward and took the forlorn figure of her sister in her arms. 'I know it will be hard,' she said quietly, 'but it has to be done.'

'I could disappear.' Harriet grasped at a possible solution.

Arabella pushed her gently away so she could look into the tear-filled eyes. 'Don't ever think of doing such a thing,' she said severely. 'It would only lead to greater grief for everyone . . . most of all Father. He's lost a son, don't let him lose a daughter.'

'But he'll cast me out and lose me anyway.'

'I don't think Papa will do that. He thinks more of us than he shows. Trust him, Harriet, trust him.'

She bit her lip and nodded.

A few minutes later they heard a door open and close and recognised it as the front door.

'That'll be Papa,' said Arabella. 'Let's get it over with.'

Harriet held back, reluctant to face the terrible ordeal. Arabella took her hand. 'Come on, it's got to be done. I'll be with you.'

They went down the stairs, knowing their father would be in his study, as was his habit when he came in from work at this time.

Harriet could feel her heart pounding; she felt sure her father would hear it immediately they entered his study. She felt her nerves stretch to breaking point. She just could not face him; she'd flee here and now, disappear, never to see anyone again. But which would take the most courage? Then she felt Arabella's hand slip into hers and knew she could not let her sister face all the questions on her own.

Their knock on the door was answered by a sharp 'Come!'

Tentatively they entered the study. At this moment it seemed a gloomy, oppressive room, its dark panelling pressing down on them, its large desk seeming to set a barrier between them and their father, who was standing behind it, fingering a document with obvious irritation.

'Well?' he snapped, wondering what brought his two daughters to see him in such unmistakable trepidation. They were trying to hide the fact that they were holding hands, as if they needed to draw additional strength from eachother.

They glanced at one another.

Harriet swallowed and then the words burst out of her – not as she had planned, but straight to the point like an arrow finding the centre of its target. 'I am with child!'

A frozen silence fell. For a moment the room seemed

to have become a vacuum. Then it filled with tension and disbelief. Benjamin stared at Harriet, frowning fiercely. 'You're what?' The two words were delivered quietly but they were charged with terrible anger.

Harriet was shaking. Arabella gripped her hand tightly, hoping she was instilling some sort of courage into her. Harriet bit her lips. Averting her eyes from her father, she repeated, 'I am with child.'

Benjamin stiffened. 'Look at me,' he snapped, 'and tell me it's not true.'

Harriet raised her eyes, which had filled with tears she had somehow managed to hold back. 'I can't,' she said quietly.

This confirmation brought Benjamin's fury bursting forth. He slapped the document he was holding against his desk with such force that both girls flinched. 'You fool! What the devil ...?' He flopped into his chair. Seeing that Arabella was about to say something, he stemmed her words with a dismissive gesture of his hand and fixed his dark eyes on Harriet. 'The scandal ... the pointing fingers ... you'll be ostracised, an outcast, unable to live in respectable company. You can't expect John to marry you now even if he does survive, which is unlikely. Did you ever think of that?' Harriet looked down and let the tears flow without replying. 'Who's the father?' She hesitated. 'Answer me!'

'Stephen Waite,' she replied quietly.

'What?' The word exploded like a thunderbolt.

Harriet held out the letter she had received from him. Her father snatched it from her. He read it quickly but didn't miss a word. He looked up at his daughter then. 'He knows?' he asked.

'Yes.'

Benjamin examined all the implications. Not coming back! So there was no chance of a business deal between them. His own hope that the loss of the *Sea King* might be offset by a deal with Stephen Waite was destroyed. Or was it? Benjamin's face was set with determination. 'I will find him and bring him back! He went north from here but will have to attend to his business in Bristol. I will leave for there tomorrow. Say nothing of this to anyone, not even Sarah, until I return.' He fixed his eyes coldly on Harriet. 'God help you if I fail. It will mean putting you away . . . in an asylum, somewhere far away.'

She shuddered at the thought and tears flowed even faster.

Arabella stiffened, drew herself up, and with a determination to match her father's said, 'If you try to do that, I will take Harriet away and look after her myself. I will not have her branded a slut.' Though she was shaking inside, Arabella kept her voice strong. 'If that happens, Father, you will no longer have me looking after you. And I'll persuade Sarah to come with us. Then you'll be alone!'

'And how will you live?' he mocked.

'You forget, Mother left each of us a small legacy.'

'That won't last long,' he sneered.

'But it would give us time to find some work, paltry though that may be.'

'And what do you know of the world? You'll be back here soon enough, pleading for help.' Benjamin sprang to his feet and stormed from the room. 'You'd better hope I find Stephen Waite!' he called over his shoulder.

22

21 January 1834. Father was not at breakfast this morn-
ing. Arabella told me he has gone away on business. She
does not know when he will be back. The weather looks
like worsening. Maybe snow is coming . . .

23 February 1834. Father is not back yet. I told Arabella
I was worried about him but she reassured me that he
would be home soon . . .

1 March 1834. Father arrived home this afternoon, only
an hour ago; he looked drawn and didn't have much to
say. The journey must have been tiring and at times haz-
ardous where snow still lay on the moors. He refreshed
himself and then disappeared into his study. After half an
hour he called for Arabella and Harriet to join him. They
are still together. I don't know what is going on. This has
never happened before.

Harriet, needing help to control her trembling, reached
for Arabella's hand as they crossed the hall to their
father's study. They paused before the door and

exchanged glances, Harriet's pleading for her sister to stand by her and Arabella's conveying sympathy as well as trying to give Harriet strength to face what was in store.

Benjamin gestured impatiently to the two chairs he had placed ready for them. Untypically he fiddled nervously with a pencil, his shoulders hunched. He looked pale, gaunt, as if the blood had been drained from his veins. His forlorn look aroused Arabella's sympathy even as she waited to hear what he had learned.

In spite of her own situation, Harriet too noticed the change in her father. Knowing she was the cause of it, she wished with all her heart she could turn back the clock.

'I failed to find Stephen Waite,' he announced dejectedly.

His daughters' expressions betrayed astonishment bordering on disbelief.

'Was he not in Bristol?' gasped Arabella.

'Not only was he not there, he wasn't even known there,' replied Benjamin, annoyance in every word.

'But what about his firm?' asked an incredulous Harriet.

'It doesn't exist. Never has. Oh, there's a firm called Waite and Son, but when I went there and saw the owner, he did not know of any Stephen Waite. He said there was no Stephen in the family and never has been.'

Arabella and Harriet were both shocked into silence by this revelation.

'It seems we were all duped by him,' muttered Benjamin, with a trace of embarrassment.

'But he seemed so genuine,' commented Arabella.

'He told me he loved me.' Harriet's words were full of

emotion. Seeing a bleak and horrible future stretching ahead of her, she could not hold back the tears.

'I searched for leads in Bristol but it was in vain,' her father continued. 'From what he told me of Bristol, I believe he had been there but more likely than not under a different name. He seemed so genuinely interested in a partnership between us . . . I wonder if he had some underlying scheme aimed at taking the firm from me . . . by using you, Harriet, to that end?'

'If that was so, Father, why abandon her?' put in Arabella.

Benjamin shrugged his shoulders. 'Who knows? We could speculate until kingdom come and still be wide of the mark, but whatever or whoever it was must have had a powerful hold over him. We may never know.' He paused as if trying to banish all thoughts of the episode from his mind forever. He looked sharply at Harriet. 'Stop crying, girl! Now we have to face your dilemma.' The announcement was made with all the severity he could muster. Wanting to thrust home his authority, he continued before either of his daughters could speak: 'Her situation here is untenable. She cannot remain. An asylum far from here is the only answer.' Shock and horror were evident on Harriet's face but she dared not protest in the middle of his tirade. 'Where that is will remain a secret. We will make up some explanation for her absence. I will do my best to have the . . .' Benjamin left an almost imperceptible pause, as if he abhorred the next word 'child adopted or put into a home for such as they.'

'No, Father, no! Not an asylum!' Revulsion filled Harriet's protest.

'There is nothing else for it,' he replied coldly.

'Yes, there is.' Arabella's defiance was sharp as a rapier. 'Remember what I told you before, Father?' She did not wish to do this but knew if she submitted to his will, she would regret it for the rest of her life. 'I meant it and I still do. No matter what you say, you will not divert me from that course. I will not abandon Harriet to an asylum.'

Benjamin glared darkly at her. 'Don't you dare defy me! Your sister has brought scandal on this house and must pay the penalty!'

It was only then that Arabella realised she was gripping the arms of her chair so tightly that her knuckles were white. She pushed herself up from it, saying as she did so, 'Come, Harriet!'

She was so astonished by Arabella's boldness that she hesitated.

In that moment, shocked by his eldest daughter's defiance, Benjamin ordered, 'Sit down, girl!'

Arabella met his enraged gaze with a calm expression. 'Only if you will listen to me without interruption.'

He glared at her, growling, 'Say what you have to say.'

Arabella sat down slowly, allowing herself a moment in which to gather her thoughts. 'No one knows of Harriet's condition but us. And no one need know until it becomes obvious. That will give us all the chance to work out what is best for her and all the family. Who knows? Something may yet turn up that will solve the problem.'

'I may lose the baby,' put in Harriet quietly.

Arabella scowled at her sister. 'Give no consideration to that unless it happens naturally!'

'No more scandal,' hissed Benjamin, eyeing Harriet with a penetrating gaze that warned her not to seek to lose the child. 'Tongues wag, and there are people in Whitby who would just love to let them.'

'There is one more thing, Father,' said Arabella, sensing she had gained some measure of control. 'I think Sarah should be told. She may even now be wondering what is going on. It is unusual for you to keep us in your study for so long.'

Benjamin pondered a moment. 'I suppose you are right. Arabella, you explain to her.'

She took that as a dismissal, nodded and rose from her chair. Harriet followed her sister's lead but paused at the doorway. 'Father, I'm sorry. I did not mean to hurt you.'

He met her eyes for a brief moment but turned his gaze away as they left the room. When the door closed behind them, the severity of his expression faded. Dampness dimmed his eyes and he murmured, with heartfelt regret, 'Oh, Jane, I need you. Why did you have to leave me?'

23

1 March 1834. This is unusual for me – a second entry in my diary on the same day – but after what Arabella told me I just had to write some more before I go to bed so that the story will be complete. I'm glad I have been told – now I can help; I would like to. I hope a solution may be found, but if Arabella's threat has to be carried out, I have pledged myself to her and Harriet, sad as I am for Papa. What would John have made of this if he had been here?

John drowsily checked his watch and the calendar. Seven a.m., 1 March. It was a time and a date he would always remember. His door creaked open; mist swirled around a female figure standing on the threshold; sleep was driven from his disbelieving eyes. She vanished again. Harriet? Arabella? Or some shipboard haunting?

Then the cold bit into him and he remembered where he was. This was the Arctic. There couldn't possibly have been a woman here. Was it just a dream? It must have been, but he'd sensed something different about it. Whoever it was, he felt certain that she'd been trying to tell him something. He looked towards the door again. It was closed, only the early-morning light filtering through the cracks.

The ship juddered. John's mind was yanked back to the present. The ice sounded different this time. He swung from his bunk, taking little time to dress, for he slept almost fully clothed. He hauled on an extra pair of socks, pulled on the thick jersey that Arabella had knitted him, and slid his feet into his sea boots.

The floor heaved under him, sending him stumbling across the cabin. Alarm set his heart and mind racing. Was the ship breaking up? He rushed on deck, cautious to keep a foothold.

The ice was on the move! He surveyed the scene as quickly as he could. He felt some measure of relief when he saw that the ice was not piling up and encroaching on the ship. Instead it was moving in a steady drift, with the *Sea King* held firmly in its grip. Hope rose in him. Was this the first sign of a possible escape after the endless Arctic winter had taken its toll? Six lay dead, awaiting open water; the rest of the crew were emaciated, some barely able to move from their bunks. Others, like Charley, found strength from somewhere to see to the needs of their mates. The ship had been stripped of much timber to meet their need for warmth but still had its masts rising proudly, sails stowed safely in case they were needed. Now they might be! John offered up a silent prayer to God to make it so.

Mr Chapman appeared beside him. 'Mose, what do you think?' John asked excitedly.

The first mate needed no further encouragement. 'The movement is good. If it continues and there is no drastic change in the ice's hold, we may survive.'

John nodded. 'Let's tell the men. Give them fresh hope.'

The two men did the rounds, imparting their observations on the latest conditions and what they could mean. The crew received their news with relief, everyone's hopes now running high that they could escape the grip of the treacherous ice.

Twenty-four hours later, during which time the ship was held firm in the steady drift, the elements mocked them. The wind rose, driving a thick snowstorm across the vessel. The waters could do nothing but fall under the spell of the wind, and even the ice could not resist its power. The grinding and groaning, scraping and slithering sent the hopes of the crew plummeting. The unrelenting howl of the wind, and the answering chorus from the ice, brought despair to the listening men.

Though weak themselves, the captain and first mate moved continually among the crew, encouraging them, instilling confidence, listening to their hopes, and noting their requests. They found an able ally in Charley, until finally all three of them sank exhausted into their bunks.

John stirred. With the panacea of sleep slipping away from him, his eyes flickered open. He stiffened. Once again a female figure stood by the door, but before he could see her more clearly she had vanished. He came wide awake. Who was she? If an answer was to be found, it was prevented by the realisation that the wind had dropped and the ice no longer made its ominous sounds. He needed to assess their situation. In a matter of moments he was on deck. The morning sun cast a welcoming glow across the ice, which stretched ahead as far as he could see from the deck.

'Varley! Varley!' John did not hold back the urgency from his voice.

'Aye-aye, sir!'

John was thankful there was still briskness in the man's voice and that their recent trials had not taken as great a toll on him as on some of the others.

'Aloft?' John made the order more of a request; he knew the ropes could be lethal, caked as they were with deep ice.

Varley, reading and appreciating his captain's concern, nodded as he said, 'Aye-aye, sir.'

John, with Mose and Charley beside him, watched Varley climb to the masthead and awaited his observation.

'Land, twenty miles port quarter!'

'Know it?'

'Could be Disco, sir.'

'Disco!' John and Mose spoke together, their eyes bright. John saw Charley looking at him questioningly. 'Island off the Greenland coast, Charley,' he explained. 'It means our drift has always been in a favourable direction.'

'Ice?' yelled John, peering up at his lookout.

'It's solid all round, but there are no large bergs in sight.'

'Thank goodness for that,' muttered John. A few moments later he felt the wind change direction and quickly estimated it would be beneficial. Even as he thought that, he recalled his waking sight of the woman. Was she a portent of good luck? Was she watching over them in some mysterious way? Let's hope she keeps the wind blowing from that quarter, he told himself, lips moving silently, and concluded with a word of thanks. But to whom? He wished he knew.

*

315

John slid out of his bunk, only just managing to stop himself from falling. He winced as he straightened up, fighting against the pain in his back and trying to draw strength into his legs. He must not surrender now.

He struggled into his thick jacket, pulled on his cap, and went on deck. As he stepped into the cold air he saw Mose coming towards him, his usual brisk step replaced by the shuffle that was growing worse each day. But this morning John was struck by the brightness in the first mate's eyes.

'Captain! Captain!' Mose croaked between cracked lips. 'I sent Varley aloft. He signalled open water dead ahead.'

The news flooded John's mind with joy and eagerness to learn this was true. This must not be another false hope. After all his crew had endured, through a terrible winter, they deserved this to be God's answer to hopes balanced on a knife edge above the depths of despair.

As weak as he was, John must have confirmation. He mustered the energy to climb the ratlines until he could view the sea ahead and was within hearing distance of Varley's feeble voice.

'Open water about three miles ahead, sir.'

'Any threatening ice, Varley?'

'Only astern, sir, close to the ship. More to the east, but our drift is south and the wind is from the north-east. In our favour, sir.'

'God be praised!'

'Amen, sir.'

'You all right up there, Varley?'

'Aye-aye, sir. I'll keep watch for any change but it looks good to me.'

John was soon back on deck, imparting Varley's observations to Mose. Then he added, 'Let's break the news to
those confined below decks.'

Those members of the crew who were on deck were
already celebrating their possible escape from death.
Once that news was passed on to those too exhausted or
ill to be on deck, the mood aboard the *Sea King* changed.
Hope charged the atmosphere.

Two hours later they were reminded that they were not
out of danger yet when Varley reported seeing broken
masses of ice moving in from the east. The men held
their breath when, during the next hour, they ran close to
heavy fragments, some of which sent the fragile ship and
her crew's hearts trembling. But the Whitby-built ship
had a stout heart and fended off the last attempts of the
Arctic to overcome her.

That hour was a long one and relief was general when
Varley announced they were clear – only open water lay
ahead!

John, knowing that he still had a responsibility to get
his crew safely home, methodically organised jobs to
keep those who were capable occupied. He delegated
men to help Charley see to the needs of the incapacitated,
and contest the possible spread of scurvy when the frost
of the Arctic succumbed to the damp and fog of the open
water. The sleeping berths that had been coated with ice
became dripping wet as the ship, a proud skeleton
stripped of much of its timber, sailed steadily south.
John's most heart-breaking role was to confine to the
depths of the sea those who had not survived.

After escaping from the ice, they endured two more
weeks of hardship, when more fell to scurvy and those
still capable of it found the work growing harder and

harder. Finally a shout from the lookout of 'Land ahoy!' brought indescribable joy to men who had never expected to hear that cry again.

Just as indescribable was the incredulity of the small community of Ronas Voe, in the west of Shetland, at their first sight of the returning *Sea King*. Few could believe their eyes that a ship in this state could keep afloat, let alone survive a winter in the Arctic.

Help was swiftly at hand. The inhabitants of Ronas Voe organised all the aid that they could and dispatched one of their men to Lerwick to break the unbelievable news that the *Sea King* of Whitby was back, asking that word be relayed to Whitby by the first possible ship.

After a week in Ronas Voe, when the crew were offered every care and attention to prepare the ship for sea again, some Shetlanders were engaged to help sail her to Lerwick. There she was given an equally warm welcome, even though her emaciated crew presented a ghastly sight. The need for medical care and building up the men's strength was paramount.

John decided to remain in Lerwick until his crew were sufficiently recovered to sail their ship back to her home port at last.

24

5 March 1834. If we nurtured any hope of the Sea King *returning now folk would say we were fools . . .*

30 March 1834. The last of the whale-ships sailed today. They have been leaving during the last five days and all received their usual send-off, but none of us went to see them go; it would have revived too many painful memories. With their departure it seems as if the old life has ended for us. I suppose in time we will come to terms with it and be able to look ahead, but of one thing I am certain: my love for Jim will never falter; no one will ever take his place in my heart . . .

'Sir! Sir!' Jake Carter burst into Mr Brook's office without knocking. Benjamin looked up sharply, irritated by this unexpected and unusual interruption by his excited manager. 'There's a Captain Baron to see you!' Without waiting for his employer's approval, Jake turned back to the open door and said, 'Come in, sir, come in.'

A bewildered Benjamin fixed his eyes on the man who walked into his office. He was a tall and imperious figure; thin-faced with sharp dark eyes. Immaculately dressed, with his coat buttoned to the neck, he held his hat respectfully under his left arm.

'Sir, I bring you good news. I left Lerwick ten days ago, on the twenty-sixth of March. I had to put into Newcastle and was delayed, for which I apologise.' As he was speaking he held out his hand, which Benjamin took, feeling his strong grip.

'Good news?' Benjamin asked with a frown, casting a quick glance at his manager who stood fidgeting beside the door.

'Yes, sir. Your ship the *Sea King* is in Shetland!'

Benjamin felt the coldness of disbelief sweep through him. The dread of hearing confirmation of what he had long accepted as the *Sea King*'s fate still gripped his heart and tied his tongue. What he had just heard could not be true. It was impossible. Thinking this raised his ire and caused him to show hostility. 'Sir, don't play me for a fool!'

Captain Baron showed sympathy; he could understand what a shock this must be for Mr Brook. 'I do not think you a fool. Would I be standing here if the news I bring were not true?' He pressed his meaning home.

Still filled with disbelief, Benjamin sank back against his desk. 'Sir, I apologise for my reaction. Pray tell me what you know?'

'I was preparing to leave Shetland when word came that your ship had arrived in Ronas Voe and was receiving help. I was asked to call in at Whitby on my way to London and inform the owner.'

'What about the crew?' Benjamin asked, his voice full of concern.

'I have not seen them but I'm told they were in a

terrible condition. There had been deaths, which I suppose was to be expected.'

'You were given no list of survivors?'

'No. I had no contact with the crew and left Lerwick while they were still in Ronas Voe. It was expected they would be taken on to Lerwick. From what I heard about the state of the survivors and the ship, I think they will be there for a while, recuperating and engaging some Shetlanders to help sail her here.'

Benjamin nodded. 'I thank you for this news but my full joy must be tempered until I see my ship sail into Whitby and learn the condition of my crew.'

Shortly after Captain Baron's departure, Benjamin left behind his excited employees and walked home. Word about the *Sea King* had spread quickly and Benjamin had to endure the congratulations, hopes and queries of many people, until he had crossed the river and traversed the centre of town. In the quieter area his thoughts ran to his family. Had Charley survived? Was John still alive? Question after question flooded his mind until he realised he was only speculating about the possible answers. He needed Charley to step into the business he had created for the family. And John? He could be the answer to Harriet's trouble, but would he be prepared to shoulder the burden of another man's child? How he wished Jane were still with him, to share the tremendous news delivered by Captain Baron but also to give him strength and support in facing what lay ahead.

Immediately he'd entered the house Benjamin sent a maid to summon his daughters to the drawing-room. As he waited for them, his thoughts turned to the state of affairs with them. He judged himself to have been a good father – he had provided well for them, given them a good home, security – but recent events had made him see that maybe he had been too strict, too severe, and, though he loved them, had been too slow to show affection. He had always excused himself with the thought, I'm not made to be demonstrative except in privacy with my wife. Now, needing their closeness, he realised he should make an effort to overcome the barrier he had unconsciously created. He could see the first step must be to give them his full support in the uncertain time ahead when he had announced his news. Then he would have to combat the threat that Arabella had made. He had not believed that she would carry it out until he saw the three sisters supporting each other, united in their determination to confront him. Once he had considered this, he found himself pleased by their sisterly love and admiring of their resolve to see this through together. But now the survival of the *Sea King* might throw a different aspect on the situation.

His thoughts were interrupted when Arabella arrived. Benjamin indicated a chair without saying a word. Puzzled that her father was home at this time of day, she sat down primly, her hands clasped together in her lap. Harriet came in, casting a quizzical glance at her sister when her father said nothing but turned to the window and looked out. Arabella shrugged her shoulders and silently indicated that she did not know why they had been summoned. Sarah hurried into the room. As she sat down, Benjamin turned from the window.

'I have come straight from the office to tell you that a ship under the command of a Captain Baron has recently arrived in Whitby, bringing news that the *Sea King* has arrived in Shetland.'

322

Speechless with disbelief, the girls exchanged astonished glances. Then, with the implications of their father's announcement sinking in, they all started to speak at once.

'When will she be home?'

'Are the crew safe?'

'What news of Charley?'

'Is John all right?' Harriet put this question, already thinking that, if he were still alive and she had lost none of her persuasive charm, her dishonour could yet be overcome.

Harriet's query was one that was on Arabella's lips, too, but was never spoken. Her heart was pounding and she prayed for him to be safe as she waited for her father to answer them. In that moment she saw that Sarah's face had drained of colour and knew her thoughts were centred on Jim.

'Captain Baron was on the point of sailing from Lerwick when he was asked to bring the news to Whitby. The *Sea King* was in Ronas Voe. He was told the survivors were in poor shape, and the ship . . . well, it was a wonder she had reached Shetland. He could not wait for a list of survivors.'

The sisters did not hold back their disappointment.

'I know how you feel,' Benjamin announced, and went on, 'I feel the same way. I want to know what happened, what the news is of . . . oh, everything.' His voice faltered as one word escaped him. 'Charley?' He slumped into his chair and his daughters saw tears in his eyes. They came and knelt beside him, held his hands and put comforting arms around his shoulders.

'He'll be all right, Papa. Charley will be back.'

Benjamin gave a wan smile, looked gratefully at them

all, and knew that Jane's influence was still at work in his life even though she herself was gone.

5 April 1834. What news Father brought today! What joy! I hope Jim is safe . . . and of course Charley and John too.

25

14 April 1834. The same entry as before: I wish the Sea King *was back. I want to know that Jim is safe. Father is growing impatient. Harriet is more anxious each day. Arabella is quiet. We are . . . oh, there's shouting in the street!*

'Whale-ship! Whale-ship!'

Sarah raced down the stairs and Arabella rushed out of the dining-room, leaving Mrs Ainslie hoping fervently that the ship was the *Sea King*. Then the house might get back to some sort of normality, no matter what the news. Sarah did not wait for her sister, whom she saw turning into the drawing-room.

'You heard?' Arabella asked when she saw Harriet still seated in a chair beside the window.

Her sister nodded, her face expressionless.

'You're coming then?'

'No. I can't face John.'

'You'll have to some time.'

'I know. I'd rather it be here than on the quay.'

Arabella nodded. 'I understand. Maybe that's the wisest course.' She started for the door but was halted by a request.

'Will you break it to him, Arabella, please?'

Arabella hesitated. It was something she did not want to do but her sister looked so pathetic that she could not find it in her heart to refuse. 'Very well,' she said, and rushed from the room.

She hurried through streets already filling with people drawn by the cry that had echoed throughout Whitby. Because they had all assumed it was the *Sea King* returning from the cold jaws of death the town was already celebrating, but it was a relief nevertheless when confirmation of her identity came from the nearest onlookers on the East Cliff.

Arabella crossed the bridge with the flow of people. She turned away from the quays and joined those who had the same intention as she – walk down Church Street to the Church Stairs, then climb the one hundred and ninety-nine steps to the clifftop to get a first sight of the *Sea King*.

She gasped when she saw it. How had this ship survived? Even with some repairs carried out and new sails, she still presented a chilling sight. So much timber gone . . . it was a wonder she had been able to manage the long voyage out of the Arctic. Arabella was sure the *Sea King* would have met terrible seas on her way back and yet here she was, sailing with pride into her home port. But even from this distance Arabella could sense sadness and regret, too. Who was missing? Who was not returning home? She searched the decks as the ship moved between the piers to meet the waters of the river.

The relief that surged through her then almost caused her to collapse. John was standing beside the helmsman. Oh, he looked so thin, even from this distance. She turned to go; she must be on the quay to greet him! Then she stopped and searched the crew again. Charley? There! He was safe! Thank goodness. Jim . . .

Further along the cliff, Sarah had pushed her way to the front of the crowd. Her eyes too sought feverishly for Jim. Charley and John were safe, but where was Jim? He would usually have been on the ratlines. Maybe he was too weak to climb, but he wasn't on deck either. He must be below deck, too ill even to see his home port and the girl to whom he had expressed undying love. She had to get to the quay. She pushed herself free from the crowd and ran, unaware that her sister was not far behind her.

A call came to Arabella's lips on seeing her go, but she stifled it. She recognised the intensity of Sarah's concentrated dash and knew she would be oblivious to anything else but reaching the quay before the *Sea King*. Arabella quickened her own pace without breaking into a run.

Sarah's feet barely touched the ground as she went down the steps and along Church Street until she reached the quays along the east bank of the river. A crowd was already gathering where the *Sea King* would tie up. Her father was there. Seeing his face creased with anxiety, she slipped past the press of onlookers to stand by his side. He glanced at her.

'You heard . . .'

'Yes, Papa.'

'You've been running, I see.'

'I was on the cliff but wanted to be here when the *Sea King* docked.'

'Then you've seen her?'

'Yes, Papa.'

'She's . . .?'

Benjamin left his question hanging.

327

'Not the best of sights.'

He grimaced then asked, 'See anyone?'

'Charley and John.'

She saw him close his eyes in relief. 'Thank God,' he whispered. When he opened them a new light was evident but, looking at Sarah, he grew concerned.

'You seem worried. What is disturbing you?'

'Nothing, Papa. They looked very thin, but all right as far as I could see.'

'So what troubles you?'

Sarah had been determined to keep her relationship with Jim a secret until he returned and could be by her side when she told her father. But the different anxieties the family had faced throughout the winter had brought them closer. Now Sarah felt the urge to tell her father and satisfy her own need for him to know.

'Papa, I met Jim Barbour and fell in love with him. He sailed on the *Sea King*.' Her voice faltered. 'I did not see him on deck.'

Many questions about her association with this Jim Barbour sprang to Benjamin's lips but he held them back. His daughter was clearly afraid. 'He may be ill and confined below decks,' he offered soothingly. 'We'll know soon enough. I'm sure he'll be coming back.'

They fell silent; he knowing his son was alive, she not knowing if Jim would step on to the quay and take her in his arms.

A quality of expectancy settled over the quays, staithes and cliffs of Whitby. Then a ripple of speculation spread over them like the gentle surge of waves breaking on the shore. It reached those waiting anxiously on the quay where the *Sea King* would dock. More folk added to the crush already there, though that press held back from the anxious relatives of the crew. The bridge opened, the buzz of conversation heightened. Then the *Sea King* was there, and with her arrival a silence full of disbelief and horror settled over the crowd. Even the repairs made in Lerwick to see her home could not hide the extent to which the crew had stripped her for fuel. And the ship's skeletal appearance was nothing compared to the evidence of what her surviving crew had suffered; it was still apparent in their hollow faces even after the sustenance they had received in Shetland.

People searched for relatives, and if they did not see them anxiously called out names.

Charley, with a half-smile on his emaciated face, stood at the rail. He raised an arm on seeing his father and Sarah, just as Arabella managed to push through the throng and join them. His eyes fixed on Sarah alone. She saw sadness in his expression and the slight shake of the head he gave her told her the answer she did not want. Her heart plummeted; shock drained the colour from her cheeks and her knees began to give way. Arabella too had read her brother's sign. As Sarah sank against her, she supported her with one arm round her waist and quietly said, 'Hold on, Sarah. Jim would want you to be brave.'

Though tears had started to flow, Sarah firmed her body and steeled her mind, thankful at that moment to feel her father's hand rest on her shoulder in a momentary display of sympathy. Then his attention, diverted for that brief instant, was fully back on his son. He indicated the gangway that was being run out. Charley came to it amidst the other survivors eager to be ashore and feel the arms of loved ones around them, but there was no disorderly pushing. The men came ashore steadily, to ecstatic welcomes, but faced sadness on all sides from those who looked in vain for their man.

Arabella's eyes were fixed on John. She knew the love she had always felt for him was still alive. All she wanted, at this moment, was to take him in her arms and nurse him back to good health, but she knew that was not to be. She had sworn to take Harriet away if her father resumed his threats against her.

John waved and indicated he would come ashore in a few minutes. She and Sarah went towards Charley. Their effusive thanks for his safe return were only shadowed by his 'I'm sorry about Jim.' Charley still felt the urge to pour out the truth but knew that as a sailor he had to obey his captain's orders.

'I'm taking Charley home. I think it would be as well for you to come too, Sarah,' Benjamin said.

'But, Father, I haven't been released by Captain Sharp,' Charley reminded him.

'I'm sure he will have dismissed the crew, don't you worry.' He glanced at Arabella. 'Will you mention it to John?'

She nodded. 'I will.' Thankful that with the way things had turned out she was going to have John to herself, she resumed her wait on the quay. In her mind she reviewed all that had happened since the *Sea King* had left Whitby on what should have been a normal whaling voyage, if there ever was such a thing. Certainly this one had not been. Now the ship was back, bringing heartache, relief, sadness and joy in different measures to the people beginning to disperse from the quay.

John paused at the top of the gangway. Most of the Whitby men had gone, leaving only the Shetlanders who had helped bring the *Sea King* home still on board, awaiting the vessel from Shetland that was only half a day's sail behind. The quay was almost clear; Arabella the lone female figure visible. John's eyes rested on her. Her full-length, dark green coat was cut like a cape at the shoulders and buttoned up the front with only the top one left undone, revealing a thin white scarf tied at the neck. The coat's hood was drawn up, half hiding her face. His thoughts flew to the figure that had haunted him in the Arctic – but he was still unsure. He came down the gangway with a measured step.

'John!' She held out her arms to him.

He stepped into them and felt the comfort of hers closing around him. 'Arabella!'

As one they leaned back against each other's embrace. Arabella's eyes were filling with tears of joy, but she was determined to hold them back lest they weaken her into saying the words she knew she should not say.

Then John asked, 'Harriet . . . where is she?'

'Are you able to walk?'

'Yes. I suffered less than most.'

'The West Pier then?'

He gave a little smile. 'A return to our young days when we looked ahead to a life full of promise?'

She ignored the reference and said, 'I have much to tell you. Harriet was not on the quay because she did not want to face you there.'

'Why ever not?' he queried.

'There is no way of making this easy, John, so I am going to come straight to the point – Harriet is expecting a child.'

'What?'

'She's expecting a child,' repeated Arabella.

John gasped, 'Who has she married?' He frowned then and anger coloured his words. 'Did she not believe I was coming back?'

'The situation was . . .'

'I suppose I can't blame her for thinking I was dead,' he interrupted. 'She wouldn't be expecting a miracle. Well, who did she marry?'

Arabella ignored his observations and said, 'She isn't married.'

John looked bewildered now. This situation did not happen in their level of society, but if it did it was dealt with discreetly and pushed well out of sight of the gossips.

Before he could speak, Arabella went on to tell him the whole story.

'So this child will be born without anyone knowing where the father is?' he said at the conclusion.

'And, judging from Father's enquiries, he's not likely to be found.'

'So what is to happen to her?'

'Father wants to put her into an asylum, but I've told him I will not let that happen. I'll take Harriet away and look after her myself if he continues to threaten her with that. Sarah has said she will come with us.'

'Leave your father?'

'Yes, if needs be; if Father insists on an asylum as I think he will, especially now that Charley is safe. The decision will have to be made soon otherwise Harriet's condition will become evident and folk will talk.'

'But you can't leave Whitby!'

'We can if we have to.'

'It would be tragic.'

Arabella shrugged her shoulders. A fresh wind blew

along the West Pier, lightening her relief that the burden of telling John was over, but sending his thoughts into further turmoil. They walked on, the silence between them becoming increasingly strained until he broke it. 'I will still marry Harriet.'

Arabella's heart lurched and a chill gripped it. She stopped and caught his arm. 'You would do that?'

'It's the best solution. After all, I am still betrothed to her. Better do it soon . . . she and I will go away. Time it right and the baby will be seen as ours. Only your father, Sarah and we three will know the truth. Harriet won't be branded a slut, she'll be an honest woman, and your father won't face a scandal.'

Arabella bit her lip then said with deep sincerity, 'You're a good man, John. You deserve happiness and I hope Harriet can bring you that.'

She brushed the tears from her eyes as they left the West Pier and its bitter-sweet memories.

26

14 April 1834. What can I write when my heart aches so much? But even now, as I get ready for bed – dreaming of what might have been, I can hear Jim telling me I must go on with this diary . . .

Few words were spoken as Benjamin, Charley and Sarah walked home. Though joyful at his son's survival, Benjamin knew it was a hard homecoming for them both; Charley's experiences must still lie heavily on his mind and, from the love he had seen in Sarah's eyes when she had told him about Jim, he knew her loss would cut deep.

When Charley said he wanted to have a bath and feel the softness of his bed again, Benjamin took Sarah to his study. After they had talked a while, she knew how much her father had suffered when his wife had died and that he could understand her feelings now.

'You are young, Sarah. You have a whole life before you and will find someone else to make you happy,' he finished by saying. 'I'm sure Jim would have wanted that. Mourn, yes, but look to tomorrow also.'

When she left his study to find Charley, though, Sarah knew that for her tomorrow would always be filled with memories of the short time she had shared with Jim. No one else would ever be allowed to intrude on that.

Wondering if it was the right moment, she hesitated before Charley's door. Then, deciding she needed to know everything, she knocked. Hearing his voice telling her to enter, she walked in.

Charley, who had been lying on his bed, sat up when he saw her. Guessing what this was about, he felt his body run as cold as if the Arctic yawned around him again. He nodded and Sarah crossed the room to sit beside him on the edge of the bed.

'What happened?' she asked quietly.

Charley hesitated. He could refuse to answer, but tell her the full truth and everybody would know. Then John would feel that Charley had disobeyed a command! He could never allow that to happen. 'It's painful, Sarah,' he said, taking her hand. 'Are you sure you want to know?'

'Yes,' she said, firming her voice.

He frowned and nodded then started on his story of what had happened in the whale-boat, leaving out his own culpability in losing the axe whose absence had cost the lives of his shipmates. Charley found it hard reliving those moments; several times he faltered but, with Sarah's gentle encouragement, continued to the end. There were tears in her eyes then and Charley's face was creased with misery. 'I wish it had been me instead of Jim,' he told her, and Sarah believed him.

She took his hand. 'I know it was not easy for you to tell me that but thank you for doing so. And don't ever make that wish again. If it had been you, Father would have been devastated; he has great ambitions for you. And I believe what happened to the crew of the *Sea King* has mellowed him to some extent. He is a more understanding and kind man because of it.'

This was an observation Charley stored away for future use.

When Arabella and John reached home they saw that the door to her father's study was ajar and assumed he must have been listening for their arrival. She knocked on the door and tentatively pushed it wider.

'Come in.'

Benjamin was rising from his chair when they went in. 'John, my boy!' He came out from behind his desk, hand outstretched, eyes rapidly assessing the toll on his captain taken by a winter spent in some of the fiercest conditions on earth. Benjamin's grip was firm and he immediately regretted his lack of consideration when John winced at the pressure on his shrunken fingers.

'It's a miracle the *Sea King* is moored at her quay again.'

'God was indeed looking after us, sir.'

'Your skilled leadership played its part, I have no doubt. I will have your full report and log, all in good time. First I need a list of the men who did not return. But perhaps you could tell me about Charley?'

'He was a credit to you, sir. I could not have wished for a better member of crew. But may we go into details of that later? With your permission, I would like to see Harriet alone now?'

'Of course,' replied Benjamin. 'Arabella has told you?'

'Yes, sir.'

When John offered no more, Benjamin said, 'She is in the drawing-room.'

*

When John walked into the drawing-room he found Harriet sitting bolt upright in one of the armchairs near the window. She turned her head to look at him as he came in, and received a shock. This was a thin and worn-looking shadow of the man who had proposed to her what seemed an age ago.

'John,' she said quietly.

'Harriet.' He leaned down and kissed her on the cheek. He sensed her fill with emotion at his touch and saw her eyes brim with tears. He pulled a chair closer and sat down next to her, taking her hands in his. Before he could speak she asked, 'Has Arabella told you?'

He nodded. 'Yes.'

She let out a low moan and tears flowed silently down her cheeks. 'I'm so sorry.'

She looked so pathetic in that instant; gone was the lively, effervescent girl he had previously known, the one who knew how to exert her charm to get her own way. No longer, it seemed. But he had another proposal to make to her nevertheless.

'Harriet, I think we should marry as soon as possible,' he told her.

She stared at him in disbelief, thinking she hadn't heard properly. Surely he could not be serious?

'John, you mean . . .?'

'I'll marry you, if you'll have the wreck of a man who sits before you?'

Her face lit up with a wondrous smile that turned to tears of joy. She flung her arms around his neck. 'Oh, John! John!' Still hardly able to believe what was happening, she said, 'The baby?'

'Will be ours.'

'You'll accept it?'

'I understand only your father, Arabella and Sarah know the truth?'

'Yes.'

'Then it will remain that way. The child will be raised as mine. We should marry quickly and go away on a prolonged honeymoon. We will allow outsiders to see it as a necessary period of recovery for me. I have no other commitments. When we put this to your father, I know he'll agree. He will wish to avoid a scandal and most certainly will not want to lose his daughters in the way Arabella has threatened. We will let it be known that you had our baby prematurely, and when we return to Whitby no one will be any the wiser.'

With immense relief Harriet grasped at the escape that was being offered to her. 'Oh, John, I don't deserve you,' she cried.

He stood up and held out his hands to her. 'Come, let's tell your father now. We will need his blessing, but I don't believe he'll withhold it.'

'No, I don't think he will.' She slid her arms around his neck again and kissed him passionately on the lips. 'And I promise to be a good wife, John,' she told him joyfully.

Arabella had revealed nothing to her father of John's plan to propose again to her sister.

When he entered the study and, without any preamble, told Benjamin he wished to ask for Harriet's hand in marriage once again, for a moment Benjamin was taken off guard. Then, as this happy solution to all the problems caused by Harriet's indiscretion became evident to him, he said cautiously, 'And you'll be responsible for the child?'

'As if it were my own, sir. No one need ever know it is not.' John went on to reveal his plan, with which Benjamin fully agreed. 'There is only one thing more, sir. We should marry as soon as possible and we cannot go through all the preparations for a marriage appropriate to the standing of your family without risking discovery. I suggest we use the excuse of my condition, following my Arctic experience, to hold a small, quiet wedding.'

Benjamin agreed thankfully. 'I will see Reverend Bosworth about it. I may have to tell him the reason, but he is a good friend and I know he is capable of keeping a secret.'

28 April 1834. Harriet and John married today. Under the circumstances, a small, quiet wedding seemed appropriate. The state of John's health was accepted as the reason by all our friends. Harriet did look radiant. She wore a plain white dress with a high waist, and an over-mantle of delicate lace that had the effect of making the white appear to dazzle. Arabella and I wore dark blue velvet dresses and each carried a posy of flowers to match those carried by Harriet, though smaller. The service was short but heartfelt. It brought to me again what I am missing by losing Jim. I know Arabella felt it too – I saw her eyes were damp when John made his farewell to her. As she and I stood side by side, watching them drive away in their carriage, she held my hand for comfort. We wonder where they are going. John would not tell anyone, which I think is for

*the best. As we settled in, after they had gone, Father
called the three of us into the drawing-room.*

'After the *Sea King*'s unexpected return, and because of
what I believe to have been an attempt by Stephen Waite
to get his hands on my business, I have made provisions
that it may never pass out of family control unless it is so
agreed by all those in ownership at that time. That means
I have provided for you here and now, and secured your
future. Your income, of course, will depend on how pros-
perous the business is. For now that will depend on my
acumen. Then, after I retire, on Charley's and John's.
They will both work ashore after they leave the sea.'

Charley, grasping the inference behind those words,
gasped, 'Then, you'll allow me to go to sea again,
Father?'

'Yes, until you wish to take over the business here.
After what I heard about your conduct aboard the *Sea
King*, I realise I was wrong to oppose your ambition. If
I had insisted, you would not have become the man I see
emerging now. Let me always be proud of you, son.'

'I will, Father, I will!' In his mind he was also keeping
a pact with Jim, whose ambition to be a master seaman
had been cut short through Charley's carelessness.

'I should tell you all that I have made bequests to Mrs
Ainslie, Cook, and the staff, to be paid at the appropriate
time. As my daughters, Arabella and Sarah, you will be
adequately provided for by receiving a regular income,
with bonuses depending on the prosperity of the business. It will continue to be paid independently, for your
own use, even if you marry. Neither of you should ever
want.'

Both girls were effusive in their thanks, then Sarah

added quietly, 'I will never marry, Father, my heart belongs to Jim. But your foresight and generosity will give me my independence, and the confidence to ignore the slighting remarks about spinsters made by people who should know better.'

Arabella added nothing to this, her thoughts far away and fixed on her own likely future, which would most probably lie in this house with Sarah.

Ten days later, while they were all together at luncheon, a maid came into the dining-room. 'Sir, the landlord of the Angel has sent these.' She held out a tray on which there were three envelopes.

'Did he send a message?' asked Benjamin.

'Only to say that the mail-coach arrived half an hour ago and, in accordance with your arrangements, he sent them immediately he'd sorted them.'

Benjamin looked at the envelopes as the maid left the room. He dropped two on the table, keeping one. 'It's from John.'

That sent a buzz around the table. Arabella, Sarah and Charley watched as he withdrew a sheet of paper and stared at the words.

'Tell us, Papa,' prompted Sarah, eager for news.

'Where are they?' asked Arabella.

'Cornwall,' he announced, scanning the letter. 'They had a good journey with no delays. The accommodation is excellent and they are both in high spirits. John says, "Excuse the short message; I will keep you informed of our well-being."'

There was a sense of relief around the table. They knew where Harriet and John were and now awaited regular updates.

These came at fairly regular intervals, with nothing to raise undue alarm as the estimated date for the birth drew nearer.

Then, one day in late July, Benjamin slit open an envelope, unfolded a sheet of paper and read out, 'It's a girl! Harriet and Caroline are both very well.'

'A girl!'

'Caroline!'

Excitement filled the room.

Sarah, with teasing laughter in her eyes, said, 'You'll be Uncle Charley!'

Charley said grumpily, 'Should have been a boy. I've had enough of girls around me.'

'You won't say that one day,' laughed Arabella.

27

8 September 1834. Harriet and John came home today. Harriet is in good health and John looks much recovered from his terrible experiences in the Arctic. Caroline is beautiful. I can see she will rival Harriet as the beauty of the family. Her pale blue eyes and ready smile would melt anyone's heart. I had worried how Arabella would react, but I need not have done. She was the epitome of a loving sister, sister-in-law and aunt. How she fussed over Caroline; maybe more so than if she had been the mother herself. Did I detect a touch of envy in this reaction? If so it was well disguised. Father is delighted with the way things have turned out and is much more relaxed now he has come to terms with all that has happened. He is pleased that the new family will be living only two doors away in John's family home. He has had Mrs Ainslie and Cook prepare an exceptional meal for the family this evening. I believe he is going to make a special announcement.

Benjamin leaned back in his chair at the head of the table. As he cast his eyes around his family, who were all enjoying being together again, he counted himself lucky, and resolved to do all he could to maintain the mood of the moment. He sat for a few minutes contentedly listening to their good-humoured banter, wishing only that Jane could share this happiness too. Finally he reached out, picked up a knife and tapped the table with the handle. Everyone stopped talking and looked at him.

'I have something I want to say, apart from welcome home to Harriet, John and Caroline, of course. Some of you know or will have guessed what it is to be.' He left a little pause, sufficient to accentuate the importance he attached to what he was about to disclose. 'John, I am offering you a captaincy I would very much like you to accept. The *Sea King* will be ready to sail again in March.'

'The *Sea King*!' John's eyes lit with enthusiasm. 'A new ship, sir?'

Benjamin smiled and shook his head. 'No.'

John looked at him doubtfully. 'You mean . . .?'

'I'm having her repaired, brought back to her former glory. She was a stout-hearted girl; I couldn't see her broken up. She's yours to command again, if you want the position.'

'Sir, what can I say? I never expected to see the *Sea King* again, let alone stand on her deck as her captain. Of course, sir, I'll accept your offer and your trust.'

Sarah's glance at Harriet, brief though it was, caught a passing expression of displeasure. She knew her sister did not want him to go back to sea, but no one else, with their attention on Benjamin, noticed, so skilfully did she hide her disappointment. Sarah hoped this would not cause friction between Harriet and John.

All such thoughts were banished by Benjamin's next words. 'Good, that pleases me immensely. You have plenty of time to see to everything . . . hiring a crew . . .

well, you know what is entailed. There is only one thing more: you must sign Charley on!'

'I couldn't sail without him.'

20 October 1834. We are enjoying a pleasant time. Caroline is adorable. Father is content in his work, especially overseeing the refitting of the Sea King, *which he tells us is going extremely well. John spends a lot of time with him as well as dealing with other matters relating to the ship and its forthcoming voyage next year. Charley is delighted that Father is allowing him to go to sea again. I think he misses Jim and hope he finds another friend to take his place.*

Arabella and I have visited Harriet on numerous occasions. Most of them are short visits, but every Thursday we take tea with her and are able to spend an hour with Caroline before she is whisked away by her nurse. Yesterday, however, Harriet gave us cause to be disturbed. I felt something was not quite right when we arrived, but it was not until tea was poured that she voiced her concern . . .

'You must be pleased that John and Father seem to be getting on so well,' commented Arabella as she stirred her tea. 'The renovation of the *Sea King* has brought them closer. John must be delighted to be her captain again.'

'I wish he'd never accepted,' complained Harriet. 'He knows his real future lies in working with Father ashore. Why run the risk of the events of his last voyage happening again? It nearly killed him. And I'll have to suffer all the worry while he is away . . .'

'Harriet, you can't think like that. The sea is John's

life; he'd be miserable away from it. The time will come when he will retire, but until then you've got to support him.'

'It's all very well your talking like that, you haven't a husband who's leaving you for six months at a time, risking his life, and for what? To bring a few more barrels of oil into Whitby!'

'You know it's much more than that,' Sarah put in.

'I thought you'd understand my feelings,' Harriet said sharply. 'You lost Jim.'

The reminder hurt, but Sarah remained composed. 'I knew what Jim wanted from life. It would have stifled him if he couldn't have pursued his dreams.'

'You should give John every support,' chided Arabella. 'You must remember what he did for you.'

Harriet tightened her lips, irritated by the reminder. 'Oh, why do men always have to have their own way?'

The subject was never mentioned again. Though Arabella and Sarah knew the undercurrent was still there, they realised they were the only ones who sensed it. They never knew if words about it passed between Harriet and John; the privacy of their relationship was maintained.

26 December 1834. Christmas Day was splendid. We were a happy family spending the day together. What a difference baby Caroline made, even though she was too young to know what was happening . . .

1 January 1835. A new year. I wonder what it will bring for all of us?

14 March 1835. The Sea King *sailed today. How fine she looked! Father's delight was plain for all to see. How proud John was to be taking her back to the Arctic. Charley was full of excitement, too. I could tell Arabella was tense though she did not show it; her parting from John on the quay was brief. Only she knew what her thoughts were at that moment. Mine had slipped back to the moment I said a last goodbye to Jim. I wished I had him in my arms again when I saw Harriet and John embrace and make their farewell kiss. Then John made Caroline giggle and went aboard to join his crew. As the ship slipped away downstream Harriet held the baby high for him to see and for her to make her first goodbye . . .*

'Harriet, pull that shawl round Caroline; there's a bite in the wind.'

Sarah saw Harriet frown. She did not like being told what to do by Arabella.

'Give her to me while you button your coat up.' Her sister held out her arms for the child.

Harriet hesitated then half-heartedly did as Arabella suggested, though as a show of defiance she left the two top buttons undone. She took Caroline back without a word and strolled a little further along the pier, away from Arabella and Sarah.

Arabella raised an eyebrow as she exchanged a look with Sarah.

'Don't worry, Harriet doesn't mean anything by it. She's tetchy because of what happened last time. It must weigh on her mind.'

'I suppose it will be like this until the *Sea King* sails back into Whitby again. We must accept it and look after her.'

20 March 1835. Harriet has come down with a heavy cold, and, much to her annoyance, Arabella has sent for Dr Fenby, though Arabella did so with every good intention . . .

'Stop fussing!' complained Harriet. 'I don't want the doctor. I'll be all right.' Reluctantly she obeyed her sister's order to return to bed.

'Take care of yourself, Harriet. You've Caroline to think about now. I told you on the pier to fasten up your coat. The bite in that wind has got on to your chest.'

'Yes, yes, yes, Miss Know-all!'

Arabella ignored the double taunt and attained some satisfaction when the doctor insisted that Harriet should remain in bed.

On leaving, he said to Arabella and Sarah, 'See that your sister does as she's told. There is a nasty cough developing there. She should take care.'

A fortnight passed before he allowed Harriet out of bed again, though she kept insisting she was better. On first putting her feet to the floor she realised how much of her strength had been drained, but after a couple of days she was able to disguise the fact and indicate to Arabella and Sarah that they need not spend so much time with her. 'I can look after myself now.'

Both sisters recognised the dismissal intended and exchanged the same thought: Let her get on with it then. She could have said thanks. But even as they voiced this later they excused Harriet's attitude, blaming it on her worry about John.

20 April 1835. Arabella and I have received invitations to an engagement party for Sophia Stewart, to be held at

*the Angel Inn a month from now. Knowing Sophia as I
do, it will be a splendid occasion, with dancing and a
sumptuous buffet . . .*

'I don't think I want to go,' said Sarah when she and
Arabella exchanged thoughts about the invitation.

Arabella, recognising that her sister's attitude
stemmed from her resolve to be true to Jim's memory,
made the point, 'I think you should begin to meet more
young people, and this is a good opportunity.'

'But . . .'

Arabella interrupted her quickly. 'I know – Jim. But he
would not want you to remain a spinster.'

'That is my choice,' Sarah returned calmly, 'just as it's
my choice not to accept this invitation.'

Arabella, recognising she could not argue this point,
took a different tack. 'Please come, Sarah. I don't want
to go on my own.'

Sarah's reply was pre-empted by Mrs Ainslie's
arrival for a prearranged consultation with Arabella,
who soon seized the opportunity to recruit an ally in
her. 'Mrs Ainslie, Sarah and I have received an invitation to a party. She doesn't want to go; I do. But not on
my own.'

'Oh, Sarah, I think you should go,' agreed Mrs Ainslie.
'It will take you out of yourself. You'll enjoy it. It will be
good for you to dance again.'

Sarah hesitated, then said with a wry smile, 'All right,
I can't stand against the two of you.'

'Splendid! And thank you, Mrs Ainslie.' Arabella
secretly hoped that something would come of the event
that would brighten Sarah's future.

*

Everyone at the party was in a jovial mood and the sisters were made so welcome that they were quickly caught up in the spirit of the occasion. They were both good dancers and most of the men knew this so they were never short of partners. Arabella was delighted to see Sarah swept into every dance and fussed over whenever there was a break for refreshments. Watching her float effortlessly through every step, with laughter on her face and merriment in her eyes, Arabella thought this might well be the turning point in her sister's life. While Jim would always have a place in her heart, tonight could be her first step outside the cocoon of spinsterhood.

'That was a splendid evening,' commented Arabella, flinging herself into an armchair when they returned home in the early hours. 'I'm about exhausted after all that dancing.'

'So am I,' laughed Sarah.

'You looked to be enjoying yourself.'

'I did.'

'Good. And you weren't short of attentive beaux.' The query in Arabella's eyes was not lost on Sarah.

She grinned. 'They were all most attentive, every one of them wanting to meet me again.'

'And?' prompted Arabella.

Sarah laughed. 'I said yes to them all, while giving them to understand that we could have a good time together so long as they knew that it was in friendship only.'

'And they accepted that?'

'Oh, yes. I used my charm to make them agree.' Then Sarah turned serious. 'Arabella, I will enjoy myself; tonight has proved that to me, and I'm grateful to you for insisting I accept the invitation. But I will never be false to Jim. He will always remain in my heart.' Having made that announcement, she changed the subject. 'What about you? Are we going to be two old maids together?'

Arabella laughed. 'That's a thought. Maybe it's the right course for us. Like you, I enjoyed this evening and I don't intend to sit around and mope. I know I need not be short of escorts, but as for anything more . . . Life will be easier now Papa has accepted that we need more freedom and he trusts us. And we have Caroline to keep us—'

Sarah cut her short. 'Be careful, Arabella. I've seen how much you dote on her. Don't take over Harriet's role. After all, she is the child's mother.'

28

10 July 1835. Arabella called Dr Fenby today, worried about Harriet. She doesn't really seem to have got over the cold she had at the end of March. It developed into a cough, not a bad one but it did not seem to get any better. Harriet insisted that she was all right, but finally today Arabella took the responsibility into her own hands. Dr Fenby has just left. He prescribed some medicine for Harriet, and insisted that she rest as much as possible, which irritated her . . .

'Harriet, you've not touched your lunch. Cook made some broth especially for you. You really must try and eat more.'

Harriet eyed her sister from the pillows. 'Oh, don't fuss! I'm not really hungry now. I'll have something later.'

'You've been saying that for a few days. You worry me. When Dr Fenby left today, he told me he is going to call in again tomorrow.'

Harriet shook her head with annoyance. 'I wish he wouldn't. I'm going to be all right.'

'It's for your own good. Caroline doesn't want a sickly mother, and Father's worried about you.'

Any retort that Harriet was about to make was stopped by a bout of coughing. When it was over she lay back on the pillows, exhausted. Arabella smoothed her sister's forehead with a comforting hand.

The next day Dr Fenby arrived with a younger man whom he introduced as Dr Conan Wentworth. 'He is my nephew. He trained in Edinburgh and is currently helping with a practice there. He is due to return tomorrow. I'd be glad to have his opinion before he leaves.'

The young doctor was impeccably dressed, his well-fitting clothes revealing an athletic figure. His smile was warm and his handshake inspired confidence.

'Before we go up, Miss Brook, will you tell me your observations of your sister since Dr Fenby's visit two days ago?'

'She is no better. Has to be persuaded to eat, and then only picks at her food.'

'Her cough?'

'No better, no worse.'

'But still troublesome?'

'I would say so, though my sister does not complain. In fact, she hates any fuss.'

'Thank you, Miss Brook. We must reassure her we are not fussing but want to see her returned to good health as soon as possible. Now, let us see the patient.'

At that moment Sarah appeared on the landing, looking distraught.

'Harriet's coughing blood!'

'Quick, where is she?' asked the young doctor.

'I'll take you,' said Arabella. 'Sarah, go for Father.'

When they reached the bedroom they found Harriet, her face drained of colour, gasping for breath. Her head lay on a pillow that was flecked with blood; a saturated handkerchief was clutched in her hand. Arabella's heart missed a beat – her sister looked so forlorn and helpless.

The two doctors went to the bedside. Arabella made to leave the room, to allow them to make their examination and diagnosis in privacy.

'Miss Brook, I would like you to stay.' The request came from the younger man and was couched in a way that could not be refused.

She stood to one side of the room, only speaking when asked a question. As the two doctors conducted their examination they conferred in lowered tones until Dr Wentworth finally said, 'Mrs Sharp, I will not hold anything back since it is neither in your interest nor in mine. Your condition is serious. Your lungs are infected. You must take exceptional care, rest and try to eat more; you need to get your strength up. Whenever you cough, use a handkerchief. Take great care whenever other people are in the room. It is out of the question for you to hold your baby.'

Harriet's face creased with distress. 'But . . .'

'I'm sorry, Mrs Sharp. The nurse or your sisters can bring her to the door for you to see her, but not into the room. That is too unsafe.'

Harriet bit her lip to hold back the tears. With a heartrending sigh, she sank her head deeper into her pillows.

Arabella made for her bedside.

'I'll see you in few moments downstairs, Miss Brook,' said Dr Wentworth.

When Arabella came down she saw him standing alone in the hall.

'I've sent my uncle to see your father. Is there anywhere we can talk?' he asked.

'In the small parlour.' She led the way and closed the door behind them. 'Please be seated.'

'Thank you,' he replied. 'Miss Brook, as I said to your sister, I don't believe in holding back the facts but I only went so far with her . . . far enough to make her realise that her situation is serious. Now I wish to explain that I have seen many cases like this in Edinburgh. Her lungs are in a poor way . . .'

'Consumption?' interrupted Arabella.

'I cannot say definitely but it is more than likely. Little is known about the best way to treat it. From what I have seen, it is largely up to the patient themself. Only they can act to build up their strength and fight the disease.'

Arabella's face had paled. 'What chance has Harriet got?'

Dr Wentworth shrugged his shoulders. 'I wish I could tell you something positive but I can't. We must keep careful watch on her. I will visit her daily to monitor her progress.'

'I thought you were returning to Edinburgh tomorrow?'

'I cannot leave without knowing more.'

Realising he had been gentle by using the word 'more' rather than being specific about Harriet's disease, she appreciated his thoughtfulness. 'You are most kind, Doctor.'

He stood up. 'You may find she perspires a lot, so frequent changes of clothes and try to keep her cool. The importance of eating regularly goes without saying.'

'Anything special?'

'Whatever you can get her to eat; the more nutritious the better.'

Arabella escorted him to the drawing-room where he

was introduced to Benjamin, and then the two doctors took their leave.

Seven days later, after Dr Wentworth had paid his daily visit, he spoke to Arabella in the hall. 'Your sister seems very much better. I know you will continue the care and attention she has been receiving. I must return to Edinburgh now but leave you in the capable hands of my uncle. I have passed on to him notes about the course I think the disease will take and how I believe it should be treated. So I must say goodbye.'

'We will miss your visits,' Arabella told him. 'We owe you a great deal of thanks for what you have done, and for staying in Whitby when you should have been in Edinburgh.'

'There was nothing my fellow doctors there could not take care of, and it has given me the opportunity to see more of what my uncle's practice entails. I am considering moving here when he retires.'

'Then I hope your decision is favourable to us and that in the future we may be able to repay you for your kindness.'

'We shall see, Miss Brook, we shall see.'

She offered her hand. He raised it to his lips and said goodbye.

Ten days later Arabella paid her usual morning visit to Harriet and was pleased to see her looking more relaxed, with eyes that shone a little more brightly. Her spirits lifted at the sight. It therefore came as a shock when Harriet very calmly said, 'Arabella, will you please look after Caroline when I'm gone?'

'What?' She frowned. 'You'll be doing that, surely.'

Harriet gave a little shake of her head. 'No, I won't. I'm dying.'

'Don't talk nonsense!' Arabella's thoughts raced. This was so unlike Harriet, but there was something about her tone that revealed she was fully aware of what she was saying. How Arabella wished Dr Wentworth were there!

'I'm not.' Harriet softened her voice. 'Arabella, I'm sorry for causing trouble between us . . .'

Arabella brushed the apology away with a wave of her hand. 'Sisterly squabbles,' she said casually.

'It was sometimes more than that, and I know I hurt you. I'm sorry for it. But please say you will look after Caroline for me?'

'Of course I will. I promise you.'

Arabella saw relief and contentment suffuse her sister upon learning that her daughter would be safe; Arabella had never been one to break a promise.

'Thank you.' Harriet reached out for her sister's hand. Arabella took it and squeezed it lovingly. Then Harriet smiled and said, 'Now fetch Papa, and Sarah, and Mrs Ainslie. I want to say goodbye.'

28 July 1835. It was a terrific shock when Arabella summoned us all to the bedroom, informing us that it was at Harriet's request because she believed she was dying. She had seemed so much better of late. We could not understand her wish. But she was right. She died peacefully that day after saying goodbye to each one of us in turn. My thoughts went to Caroline and John. What will they do now? My concern for Caroline was eased when Arabella informed me that she had promised Harriet she would look after her. I said I would help in any way possible. We were both thankful when Mrs Ainslie offered her help, too, and said if it was Father's wish to re-engage the nurse she would see to it. Father is not looking at all well himself, which I suppose is only natural after such a shock. I feel it deeply; I have lost a mother, a sister and Jim in a very short period of time. It weighs heavily on my heart. And we still face breaking the bad news to John and Charley. It will soon be time for their return.

'Another whale, Mr Chapman, and we can head for home.'

'Yes, sir. The crew know it. There are a lot of sharp eyes out there eager to shout, "Thar she blows!" I'll get Varley's report. He did sight ice late yesterday but has not reported any this morning.'

'We want to keep away from that stuff,' John commented wryly.

As the first mate closed the door behind him, John leaned back in his chair, his expression pensive.

He was surprised by the way he had taken to Caroline – another man's child. Harriet's, yes, but . . . At first he had expected to feel awkward with the baby, but loving her had proved to be easy. And loving Harriet? Sometimes he thought he had never really known her, and yet was it not her benign, loving presence that had visited him, here in this very cabin, in the depths of his despair?

'Thar she blows! Thar she blows!'

All personal thoughts were driven from John's mind by the cry from the masthead.

29

4 August 1835. We laid Harriet to rest today. The weather matched the occasion. In spite of its being summer a bleak wind blew across the clifftop cemetery. Father is privately devastated but bore up well in public and, with calm fortitude, greeted the many people who came to pay their respects. Gloom hangs over the house. We are dreading having to meet John on his return . . .

20 August 1835. Today Arabella received a letter from Dr Wentworth which she read out to us.

Dear Miss Brook,
My uncle has informed me that your sister passed away. It was a surprise to me as his previous report (I had asked him to keep me informed) indicated that there were good signs of recovery. I am at a loss, as is he, to say why this happened. I am afraid we do not know enough about this scourge to mankind but hopefully, one day, following more research, we will find a way to combat it.

Please accept my sympathy and pass it on to your father and sister. Also, of course, to your

brother-in-law and brother when they return from
the Arctic.

I hope to meet them one day when I return to
Whitby to join my uncle at the beginning of
December. I look forward to renewing your
acquaintance at the same time.

    Yours humbly,
    Conan Wentworth

2 September 1835. Only one of Whitby's whale-ships has
not returned and, though no one voices it as yet, we are
beginning to think, Oh, not again. Surely life cannot be
so cruel, especially to baby Caroline who, all unknow-
ingly, adds brightness to our days. She and her nurse
have remained with us. It was the sensible thing to do.

3 September 1835. What excitement! The cry of 'Whale-
ship!' is resounding through the town. It must be the Sea
King*!*

Sarah threw down her pen and raced down the stairs.
Arabella was already in the hall, shrugging herself into
her coat.

'Are we taking Caroline?' Sarah asked, grabbing her
own from the closet.

'I think it may be wiser not to on this occasion,' replied
Arabella. 'John will have enough to take in as it is.
Seeing Caroline under these circumstances could make
it worse for him.'

The sisters hurried from the house together.

People were already flocking to the quays, staithes and

clifftops. Sarah and Arabella could feel waves of relief coming from the crowd; the ship had been identified; the name *Sea King* was flying from person to person.

'It will be a little while before she reaches the river,' said Arabella. 'Let's call on Father.'

They hurried to his office, where they found Benjamin seated at his desk with his head in his hands. When he looked up, they saw he was drawn and pale at the thought of telling John the dreadful news.

Arabella, realising that he was reliving the loss of his own wife, said gently, 'Would you like me to do it, Papa?'

He looked at her with an expression of shame. 'I shouldn't transfer the burden to you.'

'We'll both do it, Papa. I'll be with Arabella.' Sarah came round the desk and left a comforting kiss on his forehead.

His eyes expressed the thanks he felt. He patted Sarah's hand and gave Arabella a wan smile.

When they left the office, Sarah asked, 'Are we going to the clifftop?'

'We usually do; it's better than hanging around here.'

Before they reached the top of the cliff, breathing heavily from the exertion of climbing the crowded Church Stairs, they could hear the buzz of excitement rising from those already on the clifftop. Whitby was preparing to welcome home one of her own. They remained among the crowd, a little way back from the cliff edge, hoping their mourning dress would not be noticed by John and Charley. They allowed excitement to charge their feelings as they watched the *Sea King* slip between the piers to meet the river. By the time they had descended to the quay they were in a sombre mood, while all around them the atmosphere was light-hearted.

As the ship manoeuvred through the bridge into the upper reaches of the river, to be brought alongside the quay, the joy of her crew was more than evident. Charley waved excitedly to them, then hurried across the deck to point out his sisters to John, who raised his arm and smiled . . . only for his expression to freeze. Arabella and Sarah knew he had noticed their mourning dress.

He issued orders and, leaving the first mate to oversee the final docking, was down the gangway with Charley immediately it was run out.

'Your father?' It was a natural assumption but John's question was immediately followed by another. 'Where's Harriet?' He looked around expectantly. At any moment he would feel her arms around him, her mouth ready to trade him kiss for kiss . . . When he turned back to her sisters his eyes were wild with disbelief. 'No! It can't be true.'

Arabella placed a hand on his arm. 'I'm so sorry to have to meet you with such news.'

Charley gasped as he realised what she meant.

John dashed his sleeve across his face and pleaded: 'Walk with me, Arabella. Tell me everything that happened.'

10 January 1836. Christmas and New Year have been quiet for us. We miss Harriet's lively spirit. As Caroline seems settled living with us, with her nurse in attendance, Father has persuaded John to leave the situation as it is and move in here for as long as he wishes. This has worked well for now but I know it is not satisfactory in the long term, from John's point of view. He is faced with the problem of being a father to a child who is not his, and without any of the help a wife could give. He has decisions to make and it can't be easy for him. Arabella tells me she has realised this, too, and has persuaded him to talk to her . . .

'It might help you to do so, John. A trouble shared is a trouble halved.'

'You are very kind, Arabella, but why should I burden you with my problems?'

'Because we were very close once and, I hope, still close enough for me to help. I would like to.'

Recognising her sincerity, he came straight to the point. 'I've given the future much thought and have come up with an answer that makes sense to me. I will leave the sea.'

'You can't!'

'I can and must. I'm jinxed. We were iced in; men died; and then, while I was away, Harriet . . .' He let the inference hang in the air. 'I've got to leave this bad luck behind.'

'But you're not jinxed, and your heart is with the sea. You'd be lost without it.'

'I must face leaving the sea one day, so why not now?'

'Because you are still a young man. Your sailing days could run to years.'

'Your father said that one day Charley and I would run his business. I plan to ask him to take me in now, though not to run it; your father is active enough still. But I'm sure he could give me something to do ashore.'

'Something to do? That's not right for you, John. You need to be more fully occupied than that. You need the sea.'

'But you're overlooking the important fact of Caroline. She needs at least one parent. I should be here to see to her needs.'

Arabella restrained herself from saying, 'She's not yours,' and said instead, 'She has her nurse to see to her welfare day-to-day. I will look after everything else. Since I already run the house it will be little trouble to me.'

'But she would be an extra responsibility and you have your own life to lead.'

'I won't neglect that, never fear. But Caroline is the flesh and blood of my sister. She belongs in this household. I will hear no more about it. You continue your career at sea, John. Keep faith with that and the memory of Harriet.' In her mind she added, 'And with me.'

John hesitated.

'It's the right way,' Arabella insisted.

He nodded slowly. 'I don't deserve such kindness.' He came to her then, placed his hands on her arms and, looking earnestly at her, said, 'If I used all the words of thanks I know, they would not be adequate to express my gratitude for what you are doing.'

'You can repay me by thinking of me and Caroline wherever you sail.'

30

10 February 1836. Arabella and I were in the drawing-room early this afternoon when Lucy came in to present Arabella with a calling card. Father, John and Charley had gone to the Sea King, *something to do with her forthcoming voyage, and Nurse had taken Caroline out to enjoy the first warm sunshine of the year . . .*

Arabella's glance at the card elicited an expression of surprise. 'Show him in, Lucy.' As soon as the door closed behind the maid, she said quietly, 'Dr Wentworth.'

Before Sarah could comment the door opened again and Lucy announced the visitor.

He strode in, handsome features made more attractive still by his warm smile. Arabella suddenly realised she had not seen him smile before; the circumstances of their previous meetings had not merited it. True, she had noted in passing how good-looking he was, but with that smile . . .

He bowed to her. 'Miss Brook.' He turned to Sarah and made a similar greeting.

They both acknowledged him with a smile and an inclination of their head.

'This is a surprise and a pleasure, Dr Wentworth,' Arabella told him. 'Please do be seated.'

'Thank you. The pleasure is mine.' He chose a chair that allowed him to keep both sisters in his line of vision.

'When did you arrive in Whitby?' Arabella asked.

'Late the day before yesterday. I have been settling in with my uncle. Today I thought I must renew our acquaintance. I hope I am not disturbing you?'

'Not at all. I recall in your letter you said you would be joining your uncle in February.'

'I am honoured you remembered.'

Sarah, sitting silently, was entranced by the scene being played out before her. Oh, she remembered him from last year, but under these circumstances he seemed like a new man, with a smile that set her heart racing. Then she restrained her thoughts, remembering the promises she had made to herself about Jim.

Arabella was offering him tea.

'That would be a pleasure, Miss Brook. But only if you are taking it too?'

Sarah rose from her chair and went to the bell-pull to summon a maid, saying as she did so, 'It will be our pleasure also.'

The rest of Dr Wentworth's visit passed pleasantly and left the sisters exchanging excited comments about him once he had taken his leave, but that was only after Arabella had invited him and his uncle to dine with them two nights hence, in order for him to meet John and Charley and reacquaint himself with their father.

Once the formalities and commiserations to John were made, the evening moved on in an agreeable and satisfying manner. Coming as he had to settle in a thriving port, the young doctor was keen to learn all about it and the seafaring life, and found a ready tutor in John. He noted Mr Brook's evident pride in Charley and the lad's own enthusiasm for all things maritime.

Dr Wentworth found he could not reach a conclusion about the precise relationship between Arabella and John. He knew from his uncle that they had been more or less brought up together, but it was Harriet he had married. Now, with Captain Sharp free again, was the old easy relationship likely to strengthen and take a new turn? Or did the fact that he had been married to her sister raise a barrier between them? If so, Conan wondered if there was a chance for him; he did have one advantage, given that he would never be out of her life for six months at a time as Captain Sharp would. He had admired Arabella from the first moment he had walked into this house to minister to Harriet, and she had occupied his mind while he was laying his final plans to join his uncle in Whitby. But, being the person he was, he knew he must tread carefully; the last thing he wanted was to alienate her and lose her friendship.

18 March 1836. The Sea King *sailed today. When we reached the quay to make our goodbyes we found Dr Wentworth already there, speaking to John. After greeting us most pleasantly, he thanked us again for our hospitality and said our friendship was making it easier for him to settle in Whitby. He then politely left us to make our private farewells. We had decided to watch the* Sea King *leave from the West Pier so as to be close to the ship as she neared the sea. The walk was easier than climbing to the clifftop for Father. Arabella and I took turns to carry Caroline. I must say, she looks more natural with a child than I do. We gave Charley and John a*

*royal send-off, hoping that on their return we would not
be the bearers of bad news again . . .*

*31 August 1836. The cry of 'Whale-ships!' is ringing
through my window again. Thank goodness we have
nothing but good news for the returning sailors. I hope
theirs too is good. I'm off to meet them.*

Arabella was trying to tie a bonnet on Caroline, who was
growing excited at the prospect of going out. 'Keep still,
Caroline, otherwise we'll never get to see your daddy
sailing into Whitby.'

'He's coming home to see us. We don't want to be
late,' said Sarah, trying to calm the child.

Bonnet on, coat buttoned up, Arabella raised her eyes
in relief as she glanced at her sister and asked, 'The West
Pier?'

'It will be the best place for Caroline,' replied Sarah.
'We can come back to the quay and join Father there.'

People were already making their way to their
favourite places from which to greet men returning from
the Arctic. Bone at a masthead signified a full ship, and
all four ships today carried that token of good fortune. In
spite of the financial problems troubling the country,
Whitby's economy would be boosted by these ships and
there would be money in the crewmen's pockets to ease
their families' winter.

As the *Sea King* approached the gap between the piers
they were delighted to see the elation being expressed by
John and Charley; nothing had gone wrong on this
voyage. Arabella and Sarah responded with equal glee.
Reading that as a good sign, John and Charley reacted

with more waves and smiles. Caroline caught the mood and giggled when Arabella grasped her hand and waved it at John, telling her to 'Wave to Papa.'

Enthusiastic greetings continued all along the quay, where their joy was mirrored again and again by the crowd who had gathered to welcome their loved ones home.

The first two ready for the evening meal, Arabella and John, found themselves alone in the drawing-room that evening.

'You were right, Arabella,' he told her.

'Right?' she queried as she sat down.

'Telling me not to give up the sea.'

'I'm glad to hear it.'

'And I'm pleased all has been well here. I hope Caroline has been no trouble?'

'None. She's such a delight. But I do have something to tell you.' Arabella made her statement light so as not to raise his expectations, but before she could continue the door opened and Caroline ran in, leaving her nurse standing by the open door.

'Mama, Mama!' called Caroline, her face one big smile as she went to Arabella and flung herself into her arms.

Wondering what John's reaction would be, an embarrassed Arabella glanced across at him while hugging Caroline. She eased the child away and said quietly to her, 'Go and look at your picture books.'

Obediently the little girl went to the books piled in one corner of the window-seat.

'John, you need an explanation.'

He shook his head. 'Who else should she call Mother?'

'That is what troubled the nurse. They were spending so much time together that she feared Caroline might begin to regard *her* as her mother. And, as I am very much a part of Caroline's life, Nurse saw no harm in allowing her to refer to me as Mama.'

'Quite right. There's no harm in it.'

'I pointed out that the situation would change if either of us married, but the nurse said she was convinced Caroline would be able to cope with an explanation if and when that happened.' Arabella left a slight pause but John did not speak. 'It came about naturally. I hope you don't mind.'

'Far from it. There couldn't be a better person to take Harriet's place. You are . . .' But John could not finish his sentence then as the other members of the family appeared.

After the setbacks of recent times, they were all enjoying being at peace together. John added to their joy when he announced, 'Charley has become such a hard-working and exemplary member of the *Sea King*'s crew that I am going to promote him to a more responsible job as one of the boat-steerers.'

Charley gasped. He had not expected this so soon; one day maybe, but not yet. Amidst all the congratulations and clapping, he managed to splutter his thanks to John.

'Is he strong enough?' Benjamin asked cautiously. 'Steering-oars are heavy.'

'He's toughened up considerably,' John reassured him. 'He'll manage. Of course he'll get a lot of practice before I put him with his boat-crew.' He turned to Charley then. 'I've watched you carefully. I've noted you have the respect of the men for your ability, and I know from the way I've seen you studying the boat-steerer when you have been rowing in my boat that you'll be good at it.'

Charley filled with pride at these words, but gained even more from the delight and approval he saw in his father's eyes.

20 March 1837. The Sea King *sailed today, along with two other ships. My parting from Charley was particularly poignant. We were on the quay and, when I finally hugged him and wished him well in his new position as boat-steerer, he said something that brought tears to my eyes and a lump to my throat. 'Sarah, I feel this promotion is as much for Jim as for me. He could easily have been in my place. I owe you both so much for helping me to stow away.'*

29 March 1837. Arabella has received an invitation to accompany Dr Wentworth to a musical evening at the Angel, and Father has approved. She hesitated to accept even though I told her I thought she should . . .

'Arabella, he's an eligible young man. You should make something of your chance to get to know him better. And, oh, he's so handsome!'

Arabella gave a small laugh. 'Don't think I haven't noticed.'

'And he's been very attentive.'

'Don't think I haven't noticed that too. I'm flattered but . . .'

'John?'

Arabella did not answer.

'You can't live on past dreams. Has he shown any feelings towards you, apart from natural gratitude for all your care for Caroline? And he chose Harriet, remember?'

'I know.'

'Arabella, you cannot go on like this. Life will pass you by. You cannot hang on to a love of yesteryear.'

'Aren't you doing just that?'

'It's different; Jim died, and no one else is paying me marked attention. John is still alive but not reciprocating, and someone else positively wants your company. You should accept his invitation.'

Still voicing a little reluctance, Arabella agreed. She found she passed a pleasant evening with a man who was considerate but not overwhelming in his attentions. He was most courteous when he escorted her to the front door.

'Dr Wentworth, I must thank you for a most enjoyable evening. It has been a pleasant change for me,' she said.

'The pleasure has been mine. You are a charming companion. If I may be so bold, may I ask you to accompany me again?' He hastened to add, 'If you agree, then I will approach your father for his permission.'

'Then do so, Dr Wentworth.'

'Miss Brook, you have afforded me a pleasure to look forward to.' He took her hand and raised it to his lips. 'Good night.'

She watched him for a moment as he walked away. Finding herself making comparisons with John, she turned back sharply and entered the house.

Two days later, at the end of their evening meal, Benjamin asked his eldest daughter to come to his study.

When she was seated facing him he said, 'I had a visit from Dr Wentworth at my office today. He came seeking

372

my permission to ask you to accompany him to social functions and house parties throughout the summer.' He paused, letting his gaze rest on her, trying to gauge her reaction to the request. All he saw was polite enquiry, so he continued, 'I gave him permission to do so.'

'Thank you, Papa.' Arabella's tone revealed nothing either, because she did not know whether she was elated or not. Oh, she knew she would enjoy these events, whatever they may be, but there was something telling her that there could be more behind the doctor's request and, if her surmise was correct, she was not sure how she felt about that.

'Arabella, as your father, I must say this. Dr Wentworth is a charming, handsome and courteous man. His medical experience and knowledge will be an asset to Whitby. He will follow in his uncle's practice so his prospects are good and his future assured. He must be attracted to you in some way or he would not have made this request. I am not questioning his feelings, or yours; such things take their own time. All I want to say is, don't lead this young man on; do not give him hope if there is none. Be careful how you display your feelings.'

'I do not know them myself, Papa. But I will heed your words.'

Benjamin stood up and held out his hand to his daughter to help her to her feet, indicating the interview was over. Then he kissed her on the forehead. 'I think only of your happiness.'

'Thank you, Papa.' She walked from the room wondering what the future might bring.

It brought pleasant times with the young doctor throughout the summer. He did not overwhelm her with invitations but chose the occasions he knew she would enjoy – something Arabella appreciated.

Sarah was always eager to hear about these occasions, but when she tried to sound out her sister's feelings, Arabella always countered with, 'We're just good friends.' Then she would switch the conversation to Sarah's life, hoping she would encourage her sister into finding love with one of her friends.

Sarah, for her part, was perfectly happy with her own situation, fulfilling the promises she had made to herself when Jim was lost. She was happy, but she wondered if her sister ever would be. Arabella still dwelt in the past, and thought of John too much, in spite of Dr Wentworth's attentions. Though Arabella enjoyed these, she held herself always just out of reach. Sarah recognised this and wondered if the doctor's patience would eventually give way.

Then the *Sea King* returned.

31

*29 August 1837. The shout we have waited for: 'Whale-
ship!' I hope it's the* Sea King!

'I'm going, Sarah, and taking Caroline!' The shout from
Arabella came as Sarah emerged from her room and hurried to the top of the stairs.

'All right. Go to the West Pier. I'll catch you up.'

Arabella was out of the front door carrying Caroline
before Sarah was halfway down the stairs. She ran to the
closet, swung a cape around her shoulders, covered her
hair with a scarf and knotted it at her throat. She'd caught
up with Arabella before she reached Pier Road but had
already gleaned from the chatter of people flocking to
greet the returning whale-men that only one ship had
been sighted . . . and it was the *Sea King*. Hearing this
brought great relief to Sarah, who saw the same feeling
reflected in Arabella when she took Caroline from her.
This was going to be a joyous homecoming; they knew
it would be even more so when they saw bone at the
masthead.

They found a good position on the West Pier; the *Sea
King* would be close as she headed for the tranquil water
of the river.

People around them were cheering and calling to members of the crew, who were equally enthusiastic in their acknowledgements.

Caroline was swept up in the excitement and was laughing when Arabella took her from Sarah and pointed out John, saying, 'There's your father! Wave to him! Wave!'

Caroline waved vigorously, but Arabella's smile died on her lips. John was waving back but it appeared to her only a token gesture. A chill settled around her heart. Something was wrong, but what? Her eyes swept the deck. She grasped Sarah's arm with her free hand. 'Where's Charley?'

'Charley?'

'Yes, yes.' Her urgent tone startled Sarah. 'Where is he? He's usually somewhere to be seen.'

Even as Arabella spoke, Sarah's eyes were quickly ranging across the crew of the *Sea King*. 'Oh, my God, where is he?' Cold fingers brushed her heart and mind, numbing all feeling.

'Sarah! Come on! To the quay!' Arabella's shout roused her sister out of her stupor of disbelief.

The sisters ran for the bridge but, before they reached it, it had opened to let the *Sea King* get to her berth. They waited impatiently while the ship was manoeuvred through the narrow opening. Once the bridge was closed again they pushed and twisted through the crush of people, most of whom were equally anxious to reach the quay and greet their men-folk.

'There's Papa,' said Sarah when they had reached the crowded quay.

'Have you seen Charley?' he asked when they joined him.

They shook their heads but did not express their fears.

376

A few minutes later, when John came down the gang-way, they were all alarmed by his serious expression.

'Sir, I've news about Charley. I'm afraid he's in a bad way. A whale smashed his boat and he bore the brunt of it. He should have had a doctor straight away. I did the best I could, but . . .'

'I'll get Dr Wentworth straight away,' said Arabella. 'John, do you want him here or at home?'

'I've put things in motion for him to be taken home. The men who volunteered will be setting about the task immediately they have greeted their own folk.'

'Take Caroline home, Sarah,' instructed Arabella, thrust-ing the child at her sister, 'and warn Mrs Ainslie what is happening.' She saw all the colour drain from her father's face. The man who generally would be in charge looked lost today. 'Papa, I'm sure Charley will be all right.' She tried to sound convincing even though she had no idea of her brother's true condition. 'Go with John; be at Charley's side.' She turned to John next. 'Look after Father, please?'

'Of course I will,' he replied, his eyes telling her that he wished he wasn't bringing such dreadful news.

Arabella hurried away from the quay hoping she would find Dr Wentworth at home but, when she reached the West Side, saw him hurrying towards her.

'Miss Brook!' There was concern in his voice and clouding his eyes. 'You look flustered, what is wrong?'

'Oh, Dr Wentworth, I'm so relieved to find you!'

'What is wrong?' he repeated, reaching out his arm to support her.

'It's Charley! He's been injured.'

'What happened?'

'I don't know. John's having him taken home, but they won't have left the ship yet.'

377

They reached the quay just as some of the crew were carefully manoeuvring down the gangway with the ladder on which Charley was lying. Groups making their reunions moved aside, fell silent or spoke in hushed whispers, eyeing him with curiosity and pity.

Arabella felt a chill sweep across her when she saw her brother. This was not the young man she had seen leave Whitby on the *Sea King*. Then he had been vibrant, full of energy and laughter. Now he lay inert, unable to muster even the faintest of smiles, though through her tears she believed he was trying. She glanced at her father, who stood beside his son holding his hand; she saw worry etched so deep on his face that it frightened her. He had aged years beyond measure in a few minutes.

'Lay him on the ground.' Dr Wentworth took charge. Arabella felt some relief but not enough to overcome the anxiety that haunted her at the sight of her helpless brother.

Dr Wentworth knelt down. Arabella took her father's hand in hers, seeking comfort and conferring it. As the doctor gazed intently at Charley's ashen face he asked, 'Captain Sharp, what happened?'

'Charley was boat-steerer. They were on to a whale, which sounded. When it surfaced it was close, flukes high – they smashed down on the stern of the boat. Charley took the full force . . . it's a wonder he survived. The crew were thrown into the water. Fortunately there were two other boats close by and they got everyone out quickly. Charley was in a bad way but we did what we could for him. Left for home immediately. I was heading for Shetland given his parlous state, but in his delirium Charley was calling out for Sarah with such anguish that I thought it best to head straight for home. I crammed on all sail and here we are. I hope I did right?'

Dr Wentworth, who all through the explanation had been examining Charley, nodded. He was not sure if Captain Sharp had made the right decision or not, but was not about to voice any doubt. There was probably no means of knowing, but one thing was certain: Charley had been granted his wish. The doctor looked round. 'Where is Miss Sarah?'

'I sent her home with Caroline and to instruct Mrs Ainslie to have things ready for Charley.'

'Then let us get him home.'

Fear for his son's life gripped Benjamin, who moved closer to him.

Arabella's face reflected her anxiety and alarm; her hand gripped Dr Wentworth's arm as she asked, scarcely above a whisper, 'Is he as bad as that?'

'My first examination tells me he is, but . . .'

'Oh, no. No!' She sank against him, feeling warmth and strength as his arms came comfortingly around her. She wished she might remain there forever, but, looking up, saw a look of hurt and confusion in John's face.

A frisson of alarm surged through John. Where had all the years gone? Had he allowed his life ashore to be mis-directed? Had that haunting in the Arctic been Arabella all along, trying to tell him something? Seeing her in another man's arms was torture to him!

He turned away and spoke to his men. They started off, carrying the ladder as gently as possible.

Arabella eased herself out of Dr Wentworth's arms. 'I'm sorry.'

'Don't be,' he said. 'I'm glad I was here for you. Come, my dear. We will both be needed when Charley reaches the house.'

*

379

Benjamin, his two daughters and John waited in the drawing-room while Dr Wentworth and his uncle examined Charley. It had not been easy for the ladder-bearers, knowing their crew-mate was suffering pain with every movement – not that Charley complained – but he could not hide completely the outward evidence of his distress.

Sarah was shocked beyond words when they arrived. The numbness that took hold of her body did nothing to block the anguish from her mind. Charley, with whom she had shared so much, was rendered completely helpless and she could do nothing about it. She sat silent in the drawing-room, too shocked to say anything. Benjamin was a study in desolation. The mood of anguish brought home to Arabella how much she loved her brother. If only she had told him so; she would rectify that if . . . John sat with hands on knees, staring at the carpet. Had he promoted Charley to boat-steerer too soon? Should he not have ordered the whale-boats launched when he did? Should he have gone to Shetland? If only . . . if only . . .

The door opened. They all looked up expectantly. Dr Wentworth walked in. His solemn expression did nothing to ease their minds.

'Charley wants to see Sarah,' he said quietly.

She rose from her chair. No one else moved. As much as they wanted to see Charley, they did what they felt obliged to do – honoured his request.

Sarah made her way up the stairs with measured steps. She had an urge to rush and yet there was something holding her back, too . . . She entered the room and approached her brother, pale and wan against the white pillows.

Dr Fenby moved away. 'I'll wait outside,' he said quietly.

When the door had closed Charley held out his hand to his sister. She took it, and forced herself not to show any emotion at the feel of his fingerbones through the withered skin.

'Charley.' She said his name with such feeling that it caught in her throat and caused tears to flow silently down her cheeks.

He managed a wan smile. 'Sarah.'

She felt him drawing into himself the strength necessary to go on. 'Sarah, I knew how badly I was hurt; I knew what lay in store. But I needed, and was determined, to see you before . . .' He let his words rest there.

'Charley, no! Oh, no!'

'Don't mourn for me. I'm escaping the guilt I couldn't have lived with.'

'What are you saying, Charley?' she moaned. 'Don't talk like that.'

'I have a confession to make, then you'll understand.'

With tears still streaming down her cheeks, she recognised it was vital for to him to say what he wanted to say, so she waited.

'Before I say anything, I want you to swear you will never tell anyone what I am about to tell you.' His eyes held hers while he was speaking. She could not refuse that look, pleading with her to agree. She knew if she refused he would be tormented here, now and beyond.

She nodded and tried to brush away the tears. 'I swear to tell no one.'

Charley relaxed. He knew his secret was safe with Sarah; she was someone who never broke her word.

'Everyone will want to know why you wanted to see me, though. Why must it be a secret, Charley?'

'Because I killed Jim!'

'What?' That one word was full of disbelief. What did he mean? Why would he say this? Had he taken leave of his senses, affected by the terrible wounds he had suffered?

'I killed Jim!' The words came again, with such conviction, she knew he was telling the truth.

With that realisation came a sense of horror. All she could manage to say was a weak, 'What do you mean?'

'Not only Jim but all the others who lost their lives on that dreadful first voyage of mine.'

'Now I know you are talking nonsense.'

He gave a slight shake of his head. 'No, I'm not. Listen to me.' He stretched out his other hand to her. Sarah took it, loving him still despite the shock of his words.

'I was in John's boat, we had struck a whale . . .'

Sarah listened without interruption even though she wanted to scream at him when he explained why he was to blame for Jim's death and those of the others.

There were tears in his eyes when he'd finished speaking. They were still fixed on hers. He could see how much she was hurting, but all he could say was an inadequate 'I'm sorry, Sarah.'

'Why tell me now?'

'I do not want to die with those deaths, especially Jim's, on my conscience. And please don't tell me I'm going to live. I know I'm not. I knew that when the full power of the whale's flukes hit me, but I was determined to stay alive as long as it took to confess to you. I needed to. I didn't want to cause you pain, only . . .'

All manner of confused thoughts were revolving in Sarah's mind, but one kept pushing itself to the fore. Tell him you forgive him.

She took hold of his wasted hands, more firmly this

time. 'Charley, you and I were always close. What you have told me is shattering, but I cannot bear you any malice. In a whale-man's life, things like this happen. When that boat hit the ice, things could not be reversed and put right. It's not as if you did it on purpose; if you had that would have been a different matter. I know Jim would attach no blame to you, nor do I, and nor, I believe, would any of the other men. From what I heard from the survivors of that sailing, and their relatives, you were a saviour to many men.' She saw the immense relief in his eyes and knew that something that had lain heavily on her brother's heart since that fateful voyage had been exorcised.

'But still, you won't tell anyone, Sarah?'

'Your secret is safe with me.'

'You deserve to know why I asked you that. You see, John knew what had happened, that I was responsible, but he ordered me to tell no one. If you break your promise, word will get back to him and he will know I disobeyed him . . .'

'He will never know from me.'

Charley smiled at her. 'Thank you.'

She treasured those words – the last she heard her brother speak.

When she realised they would be, Sarah hastily summoned Dr Fenby and ran downstairs to alert the others.

They each received a smile from Charley and a touch of his hand that spoke volumes of his feelings for them.

Benjamin was the last to leave. Everyone else realised he needed to be left with his thoughts as he looked down at the peaceful face of the boy for whom he had had such high hopes.

32

8 September 1837. I stood at Charley's grave, wept a while and silently renewed my promise, 'Your secret is safe with me.' But I've written it up in my diary – I felt compelled to do so. Poor Jim . . . my poor, dear brother too. That I have written this account does not mean other people will see it. The diary will be kept under lock and key and will never be out of my possession. One day I will destroy it and the secrets of the Brook family will be lost forever. If I last into old age, those around me will be dead and gone and the diary will no longer hold any significance; that may be the best time to do it.

Two weeks later, the atmosphere of gloom hanging over the Brook household was palpable. The young ones, knowing there was still a future to be faced, endeavoured to accept the tragic loss of Charley, but Benjamin saw no future for himself. The one he had planned was lost; he had no son and heir to follow him into the business he had built up. He could not be persuaded to immerse himself in work, and if Jake Carter brought him documents to sign he did so without knowing what he was doing. Any decisions that needed to be made were waved away. Jake turned to John, but he had no authority within the firm. That he and Charley should run the business had been only a promise for the future. Now Charley was gone. John hated to see what was happening, but his heart lay with the sea.

As he sat alone in his study, day after day, despondency ate away at Benjamin. Arabella and Sarah were in despair. Even his granddaughter's innocent prattle could not break down the barrier of grief he had raised around himself.

Arabella was feeling overcome, not only by the atmosphere in the house but by John's recent estrangement from the family. It was as if he wanted to be away from anything associated with Charley, as if he knew more than he had said and wanted to avoid the possibility of any questions being put to him. The links weren't completely severed; he had gratefully accepted the suggestion that Caroline and her nurse remain with the Brooks. But even that connection proved to be tenuous and did not lead to Arabella seeing him as frequently as she might have expected. She worried that something was troubling him; something besides the loss of Charley.

Today she was restless. The house was closing in on her. She needed to leave it, needed to be alone. She turned from the window of the drawing-room and strode with a determined step into the hall. The sun, high up in a clear sky, called to her. She grabbed her cape and draped it round her shoulders. She went to the front door and opened it, breathing in the fresh salt tang of the air. Then she walked briskly down the path.

She had no idea where she was going. She was aware of her surroundings but they made no impact on her. It was as if she was seeing them from afar.

After an hour the slowing of her footsteps brought the realisation that she had turned into the street where Dr Wentworth resided. She hesitated, and then something impelled her to move on until she reached his house. Arabella paused, one hand on the gate, her mind in confusion. Then she walked up to the front door and rang the bell.

On leaving the doctor's house her thoughts were no easier because now she knew she must face John. Oblivious to all the activity and bustle of the busy port, she walked down beside the quays.

She stopped in her tracks, drawn by the sight of a ship at its moorings. The *Sea King*! She felt overwhelmed by the reaction the sight of that vessel caused in her. Her lips tightened. Her mind filled with curses she wanted to fling at the ship for all the trouble it had caused, but they were never uttered. Her father loved this ship; John, as her captain, treasured it; and Charley had adored it. She strolled slowly forward, eyes riveted on the *Sea King*.

There was little activity on board. The vessel was awaiting her next assignment and, under the present circumstances, that had yet to be decided. As Arabella's mind began to ponder this problem, she saw John come on deck. Her heart lurched. They had shared so much together, surely that counted for something? She stood and watched him. He strolled around the deck, apparently deep in thought. Not wanting to intrude on him she started to turn, thinking she was far enough away to go unnoticed. But she had overlooked the sharp eyes of a sailor. John saw her. For a moment there was no gesture from either of them but their eyes were locked upon each other. Then he raised his arm in a wave and she responded. He came towards the gangway. Arabella walked in his direction.

'Arabella,' he greeted her, and paused as if looking for the right words. 'I should thank you again for looking after Caroline. I shouldn't leave all the responsibility with you. But I will put that right. How is she?'

'Very well . . . full of life.'

'And your father?' he asked as they started to stroll together towards the bridge.

'Terribly withdrawn. He shuts himself in his study, takes no interest in the business.'

'But the business needs someone at the helm.'

'He leaves it to Jake Carter. Papa only signs the necessary papers. I don't believe he even knows what is in them.'

John frowned. 'It's as well Carter is competent and trustworthy.'

'Losing Charley has hit Father hard. It is as if his whole future has been ripped away from him.'

John nodded his understanding.

They walked on in silence, crossed the bridge and, without any words being exchanged, turned towards the West Pier.

John broke the tension that was gathering between them, though neither of them knew why this should be. 'I'm giving up the sea!'

Astonished by this unexpected announcement, Arabella stopped and stared at him. 'Is it because of what happened to Charley? You can't blame yourself for that. It was an accident. Tragic, yes, but no one's fault.'

'Of course I regret what happened to him, and always will; he was like a younger brother to me. But it's the wider implications that need tackling.' He started to move again and she matched his slow steps with hers. 'What you tell me about your father only confirms the rumours I've heard along the quays. If that is allowed to continue, the firm he worked so hard to maintain will disappear. We cannot let that happen, for his sake and for the memory of Charley. Who knows what he would have achieved had he lived?'

'But . . .'

'Hear me out before raising objections. You will recall that your father, looking to the future, said he was prepared to take me into the business alongside Charley when I retired from the sea?'

She nodded.

'Well, I will suggest that if I retire now, he can take me into the business sooner than he expected. I know little about the financial side, but if he sees its future as lying with me he will have to train me, which means he will need to take a more active part in it again.'

'And banish this awful despondency that is threatening his sanity, if not his life?'

'Exactly.'

They had reached the pier. She stopped and placed a hand on his arm. 'You would give up the sea to do this for him?'

'Yes.'

'But you love the life.'

He gave a wan smile. 'I do, but there are more important things.'

'John, you came to this family's rescue once before. If Father agrees to your idea, we will be even deeper in your debt.'

'No, you won't. You have been a family to me.'

'But that was easy! Your commitment to Harriet

wasn't. It altered your life. This new one will do so too. Be sure, John. For your own sake, be sure of what you are doing.'

He made no response, but as she started to retrace their steps, stopped her. 'Walk with me on the pier.'

Arabella hesitated. It had many memories for her, some of them painful, but she could not withstand the look in his eyes. Nor did she pull away when John linked arms with her.

'Our pier,' he said quietly. 'I've something I'd like to tell you there.'

Sensing something profound or momentous was coming, Arabella gripped his arm more tightly.

'During that winter in the Arctic I was visited on more than one occasion by a shadowy female form,' he began.

'What? A ghost?'

'Who knows? Some would say that, under the conditions we were suffering at the time, I was prey to delusions. But I know what I saw and, by its dress, the figure that visited me was female.'

'Who was she?'

'I don't know. She was too hazy for me to make out her features, but I have always thought she was trying to tell me something. Give me hope that I would survive.'

'Did she make any gestures?'

'No. Just appeared briefly and disappeared. But there was something which really didn't fit in with the hope I thought this figure was offering me.'

'What was that?'

'She sobbed.'

The words stopped Arabella in her tracks. Her face registered shocked surprise and she whispered automatically, 'I wept for the morning sun.'

'What did you say?' he asked, puzzled by what he thought he had heard.

She repeated her words.

He gave a little puzzled shake of his head. 'I don't understand.'

'Many a morning I watched the sun rise and wept for it to warm you and your crew that long winter.'

'So it was you!' he gasped. 'I could never be sure who that shadowy figure was, Harriet or you. But as we sailed for home, I'd reached a decision.' He took her hands in his and looked intently into her eyes. 'When we got back to Whitby I was going to tell Harriet that I couldn't marry her, and then I was going to speak to you. I had realised during that long bitter winter that it was you I loved.'

'And you never said a word, but married Harriet to save her reputation and the family name! Oh, John, what has happened to our lives?'

'I never realised the depth of my affection for you until that terrible time in the Arctic. Now I am here I find Dr Wentworth is—'

'Say no more,' she interrupted. 'He has been very kind and was there when I needed someone, and I'll admit I find him attractive.'

'I don't like—'

Arabella interrupted. 'Don't say things you'll regret. Let me finish. I know he has strong feelings for me, I have just come from seeing him.' She sensed jealousy in John then. 'I thanked him for his friendship but told him it could be no more than that.'

Those words eliminated everything else from John's mind except for the heartfelt request, 'Will you marry me now, Arabella?'

She looked deep into his eyes and, smiling through tears of joy, said, 'Yes. John, yes.' Their kisses sealed their love and then she suggested, 'Let's go home and tell Father we'll give Caroline a brother who'll be heir to the firm one day!'

John chuckled. 'Tell him that and he won't dare withhold his permission.'

He kissed her again, his arms around her waist. Arabella felt safe and loved as she had not truly felt since her mother had died.

EPILOGUE

14 August 1901. I have made a decision. A great weight has been lifted from my shoulders. Hasty words were spoken yesterday. My fault really – the fault of a silly old fool who did not display faith in the niece she loves so much. My immediate antagonism to Esther's request made her all the more determined to see the diaries, resulting in her threat. That got my hackles up and I almost said I would not be blackmailed, but thankfully I drew back. If I hadn't there would have been a rift in our relationship, and that I could not allow to happen: the love Esther and I share is too precious to lose. Had it happened my regret would have been of short duration – at my age I cannot have long to live – but Esther would have been left with hers for much longer. So I have decided to let her have the diaries.

'Good morning to my favourite great-aunt,' cried Esther as she breezed into Sarah's room, her face filled with the joy of living.

'Hello, Esther,' replied Sarah, her own expression betraying her love for her great-niece. She held out her arms but Esther had no need of the invitation, she was already halfway across the room.

In their embrace were love, sorrow and heartfelt apologies for the hasty words spoken yesterday.

Sarah eased her niece away so they could look into each other's eyes.

'If you are so intent on knowing about your family, you can have the diaries. I will not lay down any rules as I thought I might, but will leave you to judge for yourself if there is anything to be gained by revealing what is in them.

'Esther, think carefully about your decision after reading my diaries. They may shatter what are firmly based beliefs, not only yours but the beliefs of those who are dear to you and whom you hold close.' Sarah gave a wan smile and said, 'Do what you think is best.' She pointed a withered finger at the diaries laid out on the table across the room.

Esther gave her aunt a hug and a kiss, then went to the table and picked up the diaries with what amounted to reverence. 'Thank you.' She headed for the door. 'We'll talk about them later,' she said, turning to look back.

Sarah nodded.

The door closed and Esther walked away.

Sarah gave a little smile. 'You are a sensible young woman, my love,' she whispered to herself, 'I hope you won't think less of Arabella and John when you know who your true grandparents were. More importantly, you'll have to ask yourself if your mother should know the truth.' Her lips quivered. She gave a little grimace. 'I know you'll make the right decision, but I'm sorry to disappoint you, Esther, we'll not be able to talk about what my diaries reveal. Maybe it's for the best.' She settled herself in her seat, and added, 'You see, I'm going to Jim.' She leaned back in her chair, closed her eyes and fingered the jet brooch that she had worn at her neck every day for nearly sixty-nine years.

ACKNOWLEDGEMENTS

I have been fortunate throughout my writing career to have the full support of my family. What a blessing this is for a writer. In the case of this book, my daughter Judith has been ready with suggestions and comments throughout the writing process. Geraldine, her twin sister, read the story in its entirety, offering suggestions for its final form before it went to the publisher.

My gratitude goes to Lynn Curtis, who has edited all Jessica Blair's books. It also goes to the entire Piatkus staff, who have contributed to getting this book on to bookshelves, especially Donna Condon, who has overseen the book from my initial suggestion. Thank you, all of you.

This page would not be complete if I did not thank all my readers, without whom I would not continue to enjoy writing.